Ace of Hearts

'Remember, my sweet,' everyone has their price,' said Lord Delsingham.

Marisa pulled herself together. 'I told you before, my Lord,' she said stoutly. 'No one pays me to do anything!'

'A pity,' he murmured, his narrowed grey eyes raking her. 'My imagination runs riot at the sight of you in those breeches. And the thought of you out of them is quite devastating.'

Author's other Black Lace titles:

Elena's Conquest
Elena's Destiny
The Amulet
Nicole's Revenge
Nadya's Quest
Risky Business

Ace of Hearts
Lisette Allen

Black Lace books contain sexual fantasies.
In real life, always practise safe sex.

This edition published in 2003 by
Black Lace
Thames Wharf Studios
Rainville Road
London W6 9HA

Originally published 1996

Printed and bound by Mackays of Chatham PLC

ISBN 0 352 33059 7

Chapter One

The late afternoon sun poured in through the high windows, burnishing the bare oak floorboards of the spacious attic room. From the narrow London street below came the muffled clatter of carriage wheels on cobbles, and the shrill cries of street sellers. But up here, the only sound that mattered was the delicately lethal kiss of the two rapier blades that gleamed like slivers of light in the still air.

In a sudden flurry of movement, the shafts of steel shuddered together then fell, sighing, apart. The two opponents, solitary occupants of the room, circled one another warily. One was fair, the other one dark; their features were concealed by the wire face masks they wore. Both were clad in open-necked silk shirts that were tucked into slim-fitting buckskin knee breeches. The room echoed to the soft tread of their stockinged feet on the polished oak boards as they moved gracefully, assessing one another. There was a sudden hiss of indrawn breath as the fair one's arm whipped up; blades clashed gratingly, to be followed by a moment's fierce, sinew-straining tension as both strove for mastery. Then the dark-haired man gave ground and let his blade slide gently aside. The slither of steel died away in the silent room and he said thoughtfully, 'Your riposte was good. You improve every time we meet.'

1

His opponent's fair head bowed slightly in acknowledgement of the compliment. 'My thanks, Signor Valsino. That is my intention.' Then the two blades tapped once more in salute, and once more the stockinged feet tensed and stepped sideways in their purposeful dance. Muscles flexed and rippled beneath thin silk shirts that were damp with perspiration; the room seemed charged with the energy of vital combat.

Suddenly the slighter of the two, the fair one whose face was all but obscured by the mysterious wire mask, lunged forward to deliver a lightning thrust in tierce, with arm held high and silk sleeve falling back to expose a slender yet sinewed wrist. The dark-haired man whipped up his blade in retaliation, the muscles of his forearm ribbed and hard. There was a scuffle of blades in forte, a sparking clash of metal as the rapiers jarred and adhered, to be followed by a final, deadly struggle as each combatant tried to force the other aside. A soft hiss of expelled breath was followed by a sharp clatter of steel as the fair fencer's rapier flew in a silvery arc through the air, landing with ringing finality on the oak floor.

The dark-haired man's sword flashed in for the kill, his rapier point jabbing with deadly accuracy at his vanquished opponent's heaving ribs. The moment seemed to hang suspended in the bright, thin air. Then the victor laughed. Lowering his sword, he pulled off his wire mask and tossed it onto one of the striped satin settees that lined the long wall. He lifted his sword in mock salute and said, in a musical, slightly foreign voice, 'You prove yourself a worthy opponent, my dear.'

The fair-haired combatant pulled off her mask as well and shook her long tresses out of the narrow black ribbon that restrained them. Once free, her hair clustered in thick curls round her slender shoulders, honey-gold in the spring sunshine. 'I will be a truly worthy opponent for you, Signor Valsino, when I beat you. I strive, as always, for perfection.'

Her voice was low and melodious and sent shivers down his spine, just as if he were stroking a fine rapier blade. He stood watching her in frank admiration, drinking in the pale gold silk of her cheeks and throat, lightly sheened with perspiration after her exertion. He noted her slender but deceptively strong shoulders and arms that wielded the rapier with such skill, and saw how the sinuous folds of her silk shirt clung to the contours of her body, reminding him, with a familiar, stabbing ache, that beneath the cool silk were firm, high breasts crested with darkly tantalising nipples, as luscious as peaches ripened in the warm Italian sun. And as she stood there, with her hands poised boyishly on her leather breeched hips, he realised that he wanted her now, badly.

He said, 'You seem quite perfect as you are to me, Signorina Marisa.'

She gazed coolly back at him with her devastating blue eyes. She must have seen the blatant desire in his dark gaze, but she deliberately chose to misunderstand him, because she said breezily, 'My father taught me well. You told me that yourself, the first time I came to you for tuition.'

He stirred, conscious that he was still staring at her rather besottedly, and said, 'Your father must have been skilled in the art of swordplay. He's instructed you in all the moves of someone tutored by the Angelos themselves. Fencing was a pastime of his?'

She chuckled, a richly beguiling sound that drove him wild, and ran her hand through her thick, honey-blonde hair. 'You could say it was a necessity, Signor Valsino, rather than a pastime. You see, my father was forever fighting his way out of debt. Either that, or escaping from the people he'd cheated at the gaming tables.'

As she spoke, she was moving with unconscious grace towards the ewer of water that adorned a polished mahogany stand near the marble fireplace. She poured the cold water into a bowl, then she dampened a linen towel and bathed her face and wrists with sensuous pleasure. 'Together,' she went on, 'we travelled round half the capitals of Europe. Inevitably in rather a hurry.'

'An unusual education for a girl.'

3

'It had its advantages.'

He smiled, his arms folded across his chest, taking pleasure in just watching her. She'd unfastened the top buttons of her shirt so that she could draw the moistened towel across the delicate skin of her throat, and he could see the gleam of her naked shoulder in the shaft of slanting sunlight, could see the warm beginning of the heartstopping swell of her breasts.

He dragged his dark eyes back to her face, watching her as she threw back her head in unselfconscious delight at the caress of the cold water. Her long thick hair cascaded down her back, drawing his gaze down to the handspan slenderness of her waist, to the sensual swell of her tight, firm buttocks in her clinging boy's breeches. He ached for her, and was conscious, again, of the impelling heat at his groin.

Carefully he turned towards a small gilt table set between two French settees where a decanter and two glass goblets had been left, and said lightly, 'You'll take a glass of wine with me before you leave, Signorina Marisa? My next pupil isn't due for an hour.'

She had been letting her eyes drift idly along the display of illustrious visiting cards and invitations set along the marble mantelshelf, evidence that David Valsino numbered the elite of London society amongst his clients. But at his suggestion she turned from them and smiled.

'Wine. Why not?' And without waiting for further encouragement, she flung herself cat-like amongst the plump silk cushions of the nearest settee and rolled onto her back, her head pillowed by her arms, her stockinged legs stretched out luxuriantly.

David Valsino brought her a brimming goblet of the rather good hock. She pulled herself up, leaning her elbow on the padded silk arm of the couch, and drank it all down with evident enjoyment. He watched the slight rippling of the muscles in her slender throat as she eased her thirst and he reached to refill her glass. He waited for her to drink again, then took the glass from her hand and

4

replaced it on the small gilt table. Lowering himself with easy grace onto the tapestry footstool at her side, he took her hand and began to kiss her wrist. Slowly he pressed his mouth along the soft, blue-veined whiteness of her inner arm, at the same time easing back her silk cuff with his sinuous brown fingers. His eyes were dark and burning.

She ran her other hand through his black, curling hair and leaned back against her cushions with a contented little sigh. 'Dear David. It's good to be back in London.'

David Valsino, exclusive fencing master to some of the richest men in London and discreet lover of many of their wives, felt his heart lurch like a boy's. 'We've missed you, *carissima*, these last few weeks. Where have you been?'

She relaxed contentedly on the beautiful Louis Quinze settee. 'I've been living in luxury. In the country.' She wrinkled her face exquisitely.

'And the country bored you, my dear?' said David, still stroking her wrist with his fingertips.

'Not as much as I expected. I can always find some kind of entertainment.' She laughed. 'But my companion bored me excessively. He was very rich, and very stupid.'

David Valsino grinned, his teeth white and even in the sunbrowned perfection of his face. 'Most women of my acquaintance would say that was the perfect combination.'

'Not for me.' She reached languidly for her wine and drank again, savouring the sweet, rich liquid. 'Though I miss his wealth, I could do with some money of my own.'

'Couldn't we all?' said David lightly.

She turned suddenly towards him, resting her hand on his forearm. 'David, you've got lots of rich clients, haven't you? Won't you introduce me to some of them?'

'You want to seduce them, *carissima*?'

She shook her head, smiling. 'Not unless they're very, very eligible. You know how fastidious I am, David. No, I want to win their money. I want to be invited to those

5

discreet, fabulously wealthy parties of theirs, where the gaming goes on all night, and they think nothing of wagering thousands of guineas on the turn of a single card.'

Her blue eyes were glittering, her voice husky. He said, 'My dear, I know of your reputation. I can't possibly introduce you to my patrons, because you'd fleece them all within a week.'

She pouted a little, trailing her fingers down his forearm. 'You're accusing me of cheating, Signor Valsino?'

He laughed. 'Oh, no, Marisa. You're far too clever for that. But I have heard that you have the most incredible luck. Save it for the gaming hells of Leicester Street that you and your friends frequent, eh?'

Her eyes became shuttered. There was a silence, and then, to his relief, those wonderful blue eyes glinted mischievously as she smiled up at him from beneath the thick veil of her lashes. 'Ah, well. An hour before your next pupil, you say, Signor Valsino?'

He caught his breath, then said smoothly, 'A whole hour, *carissima*.'

'And what shall we do with that hour, signor?'

His eyes darkened in anticipation. Her shirt clung damply to her skin where she'd washed herself, and he could see the dark ripeness of her nipples thrusting against the silk. He swallowed and said, 'You are the one with the ideas, Signorina Marisa.'

She smiled deliciously. 'That's true. Well, then. In view of your recent, scandalous comments about my prowess, shall we have a game of cards?'

'As I've said, everyone knows of your luck in any kind of contest, Signorina. You are bound to win.'

She clapped her hands. 'Then let it be dice. And if you provide them yourself, then how can I possibly have the advantage?'

He hesitated, then nodded. 'But what shall we play for?'

She looked at him directly with an enticingly mischievous expression in her eyes. 'Why, the winner can have exactly what he, or she, desires.'

He felt a throb of excitement. 'I still feel you are bound to win.'

'Ah,' she murmured, leaning closer to him, her fingertips trailing along the soft dark hairs on the back of his hand. 'But if we both want the same thing, then that's no problem, is it? No problem at all.'

He got up, his dark eyes smoky with desire, and walked slowly across to the inlaid walnut bureau in the corner of the room. He took his time in unlocking it, because he was only too aware that his fingers were trembling with excitement and he didn't want her to notice it. As he searched for the dice, trying to appear casual and in control, he swiftly ran through everything he could remember about Marisa Brooke.

She'd arrived in London last summer, after travelling round the continent for many years with her father. He'd gathered that it was her father's unexpected death in Vienna that had precipitated her return; but Marisa spoke little of her past.

When she'd first made contact with David through a mutual acquaintance and asked him for lessons in fencing, he'd resigned himself to a mildly entertaining session with yet another spoiled society beauty who would be anxious to toss the rapiers aside as soon as possible and engage him in another sort of rather more intimate physical combat. David Valsino had no false modesty about his reputation in fashionable circles. Women found his dark Italian good looks and lithe, graceful body intensely appealing. His discretion was an added bonus.

But when Marisa Brooke arrived on his doorstep, he realised immediately that she was quite different. He judged her to be around 23, or 24. She looked younger, because of her slender build and innocent face, but she had all the quiet self-confidence of a mature woman. She'd brought foils of her own, which he'd checked over; they were a trifle overlong for his taste, but they were wonderfully balanced. In addition, she had her own face mask, made according to the original design introduced by La Boissiere 35 years ago. 'It belonged to my father,' she'd explained simply in her low, musical voice when he admired the way the wires had been oiled and cherished.

She was also, he'd realised at that very first meeting, one of the most exciting women he'd ever met. At first, he'd thought her face to be utterly angelic; it was heart-shaped, exquisite, with a delicate tip-tilted nose and huge, thickly lashed eyes of cornflower blue, comp-lemented by a full, enticing mouth that had a tendency to part in delicious invitation whenever she smiled.

Angelic. That was what he'd thought, when she'd first come to the door of his discréet residence just off St James's Street, asking him if he really was the best fencing master in all of London.

He'd realised extremely quickly that 'angelic' was not quite the right word to describe Marisa Brooke. He realised that when she first slipped her hands down his breeches, coolly and deliberately, then bent down to taste him, as if he were some fine wine.

They'd had several encounters since then, and they were always memorable. She told him little about herself, and he asked few questions, but he gleaned that she made some sort of living amongst the gaming dens with which the back streets of London teemed. Occasionally, he knew, she allowed herself to be patronised by some rich, besotted admirer, but these affairs never lasted long. David knew that it was always Marisa whose ardour cooled first. Not many men succeeded in holding her interest.

He found the dice at last in their little leather box and walked back towards her, bending to place them on the little gilt table by the settee. As he did so, Marisa leaned forward to pick them up, and her loose silk shirt fell apart to afford him a devastating glimpse of her rosy-tipped breasts. It was done deliberately, he was quite sure. He swallowed hard, conscious of the rearing hard-

8

ness at his loins. Dear God, but she was utterly bewitching.

Marisa Brooke, watching him discreetly from beneath her thick lashes, let the dice click in her palm like old friends and smiled secretly to herself. David Valsino was very sure of himself, as always. But, though he didn't realise it, she, Marisa, was the one in charge.

Her body was still supple and warm from the fencing. Surreptitiously she'd allowed herself to become progressively aroused as the duel progressed: the lithe, fluid movements of combat, the muscular grace of her opponent, her own taut prowess as her body's balance was gracefully expressed in the very tip of her dancing rapier, never failed to excite her. And what happened next was up to her.

She tipped the two dice into their little leather box and assessed her partner thoughtfully. David Valsino was not tall, but he was beautifully made, with wide shoulders and slim, muscular hips; just as she liked her men, even if he was somewhat arrogant. His face was darkly handsome, in a way calculated to make simpering English-women melt; his skin was smooth and warm, and gilded to a light bronze by the sun of his homeland. By way of contrast, she knew that his thighs and chest were lightly matted with silky black hair, which intensified to a thick, wiry nest of delight at his loins. As she fondled the dice, she remembered their first meeting with a little quiver of amusement. He'd been desperate for her, but was uncertain about making the first move. When Marisa had slid her hand down his slim-fitting breeches, her blue eyes wide with lethal innocence, he'd cried out hoarsely in surprise. She herself had been forced to admit privately to a pleasurable sense of shock when she'd felt the size of the hard, hot shaft of his erect manhood thrusting agonisingly against her teasing fingertips. After that, she and the fencing master had proceeded rapidly to a most satisfactory mutual pleasuring, the first of several.

There was a rather promising swell at the fencing

9

master's loins now, if Marisa was not mistaken. Her eyes glinted at the thought of that excitingly eager penis, sturdy and endearingly long in erection, pushing urgently at the placket of his breeches. He sat calmly before her on his stool, with the little gilt table between them, his elbows resting on his parted thighs. She knew that he would be quite sure of triumph, one way or another.

Marisa leaned forward confidentially and said, 'Let's keep it simple, shall we? Best of three?'

He nodded. 'Whatever you say, *carissima*. You first.'

She cast a three and a four. When David reached silently for the ivory cubes, Marisa felt her nipples harden against her soft silk shirt as she watched his lean brown fingers fondling the dice, and imagined those same fingers caressing her full breasts. She was aware of a pleasant stirring of sensuality, a sweet promise of pleasure that could all too soon flare into a primitive carnality that the handsome Italian would be all too ready to assuage. He was calmly confident that he would win, and she was equally confident that she would.

He threw two fives. Trying to keep the gloating tone out of his voice, he said, 'What did you say we were playing for?'

Her shadowed blue eyes glittered. 'Winner to decide.'

'Anything?'

'Anything.'

David swallowed. Outside, the sun was starting to fade, and cool shadows stretched across the lofty room. A dust-specked shaft of light fell across the marble mantel, with its enticing array of invitation cards. Marisa let her eyes rest just for a moment on one larger than the others, importantly edged with gilt. In the street below, there was a noisy altercation between two carriages fighting for space, but the raucous oaths of the drivers seemed a world away. Marisa reached lazily across the table to place her hand on David's hard thigh, and felt him tense as her fingers travelled slowly upwards. She paused tantalisingly just before she came to the place

10

where his taut breeches strained across the thick stem of his phallus, and she saw the colour rush to his face. Marisa smiled, and took the dice box. Perhaps she should let him win after all. She knew very well what he would claim as his reward, and the idea was far from repugnant to her. She knew from experience that his fingers were gentle yet knowing, his body firm and sweet, while his penis was an exquisitely lengthy weapon that he wielded as skilfully as any rapier.

She leaned forward to make her cast, aware that the secret flesh at the juncture of her thighs, which was gently yet insistently caressed by her tight breeches, was liquid with need. She longed to feel his hands cupping the fulness of her hot breasts, longed to feel his delicious mouth tugging at her tight nipples as her secret self opened up like a nectared flower to the dark thrust of his penis.

She trickled the dice out. Five and six. She saw the brief flicker of anguish on David's face and stopped him gently with her hand as he reached out for the box.

'There's no hurry,' she said softly, sliding the dice back in. 'Do you know, I've a fancy for some more wine.'

When he came back with two full glasses in his hands, she saw the shock in his face as he realised that she was lying back casually on the settee with her shirt unbuttoned, while her hands lovingly cradled her small but full breasts. He swallowed hard.

'Your drink,' he said in rather a hoarse voice.

'Thank you,' said Marisa charmingly. She was examining her thrusting nipples intently with her fingers, knowing that her self-absorbed caresses would make his already swollen penis rear in agonised need. 'Your throw, I think, David.'

With a low groan, he seated himself and emptied out the dice. A two and a one.

'Oh, bad luck! Last throw to decide,' said Marisa sweetly. 'This is so exciting, I can hardly bear it. Come and sit beside me, David.'

He ran his hand somewhat distractedly through his

dark, curly hair and did as he was told. She nestled against him, still sipping her wine, with her pouting breasts deliciously exposed. He longed to caress them, but her cool self-possession disconcerted him.

She slanted a mischievous look up at him and murmured, 'Still as hotly primed as ever, David? How is Lady Morency? Does she still pay you to pleasure her? Does she still like to crouch on all fours for you, and call you her mighty stallion?'

He preened himself, just a little, and laughed dismissively. 'Lady Morency became rather a nuisance, so I cancelled our engagements for a while. But I'm busy enough, yes.'

'I'm not surprised. I've missed you, David. I've really missed you.' And before David could move, she'd twisted round to bend over his lap and was starting to unbutton his breeches. Within moments she'd freed his penis so that it sprang out, darkly engorged. David laughed a little weakly.

'Marisa, we've not finished the game yet. But of course, *carissima*, if you can't wait . . .'

She smiled. 'Poor David. It must be so trying to have women so desperate for you. How delicious you are. We'll return to the game in a moment, shall we?'

As she spoke, she let her fingers flicker along the dark stem of his rearing phallus. It trembled and strained towards her, and David's breathing became ragged. Marisa, her delicate tongue just protruding from her parted lips, positioned herself with great concentration so that her pink-crested breasts hovered just above the angrily swelling tip of his penis. Then she lowered herself and rubbed her nipples lightly against the velvety glans.

David clutched at her shoulders with a groan and pulled her face towards him to kiss her hungrily. She responded for one tantalising moment, her mouth yielding and her tongue flicking coolly against his. Then, almost regretfully, she pulled herself away.

'Rather a wild thrust in prime, that, wouldn't you say,

Signor Valsino? What did you tell me about fencing, on my very first lesson? "Know your opponent's weakness."'

'Dear God. Marisa, you witch!'

She laughed merrily and turned back to the dice. 'My throw, I think.'

A five and a six again. She smiled at him, letting her eyes drift down to his swaying penis as it thrust up hungrily from his open breeches.

He said, a little tightly, 'Is it really worth my throwing, Marisa? After all, we both want the same thing, don't we?'

'Possibly.' She reached for the little leather box and gave it a light kiss before passing it to him. 'Your throw.'

He shrugged, and made his cast. A three and a two.

'Well. So much for the dice,' he said dismissively, and turned swiftly towards her, his hot eyes lapping up the sight of her naked breasts pouting enticingly from between the parted folds of her silk shirt.

She put out her hands gently to stop him touching her. 'We had a bargain, Signor Valsino. And I won, remember?'

'Yes. Of course I do. But surely, this is exactly what you wanted, isn't it, Marisa?' he said, caressing her with urgent certainty.

She sighed and let her gaze linger on his quivering penis. Then, to his horror, she began to slowly button up her shirt. 'Not exactly, no, pleasant though it would be. You see, there's something I want rather more.'

'What do you want, God damn it?'

She stood up and walked casually across to the fireplace. 'I want this, David.'

And she reached for the large, gilt-edged invitation that took pride of place amongst the assorted cards and letters on the marble mantelshelf.

There was a moment's aghast silence, and then he exploded. 'But that's my card for a masked ridotto at Vauxhall tonight. Why in hell do you want that?'

She stroked the thick, creamy card with her fingers, almost purring. 'Because it looks rich and discreet. No

13

names, no identity. Just this little mark of the ace of spades in the corner. A masked ridotto at Vauxhall, you say; it's ideal for me, David. Will there be card play, do you think?'

David stood up, his handsome face dark with annoyance and disappointment. He started to rearrange his clothing, and his penis throbbed angrily as he forced it back inside his breeches.

'Undoubtedly,' he said bitterly. 'So that's it. You want to make a fool of some other unwary punter, just as you've made a fool of me.'

She walked to where he stood and reached up to draw a finger softly down his lean, smooth-shaven cheek. 'Now don't be like that, David darling. I did ask you earlier if you'd introduce me to some of your wealthy friends, but you refused. Then I caught sight of that invitation, and decided I'd have to take matters into my own hands. After all, it was a fair contest, wasn't it?'

'I don't know,' he muttered. He'd heard all the rumours, that Mistress Brooke had a range of impossibly devilish tricks that enabled her to gull the entire world at faro and hazard without a flicker of her innocent blue eyes.

'But I couldn't possibly have cheated, David. After all, they were your dice. And you did agree when we started that I could have whatever I wanted.'

'I thought,' he said stormily, 'that you wanted me!'

'Then let that be a lesson to you,' said Marisa Brooke softly. 'Of course, I adore you, but just now, I want this invitation rather more. A masked ridotto! No-one will recognise me. The whole affair will be delightfully *incognito*.'

David said, through gritted teeth, 'I could tell the host that my invitation was stolen. I could warn him not to let you in.'

'Oh, David. That would be most ungenerous of you. By the way, who is the Ace of Spades? Is he rich and stupid?'

She was laughing at him, mocking him. He replied stiffly,

'Surely you'd rather that the identity of your host was a surprise, Marisa. You like surprises, don't you?'

Her husky laughter tinkled around the darkening room. 'Yes. Yes, I do like surprises. Dear David, you are still my friend, aren't you? You're not really angry with me, just because I want to win lots of lovely money off a crowd of drunken, aristocratic fools who are only to eager to lose it all anyway.'

He struggled, then laughed ruefully at her deliciously expressive face. 'I'm not angry. Just incredibly disappointed,' he said frankly. 'Dear God, Marisa, you must be the most tantalising woman in London.'

'In that case our next meeting should be something for you to look forward to,' she smiled. She'd walked across to the doorway and was pulling on her supple leather boots.

'Perhaps we can play piquet next time,' said David, following her. 'I'm quite good at that. I might even win.'

'Don't count on it,' Marisa laughed. She was easing on her long, silk-lined greatcoat, cut to look like a man's, and then she pulled on her curly-brimmed hat, tucking her hair up into its crown so that she looked like some exquisite blond youth. She reached up to kiss him affectionately on the cheek. Then, without waiting for his footman to show her out, she ran lightly down the stairs.

'Enjoy yourself tonight,' called out David suddenly, but he wasn't sure she'd heard him.

Marisa paused for a moment on the pavement outside the row of tall stuccoed houses where David lived. The sun was setting now behind the rooftops; the grey light of the London dusk softened the hard outlines of the busy street. A fruitseller went by, singing out her wares. Marisa bought an apple, and bit contentedly into its crisp, juicy flesh.

As usual, she'd got exactly what she wanted. She glanced up affectionately at the high windows of the lofty room where Signor Valsino gave his expensive private fencing lessons. Dear David. She'd almost given way to temptation and pleasured herself with him, against all her resolve; the rapier-play had excited her, as it always did, and he was exceptionally handsome.

But he was also rather conceited. And from the moment she'd caught sight of that mysterious invitation from the Ace of Spades, displayed so enticingly on his mantelshelf, she'd wanted it badly, so she'd played to win. The exquisite thrill of uncertainty as she'd substituted her own weighted dice just before each of her own throws sent the blood racing through her veins. In fact, it was almost as exciting as the proximity of David's warm, virile body.

She'd heard once of a man who'd orgasmed at his moment of triumph in a low-class gaming hell in Southampton Street. She'd laughed when she heard of it, but secretly she could understand. Poor David wouldn't understand. He'd not suspected her of cheating at all, and that was part of the joy. He never had the slightest idea that each of her daringly intimate caresses was intended to distract him, while she dexterously replaced his innocent dice with the pair she always carried in a tiny secret pocket in her breeches, the pair that were weighted so that they never gave any result but a five and a six.

Marisa was gifted with luck and skill, a lethal combination. She considered that it had been a successful afternoon, but it could have been better. Her body told her so as it twinged softly with regret at what might have been. She frowned as she finished the apple and tossed the core into the gutter, only too aware that her secret feminine parts were still moist and swollen, still anticipating the delicious caress of David Valsino's serviceable penis. But she'd been right to turn him down on this occasion. Sex was without a doubt the supreme pleasure, but as with all pleasures, Marisa's greatest strength was that she could take it or leave it, depending on how it fitted in with her plans.

Today, David had been oversure of her. And besides, from the moment she'd seen that invitation beckoning her from his mantelpiece, she'd wanted it badly. With a quickening of her pulses she reached into the silk-clad inner pocket of her coat and drew out the gilt-edged card with its intriguing instruction to admit the bearer to a masked ridotto at Vauxhall Pleasure Gardens that very evening. There would be supper, dancing and cards, and from what she knew of such occasions, all the guests would be expected to remain anonymous, not revealing their names unless requested by their host, the ace of spades himself.

The Ace of Spades. Probably some fat, aging old roué, a contemporary of the Prince Regent, Marisa told herself dismissively. But at least he and his guests would be rich, and she could win lots of money off them and depart swiftly into the crowds at Vauxhall, with no-one being any the wiser as to her identity. No-one would even guess she wasn't a genuine guest, unless, of course, the ace of spades himself challenged her.

She shivered deliciously as she contemplated her evening, feeling as though she was on the verge of some exciting new world, where absolute discretion was the unstated rule, and not an eyelid flickered as fortunes were won or lost at the turn of a card. Where the winnings might be so great that she would never have to play again.

Her thoughts were interrupted as an open chaise, coming from the direction of St James's Square, edged rather too close to the kerb in order to avoid a milkman's dray. Marisa jumped swiftly back out of the way, at the same time instinctively assessing the fine equipage. The chaise was of bottle green, with glittering brass lamps and high yellow wheels. It was drawn by two handsome chestnuts, and its driver was swathed in a many caped greatcoat of fine broadcloth and a tall crowned hat. He handled his spirited team with consummate skill, avoiding the big dray with inches to spare.

And then, she realised that he was drawing up outside

David's house. She felt a moment's unease, then shrugged. Another of David's rich clients, no doubt. She turned to walk on, away from the splendid vehicle, but she pulled up in surprise as the driver's peremptory voice followed her down the street.

'Here, boy. A shilling for you to hold my horses.'

Marisa whirled round to see that the man in the fine green chaise had swung himself down from the box and gone to his horses' heads. She said darkly, 'Are you by any chance speaking to me?'

He didn't even look at her. He was too busy attending to his horses as they restlessly champed at their bits. 'I am indeed. Be quick about it, will you?'

Marisa caught her breath. He hadn't realised she was a woman. No fault there, as she knew she looked very much like a youth with her man's greatcoat concealing her feminine curves and her wide-brimmed hat hiding her long hair. But she burned with indignation at the arrogance of him. Why, he hadn't even bothered to look at her as he issued his command. She said, with slow deliberation, 'I think you've made a mistake. No-one pays me to do anything.'

His face jerked towards her at that, his attention drawn at last from his precious horses, and Marisa had the satisfaction of seeing a pair of world-weary grey eyes open rather wide as he realised his mistaken assumption as to her sex. 'Really?' he murmured in a silkily cultured voice. 'You surprise me. I should think that quite a few people would pay a small fortune to see you out of those clothes.'

She caught her breath, and gazed calmly up at him. '*You* certainly couldn't afford it.'

'You think not?' His wide, thin mouth mocked her. 'In my experience, everyone – but everyone – has their price.'

He'd taken off his high-crowned hat, and laid it on the driver's seat of his chaise. Marisa, her practised eyes assessing him narrowly, took in the fashionably short dark hair that was cut in a Bedford crop, the pristine

18

folds of his white lawn cravat, and the luxurious shine of his top-boots that gleamed beneath the sweeping folds of his coat. An aristocrat, thought Marisa grimly, in his early thirties, awash with money and self-importance. Rich, powerful and utterly arrogant.

'How very sad for you,' she said sweetly, 'that you have to pay for your pleasures. But of course, I can understand it. After all, no self-respecting female would come to someone like you of her own accord, now, would she?'

The cold perfection of his haughty features seemed chiselled in ice. 'And what exactly do you mean by that, Ganymede?' he said softly.

Ganymede, the boy beloved of the gods, a kind of bisexual concubine. How dare he address her thus? Marisa's mind crept tantalisingly over all the backstreet cant she knew by way of revenge, but she rejected it all as being too subtle a form of insult. Instead she said pityingly, 'I mean, of course, that it's quite evident that you must have a very small penis.'

His face seemed to blaze. Then his eyes flickered over her thoughtfully. 'Well, I do believe I should horsewhip you for that,' he said in the same level, silky voice.

'Ah. You enjoy that kind of thing, do you?' said Marisa in wide-eyed innocence. 'Do you pay for that as well? There are some women in a house in Vere Street, most discreet, I believe, who'll not charge you overmuch.'

The man's hand was tightening ominously on his riding crop just as the big door of David Valsino's house flew open and a flustered footman came hurrying out.

'Lord Delsingham,' the footman uttered in distress. 'A thousand pardons, my lord, that no-one was here to greet you. Signor Valsino is expecting you, of course. If you would care to go inside, my lord, a groom will take your carriage to the stables round the back.'

Marisa stood transfixed. Lord James Delsingham, one of the richest, most fashionable men in London. She felt rather faint.

Delsingham was saying coolly, 'No need for the stables. My visit is only a short one. Tell the groom to walk the horses up and down until I return – with care, you understand, or believe me, there'll be the devil to pay.'

'Yes, my lord. This way, my lord.'

Lord Delsingham turned to go up the steps to David's house. Then, seeing Marisa still standing there transfixed, his mouth twisted in unexpected acknowledgement, and she felt a sudden wild racing of her pulses.

'Remember, my sweet Ganymede,' he said softly. 'Everyone has their price.'

Marisa pulled herself together. 'I told you before,' she said stoutly. 'Nobody pays me to do anything, my lord!'

'A pity,' he murmured, his narrowed grey eyes raking her. 'My imagination runs riot at the sight of you in those breeches. And the thought of you out of them is quite devastating.'

Hissing, she lunged forward while at the same time whipping back her hand to strike him across the cheek, but he caught her arm effortlessly to parry her blow, and even as she gasped in surprise, he bent his dark head to plant a kiss on the inside of her wrist. As she struggled to free herself, he parted his lips to let his tongue trail insolently along the delicate veined skin, and she felt the wicked warmth of his caress burning her, melting her insides. She couldn't move. She couldn't speak.

He straightened up, still holding her hand. He seemed to tower over her. 'I'll wager,' he said thoughtfully, 'that mine is the best offer you'll get all day, Ganymede. And by the way, you are quite wrong about my physique.'

With that, he smiled coldly and let her go.

Marisa watched rather weakly as he strode up the steps to David's front door, his beautiful long coat swirling behind him. She made an obscene gesture after his retreating back, but he was sublimely unaware of it. 'Hell and damnation,' she muttered angrily.

Her good mood was quite, quite broken. Before, she'd felt in charge, even triumphant after the success of her encounter with David. But now this insolent aristocrat, with his jeering mockery, had quite subdued her spirits.

Lord James Delsingham, she knew, was one of the richest men in London. He was also, Marisa was quite sure, the type of man who would be a hard, selfish lover, taking his pleasure with little regard for the feelings of the woman he was with. Cold, powerful, arrogant. She had a sudden fleeting vision of him in bed, with that hard, muscled body naked and aroused, and she shivered and shut her eyes. The tiny, insolent caress of his lips and tongue had disturbed her senses in a way that David's more obvious approaches had quite failed to do.

Well, damn him, she wouldn't let him spoil her day. She set off at a brisk pace towards Pall Mall, looking forward to the bright, candlelit shop windows that would brighten her journey home as dusk fell. Feeling almost calm again, she searched for the invitation in her pocket and stroked it. The cold, silken feel of the thick card against her fingertips soothed her. Tonight, she would be going to Vauxhall Pleasure Gardens, where amongst the lamplit shrubberies, rich and poor, pickpockets and the highest in the land, would mingle with one another in normally unheard-of freedom. The occasion would suit her purpose very well indeed.

At the thought of that tiny but elegant ace of spades emblazoned mysteriously in one corner of the card, she felt a little shiver of excitement that put Lord Delsingham almost completely from her mind. But not quite.

After David Valsino had heard Marisa's light footsteps retreating down the staircase to his front door, he'd slumped back rather despairingly on the settee. The silk cushions still smelled tantalisingly of her hair and her skin, driving him wild.

He remembered again the first time they'd met, one day last summer. She'd taken him completely unawares when, just as he was putting his precious rapiers away, she'd sunk to her knees at his feet and carefully released his penis. It was already engorged, inevitable in her exquisite presence, and she'd smiled at it happily, approvingly. Then she'd licked him quite deliciously,

21

running her tongue around his swollen glans and driving him demented as her moist lips glided up and down his straining shaft. That had been their first meeting, and he was still just as helpless in her presence. And now she'd fooled him yet again with that infernal dice game, and stolen his invitation as well. All in all, he'd been utterly routed.

As soon as the big front door banged shut behind her, he surreptitiously released his painfully engorged genitals and began to caress himself. Damn her, with her infernal teasing. She'd utterly bewitched him, and there would be no peace for him until the fire in his loins was extinguished. Lying back tensely against the cushions, he pumped his foreskin up and down the bone-hard core of his penis with swift skill until he ejaculated. And at the very extremity of his pleasure he imagined he heard Marisa's light, melodious laugh, almost as if she knew what he'd been reduced to, damn her.

Then he heard the front door again, and he sprang guiltily to his feet as he heard slow, steady masculine footsteps coming up the stairs. Swiftly wiping himself with his handkerchief, he struggled to rearrange his clothing, and had only just succeeded when his footman knocked at the door. 'Lord Delsingham, Signor Valsino.'

Delsingham. Damn. He'd almost forgotten that they had a rapier practice arranged for this hour. And then Delsingham was in the room, imperiously sweeping past the hovering footman as David stammered out, 'My lord. You are a little earlier than I expected.'

Delsingham's cold grey eyes assessed the fencing master's somewhat dishevelled appearance with amusement. David wondered despairingly if the room smelled of sex.

'No matter,' said his lordship evenly. 'I can tell I've taken you by surprise. I've just called by to postpone my rapier session with you until another time. I find myself somewhat pressed. I have certain preparations to set in order for this evening.'

'Certainly, my lord. Whatever you wish.'

Delsingham was lazily scanning the room. 'If I didn't

know better, Valsino, I'd say you'd just had some woman up here. You are coming tonight, aren't you? I don't see my invitation on your mantelpiece.'

'T-tonight, my lord?' stammered David.

'For a fencing master,' drawled Delsingham, 'you seem somewhat slow witted today. To my masked ridotto at Vauxhall, of course.'

'Of course, my lord! The invitation is – is downstairs, in my front parlour. How many guests have you invited?'

Delsingham shrugged, his wide, powerful shoulders rippling beneath the fine cloth of his greatcoat. Taller than David, he was unusually fit for a man of his height. He had considerable skill with the foils, and David normally enjoyed their encounters. But not today.

Delsingham said carelessly, 'I'm not sure of the exact numbers. Fifty or sixty, I think.'

In that case, thought David, with a sigh of relief, he won't even know if everyone's there, especially if all his guests are in masquerade, and he won't notice Marisa's there instead of me. 'I look forward to tonight, my lord,' he said aloud.

'Good. So do I.' Again Delsingham smiled, that wide, thin-lipped smile that made him look even more dangerous than usual. 'Well, I'll leave you to carry on with whatever it was I interrupted.'

Then, thank goodness, he was gone. A few moments later David heard the sound of his chaise drawing away down the street, and wondered if perhaps Delsingham had passed Marisa earlier. He wondered what Marisa would say when she found out that the ace of spades whose invitation had so intrigued her was in fact one of the richest men in London.

David supposed he ought to have warned her, but he was damned if he would. After all, it was a subtle kind of revenge, to let her go unprotected into the lion's den. If any man could sort out Marisa Brooke, he reflected ruefully, then it was James, Lord Delsingham.

Chapter Two

Marisa was almost home. As she made her way purposefully through the labyrinth of narrow streets that lay behind the Strand, she felt her spirits rise inexorably in spite of the gathering darkness. Here the shabby houses pressed in on one another in crowded disarray, a world away from the spacious residences of the area where David lived. But as the lamplighter did his rounds, there was an air of vitality, of things about to happen amongst the crowds who passed between the low taverns and gaming hells that clustered in this quarter of London. Already the noise of music and laughter came from lighted doorways, and as Marisa passed Bob Derry's notorious cider cellar on the corner of Maiden Lane and Half-Moon Alley, a bunch of drunken young bucks spilled out noisily, their purses no doubt considerably lighter than when they went in. Realising that Marisa wasn't a boy, as they'd first assumed, they gaped at her with lecherous eyes, but she merely laughed at them and carried on, her long coat swinging jauntily around her calves, her boots sturdy and comfortable as she walked swiftly on towards Covent Garden, where an unsavoury collection of wine booths and tumbledown shacks now mocked Inigo Jones's beautiful square and piazza.

Her pace quickening, she turned at last down a narrow alleyway where scruffy urchins played with broken skittles outside an ill-lit local tavern, and here she came to a halt. The Blue Bell was popularly known as The Finish, because it was open all night, and harboured drunken punters who'd been kicked out of everywhere else. Marisa was fond of it. Pushing open the battered door, she made her way along the grimy passage that led past the tap room, breathing in the familiar strong odours of beer and tobacco smoke.

She didn't pass unnoticed. At a nearby table, she observed the flash of cards and the gleam of coins changing hands. She paused as someone called out to her, 'Marisa! Marisa, darling, you'll join us for a game?'

She turned, grinning. 'And play with your marked cards? Not tonight. I'm on my way out again soon. I have higher stakes in mind.'

'Then we wish you luck,' came the friendly response. Marisa, who'd moved into rooms above the inn some months ago and used it as her base, had quickly become a favourite with all the Blue Bell's patrons. They'd been suspicious of her at first, and then they'd tried to fleece her. But she'd calmly beaten them all hollow at cards one night, and then coolly tongue-lashed a drunkard who tried to kiss her, until he crept from the crowded tap room for ever. After that, she had quickly become a firm favourite, almost a kind of talisman for the patrons of the inn.

She picked up a lighted tallow candle and hurried quickly up the narrow, twisting staircase to her rooms, feeling in her pocket for the key. The door creaked open into the darkness and she stepped inside, setting her candlestick down on the battered oak table against the wall. Then she stiffened.

Instantly, she knew beyond doubt that there was someone else in her apartment. A soft light came from the bedroom door, which was slightly ajar, and she could hear the secretive murmur of voices. She frowned and moved lightly across to a chest of drawers, opening it

25

silently and drawing out a gleaming flintlock pocket pistol, her only tangible legacy from her father, who'd also shown her how to use it. If there were intruders, then she would deal with them. Easing off her big coat and laying it across a chair, she walked quietly towards the half-open bedroom door, relishing the warm, smooth walnut grain of the pistol against her palm, and stole a look inside.

The light came from one solitary oil lamp flickering on a small table in the corner of the bedchamber. She rarely used this room, because she found it oppressive and preferred to sleep on the comfortable day-bed in the small front chamber that she laughingly referred to as her parlour. This room was filled with heavy oak furniture and dark faded draperies dating from the last century, when the inn was a relatively respectable posting-house and the chamber was used for overnight guests. Tonight, Marisa realised as she fastidiously wrinkled her tip-tilted nose, the fusty smell was stronger than ever; in fact, the room reeked of sex. Her cornflower-blue eyes opened wide and, holding her breath, she edged further inside.

In the far corner of the room was a solid four-poster draped with threadbare silk hangings that almost concealed the interior of the bed from her view. But it was quite evident that behind the hangings, two people were moving in the unmistakable preliminaries to copulation. Marisa, frowning, moved silently sideways so she could see them, and her finger caressed the trigger of her pistol.

A man was sprawled back on the bed, moaning aloud. He was a servant, to judge by his coarse homespun shirt and baggy breeches, and his clothes were fairly insignificant anyway, mused Marisa wryly, since they were almost off him, thanks to the endeavours of the plump young woman who knelt on the bed beside him. Her long dark curls tumbled loosely round her shoulders as she dipped her head to flicker her tongue enticingly round the man's exposed, fully-erect penis, and in response the man was arching his hips distractedly towards the woman's mouth, reaching out for her generous breasts as they spilled from her bodice, his fingers squeezing avidly on the dark crimson teats.

Marisa's delicate blonde eyebrows lifted. The man was undeniably well made, she decided. His member certainly matched his big, muscular frame. In fact, it was of mouthwatering proportions, meaty and gnarled and stout enough to satisfy the most lascivious of women. His dark-haired companion was evidently of the same opinion, because she was uttering little whimpers of delight as she released the man's engorged shaft from her teasing lips and dangled her ripe breasts against his sturdy, thrusting phallus. The man clutched convulsively at her mane of loose brown curls and groaned aloud at her lewd caresses.

Marisa considered it a pity to interrupt them at this point in the proceedings. Feeling suddenly generous, she settled herself quietly in a big, carved oak chair in a shadowy corner by the door and watched them contemplatively.

The couple were still quite unaware of her presence, and were anyway quite beyond caring, which Marisa found rather endearing. The woman had rolled over onto her back, pulling her legs apart so that her full skirts fell away to reveal the dark serge stockings that were gartered just above her knees. The man grunted aloud and the perspiration stood out on his brow as he hurriedly knelt between her plump, fleshy thighs and gripped his hugely throbbing penis in his fist, pulling down his breeches with his other hand so that Marisa was given a shameless view of his muscular, hairy buttocks.

Marisa let out a little sigh as the man tenderly fondled the woman's lush secret parts with his swollen purple rod, liberally adorning its tip with musky female juices. Then, as the woman scrabbled desperately at his broad shoulders and clasped her trembling calves round his waist, he held his breath, and slid himself slowly into her. 'Now, then, my darling,' he was muttering hoarsely, 'easy does it, now.'

Marisa felt a reluctant stab of desire as her own nipples tightened hungrily at the sight. She wished it was her. She wished she was experiencing that fine, manly shaft sliding roughly up inside her, pleasuring her already moist vagina with delicious thrusts. Her hand stole to her aching breasts, caressing their fulness beneath the silk of her shirt until her nipples were hard as stones; then she pulled her hand away.

No. Better by far to be the one in charge, to be coolly aloof. She always chose her men carefully, and this muscle-bound peasant wasn't for her. But in spite of her resolve a soft flush rose in her cheeks. As she leaned forward slightly to get a better view, her tight buckskin breeches seemed to caress her moist, swollen labia, and she felt the ridged seam at her crotch pressing relentlessly against her heated clitoris, the sweet kernel of all her pleasure. She bit softly on her full lower lip and stroked the warm wood of her pistol, frowning as she watched.

The woman was on the very brink of her extremity, tearing at the man's broad shoulders with her hands and bouncing fiercely on the brocade covers of the bed as she gasped aloud. 'Dearest John! That's what I want; give it to me, give it to me now. Let me feel your fine fat prick deep inside me. Oh, yes . . .'

The man was certainly doing his best, thought Marisa wryly. His muscular bottom was pounding away dementedly, and his face was dark with the approaching onslaught of rapture. They were both nearly there. Marisa looked forward to seeing the looks on their faces when they realised they had an audience. Then she stopped thinking, because the man had withdrawn almost completely, preparing himself for a final, mighty assault. Marisa's pulse quickened helplessly as she caught a mouthwatering glimpse of his massive penis, its gnarled purple length sleekly coated with the woman's juices. As he slowly drove it back in between her fleshy lips the woman writhed and squirmed beneath him in delight, and Marisa felt an ominous tightening at her own belly, felt a warm, liquid melting between her thighs. Suddenly

28

she could imagine all too vividly what it would be like to enfold that mighty rod within her own silken flesh.

She closed her eyes tightly, fighting down her arousal as the couple on the bed bucked in frantic ecstasy, making the faded silk hangings ripple and sway as they shouted aloud in the extremity of their pleasure. But Marisa soon realised that closing her eyes was a mistake. Because, inexplicably, she was suddenly assailed by a vision of the man who had insulted her outside David's house. She saw his arrogant, aristocratic face with its chillingly handsome features, saw the cold mockery in his grey eyes as he murmured, like a wicked promise, 'I assure you, you are quite wrong about my physique.'

Lord Delsingham. Helplessly she remembered the wicked feel of his flickering tongue against her inner wrist, and imagined that same velvety tongue dancing between her swollen labia, parting them, finding her exquisitely engorged clitoris and bringing her, with long, rasping strokes, to the very brink of orgasm. At the same time she rocked forwards helplessly in her chair, so that the tight seam of her breeches pressed insistently between her thighs at all her most secret parts. She ground her fingers down helplessly against her clitoris, pressing herself through the leather into a sweet, hard little climax, and her body leaped and quivered silently as she imagined Lord Delsingham smiling triumphantly down at her with his beautiful, devilish grey eyes.

Utterly shaken, she drew herself dazedly back into the present, her body still flushed and trembling as the couple on the bed shuddered finally to their release and then collapsed in exhaustion.

Marisa let them lie there for one minute on the rumpled bedcovers, their bodies sheened with perspiration. Then, recovering her composure, she got up and sauntered across the room, holding her pistol lightly in her right hand.

The man saw her first. He practically fell off the bed in alarm, and as he started to fumble with his disarrayed clothes his face was dark with consternation. The woman whipped round and gasped when she saw Marisa.

Marisa put her hand on her hip as she surveyed them. Then she said calmly, 'Lucy. Dearest Lucy, if you're going to continue as my maid, or companion, or whatever you wish to call yourself, then you really will have to learn to control your lascivious impulses. Who is it this time?'

The young woman, pulling her skirts down and her bodice up, slipped hastily from the bed and bobbed a hasty curtsey. Her pretty face was flushed with embarrassment. 'Oh, Mistress Brooke! Don't be cross with me, please don't. I thought you wouldn't be back till much, much later. I was just tidying your rooms, you see, and then I saw John the new coachman cleaning the harness out in the back yard, and – and –'

Marisa said sternly, 'You have been very wicked, to pleasure yourselves so lewdly in my private rooms.'

Lucy's hot brown eyes gleamed with excitement. 'Will – will you punish us, Mistress Brooke?'

Marisa considered. 'Perhaps.'

Lucy's tongue flicked across her lips as Marisa went on, 'But not now. I have to go out very soon, Lucy, and I need you to help me get ready.' She turned to the coachman, who'd dressed himself hastily and was gazing in fascination at her slender, boyish figure. 'As for you, John,' she said softly, 'you'd better get back to your duties, hadn't you? I assume you weren't hired by the landlord solely to pleasure the women of the house, in spite of the generous size of your manhood.' She fingered her pistol gently. 'And if you've any thoughts of pleasuring me, then you'd better think again. You see, I prefer a little finesse in my men.'

He blushed and looked alarmed. 'Yes, Mistress Brooke. I'm truly sorry!'

She gestured silently towards the door, through which he made a hasty exit, and moments later Marisa heard him thudding clumsily downstairs.

Marisa and Lucy burst out laughing and fell into one another's arms.

'Oh, Marisa,' giggled Lucy, 'dearest Marisa, he couldn't take his eyes off you, with your tight breeches and boots and that lovely silk shirt that gives just a glimpse of your breasts. You look absolutely delicious, my dear, and that pistol is a wonderful touch. It was all so exciting.' She sighed. 'I only wish you'd come to join us instead of just watching.'

'I did consider it,' admitted Marisa, her blue eyes glinting as she threw herself on the big bed and lay back against the pillows, her hands behind her head. She grinned at Lucy. 'He looked extremely well endowed.'

Lucy's brown eyes shone. 'Indeed, he is. He's rather slow-witted, but his penis is quite delicious, my dear, so hard and rampant, and he seems to be able to go on for hours. You would have loved him.' She sighed happily and drew herself cosily up on the bed beside her friend. 'But of course, you have more self-control than me.'

I didn't have a moment ago, thought Marisa with a twinge of shame as she recollected her brief, excruciating moment of pleasure. But already Lucy was chattering on, saying happily, 'Marisa, you said you had to get ready to go out shortly. Yet you mentioned nothing about it this morning. Where are you going?'

Marisa went quickly into the other room to fetch the invitation from her coat pocket. She had few secrets from Lucy, who had become her ally and her friend on almost her first night in London. Lucy had been fleeing from the watch, after rather clumsily picking a stout gentleman's pocket as he emerged from the theatre in Drury Lane. Marisa, quickly assessing her plight, had hissed to the panic-stricken girl to hide in a doorway behind some winecasks, and had then told the constables that the young woman they were after had tried to pick her pocket too and had run off into the seedy depths of Martlet Court. Lucy, emerging from her hiding place when all was clear, had vowed eternal gratitude; and Marisa, taking a sudden liking to the girl's mischievous brown eyes and merry face, had taken her into her employ as servant, companion or whatever the occasion required.

Now, with the embossed card in her hand, she returned to the bedchamber and climbed back onto the high bed. 'Look, Lucy. Look what I've got here.'

Lucy scanned the card eagerly. 'Who's it from?'

'I've really no idea. And that's all part of the fun, don't you think?'

'But – how did you get it?'

'No more questions, now, Lucy. It would take far too long to explain. But I'm going, and that's all that matters.'

Lucy sighed longingly. 'A masked ridotto – at Vauxhall. How very exciting! But you must be in costume, Marisa, what will you go as?'

'Why, I'll go as a 'bridle cull' – a female highwayman, of course. I'll wear my black riding habit and a tricorne hat. After all,' she smiled wickedly, 'they'll no doubt consider me a thief by the time I've stripped them of all their lovely guineas.' She leaned forward a little, her smooth brow puckering, and said more seriously, 'I need a lot of money, Lucy. Really a lot. The trouble is that people round here are starting to know me. They suspect me of trickery, and are wary of playing deep if I'm at the table. I need to win so much that I don't have to play again for a long, long time.'

'But they'll never catch you cheating – you're far too clever for that.'

'I certainly hope so. But anyone who wins steadily is always suspected of some sort of trickery; it's only natural. And last week, at that private card party I went to in Hertford Street, Sir Peregrine Thickett was muttering darkly to anyone who would listen about innocent-looking females who weren't what they seemed. He'd just lost 200 guineas to me, you see.'

Lucy frowned fiercely and put her arm around her friend's shoulder. 'Oh, Sir Peregrine, I remember him. He's nothing but a fat, foppish fool. I was talking to his coachman once, and he told me that Sir Peregrine likes

32

nothing better than to invite some plump young serving maid to his bedroom and make her pretend to be his nurse.'

Marisa wrinkled her tip-tilted nose in distaste. 'No!'

'But yes,' Lucy smothered a giggle. 'Whenever his wife's out of the house, he calls his favourite maid up to his room. He makes her unlace her bodice so he can suck at her titties, and she reaches into his breeches to fondle him till he grows nice and hard, and tells him he's a naughty boy. Then he crouches on the floor in front of her, grovelling, and she has to smack his bare bottom until he goes very red in the face and calls out, "Please, nursie, please don't smack me," but she beats him harder and harder until he spurts out all over the floor.'

'Gods,' said Marisa disgustedly. 'And to think that earlier that night, before I won all that money off him, he was offering me 50 guineas a month and a house of my own if I would become his mistress.'

'Nursie, nursie,' crowed Lucy, and they both exploded with laughter.

Eventually Marisa went on, more seriously, 'Anyway, Lucy, Sir Peregrine was cross when I turned him down, and after that I could see he was watching me very closely each time I dealt. He couldn't see anything, of course.'

Lucy breathed in awe, 'Had you bent the cards?'

'Used the Kingston Bridge trick, you mean? No, they were all watching too closely for that. But I employed this little toy, very discreetly.' As she spoke she pulled a small gold ring off the little finger of her left hand, twisting it to show Lucy how it contained a tiny, retractable steel pin that could be hooked out with the flick of a fingernail.

'It's wonderful,' said Lucy. 'So you use that little pin to prick certain cards?'

'Yes. Just at the very edge, and then I can feel with my fingertips as I deal. A man in Drury Lane made it for me, and it's been worth every penny.'

'So you'll wear the ring tonight? At Vauxhall Pleasure Gardens?'

'Certainly.' Marisa smiled demurely. 'It should go well with my highwayman's outfit, don't you think?'

Lucy leaned back on the pillows, sighing with satisfaction. 'Oh, Marisa, you are lucky. I went to Vauxhall last spring, it was beautiful, like fairyland, with hundreds of lanterns lighting up the trees as darkness fell, and people dancing in the pavilions, and fine lords and ladies strolling up and down the avenues.'

'And tricksters, and knaves, and females of the very lowest kind lurking in the woodland walks,' said Marisa, swinging her legs to the floor and getting to her feet. 'Just the right kind of place for me, don't you think? Come on, Lucy, it's time for me to get ready.'

Lucy, still in a happy dream, nodded and pulled herself reluctantly up. Then she suddenly clapped her hand to her mouth. 'I almost forgot – a letter arrived for you while you were out. I put it over there, on that chest of drawers – it looks rather important.'

Marisa went to pick it up, turning it over slowly in her hands before opening it. The spidery, close lines of writing were little more than a blur to her. She'd always admitted, laughingly, that the one thing that frightened her was a lawyer's letter. She scanned it slowly, feeling the familiar regret that the rather unusual education she'd received hadn't equipped her to deal with such things. She hated these long, awkward words that leaped up from the page at her and mocked her with their incomprehensibility.

'It's from my attorney,' she said slowly, running her finger tortuously along each line. 'Mr Giles, of Bedford Street. He handled all my father's finances, or perhaps I should say all of his debts. I think – ' and she pored impatiently over the last sentence, 'I think he's saying that he wants to see me at my earliest convenience, about some sort of bequest.'

Lucy frowned. 'A bequest? What can it mean?'

Marisa shrugged and tossed the letter into the fire.

'That yet more of my father's debts have come to light, no doubt. That's the only kind of inheritance I'm ever likely to come into.'

Lucy had already lost interest and was looking longingly at the invitation instead. 'The Ace of Spades,' she was murmuring happily. 'How really, truly exciting, not to know who he is. He might be some rich, powerful lord, Marisa. You'll ensnare him tonight with your bewitching beauty, and his noble heart will be yours forever.'

'I'd rather have his money than his noble heart, thanks,' responded Marisa dryly as she picked up a silver hairbrush from the dressing table and started to draw it through her thick, luxuriant locks. 'In my experience, most members of the nobility are fatuous, incompetent fools.'

But then suddenly, she remembered Lord Delsingham. As she gazed at her candlelit reflection in the mirror, her blue eyes seemed to grow hazy with desire. She remembered the way his aristocratic face had been alive with intelligent irony as he bent to caress her wrist in that subtly insulting way. Lord Delsingham, she was quite sure, was neither fatuous nor incompetent at anything.

Her preparations all complete, Marisa set off in a hackney carriage across Westminster Bridge to Vauxhall at nine that evening, with Lucy as her maid and John playing the part of her strapping manservant. Never having visited Vauxhall before, Marisa had gone prepared to be unimpressed, but as she showed her invitation at the gate and entered the gardens at last, she caught her breath in wonder. As Lucy had promised, it was like entering an enchanted world, a world illuminated by hundreds of golden lanterns strung between the lines of trees, with leafy walks winding enticingly away into the darkness. Half hidden by foliage, elaborate pagodas and secret bowers glimmered enticingly in the distance, while above the noise of the crowds that milled excitedly round the main walks could be heard the sweet, liquid notes of groups of musicians playing in the shady groves.

The sky above them was studded with stars; the evening air was still and warm. 'Just perfect,' declared Lucy happily, 'for Vauxhall!' They stood for a moment, taking it all in as the other visitors to the gardens swept past them. Quite a number of them were in masquerade, or all-concealing dominos; Marisa wondered which of them were in the Ace of Spade's party, and she felt a frisson of excitement as she wondered if he himself was here yet. Lucy was in a desperate hurry to reach the main pavilion, where the invitation had instructed them to gather; but Marisa wanted to take her time. With a sigh of satisfaction she smoothed down her elegant, severely cut black riding habit with its short, tight-fitting jacket and full skirt, and adjusted her neat black tricorne at a rakish angle over her blonde, piled-up curls. Her pistol was tucked in at her waist, together with her money-purse, and the upper part of her face was concealed by a black velvet mask. She was aware of a number of men glancing at her with open admiration in their eyes, and she smiled coolly, feeling herself to be the epitome of an elegant, discreet lady of fashion.

She had come a long way, she decided. A long way since the wild, rollicking journeys from one city of Europe to another as her careless, charming father, a former cavalry officer who had gambled away his pay and run from his regiment in disgrace, concentrated his considerable energies on evading his creditors and escaping from former gaming companions who suspected him, quite rightly, of cheating them.

The youthful Marisa, utterly devoted to her handsome father, had assumed that there was no other way to live. She'd picked up an education – of sorts – from the various women who sometimes joined their entourage, the women her father referred to as governesses. But Marisa quickly realised that these governesses were there to attend to her father rather than herself, hence her haphazard inadequacy in such basic skills as reading and

36

writing. Of far more use to her than the education offered to her by these governesses were the skills she learned from her father. He was a fine swordsman, and taught her all that he knew about fencing without making any allowances for her sex. He also taught her how to shoot and ride, and introduced her to the art of gaming, of knowing when to take a risk not only with cards and dice, but also with life.

Unlike her father, Marisa usually won. She learned from his mistakes. Her combination of a cool, natural intelligence together with her stunning, innocent-looking beauty, which inevitably distracted her male opponents, made her a formidable opponent in any kind of game.

She'd learned the pleasures of the opposite sex from a charming young Polish cavalryman called Frederic, who'd introduced her most sweetly to the delicious sensations of her own body one night when she and her father were staying at a roadside inn on their way to Hanover. Her father was deep in vingt-et-un in the coffee room below when the handsome Polish cavalryman, with whom she'd made a whispered assignation earlier, had romantically climbed up the balcony to the window of the room she shared with her governess. Marisa felt quite dizzy with power as he speedily undressed her and adored her body with his mouth and lips and tongue.

At first, when he'd drawn out his penis, she'd been startled, because it looked so hot and angry and huge. But he'd continued to caress her gently, stroking his big, calloused horseman's hands over her pouting breasts, and encouraging her to touch him down there. She'd gasped with shock, because his flesh quivered at her touch and throbbed angrily against her tremulous palm, but it felt lovely as well, velvety and powerful and strong, and she ached with an indescribable longing that melted her insides. When he finally laid her gently on her little bed and sheathed himself inside her, she'd gasped and gone very still.

'I am hurting you, darling?' Frederic had said in his husky Polish accent.

'Oh, no.' Marisa had sighed happily, running her fingers over his lovely strong shoulder muscles. 'Far from it. Oh, very far from it.'

He'd caressed her skilfully with his hands, gently thrusting with his silken penis and stroking the tender nub of her clitoris until she'd arched herself dizzily towards him, feeling the sweetest ripples of ecstasy surge through her melting flesh as his bone-hard member eased away her tight virginity. Then she'd exploded, rubbing her small breasts against his hard chest, extracting every last, delicious ounce of rapture from his pulsing rod as he pleasured her into oblivion.

They'd been disturbed at that point by a gentle knocking at the door. They flew apart, Marisa giggling as she pulled the sheets up to her chin and Frederic cursing as he struggled to fasten up his tight cavalryman's breeches.

'Frederic,' a soft feminine voice called. 'Frederic, my dearest, are you there?'

It was Isobel, Marisa's latest governess. Marisa, with a quick look at the handsome Frederic's guilty face, realised instantly that the plump, pretty Isobel was also in receipt of the Polish officer's favours. Pointing quickly to the open window, Marisa hissed, 'Out!' and Frederic fled, scrambling over the balcony. Then, with a sheet draped carelessly around herself so that her flushed, still swollen breasts were just peeping over the top, she walked slowly to the door and opened it. Isobel, an insipid brunette who was some ten years older than Marisa and had often chided her tartly for various minor misdemeanours, stood there with her jaw dropping open stupidly at the sight of Marisa's near nakedness.

'Were you looking for Frederic?' enquired Marisa sweetly.

'Why, yes. We – we had some business to discuss.'

'He has already settled that business. With me.' Marisa smiled secretively. 'I wouldn't bother him again if I were you, Isobel. He told me that you are a shrivelled, passionless spinster, and that he would rather have a good bottle of claret for company than you.'

Isobel fled with a smothered cry of distress, and neither Marisa nor her father ever saw her again. Frederic secretly visited Marisa the next day, bringing her flowers and begging her to meet him again, but Marisa had coldly dismissed him, saying that she had taken a sudden unaccountable dislike to Polish cavalrymen. She'd smiled as he rode off, having listened impatiently as he declared himself to be quite heartbroken, and she relished her moment of power, the power of being in charge. She decided then that she was never, ever going to relinquish that power to anyone.

She'd been sad when her father died unexpectedly just over a year ago, soon after Napoleon had been finally defeated at Waterloo, but she'd not wasted time in grieving, resolving instead to return to London, a city forbidden to Captain Brooke because of his desertion from his regiment. London was undoubtedly the capital of Europe, awash with pleasure-seekers and gamblers now that the long European war was finally at an end. And here, Marisa was convinced she would finally find her destiny.

She was brought abruptly back to the present by Lucy's excited chatter. 'Over there,' Lucy was pointing happily, 'that's where the tightrope walkers will perform. There may even be fireworks later. And down here is the grand pavilion, where the dancing takes place.'

'And the card rooms?' queried Marisa, suddenly alert again.

'There are several private card rooms leading off the pavilion. But Marisa, how will you know which party to join, when you don't even know who your host is?'

Marisa laughed, suddenly feeling calmly confident. 'I would imagine that the Ace of Spades will make quite certain that his guests can find him.'

She was right, of course. She had scarcely entered the brilliantly lit rotunda, where sets of people glittering in silks and satins danced to the lively music, when a liveried footman moved discreetly towards her. Glancing decorously at the invitation which she held in her hand, he indicated the curtained doors of a private room. 'Please to proceed this way, my lady.' And then Marisa noticed that his cream silk waistcoat was embroidered with tiny black spades.

Her heart fluttered unaccountably, but her voice was cool as she turned to dismiss Lucy and John. 'Be near at hand in case I need you,' she said softly. Then, as the footman held open the big door, she walked slowly into the room, conscious of many masked pairs of eyes upon her as bowed heads were lifted from their study of the green baize gaming tables, and cards were held delicately poised in mid-play.

She was late. And by being late, she'd made herself conspicuous; not a good start. But she outfaced them all, men and women, young and old in their assorted costumes and disguises, reminding herself that anonymity was the unspoken rule at a discreet affair such as this, and that no-one would dare to challenge her if she only brazened it out. She looked round disdainfully, handing her hat and gloves to the footman, and felt a secret shiver of excitement as she sensed the men assessing her slim figure in her tightly cut black riding habit with open greed, while the women's eyes glittered with jealousy behind their masks. Was the Ace of Spades here yet? Which one was he? Somehow she imagined him to be mysterious, powerful, utterly irresistible.

The room settled slowly back into play. Everyone was seated, except for the hovering groom-porters who sternly called out the odds and provided fresh packs of cards as required. Marisa paused, wondering whether to join the hazard table, or try her luck at the faro bank.

She jumped as she felt a hand touching her arm. A light, amused male voice drawled in her ear, 'You must forgive them, my dear, for staring at you so when you first came in. But I rather think they were unsure whether you had come to play cards with them, or to rob them. Your costume is quite divine, by the way.'

Marisa whipped round. She was confronted by a man: a tall, formidable man in an enveloping black domino and mask, though in spite of that mask she would have known those alert grey eyes, that cultured, mocking voice anywhere in the world. They belonged to Lord Delsingham, the man who had been so hatefully insulting to her earlier that day.

She hoped desperately that he wouldn't be able to recognise her in her mask, but that hope was swiftly dismissed as his mouth curled in sudden amusement and he said, in a more intimate tone, 'Well, well, fair Ganymede. Fancy seeing you here.'

'It is no more surprising, my lord,' snapped Marisa, 'than for me to see you here. But then, I suppose you think that your money gains you entry everywhere.'

His eyes glinted. 'What a pleasure it is to have the chance to exchange sweet compliments with you once again. You have an invitation to this little entertainment?'

Marisa felt herself colour. 'Of course I have!'

'How very intriguing.'

'Have you?' she said hotly, stung by his disbelieving tone.

'In a manner of speaking, yes, I suppose I have. Let me offer you a glass of champagne. And then, fair Ganymede, you must come and join me at the hazard table.'

She lifted her chin defiantly as he handed her a crystal glass of champagne. 'Actually, I prefer cards to dice.'

He shrugged his wide shoulders. 'As you please. Perhaps you will honour me with a game of piquet later.'

Marisa smiled sweetly. 'If I do, you will regret it, my lord. I must warn you that I'm rather good.' Then she swiftly turned her back on him and headed for the twenty-guinea hazard table, just to annoy him.

Once seated at the circular table, she played a quiet, steady game so as not to draw attention to herself, losing an insubstantial sum that caused no comment, and giving herself time to recover from the unpleasant shock of Delsingham's presence here. As the dice box moved steadily round, she assessed the room quickly, seeing how the punters' tokens were accumulating at the faro-bank, and how they were betting heavily at the vingt-et-un table. Deep play indeed, just as she'd hoped. She felt a quiver of excitement as she breathed in the heady atmosphere of risk and tension. And then, slowly and carefully, she began to win. She knew she had no hope of using her weighted dice here, because it was too risky in this expert, watchful company, but nevertheless she concentrated on using all the subtle techniques for casting the dice that her father had taught her, placing the cubes nonchalantly in the box and just trickling them out with a deceptive flick of her wrist so that they fell exactly as she wanted. If she used the trick sparingly, then no-one would suspect, and even if they did, they wouldn't have a shred of evidence against her.

She was starting to win. Carefully she piled her guinea tokens in the little mahogany stand that a manservant had placed beside her, with its rimmed cavity for holding her champagne glass. The click of the dice thrilled her; she waited her next turn with excitement as the groom-porters impassively intoned the odds.

Then she looked up and saw Lord Delsingham watching her, his grey eyes steely behind his black mask. She felt a tiny shiver of fear assail her, and something else – a sharp, febrile stab of desire. Helplessly she remembered his challenging caress earlier that day, and remembered her wicked fantasy about him making love to her with his delicious mouth and tongue. A sudden, awful thought struck her. What if he were the Ace of Spades?

No. Impossible. If he was the host, then he would have known immediately that she was not an invited guest, and would have had her thrown out bodily. But he was still watching her, and it unsettled her badly. It was her turn to play. She coloured beneath her mask, and threw so clumsily that one of the dice landed on the floor. She saw Lord Delsingham murmur to a groom-porter, who hurried to pick it up. In the darkened gaming hells, a dropped die was a well-known opportunity to cheat, but there was no earthly chance for substitution in this watchful company, thought Marisa somewhat faintly.

Shortly afterwards Delsingham left with some other

guests for the supper boxes and Marisa, feeling more relaxed, moved across to the faro bank. Her choice of numbers was good; her guinea tokens continued to accumulate satisfactorily. And then her concentration was broken as a cluster of new arrivals burst into the room, their voices loud with the champagne they'd consumed. Marisa, placing her token carefully on a seven, tried to ignore them. But she jumped when a shrill male voice called out, 'That woman there with the blonde hair, the one in the highwayman's rig. She's a cheat, a vicious little cheat! I'd recognise her anywhere.'

Marisa spun round to see a plump, foppish man dressed in a scarlet domino. Sir Peregrine. She felt rather faint. An elderly man who had been sitting beside her and watching her play with an appreciative eye got to his feet and said, 'That is rather a grave accusation, Sir Peregrine.'

'Grave it might be, but it's true, by God!'

Marisa laughed shortly. 'Prove it.'

'I most certainly will. Last time I played with you, madam, you trounced me so roundly that after you'd left I picked up the discards and checked them. And I found a tiny mark at the corner of each picture, made with a pin.'

There was a hiss of indrawn breath around the room. The liveried groom-porters had moved to stand in menacing fashion on either side of Marisa. Somehow she forced herself to stay calm, although the little gold ring on her finger seemed to burn her.

'I challenge you', she said, 'to discover any such mark on the cards here.'

Sir Peregrine hesitated then lunged forwards. 'Her ring,' he shouted. 'Look at that ring. I remember how she fingered that little trinket all the time we were at play. Examine it, will you? If she's innocent, she'll make no objection to that.'

Marisa did have objections – plenty of them. Springing quickly to her feet so her fragile gilt chair fell backwards, she kicked at the nearest groom-porter's stockinged shins

43

extremely hard with her pointed little boot. He howled with pain and stumbled backwards, crashing into several astonished guests. Before anyone realised what was happening, Marisa had charged for the door to the ballroom, pushing her way between the startled dancers and out into the clear night air.

Damn, damn, damn. Of all the ill luck. She cursed stupid, fat Sir Peregrine, who was so hopeless at cards that on the night he spoke of she hadn't really needed to cheat at all to relieve him of his guineas. She cursed the Ace of Spades, whoever he was, for inviting such a stupid booby to his card party. Her one consolation was that the hateful Lord Delsingham hadn't been there to witness her humiliation.

She heard shouts behind her and set off down a narrow path towards a Japanese pagoda, conscious of passers-by turning to gape at her as she flew past them, her hair streaming out behind her as her lovely little hat tumbled to the ground. In no time at all, the whole place would be on the alert for her. No good trying to get out through the main gates again. No good relying on John and Lucy, who were no doubt engrossed with each other in some dark corner. They had the brains of a pea between the two of them, with all their mental activity concentrated in their loins.

'There she is,' someone yelled. 'Stop her!'

Marisa plunged down yet another twisting path, the now hateful, coloured lanterns winking at her, the fiddlers in their cocked hats seeming to mock her as they played their jaunty music in the leafy glades. Two young, drunken bucks ogled her and tried to block her path, but she stunned them with a vicious stream of invective and ran on, her heart pounding against her ribs, until at last she became aware that the lights and the crowds seemed to have faded away. She pulled up, her chest heaving, and tore off her mask. She was in a wild, obviously unfrequented part of the gardens, where the tangle of undergrowth and the untamed trees told her that she must be on the very edge of open countryside. Somehow, she must get out of here. If Sir Peregrine caught her, he'd hand her over to the magistrates, and with no-one to speak up for her, that could mean a hefty fine she could ill afford, or possibly even prison. It seemed as if her luck was running out at last.

Suddenly she heard a menacing rustle in the bushes behind her. She whirled round to see two young, roughly dressed men grinning at her, openly assessing her fine clothes. Marisa's stomach lurched. Footpads, thieves. Fool that she was, she'd quite forgotten that the Pleasure Gardens were a notorious attraction for the very lowest sort of criminal, on the lookout for easy pickings.

Well, she wouldn't be anyone's easy pickings. She turned to run, but they caught her without difficulty, even though she struggled and kicked out at them. If only they knew, thought Marisa disgustedly, that she was in just as much danger from the authorities as they were.

Chapter Three

The two men dragged her along a narrow, overgrown path that was in utter darkness, laughing at her attempts to escape. At last she saw the flickering glow of a fire, in a leafy clearing. They came to a halt there, with each man gripping her arm securely, and she saw that another man sat cross-legged by the fire with two blowsily dressed girls lying on the ground beside him. The remnants of a meal lay about them, and some empty wine bottles. The man by the fire was still drinking from an almost full bottle, but he put it down when he saw them.

'Well, well,' he said softly, getting to his feet. 'Caleb, Tom. What have you brought me?'

He had dark, curly hair, and a gold ring glinted in his ear. They were gypsies, realised Marisa suddenly, vagabond gypsies on the prowl.

'We found her, Seth,' said one of the men, the bearded one. 'Found her skulking in the bushes.'

The man Seth walked slowly towards the captive Marisa and drew his brown finger down her cheek while the women watched hotly from the fireside. Marisa felt a sudden quiver of awareness as he touched her. His smooth, hard-boned face was tanned nut-brown from the sun. He was young, with a lithe, muscular body that was clad simply in a loose, open-necked white shirt and corduroy breeches that were tucked into soft leather boots, and his dark eyes seemed to glitter with sensual awareness as they assessed her slender figure in her severely cut, black riding habit.

Then his hand slipped to her shoulder, and Marisa spat at him. He looked surprised for a moment, then drew out his handkerchief and brushed the moisture away from his jaw. 'A spirited little beauty,' he laughed softly. 'Calm yourself, my pigeon. We'll do you no harm. All we want are your money and your jewels.'

Marisa glared at him defiantly, remembering her abandoned winnings in the card room with acute regret. 'I've nothing, you brute!'

For answer, he lifted up her hand and pulled off her precious little gold ring, which he silently pocketed. Then he ran his hands softly beneath her tight-fitting jacket and over the silk shirt she wore beneath it. Her small breasts tingled suddenly as his palm brushed them, and she caught her breath, not knowing if the intimacy was deliberate or not. And then, he found her pistol. 'This looks worth a good guinea or two,' he said appreciatively, weighing it in his strong hands.

Marisa lunged to retrieve it, twisting free of her captors. 'Give it back to me.'

'I might consider it,' he said. 'But what are you going to offer us in exchange, fine lady?'

Marisa caught her breath. There was something about the way he looked at her that made her feel strangely excited. A game. A challenge.

The women were watching her from the fireside. There was a young slim one with long dark hair, and a slightly older one, a plump, brazen beauty with loose red curls and a low-cut lace bodice that exposed the upper portion of her full breasts enticingly as she rested her chin in her hands and gazed up at Marisa.

'I like her fine clothes, Seth,' the woman said enviously. 'Let's play for her clothes.'

The bearded man, who'd seized hold of Marisa's arm

again, laughed aloud. 'Aye. Rowena's right. Let's play for her clothes, and then for her. I've a fancy for a little sport, and it's a long time since we had such a fine, aristocratic wench on our hands.'

Marisa felt a momentary spasm of fear. Then she met the eyes of the dark-haired man Seth, and realised that he was saluting her in challenge, as if they were opponents before a duel. She drawled coolly, 'I hate to disappoint you all, but I'm no aristocrat.'

Seth said, 'Anyone out looking for you?'

She smiled up at him. 'I sincerely hope not,' she said, and he laughed. She could hear the faint strain of violins, ghostly in the distance, but the Pleasure Gardens seemed a hundred miles away to her just then.

'I want her clothes,' drawled the redheaded Rowena petulantly, getting up and coming over to lean her head coquettishly against Seth's shoulder. Marisa realised she was rather drunk; they probably all were. 'Make her give us her fancy clothes, Seth darling!'

Marisa gazed at Seth. 'If you tell these men to unhand me,' she said evenly, 'I'll take them off myself.'

There was a hiss of surprise from the others, but Seth nodded thoughtfully and the men released her. Slowly, in the hypnotised, heavy silence of that little wooded clearing, Marisa started to ease off her beautiful riding habit, feeling unaccountably excited as their hungry eyes devoured her. The odds were stacked against her this time, but she was used to that. Her eyes rested briefly on her father's pistol, which the man Seth had laid on the grass beside the fire. She would get that back very soon, she promised herself silently.

Seth took her jacket and skirt from her, and then her silk shirt. She stood there demurely in her chemise and tight-laced corset and stockings, feeling how the cool, night air made her nipples surge and stiffen against the crisp, white cotton. She tossed her head so that her loose, golden curls tumbled around her bare shoulders. She could see that the big bearded man, Caleb, who'd moved back into the shadows to watch her, was rubbing surrep-

48

titiously at his groin. She was playing a dangerous game, she reminded herself. But at least, this way, she stood a chance. She felt the familiar, nerve-tingling excitement of pitting her wits against the odds. Then the bearded man stepped forward, his genitals an ominous bulge against the tight crotch of his breeches. 'Let's dice for her, Seth,' he said, his voice coarse with lust. 'The man with the highest throw gets to have the wench.'

But Seth, with a dangerous smile playing around his beautifully curved mouth, held up his hand in restraint. 'Hold, Caleb.' He turned to Marisa. 'What do you say to that?'

Marisa shrugged her deliciously bare shoulders. 'I think', she said, 'that you're all disappointingly devoid of imagination. You really want just one person to win, so that all the rest are losers?'

'Then what do you suggest?' said the man Caleb roughly.

'Have you ever heard of the game King's Pleasure?' queried Marisa demurely.

They shook their heads, all of them hanging on her every word, even the young, dark-haired woman who still sprawled lazily by the fire.

'You play it with cards,' said Marisa Brooke. 'You've got some cards?' She smoothed down her simple white chemise over the narrow, boned corset that encased her ribs and thrust her breasts upwards, revelling in the gypsies' avid attention. 'All you have to do is pick two cards in turn. Ace is high. And the winner of each round can order any other player to do anything. Anything at all.'

'Anything at all?' echoed the redheaded Rowena incredulously, still raptly stroking Marisa's discarded riding habit. The other woman had got to her feet as well and was listening open mouthed.

'Exactly,' said Marisa softly. 'But only one command can be given at a time, so as to make the game last, and give everyone a chance.'

There was a moment's tense silence as they considered

her proposition. Caleb and the younger man, Tom, who had been silent up to now, seemed to be muttering together in consultation. Marisa went on in her low, musical voice, 'Of course, I'm bound to lose, because there's only one of me, and you'll all be playing against me.'

Seth, their leader, was watching her carefully. He was nice, thought Marisa with a sudden shiver of delight. He had a strongly made, sinewy body and a mobile, striking face, with high cheekbones that somehow added to the exotic allure of his rough mop of curling, dark hair and his gypsy earring. 'You're quite sure about this?' he asked Marisa softly.

Rowena was watching Seth angrily. Marisa realised that Seth must be Rowena's man, and the redhead was fiercely jealous of Marisa. Something to watch out for there.

'Of course she's sure, Seth,' Rowena hissed out. 'Can't you see she's nothing but a high-class whore?'

Marisa said cuttingly, 'I'm neither high-class nor a whore. Nobody buys me with their money, which I'm quite sure is more than can be said for you.' Rowena swore aloud, but Seth restrained her as Marisa went on calmly, 'However, I am fond of a wager. Shall we play?'

They settled themselves round the fire, and a pack of worn cards was brought out. In spite of her apparent calm, Marisa's heart was thumping so loudly that she was sure they must hear it. She tried to steady herself, because the stakes were too high for her to make any mistakes.

Seth dealt. They each drew two cards, and the bearded man Caleb won the first round. He drew a deep breath and gazed hotly at Marisa. Then he said gruffly, 'I want you to pull that fancy garment of yours right down to your waist and show us your ladylike titties.' He leaned hungrily across the circle towards her. 'And then I want to play with them, and suck them, and – ' Seth struck him back brutally with the back of his hand so that the older man groaned with pain.

'One thing at a time, Caleb, remember?' Seth said flatly. He turned to Marisa, his dark eyes quite calm. 'You heard, I think, what he said.'

Marisa met his gaze steadily. He was different, this one. Quite, quite different. She suddenly imagined him without his clothes, sunbrowned, muscular, lithe. His penis, she knew, would be deliciously smooth and lengthy, and he would smile as he pleasured her. Keeping her eyes locked with his, she calmly pulled her thin-strapped chemise down to her waist. Underneath it she wore a short, tightly laced corset that encased her ribcage, its upper rim cunningly shaped and boned to push up her naked breasts. She felt her exposed nipples tighten rosily in the cool night air, and heard a hiss of appreciation from her audience. She saw that the third man, Tom, was watching with desperate intensity, his silky brown hair falling across his flushed, beardless face as he gazed at her. Another one who couldn't wait to get his hands on her. She felt a fierce lick of excitement at her belly and allowed herself, just for a moment, to fantasise about having all three of them, all three sturdy, rampant cocks only too eager to pleasure her in any way she wished. She pulled her attention back to the game with an effort. This time, she must win. The pack lay loosely beside Caleb, ready to be shuffled and re-dealt. As she slipped her own card casually back into it, she checked that no-one was watching her. Then she splayed the cards rapidly and managed, within the blinking of an eye, to mark the corners of two kings and an ace with her sharp thumbnail. 'Sauter la coupe,' her father had called that particular little trick.

In the flickering firelight, none of them seemed to notice how piercingly she scanned the fan of cards that was offered to her. The pack was badly scuffed and worn, but even so within seconds she'd caught sight of her own familiar tiny marks. Two kings: that should do.

And it did. She'd won. When they'd all drawn and thrown back their cards in disgust, she turned to the woman Rowena and pointed towards Tom. She said

51

silkily, 'I want you to pleasure him, Rowena. With your mouth.'

A flicker of astonishment crossed the woman's plump, lascivious face. 'Now?'

Marisa smiled sweetly. 'Yes, indeed. Do it now. And here, so that everyone can see you.'

The man Caleb laughed, jealous. 'You chose the right one there, didn't you? Sucking cocks is a favourite occupation of Rowena's. Only usually she gets paid for it.'

'And deservedly so, Caleb,' said Rowena, shooting him a fiery glance.

Tom was already shivering with excitement. Rowena swaggered around the hushed circle towards him, her hips swaying enticingly, her breasts peeping curvaceously above her lace bodice. The stillness was painfully intense as she slowly sank to her knees before him and worked to release his penis from his breeches. It was already erect, but Marisa saw that even so it was small and white and slender; a boy's weapon rather than a man's. Nevertheless Rowena took it in her mouth with evident satisfaction, licking and teasing with her pink little tongue. Tom came almost immediately, groaning as he spurted his seed into her hot mouth, but Rowena, instead of abandoning him, started work on him again, nipping and teasing with her salacious lips until his cock started to grow once more. Excellent, thought Marisa quickly, she's going to make it last. And the others were watching with glittering eyes. So far, so good. She let her eyes rest just for a moment on her precious pistol, lying on the ground almost within her reach.

Seth won next. Marisa felt a dark flicker of excitement as his gypsy's gaze roved her vulnerable body, and then he said to her quietly, 'Your breasts are exquisite. They must give you great pleasure. I would like to see you fondle them yourself.'

Marisa met his gaze steadily and started to run her palms over her upthrust breasts until they ached with sweet fullness. She imagined Seth's beautiful mouth

52

paying homage to her nipples, and they stiffened hungrily against her fingers. 'Like this?' she murmured.

He leaned back against a low tree stump, quite relaxed, his shirt gleaming whitely in the firelight against the smooth brown of his face. 'Exactly.' He smiled, and Marisa, imagining how his beautiful cock must be stirring and thickening as he watched her lewd behaviour, swallowed hard.

Underneath her outer calm, she was seething with desire. She was desperately excited by the gypsies' hot enjoyment of her bare flesh, by the atmosphere of open sexual hunger that filled this secret firelit glade. She could hear the soft moans of the youth Tom as Rowena tortured his slender penis exquisitely with her hot mouth, while Seth, lovely, dangerous-looking Seth, was just watching her, a small smile playing around his lips. She found his smile the most exciting thing of all. She kept her eyes deliberately on his face as she played with her nipples, twisting them and sending delicious little shafts of pleasure-pain shooting through her body. But inevitably her eyes slid down to his groin, where beneath his skintight breeches she could see the wicked promise of a fine, thick rod of swollen flesh pushing against the confines of the straining fabric.

Licking her lips, she shifted her stockinged thighs beneath her chemise, feeling her labia swell and moisten. She had to stay in control, because this was one game she had to win, and strategy, as ever, was all-important. She knew that she could quite easily win every draw of the cards by marking more and more of the pictures each time she slipped her cards back into the pile, but the gypsies might lose their easy-going good humour if they suspected they were being duped. And yet it was essential for her to win just one more time if her plan was to succeed.

She drew a king and an ace. Her father would have been proud of her. Now it was her turn to give instructions, and she must do something about the bearded one, Caleb, because he was the one most likely to turn nasty if he didn't get some sort of satisfaction very soon. She leaned towards him, her pert breasts pouting enticingly above her tight-laced white corset, her nipples tawny as wine in the glow of the fire. 'Do you know, Caleb,' she breathed, 'I have a real fancy to see your cock in action.'

He grunted and lurched towards her hotly but she laughed and slipped to one side. 'Not with me, my fine stallion,' she said archly, 'at least, not yet.' She pointed at the dark-haired girl by the fire, who had so far stayed silent but was eagerly watching every move. 'I'm sure you're well primed already, Caleb. Use your weapon on her, will you? Then I can watch, and I'll know what I've got to look forward to, won't I?'

He grinned avidly. 'Oh, you can look forward to this, my fine lady,' he breathed. 'Imagine being pleasured by this mighty weapon, eh?' And without hesitation he pulled out his penis and began to stroke it fondly.

Marisa felt her breath catch in her throat. Caleb's phallus was already hotly engorged, but his loving caresses made it swell to an even greater size. It was a great, purple-headed monster that strained upwards from his breeches, swaying hungrily. She felt her moist secret parts twitch and run with juices as she imagined that thick, veined shaft sliding up between her own hungry sex-lips and pleasuring her into delicious oblivion with each virile thrust. Her nipples tightened painfully, tugging at her breasts, and with a supreme effort she tried to ignore the sweet, pulsing ache at her body's core. She couldn't afford to indulge herself yet, it wasn't part of her plan. And anyway, the dark-haired woman had already moved in on Caleb with burning eagerness. She stood on tiptoe to whisper in his ear, giggling, then she dropped swiftly to the ground on all fours, casting a mischievous glance behind her.

With a low growl, Caleb pulled up her crimson skirt and lace-edged petticoat to expose her ripe, flaring bottom. Kneeling behind her, he gripped his lengthy penis in his hand and lunged towards her, prodding hungrily towards the lush folds of her vulva. The woman was hot for him; her body's nectar anointed him lasciviously, and he drew back for a moment, using his palm to slide the glistening moisture up and down his quivering shaft, muttering hotly to himself. Then, with a great cry of satisfaction, he gripped her bottom and slid himself into her, inch by delicious inch. The woman moaned softly and writhed in delight as he impaled her, playing hungrily with her own nipples to heighten her ecstasy.

Caleb hissed, 'Steady now, my little beauty. No rush.' He drew himself out, very slowly, so the woman whimpered out her loss and thrust back towards him, but Caleb was taking his time. He gazed down, openly admiring his own meaty weapon as it nudged at her buttocks. Marisa was unable to drag her eyes away from the sight of it, and she moistened her lips as she caught a glimpse of his hairy balls swaying at the root of his glistening shaft. She shivered as she watched him slowly slide himself back inside the girl, wishing that it was her being ravished by that delicious weapon. Then she dragged her eyes away with an effort to quickly assess the rest of the little group.

Rowena was still playing with Tom's slender cock, reducing him to a helpless, quivering mass with her tormenting caresses. Tom had orgasmed violently yet again, his seed spilling on the soft ground, but still Rowena would not let him go. Now she was stroking his small, firm buttocks, pulling them apart and sliding her finger tormentingly into his tight anal crevice so that he was groaning with excitement. So, thought Marisa. They were busy for a while yet. Only Seth to deal with. She would have to win one more time, and hope that he didn't suspect.

Seth drew a king and a ten. She found it difficult to discern her marks, because Seth was watching her, and he was the most dangerous, the most handsome of them all. She wanted him badly, which affected her concentration, but she won, with a carefully drawn queen and ace. Seth watched her all the time, his dark eyes inscrutable, and she thought desperately, He knows! He knows that I've tricked them all. But she had to continue brazenly with her game. She had no alternative. Leaning towards him huskily, she whispered, 'Seth. You know what I'd really like?'

He shook his head, his eyes glinting. 'Tell me.'

She slid her hand along his forearm, pushing back his loose sleeve. His sinewy skin was brown from the sun, and lightly sprinkled with silky dark hairs. 'Seth,' she whispered, 'I'd like to see your lovely penis. And then, just to start with, I'd like you to rub it against my breasts. That drives me wild, really wild.'

He gazed at her stiffened nipples as they poked out from above her corset, but his face was still cool and impassive, which worried her. He was nobody's fool. Then she glanced at his groin, and saw the thick knot of his penis straining against the fabric of his breeches, and felt much happier. He was just as easily manipulated as the rest of them. She crouched over him and reached carefully to unfasten his breeches and draw out his cock. It was lovely, just as she'd imagined it, long and hard and silky. Her hand trembled as she caressed it with her cool palm, feeling its heat burning into her; on a sudden impulse she dipped her head and tasted it, wrapping her tongue round its swollen head and sliding her parted lips down over the sturdy flesh. She felt him shudder as his penis swelled yet further and thrust against the back of her mouth. Then gently, still not saying anything, the gypsy withdrew himself and laid her down on the soft turf, kissing her exposed breasts with his long, expert tongue until they were slick with his mouth's moisture. Marisa moaned softly, running her fingers through the tangle of his silky dark curls, aware that he was shifting himself slightly in order to position his velvety penis just above her swollen breasts. He circled her nipples with its smooth glans, each in turn, while gazing intently at her face.

Marisa wanted to climax there and then. The delicious sensations arrowed down to her womb, and gathered hotly in her throbbing clitoris. She wanted to pull him down onto her, to thrash wildly against him until she felt his delicious shaft sliding deep into her vagina so she could clutch at it with her quivering inner muscles and pleasure herself with it until the waves of longed-for rapture rolled through her. Her honeyed vulva spasmed with tension as she desperately ground her thighs together. She could see the whiteness of his teeth in his dark face as he smiled down at her, deliberately teasing her aching nipples with the smooth head of his penis, making sure that she could see every inch of the long, thick shaft as he slowly rubbed it only inches from her face.

Marisa gritted her teeth and reached out with cold deliberation to caress the heavy sac of his testicles, stroking and pinching the hairy flesh and letting her fingers slide round behind into the musky cleft of his buttocks. Seth groaned aloud and convulsed almost instantly into orgasm. He threw his head back in despair as his lengthy penis started to twitch sweetly against Marisa's taut breasts and his semen spurted out in hot, delicious bursts.

Marisa felt the sticky heat of it on her nipples and rolled away from under him. Then she jumped to her feet and swiftly picked up her discarded clothes and her precious pistol.

He was groaning softly on the ground, pumping himself to expel the last trickle of his semen, too engulfed in the throes of pleasure to move. And the others were certainly beyond caring, noted Marisa swiftly, seeing how they were still avidly pleasuring themselves in the shadows. 'Sorry, Seth,' she whispered. 'Hope you enjoyed it.' And then she ran, twisting through the trees and bushes until the firelit glade was far behind her.

After a few minutes, she paused behind some trees to pull on her clothes and get back her breath. She was genuinely sorry to have duped Seth, but she had more important things on her mind than pleasure, such as how to get out of this damned place. She had no idea where she was, or what to do next, but on coming across a narrow path between the bushes, she decided to take a chance and follow it, every sense alert for the gypsies' pursuit.

Too late, she realised she'd made a mistake. This path was leading her back towards the lights, and the crowds, and danger. On turning a corner, she found herself suddenly amongst a crowd of revellers, and almost instantly she heard a man cry out, 'There she is. There's the blonde wench who gulled Sir Peregrine. Catch her!'

And then they were all around her: men, women, servants, even a man brandishing a violin, all of them screaming at her and blocking her escape until she wanted to put her hands over her ears and shut them all out. 'That's her,' they yelled in chorus. 'She's nothing but a vile little cheat. Take her to the magistrates!'

Marisa's mind whirled with desperate plans, but she was totally surrounded by her captors, and this time even she had to admit that it looked as if she was finished. Damn that mysterious invitation from the Ace of Spades, whoever he was. Damn stupid Sir Peregrine. Damn them all.

Then a new yet somehow familiar male voice broke in on the cacophony, saying coolly, 'Is there some problem here?'

The crowd seemed to part at the sound of that voice, giving Marisa space to breathe. 'Why, yes, my lord,' someone called out eagerly. 'This is the wench who cheated Sir Peregrine, remember?'

'There has, I think, been some mistake,' said the unseen man. 'This wench, as you call her, is with me.'

'But, my lord!'

'You heard me.' The authoritative voice was colder now. 'The lady is mine. If Sir Peregrine has any problem regarding her behaviour, then he can sort it out with me.' The mob fell away from her, and at last she was able to see the man who spoke. Still trembling with defiance and fear, she gazed up at the painfully familiar figure of Lord James Delsingham, who had removed his black cloak and mask to reveal the undoubted sartorial perfection of a superbly cut coat of grey, superfine wool worn over tight-fitting cream breeches and gleaming black hessians.

He gripped her arm. 'Take your hands off me,' she hissed, but his fingers tightened painfully around her wrist.

'Come, my dear. My carriage awaits, and I rather think it's high time we left the pleasures of Vauxhall, don't you?' he said, in a loud, clear voice that was as brittle as ice. 'Believe me, I can't hold them off for ever,' he added curtly in a lower voice. And with steely purpose he escorted her through the gaping crowd.

'Damn you, what are you playing at?' demanded Marisa, stumbling along beside his tall figure but still struggling to pull her arm away. 'You expect me to go anywhere with you?'

Looking straight ahead, he said, 'They're still following us, my Ganymede. And I feel quite sure that they will follow us at a respectful distance all the way to my carriage. Try to look pleased to be with me, will you?'

'You must be mad to interfere,' she said scornfully. 'Didn't you hear that Sir Peregrine has threatened to set the magistrates on me? You'll only get yourself into trouble for getting involved with me.'

He was steering her relentlessly along the thronged path towards the exit. 'I hardly think so, my dear. I fancy my station in life is a little higher than that.' He smiled gently down at her. 'And while you're under my protection, you are quite immune from further provocation, believe me.'

Marisa dug her heels angrily into the gravel path, bringing him to a halt. 'Under your protection? Let me assure you, I need no-one's protection, my lord.'

'Is that so? Well, we're almost at the exit.' He pointed calmly at the tall redbrick building which housed the official entrance gates. 'Since you insist you can look after yourself, prehaps you'd rather I left you to make your own way out.'

She hesitated, knowing very well that they might have been alerted at the gates to look out for her. On her own, she had no chance. Almost fiercely she thrust her arm once more through his as he escorted her out towards the line of waiting carriages while he continued conversationally, 'I assume you'll deign to take a lift in my carriage? Or would that offend your principles too?'

She had no money at all for a hackney, and he must know it. 'I'll take a lift, but only across the river. After that, I can walk.'

He gazed down calmly at her defiant expression. 'You look remarkably beautiful when you're angry, Ganymede. I take it you've not enjoyed your sojourn in Vauxhall Gardens?'

'I wish I'd never, ever come to this vile place. I wish I'd never even heard of that detestable card party.'

'Presumably,' he said with interest, 'you inveigled your way inside in the hope of duping yet another poor gull like Sir Peregrine, and making off with your winnings.'

'I didn't inveigle my way in. I had an invitation, from the Ace of Spades himself. Damn you, why are you laughing at me?'

He stopped by a beautiful, black glossy carriage, with a coat of arms emblazoned on the door. 'Perhaps,' he chuckled softly down at her, 'because *I* happen to be the Ace of Spades.'

Marisa gazed up at him blankly, feeling as if a bottomless pit was opening up beneath her feet. 'Then – then why didn't you say something?' she whispered. 'Why didn't you have me thrown out when you first saw me amongst your guests?'

Four liveried manservants were waiting impassively by the carriage for Lord Delsingham's command, but, ignoring them, he said to Marisa, 'I suppose I wanted to see what game you were playing. I felt a certain curiosity about you, you see. And I also wanted to know how the devil you contrived to get into my private party when I'd not invited you.' Marisa started to speak, but he held up his hand quickly. 'No. Don't tell me yet. I'm sure the story of how you obtained your invitation is quite fascinating, but we've no time for it now.'

One of the manservants was silently holding open the carriage door. Marisa tensed, looking round wildly for escape, but Delsingham murmured in her ear, 'Better get in, my dear, before Sir Peregrine arrives. Am I really such a vile prospect?'

Marisa gazed up into his shadowed face, feeling dizzy with danger and excitement and the heady arousal of her encounter with the gypsies. Lord Delsingham, the Ace of Spades, was most definitely not a vile prospect. In fact, he was quite spectacularly handsome, but she wasn't going to let him know that. She said angrily, 'I don't appear to have much choice, do I?'

'Correct,' he acknowledged, his steely grey eyes glinting. Then he handed her up into his carriage, nodding curtly to the driver up on the box who was holding the four beautiful greys in check. Lord Delsingham stepped up behind her. The door closed and Marisa settled down rather faintly against the thickly padded velvet upholstery, her heart beating wildly.

Then suddenly, she heard the pounding of heavy feet outside, and several fists banged roughly on the door. Delsingham opened it so swiftly that it slammed into someone's face. 'The next knave to damage my paintwork will be horsewhipped,' he said. 'What is it?'

Marisa saw the men grovelling as they recognised him. 'My lord. Begging your pardon, but we are officers of the law – Sir Peregrine sent us after you. He accuses the wench in your carriage of cheating him.'

'Is that so?' drawled Lord James Delsingham. 'Then I'm afraid Sir Peregrine is going to be disappointed, because the girl stays with me. I also have business with her, as you see.' And before Marisa could even guess at his intention, he'd drawn her purposefully into his arms, quite heedless of his audience. There were muttered murmurs of 'Yes, my lord. Some mistake, my lord,' and the carriage door thudded shut as the horses strained at their harness and slowly started to pull away.

Marisa pushed fiercely at his wide shoulders, striving desperately to twist her face away, but his powerful arms tightened around her and he murmured, 'They're still watching us, Ganymede. Let's make it convincing, shall we?' and before she could draw breath to reply his mouth closed over hers in a kiss.

At the touch of his lips, something happened to her and her already overwrought senses exploded, out of control. Suddenly she was oblivious to everything except the exquisite movement of his strong mouth on her lips, the delicate flicker of his tongue against her silken, sensitive skin. His kiss intensified; she gave a little whimper, and her hands wound round the back of his neck, her fingers running through his thick black hair as his arms tightened around her and crushed her aching breasts against the hard wall of his chest. There was a dark, agonised yearning at the very core of her being that longed to be assuaged, and as the carriage pulled steadily away, her tongue entwined deliciously with his, drawing him hungrily into her. 'Steady, my sweet,' he murmured softly in her ear. 'We have time enough.' But as his fingers parted her little velvet jacket and silk shirt, and his mouth trailed lingering kisses over the soft swell of her breasts, Marisa moaned with need and pulled him towards her desperately.

With careful strength, he laid her along the soft cushions of the seat and steadily pulled down her chemise to expose her tautly straining nipples. He gazed at them silently, and Marisa caught her breath at the dark hunger in his eyes. Then, very gently, he ran his strong hand up her stockinged thigh beneath her skirt. She trembled violently as his big, strong hands met her melting flesh, and he caressed her there subtly, cupping her with his palm, drawing his long finger between her lushly nectared, flesh folds. She arched against him with a soft cry, almost ready to take her satisfaction from his probing finger, so desperate was she.

'Well, well,' he murmured as his finger did its seductive work, sending shivers of wanton desire shooting through her. 'What games have you been playing in the garden of pleasures tonight, my Ganymede?'

Marisa gasped as the pad of his finger brushed her throbbing clitoris. 'I've had enough of games, damn you. Take me. Take me, now.'

He was still watching her face, his eyes glinting as he said, 'But I thought you didn't have a very high opinion of my amatory skills. Earlier today you made a certain inference about my physique. Remember?'

Marisa groaned. Her eyes slid helplessly down towards his hips, where she could see how his slim-fitting cream breeches were straining across the mouth-watering bulge at his crotch. She replied archly, 'I'm sure you've got a sufficiently high opinion of yourself for both of us.'

He shifted her hips gently to the edge of the seat and eased her legs apart, kneeling on the floor between her thighs. 'Then you will have to decide if that opinion is well-founded, won't you?' he said gently.

He pushed her skirt back up around her waist and dipped his dark head to lick her. His tongue was long and rasping; he stiffened it cunningly and parted her labia with sweet strength as his hands fondled her stockinged thighs. Marisa clutched at his head, pressing his face down against her hungrily, but he was very careful not to bring her to orgasm.

He lifted his face, and she closed her eyes in disappointment. 'I wonder,' he said softly, 'what is your opinion of me now? Have you had enough?'

The gentle motion of the coach forced her to steady herself by hanging onto the leather straps that were fastened into the panelling. 'Bastard,' she hissed through gritted teeth, knowing that her exposed flesh was wantonly pulsing only inches from his face. 'Bastard.'

He smiled, his white teeth glinting in the darkness. 'Tell me what you want and I'll oblige. I'm a man of my word,' he added helpfully.

Marisa sucked in a long, shuddering breath. She would die if he didn't release her soon from this exquisite torment. 'I want you to push your cock into me, damn you,' she cried out at last. 'Now! Whatever its size,' she added ungraciously.

He obliged. As she gripped onto the leather straps to brace herself against the jolting of the coach over the rough road, she saw him reach down to the fastening of his breeches and draw out a long, darkly rigid penis that made her catch her breath in excitement. She felt the swollen petals of flesh between her thighs quiver and trickle with fresh moisture at the proximity of it. His face tense with control, he gripped his shaft carefully and stroked her labia with its velvety blunt tip until she arched towards him, her body shimmering with need. Then he slid his exquisite length deeply into her honeyed recesses as he crouched between her splayed legs, reaching with his hands to cup and fondle her breasts as they spilled hungrily out above the tight confinement of her corset.

Marisa was on the brink of orgasm already. She hung desperately onto the straps as the coach bumped its way along the rutted lane that took them away from Vauxhall towards Westminster Bridge, while he pleasured her slowly and sweetly, his face taut with concentration. She shivered with the warm, intense pleasure of it as he drove the firm length of his exquisite penis deep within her, and she groaned as he withdrew, only to be submerged in utter bliss as she felt him return. She held back for as long as she possibly could, hovering on the very edge of ecstasy. But then his hand slipped down to tangle in the moist, blonde curls that adorned her heated lovemound and his forefinger started to wickedly brush round her swollen clitoris. She gasped aloud and bucked against him as the searing pleasure invaded every nerveending. He was good, damn him. So good. Smiling in dark satisfaction, he began to drive himself into her, faster and faster. She glanced down and caught the thrilling sight of his lengthy shaft gliding slickly between her hungry labia. Then his mouth dipped to caress her swollen breasts, sucking and pulling at them with his thin, sensual lips and gently nipping at the hard, dark buds with his teeth. Marisa held her breath as she teetered on the very edge of the abyss. Then she began to throw herself wildly against him, shouting aloud as the fiery waves of pleasure started to engulf her, until nothing existed except the white-hot frenzy of her orgasm as she strained against the straps that supported her and bucked frantically against the exquisite rod of flesh that impaled her.

He drove himself silently to his own powerful orgasm a moment later, and she felt a renewed onslaught of delight as his lengthy penis spasmed deep within her. He lay, just for a moment, with his dark head lying against her breasts, and she felt a sudden tenderness, an unexpected longing to stroke the soft thickness of his hair. But then he drew himself up to sit on the padded seat a little way from her and began, quite calmly, to readjust his clothing. 'Delicious,' he murmured, his appraising eyes flickering over her lush nakedness. 'Quite delicious.'

Marisa's body was still purring with pleasure. She would have liked to curl into his arms, to feel his lips on her hair, her cheek, as she recovered from her rapture. But with those words he seemed to be distancing himself. He sounded like some connoisseur of fine wines, damn him. Any minute now, he would tell her how much she was worth. Swiftly pulling her own clothes back into some semblance of decency, she arranged herself with cold elegance on the seat, and gazed calmly up at his too perfect profile.

'So, my Lord Delsingham. You said earlier that you were curious about me. Is your curiosity sated?'

He smiled lazily down at her, a dark glint in his eyes. 'If curiosity is a kind of appetite, my dear, then I would say that it has been whetted, rather than satisfied. A brief taste of something exquisite makes the hunger for it all the sharper, wouldn't you say?'

Marisa gazed up at him, all wide-eyed innocence. David Valsino would have warned Lord Delsingham to be wary of that look. Pushing back her blonde curls, she purred, 'Perhaps it depends, my lord, on the kind of repast you're used to.'

Delsingham smiled and leaned back against the velvet cushions, stretching out his long, booted legs and brushing a speck of dust from his breeches. He said, 'A full night of pleasure should suit us both, I think. I've ordered my coachman to drive us back to my house in Cavendish Square. There, my dear, you'll get a chance to savour the entire feast.'

Oh, will I? thought Marisa grimly. And you don't even deign to ask me! He was just as conceited, just as impossibly arrogant as the rest of them. She felt a twinge of disappointment, because he'd been such a delicious partner. But there was no time now for regrets.

His arm had moved casually round her shoulder; he'd rested one booted foot carelessly on the seat opposite, and was gazing out of the window. 'We're just coming up to Whitehall,' he announced with satisfaction. 'It won't take us long to get to Cavendish Square.'

Marisa snuggled up to him, her cornflower-blue eyes soft with adoration. 'You're so kind, Lord Delsingham. But,' and she paused innocently, 'how did you know that I wanted to come back to your house, when you didn't even ask me?'

He laughed, his strong hand caressing her shoulder through the fabric of her jacket. 'I have yet to sustain a refusal from any female, Mistress Brooke,' he said.

Marisa patted his thigh lightly as the carriage pulled up in a sudden flurry of traffic close by the King's Mews. 'My dear Lord Delsingham,' she said kindly. 'If you had troubled to get to know me just a little better, you would soon find out that I am not like any other female in existence. In fact, I am the exception to every rule ever made.'

And with that, she jumped lightly to her feet, flung open the door of the carriage, and sprang out into the late-night crowds that were milling along Cockspur Street from the clubs and gaming dens of St James.

'Marisa,' he jumped out after her, with a furious instruction to the coachman to hold the horses. 'Marisa, wait, damn you. Marisa!'

But she evaded him with ease, darting and twisting amongst the crowds until his voice was quite lost.

So much for you, Delsingham, she thought defiantly. But at the same time she was conscious of a twinge of regret, because he really had been a delicious lover, equipped with a devastating body and the finesse to match his looks. If it weren't for his hateful arrogance, he really would rank as an ace amongst the pack.

Nevertheless, it was only a slight twinge. After all, she'd taken her pleasure with him, a fine way to end the evening, and she'd also, during that last, cosy little embrace, taken his lordship's rather fine gold watch. Patting it softly as she slipped it into the pocket of her skirt, she set off briskly for home.

Marisa knew the minute she came within sight of the Blue Bell that something was wrong. Maiden Lane itself was crowded as usual with the late-night revellers who habituated the area's notorious gaming hells and taverns; they staggered along arm-in-arm, much the worse for wear after too much rack-punch and cheap claret. Ripe for plucking, as Lucy would say. But there seemed to be a curious stillness around the narrow courtyard of the Blue Bell. A few candles guttered dimly in the grimy windows, but the front door was firmly closed.

Marisa stood on the corner of the street, frowning, all her instincts warning her of danger. Then suddenly an arm tugged at her, and she turned round to see Lucy, looking distraught and dishevelled.

'Oh, Marisa, thank goodness I caught you in time. You mustn't go anywhere near the Blue Bell – it's been raided!'

Marisa felt her heart miss a beat. 'Raided? By the watch?'

Lucy was panting in distress. 'They said they were officers of the law, but they looked more like robbers to me. John and I came back here just over an hour ago, because we couldn't find you anywhere at Vauxhall, and thought you might have come back home. We got back just in time to see it all. Those brutes were throwing people out onto the street, while they searched the place from top to bottom.'

Lucy's plump, pretty face was stained with tears. Marisa took her hand and said, 'But why, Lucy? Why the Blue Bell? I know there's some illicit gaming – but there are dozens of worse dens around here!'

Lucy gazed at her tearfully. 'It sounds as if they were looking for you, Marisa. You see, that's not all: apparently there were a couple of strangers round earlier this evening, soon after we'd gone out, asking about you. The taproom regulars sent them packing, of course, but they said they didn't like the look of them.'

Marisa's heart seemed to stop. A private vendetta; this was bad news. Who'd put the curs onto her? Lord Delsingham? No: he'd barely have had time to discover that his fine watch was missing, let alone arrange his revenge. Anyway, she doubted if a man of his standing would want to admit to the world that he'd been gulled by a light-skirt. Sir Peregrine? Now, that was more likely. The plump fool was turning out to be quite venomous. He could well have sent a couple of spies to track down her lodgings, even as he pursued her so relentlessly in Vauxhall Gardens. She said evenly, 'It's not the end of the world, Lucy. It should all have blown over by tomorrow.'

'We can stay at my sister's,' said Lucy valiantly through her tears, and Marisa nodded, though her spirits sank at the thought of the noisy, child-filled poverty of Lucy's sister's house in a narrow little alley off Drury Lane.

'That will be fine,' she said. 'Then tomorrow I can collect my things from my rooms, and we'll find somewhere else to live.'

'But they've taken everything, Miss Marisa,' wailed

Lucy in fresh distress. 'Your clothes, your papers –
everything.'

Damn, damn, damn. They'd certainly been viciously
thorough, too thorough for the stupid Sir Peregrine.
Pehaps this was Delsingham's doing after all, his way of
taking revenge for the insults she'd offered him this
morning. Tonight she seemed to have lost rather a lot,
one way or another. Thank goodness for Delsingham's
watch, at any rate. Tomorrow she'd take it to a pawn-
broker in Clare Market who would ask no questions, and
the money from that should keep her going for a while.

Then suddenly she remembered the letter from her
notary, Mr Giles, which she'd thrown into the fire earlier
that evening. At least the thieves hadn't been able to get
their dirty fingers on that. Some sort of bequest, the
notary had said. If there was anything she needed now,
it was a bequest. Some money, or jewellery? Or yet more
notices of debt? She couldn't believe that it was anything
of importance, but even so she resolved to go and see Mr
Giles first thing in the morning, before her unknown
enemy struck again.

Mr Giles was only too pleased to see Marisa, and after
some preliminary pleasantries he imparted some news
that made her frown in disbelief. For a moment there
was no sound except the ticking of the old clock on the
dusty mantelshelf of the notary's shabby little office.

'A house?' she repeated incredulously. 'And some
money?'

'Yes, indeed, my dear.' Mr Montague Giles leaned back
in his aged leather chair and knotted his fingers on the
desk before him. 'A rather substantial house, in fact: a
little remote, you understand, in the wilds of Hampshire,
but a pleasant enough situation, I believe, with nigh on a
hundred acres of parkland. And the money that comes
with it is not inconsiderable.' He coughed lightly, shuf-
fling the papers on his desk. 'A sum of 20,000 guineas, to
be exact.'

Marisa felt rather lightheaded, 'Left to my father, you say? But why?'

Montague Giles's, small dark eyes twinkled behind his pince-nez. 'It appears that the owner of the property, Lady Emily Ormond, was an elderly widow, whom your father, er, befriended some years ago when she was taking the waters in Baden. Your father continued to keep in touch with her. Their last meeting, apparently, was in Paris. You don't remember her?'

Marisa shook her head, trying to suppress the urge to laugh. Her father had always had a winning way with older women. There had been hundreds of Lady Emily Ormonds in his life, utterly besotted by his gallant cavalry bearing and his extravagant manners. But, miracle of miracles, this one was rich.

Montague Giles continued, 'She died just over a year ago, predeceasing your father by some two months. It has taken her lawyers some time to track down the beneficiary, namely, yourself. Needless to say, the terms of the will have caused some stir amongst Lady Emily's family.'

'I rather suppose they would,' said Marisa a little breathlessly. 'Who should have inherited the property?'

He shifted his papers, peering through his pince-nez. 'A nephew, I believe, Sir Julian Ormond, but of course there is nothing he can do to contest the will. It's all perfectly sound.'

Marisa nodded, still scarcely able to take it all in. A house. Money. She couldn't believe it. 'Mr Giles, when can I take possession?'

He spread his hands. 'As soon as you like, my dear Miss Brooke. The house is quite vacant. There are some formalities to be concluded, but with your permission, I can handle them easily. Would you like to read through the documents while I order you a dish of tea?'

Marisa glanced at the papers he passed across his desk and felt the familiar sinking feeling at the sight of all that close, spidery writing. She pushed them back. 'You can handle all that, can't you, Mr Giles? And as for the tea, well, I really think that I'd rather have a brandy.'

'Then brandy it shall be. Anything you wish, my dear Miss Brooke, anything at all.'

Delicious words. 'I also think,' Marisa went on slowly, 'that I should like to travel there as soon as possible. I'll perhaps take a day or two to make some suitable purchases here in London, and then I want to take up residence immediately. Will that be possible, Mr Giles?'

He poured them both a generous glass of brandy and lifted his in salutation. 'With your money, my dear,' he said, 'anything will be possible. Anything at all.'

'Oh, good,' said Marisa. She raised her glass, a mischievous smile playing round her lips. 'Let's drink to my inheritance, Mr Giles. And to whatever pleasures might be in store.'

Chapter Four

*I*t was evening and the warm dusk was just starting to enfold the wooded landscape as the big hired chaise, laden with trunks and bandboxes, left the dusty main road and turned in through the high wrought-iron gates. Birds twittered in alarm in the big chestnut trees and a squirrel scampered away towards a distant stand of beeches as the carriage swept up the long drive and pulled to a halt at last in front of the wide, stone steps that led up to the imposing entrance of Melbray Manor. The carriage door opened almost before the horses had stopped, and Lucy jumped out, gazing all around her, breathless with excitement. Marisa followed her more slowly, smoothing down her elegant brown silk travelling pelisse and adjusting her fashionable straw bonnet, newly acquired from Madame Thanier, exclusive Bond Street modiste.

Marisa's expression was outwardly calm and composed as she assessed her new inheritance in the fading light of the velvety spring evening, but in reality her heart was thumping with excitement. Melbray Manor was beautiful, more beautiful even than she had dared to hope. It was a substantial country residence, mellowed by the years so it seemed to blend in with the beautiful mature parkland that surrounded it. Built of honey-coloured stone, its multitude of ornate mullioned windows glinted brightly in the setting sun, while masses of yellow roses half-smothered the weathered stone pillars on either side of the imposing front door, spilling their lush petals across the courtyard. In the warm, still air, their scent was bewitching.

Marisa stood there, gazing silently up at it all. Mr Giles had told her how many bedrooms there were, how many reception rooms, but she'd forgotten the details. 'A gentleman's residence,' he'd said almost apologetically. 'Nothing terribly grand, I'm afraid. There are several far more imposing and palatial homes in that particular neighbourhood.' Then he'd proceeded to tell her about the kitchens and the cellars, and the storerooms and the stables, but she'd not really taken it all in, and anyway it didn't matter. To her, used to cheap lodging houses and rooms above shabby inns, it was palatial indeed. With this house and the money she'd inherited, every one of her dreams could be made reality now. Such delights in store. She drew in a deep breath as she gazed up at the magnificent chestnuts that lined the sweeping driveway, their creamy candles of blossom glimmering like the lamps at Vauxhall in the gathering dusk. All hers. It was so wonderful that she almost laughed aloud. And the best of it was that no-one here would ever, ever guess that she'd clawed her way up to all this, cheating at cards and dice, duping stupid old men, and picking pockets in the teeming back streets of London.

John the coachman, whom she and Lucy had persuaded with very little difficulty to leave the Blue Bell for good, had swung himself down from the driver's seat of the hired chaise and was starting to unharness the horses. They'd travelled post, calling at Esher and Guildford for changes so as to make the best possible speed, and stopping for a wonderful lunch of cold salmon and chilled hock in the private dining room of The Travellers' Rest on the road to Farnham. It had all been wickedly expensive, but as Marisa had casually pulled out the guineas to pay for it all she'd been overwhelmed by the delightful thought that cost was of no consequence now. Mr Giles had given her more than enough money from her inheritance to set herself up quite nicely – until the finalities were completed, he explained.

'You're sure you'll be all right going there straight-away?' he'd asked her yesterday as he gave her the keys, looking just a little anxious. 'The house has been closed up for some time, you know, ever since Lady Emily died. I really don't know what sort of condition it's in.'

Marisa had laughed. 'Dear Mr Giles. For me, it's utter luxury just to be assured of a roof over my head, believe me.'

How her father would have loved it all, she thought regretfully as she gazed up at the beautiful house. Captain Brooke would have played the role of wealthy country gentleman with as much courage and style as he brought to every other role in his crowded life. Drawing a deep breath, she took the big iron key from her reticule and moved with a rustle of silk towards the wide, shallow stone steps that led up to the imposing entrance.

Then she froze as the big oak doors swung open, and a man came out of the house and down the steps towards her, a well-dressed, elegant man with swept-back fair hair and a concerned expression on his refined face.

'Miss Brooke?' he said quickly. 'Please forgive me if I startled you. My name is Ormond, Sir Julian Ormond. I'm Lady Emily's nephew. You are Miss Brooke, I take it?'

'Yes, I am,' replied Marisa, warily holding out her gloved hand as the man bowed low over it. Dear heaven, she thought rather faintly, what was he doing here?

Straightening up, Ormond smiled down at her. 'You'll be wondering what I was doing in the house,' he went on. 'The truth is, Miss Brooke, I've been keeping a bit of an eye on the place. My aunt died some time ago, as you'll know, and there's been no-one to look after the house except me.'

'You live nearby?' queried Marisa rather sharply. This really was an unexpected complication.

'Yes, indeed. I have a place of my own: Greenfallow Park, just the other side of Crayhampton. So, you see, it's been no trouble to me to look after the old place from time to time, send my men over to tidy the grounds up a little, and so on. Now you're here, I won't need to, of course. But please, if there's any way at all I can help, then do feel free to call on me.'

Too good to be true, thought Marisa narrowly. She'd deprived him of his rightful inheritance, and here he was, offering her his help. She gazed up at him with her deceptively wide blue eyes, quickly trying to assess him. 'Thank you,' she said, still wary. 'I'll certainly remember your kind offer.'

He bowed again. 'I sincerely hope you will. And by way of a welcoming gesture, you'll find a cold repast laid out for you in the dining room, Miss Brooke. I do hope you don't mind, but I took the liberty of bringing over some food for you which my own cook has prepared. You see, I suspected you might be tired and hungry after your journey.'

Marisa nodded her thanks, feeling really mystified now. Nobody, in her experience, did something for nothing. What was Ormond after? 'You are very kind.'

'Not at all,' he responded. 'After all, we're going to be neighbours. I hope we'll meet again very soon.' Just then a mounted groom rode out of the shadows by the stable wing, leading another horse forward, a big, stocky grey. Ormond swung himself into the saddle and gathered up the reins. 'You enjoy riding, Miss Brooke?' he said quickly, seeing her watching him. 'You have horses of your own?'

'I love riding,' she acknowledged, then improvised quickly, 'But of course my horses will take a little time to arrive.'

'I have a sweet-tempered mare in my stables that you might enjoy. She could do with some regular exercise. I'll send her over with my groom tomorrow, if you like.' Before she could even think of a reply, he nodded briefly, saying, 'Welcome to Melbray Manor, Miss Brooke,' and

75

set off at a spirited trot down the driveway, his groom riding at his heels.

Lucy was watching him from Marisa's side as he disappeared round the curve of the sweeping drive. 'Something odd about that one,' she pronounced. 'A bit too smooth, if you ask me.'

'As long as he hasn't poisoned the food,' said Marisa lightly. 'I don't feel inclined to make any decisions at all about Sir Julian Ormond, except to be grateful for something to eat. I'm starving. Let's go inside and see what he's left for us.'

Ormond had left them a repast fit for a king: cold baked ham and chicken, vegetable terrines, and tiny tartlets of apricots and strawberries, along with several bottles of delicious white wine. Marisa and Lucy ate hungrily, then piled their plates with fruit and filled their glasses and wandered round exclaiming in delight over everything, while John got on with stabling the horses. The house, though shrouded in dustsheets of brown holland, was spacious and beautifully furnished. On the first floor were ten bedrooms, which Lucy counted excitedly, darting through door after door, while the ground floor contained several oak-panelled reception rooms with lovely full-length windows, crammed with old carved furniture and tapestry wall-hangings. The main reception hall, from which the oak staircase led upwards in a wide, sweeping curve, was adorned with stags' heads and faded oil portraits and ancient weapons. Gaping at it all from the foot of the stairs, Lucy drank down her third brimming glass of wine and turned to Marisa rather breathlessly. 'You'll need plenty of servants to look after a place like this.'

Marisa looked thoughtful. 'We certainly need servants, Lucy. But we'll have to choose them carefully.'

Lucy refilled both their glasses with the cool, pale wine. 'Young, strong and virile, you mean?' she breathed, her brown eyes lighting up.

Marisa laughed. 'I was thinking more in terms of discretion, dear Lucy! If I'm going to fit into local society, then there must be no hint of scandal.' She grinned wickedly. 'At least, not for a while. But you're right. We will find ourselves the most exquisitely endowed servants in all of Hampshire.'

John, who'd been tucking into a hearty cold meal by himself in the kitchen after seeing to the horses, reappeared at this point to ask gruffly if there were any more jobs to be done. Marisa set him to pushing back the big shutters, drawing off dustsheets and lighting candles to bring the old manor to life. As he worked, silent as ever, Marisa curled into the corner of a big, brocade-covered settee at the foot of the stairs and watched him surreptitiously, thinking that at least she'd made a good choice there. He looked big and strong in his corduroy breeches, with the brown leather jerkin that he wore over his white linen shirt emphasizing the brawny width of his shoulders; the candlelight flickered on his tanned face, on his sun-streaked brown hair as he moved stolidly around the room. Marisa suddenly remembered the sight of him pleasuring Lucy in her little bedchamber above the Blue Bell, vividly recalling the mouth-watering sight of his sturdily erect penis, and she felt her pulse quickening. Lucy, who had sat down beside her with yet another glass of wine in her hand, was obviously thinking along the same lines, because she pushed back her dark, loose curls from her slightly flushed face and said, a little breathlessly, 'If we get more manservants, John will be terribly jealous of them.'

'Oh, we'll hire maids as well, and John can join in,' said Marisa airily and the two of them giggled together, feeling more than a little inebriated as they watched John bringing in some logs to lay in the huge inglenook fireplace in the corner of the vast hall.

Lucy lifted up her glass a little unsteadily. 'To Sir Julian Ormond,' she pronounced. 'May he continue to provide us with food and wine – especially the wine.'

Marisa said thoughtfully, 'It certainly is exceedingly generous of him, considering I've deprived him of his inheritance. I wonder what his motive is.'

'He's probably planning to marry you and get his aunt's money back that way,' giggled Lucy, hiccuping slightly. 'Though come to think of it, he doesn't look the marrying kind to me.'

'Whatever do you mean?'

Lucy shrugged; her gown was slipping a little from her plump shoulders. 'Oh, I don't know. He was smooth enough to look at, with his fine clothes and fancy speech – proper gentry and all that – but there was just something about him.' She frowned, but was distracted as John came into the hall again, carrying a basket of logs whose weight made the muscles of his shoulders and upper arms bunch unmistakably beneath his shirt sleeves. Lucy gazed at him and licked her lips. 'Now, there's a fine man. You must try him, Marisa – he's delicious, he really is. He's so strong and sturdy, and he seems able to last for ever.'

Marisa sipped thoughtfully at her wine as she curled up amongst the cushions that were strewn across the big settee. She remembered again how she'd seen John's hot, hungry penis giving such pleasure to the whimpering Lucy, and felt the warm flesh between her thighs start to swell and throb warningly. Turning to Lucy she said coolly, 'I'm not at all sure that he's my type.'

Lucy giggled. 'Depends what you want. He's like an animal: no finesse, no conversation, just good simple pleasure, and that's why he's so valuable. He really wants you, Marisa – haven't you noticed how he's always watching you? Look, he's excited now, because he knows we're talking about him!'

They nestled close to each other on the big settee, giggling and whispering, and John glanced round at them suspiciously, the sweat beading on his wide brow from carrying in all those heavy logs, which he'd coaxed at last into glimmering flames. And Marisa saw, with a sudden dryness in her throat, that what Lucy said was true, because there was already a thick, knotted bulge at his groin, where his stalwart penis swelled and strained against his tight cord breeches. Marisa suddenly realised

78

that after the excitement and tensions of the day, with the wine singing through her body, what she needed now was sex, sex with a strong, willing man who wouldn't make life awkward. And perhaps the pleasure was there for the taking.

The candles John had lit gleamed smokily in the wall sconces, casting a golden, flickering light across the high-beamed hall and making shadows across the stone-flagged floor. John stood there uncertainly, until Marisa called out clearly, 'John. Come over here, will you?'

He walked across the hall with an anxious face, his heavy boots clumping on the flagstones. His erection seemed, if anything, to have grown more noticeable.

'Is there anything else you want me to do, my lady?' he said in his soft, burred voice. 'Just tell me if there is. I'll work all night if you want me to.'

Marisa moistened her lips and leaned forward. She'd taken off her travelling pelisse earlier, and was wearing a demure-looking gown of delicate rose crêpe with long, tight sleeves and a little lace fichu at the neck, a most suitable travelling dress for a lady of gentle birth. But if she loosened the lacings on the bodice, and removed the fichu, and leaned forward, as she was doing now, the gown was very far from demure.

John's eyes fastened dazedly on her high, small breasts as she eased them free of her bodice, with their soft, pink nipples just peeping over the edge, and the dark colour rushed to his face. Marisa saw the unmistakable stirring at his groin and said huskily, 'I don't think you'll have to work all night. But you'll certainly have to be ready for some fairly vigorous exertions. Take out your penis, John, and show it to me.'

Lucy gasped at her side, her brown eyes wide as saucers. John stammered out, agonised with shame, 'But my lady . . .'

Marisa liked him calling her 'my lady.' That, she decided, was what all her servants would call her. 'It's all right, John,' she said calmly, her hands moving thoughtfully over her own provocatively upthrust

79

breasts as she enjoyed the sensations she was arousing in her tingling nipples. 'No need to be ashamed of your virility. Unfasten your breeches, and release your penis.'

He did so with big, trembling hands, and Marisa felt her insides palpitate with lust. A mighty weapon indeed, fat and lengthy, and rearing like a live thing towards her, its bulbous head throbbing and purple. She felt her vulva tingle deliciously at the thought of sliding herself up and down on that beautifully engorged pillar of flesh. She smiled sweetly up at him through her thick lashes, aware of his hot eyes feasting on her naked breasts. 'Do you like my breasts, John?' she asked him gently. 'Would you like to lick and suck at my nipples, and rub your mighty cock against them?'

He lurched towards her, his stiff penis swaying grotesquely. 'Oh, my lady . . .'

She frowned dangerously, crossing her hands across her breasts. 'Restrain yourself, John. Learn some control. And then – ' and she let her angelic face soften again, and ran her hands slowly through her blonde ringlets, 'and then, who knows what I might permit?'

She leaned back languorously on the settee so that her breasts bobbed out pertly above her loosened bodice. Then, letting her knees spread just a little apart, she gently started to draw up the long skirt of her gown until the hem rested across her slender thighs, showing her little laced-up leather boots and her pale silk stockings gartered just above the knee. He stood transfixed, the single eye of his helplessly rampant penis weeping with frustration as he fought not to grab hold of his hot member in his big fist. Marisa saw how his face was contorted as he watched her fingers trail slowly up her leg towards the dark, secret place at the apex of her thighs. She laughed and moved her hand away, watching him all the time. Then she sucked slowly at her finger, sliding her moist lips up and down it suggestively. John groaned aloud.

Marisa said carelessly, her blue eyes gleaming, 'I can see you've got a good cock, John, but that's not always enough, is it? Lucy says you can last a long time, and I want to find out if that's true.' She leaned forward and went on in a husky voice, 'John, I want you to pleasure Lucy with your lips and tongue. If you do so satisfactorily, then I might decide to use you for my own pleasure. Do you understand?'

With a happy little cry, Lucy jumped from the settee and ran to settle herself in a small velvet chair nearby, where she could spread her legs apart and display her nest of curly dark hair to John's lust-crazed view. With an eager growl, he knelt in front of her, pulling her dark-stockinged thighs apart still wider so that Marisa could see the plump pink flesh folds of Lucy's sex, dripping with moisture, desperately craving attention. And John certainly gave her that attention, lapping and licking as eagerly as some thirsty dog at water, drawing his long, rasping tongue happily up and down between her parted labia and rubbing his nose against her clitoris. Then he began to make short, sharp tongue-thrusts deep inside Lucy's hungry vagina until she clutched at his shoulders, beating him with her clenched fists and crying aloud, 'That's it. Yes, John – right up me – oh, yes, yes!'

Marisa leaned back against the settee and sipped at her wine, frowning slightly at the dark eroticism of the candlelit scene. She could see John's ravening penis quivering between his thighs as he worked, and she continued to play lightly with herself, drawing her finger tenderly along the ridge of her throbbing clitoris and imagining the big serving man's rough tongue attending to her own hungry vulva. She could see how his heavy, hairy balls swayed between his buttocks as he worked on Lucy and wriggled his long, snakelike tongue deep inside her. She felt her own hard, keen excitement curling and gathering in the pit of her womb as the stem of her swollen pleasure bud hardened and burned against her delicate finger. With her other hand she fondled her own breasts, feeling the stone-hard nipples pouting hungrily. Nearly there – oh, nearly there. But she would save herself. She needed a good, stout male shaft to slide inside her and pleasure her moist inner flesh, to give her that final, rapturous relief.

Lucy was finished. Even as she sighed out her last shiver of bliss beneath the onslaught of John's tongue, Marisa called out sharply, 'John. Over here.'

He staggered to his feet, his breeches round his hairy thighs, his quivering penis purple with engorgement as it stood up stiffly from the thick, coarse mat of hair at his belly and loins. Marisa, her eyes shadowed with lust, gazed up at him and breathed, 'Now, John. I think it's my turn, don't you?'

He towered over her as she lay back on the settee, his penis throbbing hungrily, and Marisa drew up her skirts, teasingly splaying her thighs for him. With a throaty cry of lust he lowered his hips between her legs and started to thrust eagerly until the swollen, pulsing knob of his mighty shaft pushed its way between her soaking sex-lips and slid slowly, deeply into her aching flesh. With a gasp of rapture Marisa squeezed her inner muscles tightly around his bone-hard phallus and lifted her stockinged legs to lock them around his waist. John, uttering a husky growl, dipped his head to guzzle and suck at her distended nipples, and she felt his bristle-shadowed cheek rubbing deliciously against the soft mounds of her breasts. She shut her eyes, conscious of nothing but the throbbing force of his massive male member driving into her, ravishing her with a sweet, solid thoroughness that made her feel quite delirious with pleasure. She lifted her hips to meet him, grinding herself avidly against him in an effort to bring sharp release to her agonised clitoris, his big tongue snaked and circled at her stiffened teats, pulling them out with his lips and rolling them from side to side, and she gasped aloud, rigid with tension, almost there.

Then, with an indrawn hiss, he drew himself almost out of her, and went very still. She gazed down at his shadowy loins, her eyes hot with fascination. His penis was long and dark and thick, its base encircled by thickly curling black hair, its stalwart stem glistening with her bodily juices. She lifted herself towards him, feeling herself to be hovering on the agonised brink of rapture. Then he began to drive himself into her with strong, vigorous strokes that penetrated the very last of her self-control. Arching her hips, she writhed deliciously against him as the oncoming rapture gathered tightly in her womb, and as he continued to thrust, she reached down to touch her soaking clitoris and soared into great, engulfing spasms of pleasure that racked her whole body.

She felt him explode deep, deep within her, felt his penis twitch and spasm as he groaned in the ecstasy of release, and she lay very still, breathing in the musky male smell of him as the afterwaves of orgasm rolled sweetly through her sated flesh. A ten in the pack, she mused. No finesse, but incredibly well-endowed. Definitely a ten . . . 'Good, John,' she whispered, stroking his sweat-streaked thick hair back from his face. 'Very good.'

He lifted his head, quite dazed from his exertions. 'You are pleased with me, my lady?'

'Oh, yes.' She sighed contentedly, stretching out with her hands behind her head, and a happy smile split his suntanned face.

'You're going to let me stay here?'

'Indeed I am. In fact,' Marisa went on softly, 'I think that I shall make you my butler. Melbray Manor ought to have a butler; it's a very important post, John. Would you like that?'

His eyes glittered. 'Oh, yes, my lady.'

Marisa smiled languorously, then began to straighten out her dishevelled clothes. Lucy, who to judge by her flushed face and bright eyes had just teased herself with her finger to yet another intense little orgasm as she watched them, was leaning forward eagerly in her velvet chair. 'And me, Marisa darling? What shall I be?'

Marisa smiled at her, her thick-lashed blue eyes still hazy with satisfied lust. 'You, dear Lucy, can be my personal maid, and my companion in pleasure.'

Lucy sighed happily and went to pour herself yet

another glass of Sir Julian Ormond's fine wine, bringing the bottle over to Marisa.

'I'm hungry,' said Marisa suddenly. 'Let's go and finish off Ormond's food.'

They sat laughing together in the big kitchen, where the whitewashed walls gleamed with copper pots that softly reflected the warm candlelight. They ate chicken and ham pies off silver plates, while John, who saw himself already as the butler of the household, served them eagerly. Lucy was by now quite merrily tipsy, and John, who'd been helping himself to some ancient port he'd found, was almost as inebriated. Soon the pair of them had moved into a shadowy corner, with Lucy kissing him hungrily and running her hands all over his stalwart body.

Marisa sat and watched them thoughtfully, her mind reeling with plans. She wanted servants, fine clothes, a stable full of horses, her own carriage, but above all she wanted to be in control of everything, so she would never be at anyone's mercy, ever again. No-one would ever laugh at her for being poor, or try to take advantage of her. Not that anyone ever had, except for one man.

She found that she was thinking, rather intensely, of Lord James Delsingham. Damn him, he had been an ace indeed, the only one she'd ever known: a truly spectacular lover. A sleek, beautiful thoroughbred, compared to whom John was nothing but a sturdy if serviceable carthorse.

Seeing that John and Lucy were grappling noisily in the corner, she rose silently and made her way slowly up the broad, sweeping staircase. She and Lucy had been busy earlier that evening, finding linen for the beds. She'd left the casement window open in the spacious chamber she'd chosen for herself, and the warm night air was soft on her flushed cheek as she leant on the sill and gazed out into the silent, moonlit beauty of the rolling acres of parkland that surrounded the house. For a moment she thought she saw something moving in the shrubbery beyond the stables, and she stiffened with instinctive fear, suddenly remembering the vicious raid on her rooms in London. It was probably nothing but a breeze stirring the foliage she told herself, smiling at her own stupid nervousness. Everything was going to be wonderful here. But she did feel more than a fleeting regret that the most spectacular man she'd ever encountered was now well beyond her reach, and she would never see him again.

Out in the darkness beyond the walled shrubbery, the man on horseback saw the candles going out one by one in the windows of Melbray Manor, and as he watched his eyes were cold and bleak. When the blonde-haired woman leant out of the first floor window, he moved his horse back quickly into the dark shadows, waiting until she closed the window, gazing impassively until finally her light went out as well.

'Make the most of it all, Marisa Brooke,' he said softly to himself. Then he swung his horse's head around, and guided it swiftly away into the blackness of the enveloping woodland.

Marisa was awakened the next morning by warm sunlight flooding through the heavy curtains. For a moment she lay wondering where she was, unsettled by the silence. What had happened to the clamour of the street sellers and hawkers, the rumbling of iron wheels on cobbles, the barking of the hungry dogs in nearby Maiden Lane?

Then she remembered, and pulled herself up against her luxurious feather pillows, letting her eyes feast on the silken hangings of her beautiful mahogany bed, on the delicate rose-covered paper on the walls and the exquisite walnut furniture that was arranged around the spacious room. Hers, all hers. She drew a deep breath of satisfaction. Then she realised that she'd overslept. Outside the birds were singing and the sun was hot against the front of the house. Quickly she threw off the bedcovers and ran to the window, dressed only in her cotton shift, to tug back the heavy drapes and fling the casement wide open.

Her eyes widened when she saw that down below her in the sunny courtyard was a beautiful chestnut mare, fully harnessed and saddled, her head held by an anxious looking young groom who gazed around him uncertainly. She remembered in a blinding flash that last night Sir Julian Ormond had promised to send her over a horse, and she'd quite forgotten. Wondering with a stab of guilt just how long the young groom had been waiting there, she hurriedly dressed herself in her plainly cut, dark, cloth riding habit and pulled on her little leather boots. Then she ran a silver-backed brush through her disordered blonde curls and tied them back with a black velvet ribbon, quickly checking her reflection in a long cheval glass before running down the stairs and struggling to heave back the big bolts on the heavy front door. Where, she muttered to herself, was John? Probably snoring in Lucy's arms in some rumpled bed, utterly sated on wine and sex, damn him. Soon she would have to get the two of them into order. Swearing under her breath, she got the door open at last and stepped out blinking into the bright sunshine.

If the groom was surprised to see the lady of Melbray Manor herself opening the front door, then he made a valiant effort to conceal it, though he was obviously overwhelmed by the sight of Marisa herself.

'Sir Julian Ormond sent me, my lady,' he stammered out, his eyes dazzled by her blonde, petite figure, set off to devastating effect by her black riding habit with its long, elegantly cut skirt and tight-waisted little jacket. 'He promised you this mare yesterday, I believe.'

Marisa bestowed on him one of her most charming smiles, and saw him melt. 'How very kind,' she breathed. 'Thank him from me, won't you?'

'I will, my lady.' Eagerly he handed over the reins. 'She's a spirited ride, but she has a lovely temper. As you see, my master's already had her saddled and tacked up.

He says if there's anything else you need, then just send over to him.'

Marisa took the mare's bridle and fondled her silky nose. 'She's beautiful. Tell him that I'm extremely grateful.'

The groom, still blushing and by now utterly smitten, touched his forelock and moved away bashfully to mount his own big horse and ride off down the drive.

Marisa watched till he was out of sight, then turned to her new acquisition. 'Well, my beauty,' she breathed, running her hand down the mare's warm, sleek neck. 'Our neighbour Ormond certainly seems to be a surprisingly generous friend. I wonder why?'

The mare whickered softly and rubbed at Marisa's hand, eager for titbits, and Marisa felt her heart thrill at the sight of her lovely, clean lines, her muscular flanks and elegantly arched neck. Knowing she should have waited, or at least told Lucy or John where she was going, she nevertheless decided to take her out straight away; the prospect of a morning ride through her very own property was quite irresistible. Gently murmuring to the mare to soothe her high-bred restlessness, she led her across to the old stone mounting block in the corner of the yard and eased herself up into the side-saddle, bringing one leg round the pommel and neatly adjusting her skirt. She much preferred to ride astride, but even so it was wonderful to be on horseback again. She felt the mare move sweetly beneath her as she gathered up the reins and set her in motion. The sun was warm on her face and the air moved lightly against her cheek as she circled the gardens and headed for a wide, grassy ride that led between the trees towards a distant stand of oaks.

She still couldn't believe that all of this was hers. There was no other dwelling in sight: just the endless green turf stretching through the cool woods, and the blue sky on the horizon. Carefully, feeling the mare's willing eagerness through the tips of her fingers as they caressed the reins, she eased her into a gliding canter. To feel the soft breeze in her face, to feel the beautiful horse gather and stretch in glorious rhythm beneath her, was wonderful. Within a few minutes, Melbray Manor was out of sight, and apart from the curlews that wheeled over the distant downs, she was the only living figure in the landscape. Once, she thought she heard hooves behind her, and she pulled in to listen, but there was nothing except the melodious sound of the birds in the trees, and the ripple of the little stream that ran nearby. Her path lay across the stream; she negotiated it carefully, then brought her horse up to speed again and cantered on, her hair streaming out behind her.

And then, with unexpected abruptness, she felt the saddle lurching to one side beneath her. Gasping, Marisa clutched at the reins, but the mare, panicking at the sudden shifting of the weight on her back, shied and reared up with a fierce whinny. Marisa grabbed for her mane, but her fingers slid through it helplessly. She felt herself fly through the air, and as her head and shoulders hit the ground with a thump, she felt shooting sparks of pain, followed by absolute blackness.

Some moments later, she opened her eyes slowly to feel strong male arms cradling her and something cold and cool being pressed to her forehead.

'Marisa,' a strangely familiar voice was saying urgently. 'Marisa, are you all right?'

She nestled instinctively into the man's shoulder, feeling safe and warm. Her head still throbbed with pain, but the coldness at her temples was wonderfully soothing. 'Yes,' she replied dazedly, 'yes, I'm all right, but my head aches abominably . . .' She opened her eyes, but the overhead sun sparkling between the trees all but blinded her, and she shut them again. 'What happened?'

'You fell off your horse,' the unseen man was saying thoughtfully as he continued to dab the wet, cold muslin of his handkerchief against her forehead. 'And it must have been quite a knock to keep you silent for such a long time. My dear Miss Brooke, you've not insulted me yet, nor stolen anything. I really feel quite anxious about you.'

Marisa sat bolt upright at that, and the pain shot through her head again. With sheer disbelief, she gazed up into a pair of amused grey eyes that glinted with sparks of gold. Delsingham – Lord James Delsingham. 'Hell and damnation! What are you doing here?' she gasped.

He chuckled, but kept his arm around her shoulders. 'Now, that's more like it, my fair Ganymede. For a moment, I was beginning to think that the fall had done you irreparable damage. In answer to your question, I'm here because this just happens to be my land. But what are you doing here? I'd like to think you were paying a courtesy call to return my pocket watch, but that seems just a little too much to hope.'

She heard the gasp of her own indrawn breath. 'Your land? But it can't be.'

'Really? Why not?'

'Because,' declared Marisa heatedly, 'it's mine!'

For a moment, she had the minor satisfaction of seeing Lord Delsingham look blankly amazed, then he put his hand to his forehead and said, very slowly, 'Melbray Manor. You're the new owner of Melbray Manor. Dear God, I don't believe it.' And he began to laugh, very softly. 'No, don't tell me, sweet Marisa. You won it at cards, didn't you? Either that, or you lifted the title deeds from someone's pocket, or you blackmailed some elderly, besotted lover into giving it to you. Come on, now, which was it?'

She sat up rather abruptly, pushing him away. 'You'll just have to believe it, I'm afraid, because it is mine! It was bequeathed to my father, and now it's come to me. Whatever made you think this was your land, Lord Delsingham? Or are you just in the habit of claiming everything you set eyes on?'

Delsingham said carefully, 'I live at Fairfields, which is further down the valley. My land, Marisa, adjoins yours. The boundary between our properties,' and he lifted his hand to point, 'is that little stream back there, and you've crossed it. The land on which you chose to fall off your horse, sweet Marisa, is mine.'

She gazed up at him, still a little faint from the shock of her fall, her heart stupidly pounding. Oh, no. So Lord James Delsingham was her neighbour. And he knew her for what she was, a gambler, a trickster, a thief . . .

She snapped, 'I didn't fall off. I never fall off!'

He was getting to his feet, calmly brushing bits of grass from his beautiful grey riding coat and breeches. 'Is that your usual method of dismounting, then?'

'No,' retorted Marisa, following his example and pulling herself upright. 'It was the saddle – ' She broke off suddenly, remembering. There had been something wrong with the saddle. And where was her horse? It had been a mistake to get up so quickly; her head swam again and he put his arm round her, steadying her, but she pushed him away, saying tensely, 'My mare – was she injured?'

'I caught your horse,' he said quietly. 'She's fine; she's tethered beside mine, over by that tree. And you were right about the saddle. It came off just after you did. It's just there.' She glanced at where he was pointing, and saw the horses, and the big leather side-saddle lying arched on the grass. He went on, almost casually, 'Who saddled up that horse for you, Marisa?'

She said defensively, 'Sir Julian Ormond's groom brought her over ready saddled this morning.'

He looked astonished. 'Ormond?'

'Yes,' Marisa retorted hotly. 'He welcomed me last night, and offered to send over one of his horses for me until I could get my own.'

He looked as if he were about to say something, then he seemed to change his mind, remarking simply, 'I should be a little wary of Ormond, if I were you.'

'He's been most courteous. He brought me food, and wine, and offered his help in any way I wanted.'

Delsingham said kindly, 'He obviously doesn't know

you yet, if he thinks you need help. Where is my watch, Marisa?'

She felt herself colour faintly, then met his penetrating gaze with defiance. 'Who knows? One of the fences in Clare Market took it from me; it could be anywhere by now. Anyway, it's all you deserved, for your arrogant presumption in just expecting me to come back with you to your house for the night.'

He started to laugh, his hands resting on his hips. 'You would have enjoyed yourself,' he said.

Marisa swallowed. She had no doubt at all of that. He was still just as devastating as she remembered, his figure tall and wide shouldered in his beautifully cut dark grey riding coat, with his cropped dark hair slightly ruffled by the warm breeze. Her eyes slid surreptitiously down to his long, hard thighs, encased in tight buckskin breeches and high riding boots. She remembered how deliciously he'd pleasured her that night in his carriage, and she felt her head swim again and was only too aware that her breasts were tingling uncomfortably against the tight jacket of her riding habit.

She tossed her loose hair back and said scornfully, 'I find you quite amazingly arrogant. But then, I suppose someone as rich as you finds it hard to believe that not every woman is just waiting to fall into bed with you.'

'I don't invite every woman, by any means,' he said evenly. 'I'm actually quite fastidious.'

'And so am I. Now, if you'll excuse me, I think it's time for me to go.' And she turned to march quickly towards her waiting mare, bending to pick up the side-saddle that lay on the grass nearby.

It was impossibly heavy. Gritting her teeth, she looped her arms beneath it and struggled to pull it up, while Delsingham, curse him, was just standing there watching her with his arms folded across his chest, and that maddening smile still twisting his damnably handsome face.

Then she remembered. He'd told her the saddle was broken. She dropped it with a thud and a curse. He said calmly, 'Oh, by the way, I did fix it for you earlier. One of the girth buckles had come adrift. I replaced it with one of mine, while you were recovering from your fall.' Marisa stared at him, speechless. He said, encouragingly, 'Aren't you going to thank me? You really need to learn some manners, sweet Marisa, if you're going to be mistress of Melbray Manor.'

She clenched her fists at her sides. 'I need no tuition from you about how to conduct myself.'

'I think you do,' he said regretfully. 'For example, Marisa, real ladies don't go galloping about the countryside without a groom in attendance.'

'I haven't got a groom yet. I've not had time to appoint all the servants I need, but I will. I've got money enough for anything.'

He laughed, leaning his back against a tree, his arms still folded. 'Another mistake, my dear. Real ladies don't talk about how much money they've got. Somehow, I don't think Hampshire society is quite ready for you. What's it worth, sweet Marisa, not to tell all your fine new neighbours that you're a thieving little card-sharp from the back streets of London?'

Enough. The rage swelling in her heart, Marisa, quick as lightning, darted for the hateful man's riding crop where it lay on the ground near his feet, and lunged to strike him in a fluid, graceful movement that David Valsino would have been proud of.

But he was quick too. He parried the blow just in time with his forearm, and trapped her hand as she struggled out blindly. 'Steady, steady,' he murmured, grasping her arms easily in his strong hands and holding her firm as she twisted and writhed in his grasp. 'You seem to forget that I hold all the aces here. I know all about you, you see, and I could quite spoil all your little plans. What are they exactly, I wonder? Do you plan to cheat the local gentry at cards? Rob them of their silver and jewels, perhaps? Or maybe find yourself a rich, rich husband who'll oblige you in your every whim?'

Marisa sagged in his arms, her head bowed in defeat,

utterly silent. He frowned and relaxed his grip a little. 'Marisa? It's not like you to take a rebuke so quietly. Are you all right, Marisa?'

The minute she felt his strong grip loosen, she drew back her little booted foot and kicked him hard on the calf. His boots were sturdy, but so were hers, and she'd caught him just on the tenderest part of his leg, where the shin bone was close to the skin. As he swore vigorously and staggered back, she turned and ran desperately for her horse, stooping once more to pick up the saddle. Now that she knew it was mended, she must be able to get it back on, she must . . .

But she didn't even get to lift it from the ground. Delsingham was behind her, grabbing her by the waist. She lashed out blindly, but she lost her balance and the next thing she knew, she was sprawling face down across the arch of the saddle with its warm leather curves pressing up into her belly and ribcage. Her enemy was instantly behind her, kneeling over her, breathing hard. She could feel the substantial weight of him pressing against her back, could feel his warmth against her cheek.

'Let me go,' she hissed out, struggling desperately. 'Damn you, Delsingham, let me go!' She tried to twist round, to see her tormentor, but he'd imprisoned her quite firmly, kneeling over her as she sprawled helplessly across the steep curve of the saddle. 'Sweet Marisa,' he was saying tenderly, 'you really are quite adorable when you're angry.'

And then she realised, to her horror, that he was doing something with the stirrup leathers; he'd twisted them round her wrists, and was binding them swiftly to the pommel, tightening the straps by gradual but definite degrees so she was quite unable to pull them free. She hissed aloud and tried to twist round to face him, but she couldn't even manage that. Her long curls streamed across the saddle to the ground, blinding her: she could smell the well-oiled leather, and the grassy turf close to her face, while the steeply rounded curve of the saddle across which she lay arched her body up towards her captor. Her knees just touched the ground where the saddle rested; her buttocks were clenched high, and the underswell of her breasts was caressed through her clothing by the warm, smooth leather. She almost sobbed aloud, so trapped did she feel. What was he planning to do? She could hear him moving gently behind her, but had no idea what was going on. Would he leave her here, or perhaps beat her for her attack on him? She suddenly remembered his ominous words to her at their first, fateful meeting outside David Valsino's house, when she'd insulted him so rashly, 'I should take a horsewhip to you for that, sweet Ganymede. Some day, perhaps I will . . .'

She shivered at her helplessness. Her nipples sprang into taut life, and she felt the soft folds of flesh between her thighs pulse and tingle. What was her enemy going to do to her?

She didn't have to wait long to find out. She felt the sudden kiss of cool fresh air on her sensitised flesh as he carefully lifted up her heavy riding skirt and flimsy silk chemise to expose her bottom. She shuddered with shame as his hands slid softly over her upraised buttocks, and again she tugged desperately at the straps that bound her hands firmly to the heavy saddle. Then she gasped aloud as she felt his fingers slide down her thighs, as far as the delicate ribbon garters that held her silk stockings just above her knees, and slowly, with infinite tenderness, he eased her legs apart, and she felt all the hot, naked shame of knowing that he would be feasting his eyes on the dark, glistening flesh of her exposed femininity. Even though she couldn't see him, she could picture him gazing down at her. She could also imagine only too well the powerful stirring of his magnificent manhood, and the shaming moisture of arousal trickled anew down her thighs. Oh, but she wanted him, wanted him desperately.

His finger trailed up her thigh and brushed lightly against her silky folds, sliding in their nectar. She gasped and clenched her teeth to hold back the moan of need. He was saying thoughtfully, 'You obviously enjoy horse riding very much. Considering your low opinion of me, I really can't imagine what else can have aroused you so.'

'Certainly not you,' she hissed out. Then she moaned again as his finger slid down her juicy cleft and thrust, very gently, into her warm vagina.

'Are you quite sure?' he enquired.

She pushed back against him, unable to help herself, longing to feel more of him caressing her so wickedly, but he slowly withdrew his finger, and she slumped across the saddle in burning disappointment and shame. 'Damn you,' she muttered against her arm, the tears of shame starting to burn at the back of her eyelids.

And then she gasped, and couldn't even think of saying any more, because his warm, firm hands had clasped the creamy globes of her bottom, and were kneading and pulling gently at her sun-warmed flesh. She was aware that he was kneeling behind her, nudging her legs even further apart. And then she felt the glorious, velvety kiss of his erect penis nudging gently between her thighs and probing at her honeyed cleft, gradually easing its way with blissful skill between her swollen labia. For a moment he paused, and she groaned aloud and pushed her buttocks back against him helplessly, picturing that proud, lengthy phallus poised so deliciously at the entrance to her yearning vagina. Then she heard the hiss of his indrawn breath as he prepared himself for entry, and she realised, with a shudder of excitement, that he was every bit as fiercely aroused as she was. She held her breath, until, with incredible, measured power, he mounted her at last, sliding his exquisite length slowly into her aching vulva from behind and holding it there, very still.

She let her flesh palpitate all around him, relishing every second of the bliss of having him filling her, impaling her on his hot, bone-hard shaft. Then he began to move, very slowly. He was still kneeling on the ground behind her, tenderly gripping her buttocks as he pleasured her, powerfully driving his strong phallus in and out as Marisa, bound helplessly over the saddle in front of him, gasped out in shameful delight. Oh, but he was delicious. His penis was so firm, so lengthy, so controlled. She began to whimper aloud as he leaned into her, feeling his flat, hard belly against her buttocks and his heavy balls swinging against the backs of her thighs, while his hand slid slowly but surely up her stockinged thigh, reaching round to stroke her heated mound and delicately circle her fiercely throbbing clitoris as he continued to ravish her slowly, beautifully.

She pulled and strained in her excitement at the leather straps that bound her, throwing back her head and biting her lip. His hand moved forward to slip under her tight jacket, feeling its way under her bodice to grasp and squeeze at her stiffened nipples, twisting them gently until the darts of exquisite pleasure-pain shot down to join the fierce, demanding heat of her clitoris. Marisa writhed ecstatically beneath his body as he covered her, thrusting herself back with hungry jerks to engulf his massive penis, almost swooning with delight at the sensations aroused by the solid, lengthy shaft of flesh sliding gently but firmly inside her honeyed vagina, caressing her trembling inner core with such consummate skill that she was already whimpering and crying out his name as the hot sun beat down through the dappled shade of the trees. At last, just when she thought she would scream out with longing, his strong, teasing finger brushed lightly but persistently against her quivering bud of pleasure, and she bucked helplessly as the pleasure began, raising her bottom to him in wild abandon as he began to thrust faster, deeper. His hand pressed harder against her clitoris, and she toppled over the edge into wave after wave of excruciating pleasure, rubbing her nipples against the oiled leather of the saddle beneath her, clutching her inner muscles tightly around his delicious shaft of flesh and crying aloud all through her endless, luscious climax. Sighing, she collapsed face down across the sweat-sheened leather, dimly aware that he too was losing his iron control at last. She felt him clutching at her bottom cheeks and pounding into her until his mighty rod twitched and pulsed in release at her very core. Then he leant his cheek against her back and reached to softly stroke her aching, swollen breasts, and all she could hear was the sound of their two horses unconcernedly cropping the grass nearby.

Exquisite, thought Marisa dazedly, quite exquisite. And wholly dangerous. Whatever happened, she mustn't ever let him know how wonderful a lover he was.

Gently, he pulled down her skirt to cover her nakedness and Marisa felt a pang of extreme regret as his warm body moved away from hers, because she'd have liked him to hold her, to kiss her tenderly. Then the cold leather straps biting into her wrists brought her back to reality. How dare he treat her like some back-street slattern? Her hands were still tethered, but she managed somehow to twist her head round and face him, her blue eyes suspiciously wide and innocent.

'Well,' she said, surveying him almost with pity as he readjusted his clothes, 'it seems, my Lord Delsingham, as if I was right on our first encounter.'

His grey eyes narrowed warningly as he smoothed down his coat. 'And what exactly do you mean by that, Ganymede?'

'I mean,' Marisa said kindly, 'that you've just proved to me yet again that no self-respecting female would come to you of her own accord. You've already told me that you're willing to pay for pleasure, and now you've shown me that where money fails, you'll take what you want by force.'

His thin, sensual mouth curled slightly. 'Be careful, sweet Marisa. You enjoyed yourself rather thoroughly, I think.'

She said scornfully, wrenching at the straps, 'You think I'd have let you do all that to me willingly, my lord?'

He bent gracefully on one knee to unstrap her with his long, dextrous fingers. 'I think,' he said, 'that you are rather proud, and I simply made it somewhat easier for you to accept my advances. You can protest as much as

97

you like now that it's over, but you can't deny that you enjoyed it.'

Her hands were free. She struggled to haul herself up from the saddle and stood there before him, still dizzy with pleasure. Then she pushed her hopelesssly tangled hair back from her face and smoothed down her crumpled skirt and hissed, 'It must be wonderful to have such a high opinion of yourself. What a shame your physique and skills don't match it.'

He laughed. 'So we're playing games now, are we, Marisa? You like it that way?' He tilted his head a little to one side, assessing her dishevelled figure with mocking eyes. 'We'll come to an agreement then, since you profess you won't come to me willingly. You give me what I want, and I'll promise in return not to give you away to your respectable new neighbours. I won't tell them that the new mistress of Melbray Manor is no lady.'

She caught her breath at the enormity of his suggestion, and yet she felt the excitement curl through her entrails at the silky promise in his voice. 'If I were a man, Lord Delsingham, I'd call you out.'

He calmly strapped her heavy saddle onto her horse's back, then turned back towards her, his grey eyes dancing. 'What an enchanting idea. A duel at dawn – swords or pistols?' He laughed aloud. 'Such a pity you're not a man – in some ways, that is.' His eyes lingered on her breasts beneath her little buttoned-up jacket, and she felt hot again in a sudden shameful rekindling of desire.

'Some day,' she said shakily, 'some day, Lord Delsingham, you will receive my challenge, I assure you.' She scrambled up into the high saddle and gathered up the reins to pull away from him, her face tight with chagrin, but he held onto the bridle a moment longer.

'Marisa,' he said, his voice suddenly more serious as he gazed up at her. 'One thing you ought to know. That saddle strap was bound to break some time during your ride; there was scarcely an inch of sound leather at the buckle.'

She scanned him coldly. 'Then it was an unfortunate accident.'

'No accident,' he said curtly. 'The strap had been cut. Be careful, Marisa.'

She felt a sudden cold chill as the sun went behind a cloud. It was a lie. He was deliberately trying to frighten her. 'I'm quite used to looking after myself, Lord Delsingham, believe me,' she retorted, and turned her horse's head sharply back towards Melbray Manor.

Chapter Five

*L*ater that same morning, Sir Julian Ormond, nephew to Lady Emily, was disturbed by a tentative knock at the door of the anteroom to his bedchamber. He pulled himself up quickly, gathering his exquisite brocade dressing robe around himself and girding it at the waist. The two half-naked, tousle-haired gypsy girls he'd met the day before at the fair started to get up too, but he beckoned them back.

'Stay here,' he said curtly. 'And say nothing.' He let his eyes linger on them, just for a moment. They were a couple of sluts, but ripe and willing enough, especially the plump one with billowing red hair and mischievous green eyes. She looked as if she would enjoy anything. He smoothed his dressing gown over his slim hips, hoping the loose folds would conceal his erection, and went out into the anteroom to answer the knock. It was almost noon. The sun beat down outside, but here in the private quarters of Greenfallow Park the heavy damask drapes were all drawn, and the air was dark and stifling.

He opened the big mahogany door. It was the young groom, the one he'd ordered to take the mare across to Melbray Manor earlier. The man looked pale and anxious, not a good sign. 'Well?' Ormond questioned him softly.

The groom swallowed. 'I took the horse to her, sir, just as you instructed. The woman set off immediately, by herself, and I followed her at a safe distance like you said. She never saw me, I swear it.'

'And?' Ormond's voice was smooth, dangerous.

'She rode onto Lord Delsingham's land, sir, just across Trickett Brook, and it was over there that the strap broke. She was cantering, and she took a nasty tumble and had all the breath knocked from her.'

'So. You moved in, I take it?'

'N-no, sir,' stammered the nervous groom. 'I couldn't, because Lord Delsingham himself turned up. The last I saw, he was bathing the woman's head with water from the stream. I thought I'd better make myself scarce, in case there were some of his men around.'

Sir Julian Ormond had gone very still. A shaft of sunlight from the corridor outside caught his smooth fair hair; his eyes were pale and cold. 'So,' he said thoughtfully. 'Rather a waste of time, then, wouldn't you say?'

The groom shrugged his shoulders, his relief only too apparent because his master didn't seem particularly angry. 'I suppose so, sir. Better luck next time, perhaps – ' And then he broke off, because Ormond suddenly struck him hard across the cheek with his well-manicured fingers. The groom cried out and twisted to one side to avoid the follow-up, but Ormond had quickly grasped one of the riding whips that stood in the stand by the door and began to systematically beat him across the back and shoulders. The groom cowered, driven to his knees by the sheer force of the blows, trying to protect his face and head with his hands. He was wearing a sleeveless leather jerkin which protected him from any real damage, but even so he trembled as the lash snaked down across his shoulders again and again.

At last Ormond seemed to tire. He stepped back and said in a low, vicious voice, 'Get out of my sight.' The groom, half sobbing, scurried out and shut the big door behind him, leaving the room in heavy darkness once more.

Ormond stood there for a moment, forcing his breathing to slow down. He could feel his penis thrusting hot and urgent against the folds of his rich brocade robe. He rubbed it slowly, slipping his hand under his robe to caress the hard, silken length before returning to the curtained darkness of his bedchamber, where the air was thick with the cheap, potent scent of the gypsy girls.

Marisa Brooke had fortune on her side, it seemed. His eyes narrowed in thought as he turned back, and then he saw that the door of his bedchamber was ajar, and that the two gypsy girls had been peeping out, watching him all the time.

Their eyes were alight. The redheaded one said softly, 'We were interrupted, I think, my lord,' and he suddenly wanted them badly. They moved quickly aside as he swept back into the bedchamber and eased himself onto his huge curtained bed, letting his robe fall back from his slim but muscular body so they could see that he was fully erect. 'We were indeed interrupted. Carry on,' he said tersely.

The gypsy girls moved in on him eagerly, their imitation jewellery tinkling and the cheap, musky scent that they used wafting through the dark, airless room. The plump redhead was on his left, and the smaller, dark-haired one called Matty on his right. Both wore blowsy, full-skirted gowns in bright colours, with gaudy laces and ribbons. They'd unlaced their bodices earlier so he could feast on the sight of their lusciously naked, sun-browned breasts, and now the dark haired one was bending to take him in her mouth while the other one just watched him, teasing at her dark brown nipples with her fingers and running her tongue along her lips.

His penis strained hot and hungry beneath the girl's tongue as she avidly licked and sucked at the hardened flesh, and his testicles ached. She started to rub at the base of his engorged shaft with eager fingers and he felt the pressure building black and hard at his temples as her eager mouth danced and glided along his straining shaft.

Then the redheaded woman, the one that first caught his eye at the fair yesterday, glanced at her friend's ardent efforts, and turned to look through the open door into the anteroom, where the leather whip lay discarded on the floor. She wandered slowly out to pick it up, then came back and stood by the bed, fingering the lash meaningfully. Matty stopped what she was doing, leaving the man's cock sticking red and angry into the air, and Ormond's breath caught raggedly in his throat. His penis twitched; a fresh drop of moisture glistened at the tip of the swollen glans.

'You'd like a touch of this, my fine lord?' said the redhead softly, licking her pouting lips with her tongue as she fingered the leather lash and drew the handle meaningfully across her own lushly exposed breasts.

Ormond swallowed, his penis jerking helplessly now as it thrust up from the circle of fine, blond hair at his loins. He grated out, 'Yes. Yes, damn you.'

Rowena stood beside the bed, and used the whip to raise her own full skirt teasingly so that he could see the tops of her dark serge stockings. Then she lifted the hem even higher with the solid whip handle and slid its smooth tip between the tops of her plump white thighs, drawing it to and fro against her exposed vulva and closing her eyes in pleasure. The dark-haired one climbed onto the bed by Ormond's feet and lay on her front, her chin in her hands, watching her friend avidly. Then, suddenly, the redhead moved, flicking out the long lash so that it curled across Ormond's taut belly, just inches from the waving stem of his angry penis. He cried out in a despairing mixture of pleasure and pain. She bent over him so her ripe breasts dangled near his face, drawing the silky lash round his bulging testicles and pulling very lightly so the plump, hair-covered globes were slightly lifted from his body. He moaned softly as she tugged at the lash and it slowly came free again.

She stood there, watching him. 'On your knees, now, my lord,' she said huskily, her voice a whisper of promise. 'Matty, pull off his lordship's fine gown, will you? I've a fancy that this is what he's really after.'

Ormond slid off the bed, trembling in spite of the warmth of the room, feeling weak with desire and excitement. Wordlessly he crouched on all fours on the floor, feeling the harsh wool of the carpet scratching against his hands and his knees, and the girl Matty slipped off his dressing robe and crouched behind him, fondling the twin globes of his tight, small buttocks.

'There you are, my lord,' she whispered happily. 'Aren't you a pretty picture, now? He's all yours, Rowena dear.' And she lowered her head to gaze avidly at his yearning red penis as it thrust hungrily up against his tense belly.

It was then that Rowena struck. Standing with her legs planted firmly apart just behind him, her full breasts quivering as she moved, she used the silky lash to caress and sting alternately, to bring the heated blood to his pale taut skin, and Ormond pressed his cheek against the floor and closed his eyes. Then Matty, nodding in silent communication with her friend, slipped lithely beneath him and started to lick avidly again at his stiff, ravening member, sliding her moist lips up and down as far as the silky coronal of pale pubic hair, while Rowena, with a little smile on her rapt face, reversed the whip and started to probe at his tight buttocks with the tip of the smooth leather handle.

Ormond groaned aloud as he felt that intimate, insistent caress at his dark, secret cleft, and Rowena dropped swiftly to her knees behind him so that she could make a more accurate assault, pulling apart his bottom-cheeks and stroking thoughtfully with her fingers at the tight anal aperture. There was some balsam oil on the dressing table. She got up quickly to fetch it and kneeled down again, anointing her fingers with it and probing gently with each digit until they slipped in past the tight collar of muscle. Ormond shuddered, and Rowena, pulling out her fingers and quickly rubbing oil onto the whip handle, started to slide the thick, rounded handle into the puck-

104

ered little opening, feeling him quiver and convulse around it as she invaded him, slipping it lazily in and out while the man shuddered with torment.

'This is what you wanted all along, isn't it, my fine and fancy gentleman?' muttered Rowena under her breath, her green eyes glittering. 'I knew it as soon as I saw you yesterday at the fair, with all your grand clothes and haughty manners. All high and mighty, you pretend to be, but I've met your type before. Go ahead, Matty.'

And Matty, still crouching beneath Ormond's bowed, quivering body, nodded eagerly and renewed her efforts, sucking and licking at the man's hot, straining penis until it was thrusting helplessly at the back of her throat. He arched his back desperately as Rowena continued to pleasure him with the oiled whip handle, and clenched his buttocks so tightly round it that she thought it would break. Then he cried out, and he was spurting hotly, juicily into Matty's mouth, his hips thrusting furiously, his refined face contorted with degrading pleasure. Matty swallowed hungrily, running her fingers around his throbbing testicles, enjoying the salty taste of him and relishing his helpless spasms as his semen spurted forth.

At last, he was finished. As Rowena silently withdrew the whip handle from his quivering buttocks, he drew himself up, his face pale and expressionless, and pulled on his discarded bed robe. A strange one, thought Rowena. Handsome enough in a cool, refined sort of way, but obsessive, and maybe cruel.

She and Matty waited silently as he went over to a drawer and pulled out some coins. He was controlling his breathing with difficulty. At last he said, 'There's work for you both here, of various kinds, in the kitchens and around the house. I'll inform the housekeeper that you're staying for a while.'

They took the coins he offered and bobbed dutifully. 'Yes, my lord.'

'And now,' he went on softly, 'you can get out. And remember. If there's any hint of trouble – any theft, any spying, any gypsy mischief – then you'll regret it, believe

105

me.' He turned towards the open bottle of wine that stood on the mahogany bedside table, and started to pour himself a glass. Matty and Rowena curtseyed and hurried out into the corridor, half blinded by the noon sunlight after the artificial darkness of the bedchamber. 'Easy money,' gloated Matty.

'I'm not so sure.' Rowena pocketed the coins and began to slowly tidy up her clothes. 'He's a strange one, and no mistake. And I don't know about you, Matty, but I'm real desperate to feel a good man's cock up me after all that messing about.' She grimaced as she eased her full, sensitive breasts back into her tight bodice, tugging the fabric over her large, brown nipples. 'I wonder – why did our fine new master beat that groom?'

Matty shrugged carelessly. 'Sounds as if he was after someone, arranging some sort of accident. Nasty. Nothing to do with us, anyway.' She was much more interested in gazing about her. They were on the first-floor landing of Sir Julian Ormond's fine country house, and she loved the elegant finery of the place, with its richly gleaming furniture and all the fine gilt mirrors that reflected the glittering chandeliers. 'We'll do as he says,' Matty went on, 'and find this housekeeper, and do whatever we're supposed to do. I quite fancy staying in this big house for a while. Then later perhaps this evening, we can slip out and find the men.' She giggled meaningfully. 'Reckon Caleb and Seth'll be ready to give us what we want, Rowena, even if our fancy new master ain't up to a good straightforward pleasuring. Wonder if Seth's any nearer to finding that woman he's after? He seemed dead sure she was somewhere in these parts. Got word from other travellers, he said.'

Rowena's plump, pretty face flushed suddenly beneath her red curls. 'I still don't see why he's so desperate to find her.'

'Said he'd got a trinket of hers, didn't he? A gold ring, or something. Tells everyone he's going to give it back to her, but if you ask me, the real reason for getting us to trail all this way after her is that our randy young Seth is hot for her!' She chuckled.

But Rowena snapped, 'Then he'll soon find out that she's just a high-class whore, won't he, for all her innocent, blue eyes and pretty, golden hair and fancy manners. He'll regret the days he laid eyes on that bitch, you mark my words.'

Matty was going to say something, but then she saw the rage in Rowena's green eyes and thought better of it.

They reported duly to the housekeeper, a thin, tight-lipped woman who was no doubt well-used to her master's ways and made no comment as she found them two demure maids' gowns to wear, with little white aprons, and showed them to the two small, sparsely furnished attic bedchambers they would occupy. Then she set them to cleaning silver in the big back kitchen.

'No thieving, mind,' she said tartly. 'Your new master has his own ways of dealing with those who try to do him out of anything that's rightly his.'

Matty and Rowena exchanged expressive looks. 'I'll bet he has,' whispered Matty, thinking of the unfortunate groom cowering on the anteroom floor beneath Ormond's heated blows.

They got their tasks done quickly and efficiently during the course of the afternoon, to the dour surprise of the housekeeper. There was no sign of Ormond, and no-one noticed when the two women disappeared up to the attic to relieve themselves surreptitiously of the rather urgent sexual excitement that had been burning in them since the session in Ormond's bedchamber earlier.

'Not as good as feeling a real man's cock up me,' gasped Rowena, lying back on her narrow little bed as Matty fondled her full breasts and started to pull up her skirts, 'but I'll burst if I don't have some pleasure now. That's it, Matty, love. Run your tongue up and down me, stick it up me. Oh, I'm so hot and wet, I think I'll die ...' And she gurgled with pleasure as Matty's long, thin tongue pleasured her, running up and down the plump, fleshy groove between her thighs and wriggling about just inside her lush vulva. Rowena came quickly, panting and thrusting against Matty's face. Then it was Matty's turn, and this time Rowena pleasured her friend with her fingers, knowing exactly how to tease her soaking little pleasure bud with just the right amount of pressure, while using her other hand to stroke gently at her sex-lips and slide two, then three fingers deep inside, moving them about so Matty could clutch hard at them and bear down on them as she shuddered her way to a sharp, fierce little orgasm. They lay together for a while afterwards, flushed and sated, giggling quietly about what they'd do with Caleb and Seth and Tom that night. Then they washed and went downstairs to eat their tea of rather stale bread and slices of thin ham in the servants' kitchen. The other servants regarded them disdainfully, but Matty and Rowena didn't care.

They were just going to lay the fire in the dining room, as they'd been ordered, when they heard the clatter of horses' hooves, and the sound of a carriage pulling up at the front of the house. Rowena, ever curious, ran quickly to the nearest window to gaze out.

'Who is it?' called out Matty, who was on her knees laying kindling in the big grate. 'Some more fancy gents?' She chuckled. 'D'you think Ormond will be requiring our services again tonight, Rowena?'

But Rowena, by the big window, had gone very still. Stepping out of the carriage was a lady, a beautiful, slender lady in an elegant pelisse of darkest blue velvet, with a matching bonnet adorned with curling feathers set fashionably on her stunningly fair curls. She alighted gracefully, with her big manservant handing her respectfully down the steps. Then, after gazing around her assessingly for a moment, the lady headed towards the big front door and knocked on it decisively with her little riding crop.

'Well,' breathed Rowena, 'I'll be damned. It's her, Matty – the fancy little whore who duped us all at Vauxhall Gardens that night. The one Seth's chasing round the country after, more fool he. And would you believe, the bitch is acting like the finest lady in all the county.' She crossed her arms over her ample bosom and smiled grimly. 'Well, my proud lady. Here's two of us who know all about you. We remember how you enjoyed baring your ladylike titties and getting our fine Seth to cream all over them with his lovely big cock before you decided to beat a hasty retreat. Somehow I don't think you'd like us telling anyone round here about all that.'

Marisa stood alone on the sweeping steps of Sir Julian Ormond's imposing mansion and glanced down quickly at her velvet pelisse and elegant little boots, flicking an imaginary speck of dust from her York tan gloves. This was her first neighbourly call, and she looked right for the part, didn't she? No-one, surely, would ever guess that she wasn't born into the role of a fine lady, no matter how much the hateful Lord Delsingham might tease her about her humble origins.

A groom had come to help John with the horses, and now they were being led away round to the stable yard. Marisa gazed around with practised eyes as she waited for someone to answer the door, admiring the elegant Palladian facade. Everything about this residence spoke of easy, accustomed wealth; presumably Ormond didn't miss his aunt's legacy too much. She grinned to herself. Of course he didn't, or he wouldn't be so affable to her, Marisa, who'd inherited what he must surely have expected to acquire for himself. She hoped he was at home, because she wanted to thank him personally for the loan of the mare, and the visit also gave her a discreet chance to learn a little more about him. She wouldn't bother mentioning to him the fact that she'd taken a heavy tumble, because after all it was only an accident. Delsingham had just been trying to frighten her with his talk of deliberate damage to the saddle straps.

In fact, when she'd got in that morning from her unexpectedly eventful ride and eased herself into a deliciously scented bathtub, she'd even found herself wondering darkly if somehow Delsingham himself had arranged the accident. It wouldn't surprise her in the least, because the loathsome man seemed capable of anything. And it certainly seemed strange that he was so near at hand at the time of her fall, perfectly positioned to take advantage of her, damn him! She felt the colour warming her cheeks at the memory, and her body tingled suddenly in a renewal of sensation as she remembered how gloriously he'd pleasured her from behind as she'd lain trapped across that dreaded saddle. Well, it would be the very last time he tormented her like that. And yet, the fact that he knew exactly who she was gave him a hateful hold over her.

All of a sudden, the big front door jerked open to reveal a sour-faced housekeeper dressed all in black. 'Yes?'

Marisa, deciding immediately that she was an old witch, gave her her sweetest smile. 'Is Sir Julian Ormond at home? Pray tell him that Mistress Brooke of Melbray Manor wishes to see him.'

The woman gave a grudging curtsey, and hurried off. Marisa pulled a face at her back, and waited. Then, to her relief, she saw Ormond walking quickly across the big, tiled hallway towards her. His eyes seemed to flicker a little in surprise, and then he smiled.

'My dear Miss Brooke,' he said smoothly, reaching out to take her hand and bowing over it, 'how are you? Are you finding Melbray Manor to your liking? Please, come into the front sitting room and I will order some tea for us.'

It was very pleasant, reflected Marisa as she followed him along the hallway, to be greeted so courteously. He certainly knew his manners, unlike Lord Delsingham, and his refined, elegant welcome made her spirits rise. To be sure, the dark-haired, youthful-looking little housemaid who brought in the tray of dainty scones along with the tea looked at her a little oddly from beneath her lace cap, and for a moment Marisa could have sworn that there was something familiar about her, but then the maid had gone, and she was able to concentrate on her host. He was exquisitely dressed, in a dove-coloured coat and buff pantaloons; his silky white cravat was arranged with discreet perfection, and his smooth fair hair was immaculately swept back from his handsome, almost delicate features.

'Everything is wonderful, thank you,' she responded from the comfort of the little velvet armchair he'd shown her to, as she sipped carefully at her tea with her little finger crooked out. 'The food last night was quite delicious, and the mare your groom brought over this morning is a delight to ride.'

Was she mistaken, or did a sudden shadow cross his bland face? He put down his tea rather quickly and said, 'You've had no problems with her, then?'

'None whatsoever,' lied Marisa, pushing aside the shameful memory of her fall. She didn't want him thinking she was an incompetent horsewoman.

'I'm so glad. Keep her for as long as you wish, and if there's anything else I can do to help, please let me know.'

Marisa smiled prettily in thanks. Lord Delsingham had said that Ormond was no gentleman, but how wrong he was! Delsingham was just bitter and twisted, because Ormond's generosity showed him, Delsingham, up in such a bad light.

'You're very kind,' she responded. 'It will take me a little while to get settled in, but I'm sure I'll manage. I need to purchase so many things: household goods, clothes, horses, a carriage or two . . .'

He said quickly, 'You'll find, I think, that the tradesmen in Crayhampton will be able to provide everything you require – no need to go as far as Winchester. Before you leave, I'll ask my housekeeper to give you a list of reputable suppliers.'

'Thank you. You really are very obliging.'

'Think nothing of it, my dear Miss Brooke.' He hesitated a moment, taking a pinch of snuff from a little laquered box with his exquisitely manicured fingers. 'There is something else I might be able to help you with. You can tell me, of course, to mind my own business.

111

But I understand that you have been left a considerable amount of money by my aunt. You have probably already made arrangements to invest it, but if I can assist you in any way, please let me know. It must be very difficult for you to cope with these things now that your father is no longer alive, and I have considerable experience of such matters, so please do consult me if you are wondering how best to invest it.'

Marisa stiffened. No-one was getting their hands on all her wonderful money. But then, suddenly, she remembered the arrogant Lord Delsingham saying, 'I shouldn't trust Ormond, if I were you,' and she bridled at the memory of his autocratic tone.

'I've made no plans for investment as yet,' she said, 'but I might well be glad of your advice some time in the future.' She put her teacup down and rose gracefully to her feet. 'I must be going now. There's so much for me to do. But soon, I hope to be in a position to do a little modest entertaining, and I should be delighted if you would come and visit me.'

'I can think of nothing I'd like better,' he responded warmly as he escorted her to the door. 'I'm sure that the whole neighbourhood will be eager to welcome you, Miss Brooke.'

John was waiting, with the carriage. Ormond handed her up respectfully, and she turned to give him a little wave as John clicked on the horses and the carriage swung away down the wide drive. Lord Delsingham, she decided, was jealous and spiteful to speak ill of Sir Julian Ormond. It might be a good idea to make a particular friend of Ormond and take the advice he was offering, just to spite her tormentor Delsingham and show him that she could look after herself quite adequately.

As the carriage rolled out through the high gates, she remembered the little dark-haired maid with a sudden feeling of unease, but dismissed the memory quickly. Her mind was playing tricks on her. How could she possibly have met her before?

* * *

112

Sir Julian Ormond, standing by a tall, silk-draped window, watched the carriage disappear from sight with expressionless eyes. Then he went over to the walnut bureau in the corner and opened it, brushing his hands mechanically across the dockets of paper that lay inside.

They were all unpaid bills. His debts were such that he didn't even dare contemplate them. Soon, this house would have to go. It had been mortgaged up to the hilt years ago, on the expectation of his aunt's fortune.

He looked out of the window once more, but Marisa Brooke's carriage had long since disappeared from view. His slender, well-manicured hand tightened round the sheaves of bills one last time, then he locked up the bureau and went to tug quickly at the bell-pull by the door.

The little dark-haired maid came in, the one with the soft lips and tongue. She bobbed demurely, but he still caught the greedy glitter in her eyes. 'You wanted me, my lord?'

He shut the door. 'Yes.' His voice shook slightly.

He told her to get on her hands and knees on the floor, and he took her quickly. She was slim and almost boyish from behind, with tight, pert bottom-cheeks. She squealed and shuddered with delight as he roughly threw up her skirts and entered her from behind, pulling her buttocks apart as he thrust into her. She cried out with pleasure as he slid his stiffened penis home into her moist, tight depths, and she writhed back to meet him as he slowly withdrew then drove himself in again. The gypsy girl was hot for him. She was starting to climax already, jumping about with pleasure and sighing as she felt his slim, throbbing shaft impale her. Gripping her buttocks, gritting his teeth, he drove himself quickly to his own harsh release, pulling out his ravening penis just at the last moment and rubbing it swiftly across her ripe bottom as his semen spurted out across her creamy flesh.

When he was quite spent the girl drew herself up quickly, readjusting her crumpled black gown and pulling her lace cap back onto her disordered curls. By the time she'd done that, he was standing by the empty hearth with one arm stretched casually along the carved mantelshelf, watching her coldly.

'Will that be all, sir?' said Matty primly.

'For the time being, yes. You may go.'

She bobbed a curtsey, then picked up the tea tray and left. A find, these two gypsy girls, thought Ormond, a fortunate find, the redheaded one with the mischievous ideas especially. But he mustn't allow them to distract him from his main task, which was, somehow, to deal with Marisa Brooke.

That night, Rowena and Matty crept out of the house under cover of darkness, letting themselves out through the kitchen door round at the back. Giggling furtively, they hurried round by the stables and ran on light feet through the wooded, silent gardens of Greenfallow Park, while the moon gleamed down on them through the dark foliage of the trees.

It took them half an hour to reach the gypsy camp, which was on the common land down near the river. There were several gypsy families there, who'd all come to the Crayhampton fair to sell horses and trinkets, and tell fortunes, and hopefully dupe as many locals as possible out of their money before they moved on. Seth had decided to set their painted caravan some distance from the others, in a pretty clearing surrounded by alders and willow, and as Matty and Rowena drew near, they could see Seth and Caleb sitting cross-legged by the fire, drinking wine and talking in soft voices.

Rowena dropped to the grass beside them with a little sigh, spreading out her skirts around herself. 'Let's have the wine, then, Caleb, while there's some left. Where's Tom?'

Caleb grinned. 'Found himself a girl of his own at last. Swaggering about like he's the only man in the world to have found a use for his cock. Enjoying working for your fancy gentleman, are you?'

Matty laughed. 'He's as dirty as they come, Caleb, gent or not. Wicked, he is! Beat one of his grooms this morning, and his prick stood out all red and angry. Rowena and I could see he wanted some of the same himself. So I took his lively weapon in my mouth and tongued him, and Rowena whipped his bottom, real hard.'

Seth smiled. Caleb drew nearer to Matty, his arm slipping round her shoulders so he could fondle her breasts through her tightly laced bodice. 'Like it, did he? Did he have a good cock on him, then, this gent of yours?'

Matty ran her hand along his brawny thigh. 'Nothing as good as yours, Caleb my sweet. It was thin and red, and waved about desperately while Rowena was beating him. Then she slid the end of the whip handle into his tight little arse, and moved it in and out a bit, and he gasped and moaned so much I could hardly keep his prick in my mouth.'

Caleb's face was suddenly dark with desire. He fondled Matty's breasts more roughly as she talked, pulling them free of her gown and bending to nuzzle at their pouting crests with his bearded mouth. Matty arched against him, stroking his groin where his penis was already bulging, and whispering into his ear. 'Take me, stick it into me, Caleb, do. I'm that desperate for a real man, for a big, hard cock up inside me.'

Caleb grunted, and together they rolled into the shadows beyond the caravan, where Matty scrabbled with his breeches and pulled out his big, meaty shaft longingly. 'Ah, that feels good, Caleb. So good.' She lay quickly on her back, parting her legs for him and lifting her knees, groaning in delight as he stroked her unfurling sex with the bulbous tip of his phallus and then began to slide the thick shaft of it between her juicy flesh-lips, inch by glorious inch.

Seth and Rowena watched them, enjoying their open lust. Rowena leaned back against Seth's shoulder, her eyes green and catlike in the firelight, and took another long pull at the rough red wine, feeling it arouse her excited body still further. She gazed up at Seth possessively, drinking in his dark curls and high Romany cheekbones. He had a beautiful face and body, and he knew how to pleasure a woman better than anyone she knew, with his sensitive gypsy fingers and his lovely, long cock. 'Any nearer to finding your fine lady, Seth?' she enquired casually.

He paused. 'Not yet. But some of the hired hands were gossiping at the fair today. They were saying that there's a new lady come to live hereabouts. No-one seems to know where she's come from, except that she's young, and very beautiful. I'd like to find out more about her.'

Rowena ran her hand possessively along his forearm, excited by the feel of the silky dark hair that roughened his warm brown skin. 'You're not still hot for her, Seth, are you?' she murmured. 'You don't want her more than me, do you?'

'Sweetheart,' laughed Seth, kissing her forehead, 'at this very moment, I couldn't want anyone more than you, I assure you.'

Rowena smoothed her hand avidly across his crotch, realising that the flesh of his penis was already hard and swollen. She unfastened him with feverish haste and unbuttoned her own bodice. His erect penis jutted towards her from the dark hair at the base of his belly, and with a little moan she bent to rub her heavy, swollen breasts against it. As the velvety tip of his pulsing rod brushed her dark brown nipples, she licked her lips in anticipation, feeling the hard tightness gathering at the pit of her stomach and the moisture seeping already from the lushly tingling flesh at the juncture of her thighs. The muffled sounds of Caleb and Matty pleasuring one another nearby excited her wildly, with Matty's little whimpers rising higher and higher as Caleb lifted her hips with his hands and drove her demented with the length of his big, gnarled cock. Rowena stole a glance at them, noting that Matty was already shuddering in the throes of orgasm as Caleb slowly drove himself in and out of her. Then she saw with a thrill of fascination that Caleb had drawn out his great, glistening shaft and was rubbing it avidly all over Matty's breasts. Suddenly he gave a hoarse shout and started to spurt in great gouts all over her, his penis twitching with delight while his heavy, rounded balls grazed her tender belly.

With a little cry, Rowena urged Seth back onto the ground and sat astride his hips, pulling up her own skirt to her waist. She spread her thighs wide and stroked her own swollen labia with her fingers, tenderly drawing out the sweet, seeping nectar that coated the dark-pink petals of flesh and letting her thumb just brush the yearning little stem of her clitoris. Seth smiled up at her lazily, his hands pillowing his head, his lovely, long cock rearing upwards in anticipation. She lowered herself carefully onto him, gasping aloud as she felt the fatly rounded tip of his manhood pushing her apart, nudging its way in, sliding into her hungry vagina and filling her with delicious male power. Wriggling her hips voluptuously, she took in the whole of his lengthy shaft, relishing every rapturous inch of him and whimpering softly in delight.

He was all hers. Rowena began to ride him fast, playing with her own heavy breasts and pulling at her distended brown teats, relishing the hard, sweet delight that filled her as his sturdy member caressed the very core of her femininity. Soon, she was almost at the brink. She squeezed tightly on him with her pleasure-engorged inner muscles, and held herself very still, her head thrown back, trembling in anticipation. Tenderly Seth reached with one hand to caresss her soaking pleasure bud, and she throbbed into fiery orgasm as he started to drive himself powerfully, steadily from beneath her.

'Seth,' she gasped, 'stick it into me, Seth. Yes, oh, yes . . .'

The throbs of pleasure beat their way through her almost violently as she trembled and bucked above him, feeling his delicious pillar of flesh ravishing her as she convulsed around him. At last she was sated, though his erect cock still caressed her tenderly, begging for more attention. Rowena, slipping herself off him with a little sigh, bent her head to take as much as she could of him into her mouth, sliding her lips up and down, excited anew by the taste of her own musky juices on the silken stem, running her tongue round his straining glans and fondling his tight balls with her hand until at last his juices gushed hotly against the back of her throat and she felt his lithe body convulse with pleasure.

Afterwards she lay with her head against his chest, stroking the silky, muscle-padded flesh beneath his shirt. Her Seth, all hers.

She lifted herself up suddenly on one arm and gazed at him, seeing how his curling dark hair fell away from his sleepy, suntanned face. She said, 'You wouldn't get to like this fancy lady more than me, would you, Seth?'

He reached out to touch her cheek. 'Jealous, Rowena?'

'You know she's no good for you, Seth. She's not like us – she's dangerous. But,' and she hesitated, 'if I told you I knew where she was, would you be pleased with me?'

He was quickly alert then, pulling himself up and gazing intently at her. 'You know where she is, Rowena?'

'Better than that,' she announced triumphantly. 'I've seen her.'

And she told him about Marisa's visit to Greenfallow Park. 'Remember she's just a high-class whore, Seth,' she finished warningly. 'No better than Matty and me.'

He kissed her soundly, but his face was thoughtful. 'Nobody could be better than you, my sweet. You're staying the night here?'

Before she could reply they were joined by Matty, who'd crawled across to the fire, leaving Caleb snoring. Greedily she drank the last of the wine. 'No fear!' she laughed, picking up the conversation. 'We're going back to our fine gentleman. I've already earned two gold pieces for doing little more than talk dirty to him.'

Rowena hesitated, just a moment, then said, 'Yes, we're going back. It's nice to sleep on feather beds and be able to pinch plenty of good food and wine for a while. But we'll join you here again tomorrow night, Seth.' Seth kissed her, and she added quickly, 'You'll still be here tomorrow, won't you?'

'Of course,' he said lightly. 'Where else would I be?'

Chapter Six

A few days later, Marisa received her very first invitation.

Her eyes narrowed in calculation as she read it through slowly, word by tortuous word. She remembered Lord Delsingham's mocking laugh as he'd said, 'Somehow, my sweet, I don't think country society is quite ready for you.' Well, this prompt missive was decisive proof that he was wrong. The invitation was to Southland Grange, the home of Sir Andrew and Lady Blockley some five miles away, and it was hand delivered with some ceremony by a mounted manservant. Lucy put the gilded card proudly on the mantelpiece in the drawing room.

'Your first invitation into grand society, Marisa,' she breathed. 'How exciting!'

Marisa shrugged carelessly. 'It will be nothing of importance, Lucy. Just a few sets of country dances, and a cold supper, and old ladies playing casino and whist at a penny a point – no doubt exceedingly dull.'

But nevertheless she felt a secret frisson of pleasure. It didn't matter if the evening was as dull as ditchwater; she was on her way. She'd spent several enthralling days exploring Melbray Manor, interspersed with shopping trips to Crayhampton to order stocks of Naples soap, rolls of silk, and finest hock at thirty shillings the dozen;

in fact, all the luxuries she'd always longed for. Now she was ready to meet her new neighbours. She grinned, wondering mischievously if they were ready for Marisa Brooke.

Early on the evening of the party she took a leisurely bath, rubbing her pale gold skin with subtly scented oils until it was soft and perfumed. Then she washed and brushed her long, honey-blonde curls until they glittered in the brilliant candlelight of her room, and prepared to dress. She'd decided, after much thought, to wear the most daring of her purchases from Madame Thanier's exclusive establishment in Bond Street, an elegant ivory muslin gown with a high waist and short puffed sleeves. The sleeves and low *décolletage* of the gown were adorned with pale pink satin ribbons, and Lucy, after studying Marisa thoughtfully, found another, wider length of matching ribbon to tie round the high waistline, just below her breasts. After slipping her small feet into a dainty pair of pink shoes, and pulling on some white satin gloves that clung like a second skin as far as her elbows, Marisa gazed critically at herself in the long cheval glass.

The white muslin sheath clung beguilingly to her slender figure, making her look younger than her 23 years. So much the better. Lucy, with her customary deftness, had arranged her fair curls into luxuriant ringlets, and piled them high in a pink satin bandeau, and by the time she had draped her flimsy silk shawl in a darker shade of rose-pink elegantly over her gloved arms, Marisa decided that she looked exactly like one of the beautiful, rich ladies of fashion who visited the theatre in the Haymarket, or the opera at Covent Garden, before heading back to some grand party in Mayfair. Her new neighbours, she smiled to herself, would never guess that she was adept at mains of hazard in the dingy back-rooms of the Blue Bell, or at elbowing her way past the noisy, disreputable taverns of Covent Garden dressed in buckskin breeches and a big man's coat, matching oath for oath with all the gulls and tricksters who teemed in the narrow London alleys.

Then suddenly, as she turned in front of the mirror, the memory of Lord Delsingham's laughing sneer echoed in her ears: 'You, Marisa? A fine lady?' She clenched her small gloved fists. She would show him. Oh, yes. She wondered suddenly if he would be there tonight, and the colour mounted slowly in her cheeks at the thought of confronting him once more.

The Blockleys' house was a big, sprawling, ivy-clad grange, originally an Elizabethan farmhouse. Sir Andrew, a prosperous gentleman farmer with a stout figure and port-reddened cheeks, came warmly to the door to greet her, with his equally plump wife at his side, her grey curls enclosed in a purple silk turban that matched the colour of her dress. It was Sir Andrew himself who eagerly drew Marisa into the large, firelit hall to introduce her to his other guests. Marisa saw the male guests' eyes light up at the sight of her, while their womenfolk watched her warily.

'New little lady at Melbray Manor, Miss Marisa Brooke,' beamed Sir Andrew. 'Enchanting, eh? Know you'll all give her a warm welcome this evening.'

Marisa heard a woman just behind her whisper in an excruciatingly clear voice to her neighbour, 'My dear. Just look at that skimpy dress. Did you ever see anything so vulgar?'

She felt the colour rush hotly to her cheeks, and looked quickly around to meet the acidic gaze of a tall, thin brunette, perhaps the same age as herself, who was wearing a modest, high-necked gown of dark blue silk with long, narrow sleeves and a little muslin ruff. She gazed at Marisa almost pityingly. Marisa felt her blood churn with rage, and opened her mouth to make some angry retort. But then, as the rest of the female guests gathered together and began one by one to remove their little capes and pelisses, Marisa began to realise, with a steadily sinking heart, that she was indeed dressed far more skimpily than any of the others. No wonder the men gazed at her plunging neckline with such interest. Hell and damnation, she thought bitterly, the women here were dressed more like nuns than women of wealth and breeding.

She felt her heart thumping, but held her head high in defiance as she stood there all alone. The men didn't dare to speak to her, while the women eyed her surreptitiously and whispered viciously about her behind raised hands, encouraged by the poisonous brunette. Then suddenly kind Lady Blockley, who seemed oblivious to the gossip, was at her side again, handing her a glass of ratafia.

'Now, my dear Miss Brooke,' she said, 'I do hope you don't find cards too, too boring, because I want you to join me for a rubber of whist. A penny a point, my dear. Can you bear it, do you think?'

Marisa laughed, feeling suddenly happy again. What did she care for the gossips? 'I'll join you with the greatest of pleasure, Lady Blockley.'

'You do play whist, I take it, my dear?'

'A little,' Marisa replied, her blue eyes sparkling. 'Are you to be my partner, Lady Blockley?'

'Oh, no,' said the older woman, gleefully taking her arm. 'We have someone else for you, someone you'll like very much. Come and see.'

Marisa's heart sank again. No doubt they'd found her some hopelessly dull-witted clod of a partner. What a good job they were only playing for a penny a point.

Lady Blockley was already enthusiastically guiding her into the card parlour, where groups of guests were happily playing casino at the green baize tables. Still chattering aimlessly, Lady Blockley wove her way between the players towards her husband Sir Andrew, who was deep in conversation with a tall, dark-haired man whose back was to Marisa. Her heart lurched suddenly. Oh, no. It couldn't be . . .

It was. Sir Andrew's companion turned round slowly, as if relishing the moment, and Marisa saw that it was indeed the hateful Lord Delsingham. She caught her breath, and glared up at him with flashing eyes. No doubt he would laugh at the way she was dressed as well, just like the rest of these obnoxious people. She braced herself for his put-down.

He took her hand, his grey eyes dancing vividly in the sober refinement of his handsome face. 'Mistress Brooke,' he drawled. 'What an exceedingly pleasant surprise.' He bowed low over Marisa's fingers and she felt quite faint at the brush of his warm lips on the back of her hand. He grinned secretly at her as he straightened up, like a wolf eyeing its helpless prey. She returned his gaze furiously, waiting for him to make some jeering remark about her stupidly flimsy attire, but all he said was, 'You look quite divine, my dear.'

Marisa laughed shortly, aware that Sir Andrew and his wife were fussily seating themselves at the nearby card table and leaving them in momentary privacy. 'I look ridiculously out of place,' she replied in a cutting voice, 'and you know it, my lord. There's no need for you to sharpen your sarcasm on me.'

There was a pause as he gazed steadily down at her. Then he said quietly, 'I mean what I said, Marisa. You're the only truly lovely woman in the room. The rest of them have about as much elegance as a gaggle of farmers' wives on their way to market.'

Caught unawares by his compliment, she was aware of her heart fluttering rather strangely. The colour flooded to her face, and she tossed back her head, unaccountably disturbed. 'I think I almost prefer it, my Lord Delsingham, when you're hateful to me,' she said almost shakily.

He grinned. 'Oh, I can manage that as well, believe me. You're joining us for whist? How absolutely delightful. I have a feeling you will teach us all a thing or two, Miss Brooke.'

He started to pull out a chair for her, but she put her hand on his arm and said in a voice that was still tense, 'Just one thing. If you're going to give me away, Lord Delsingham, and tell everyone about my former life, then

I would prefer that you did so now, rather than endure an evening's charade.'

'Give you away?' he replied innocently. 'Now why should I do that, Mistress Brooke, when you and I have such a delightful arrangement?'

She felt her stomach lurch at the reminder. Damn him, he looked utterly desirable in his dark grey coat and slim breeches, with his exquisitely arranged cravat emphasizing the lean, aristocratic lines of his face. An ace indeed. He was gesturing her towards her chair, but she stood behind it and said defiantly, 'Pray, don't think you shall have it all your own way, my lord, with your talk of arrangements! It didn't take me very long to receive my first invitation into polite society, did it? Even though you assured me that I would never be accepted here.'

He smiled gently. 'Oh, you were bound to be accepted, my dear. You see, it was I who suggested to Sir Andrew that he invite you.'

Marisa gaped at him, speechless with rage. The pleasure that had lit her like a warm glow since she received her precious invitation was suddenly like cold ashes in the pit of her stomach.

'I think,' he went on smoothly, pointing delicately towards the vacant chair, 'that Sir Andrew and his good lady are ready for play.'

'So am I,' she said meaningfully. 'Oh, believe me, so am I.'

She played like a novice, deliberately throwing away her highest cards when he was winning and wasting point after point. Delsingham raised his eyebrows but said nothing; his little pile of coins diminished rapidly along with hers, and she wished, viciously, that they were guineas. He wouldn't want to be her partner again for a long, long time, that was for sure.

And then the Blockleys, having gleefully won several rubbers, rose apologetically to their feet and said they really must go to the dining hall to check that everything was in order for supper. Would Lord Delsingham and

Miss Brooke mind terribly if Mistress Caroline Henshawe and her husband Richard took their place in the game?

It was too late to object anyway, because the couple in question were already on their way over, and Marisa saw to her dismay that Caroline Henshawe was the tall brunette who'd made such disparaging remarks about her gown. Mistress Henshawe sat quickly next to Delsingham, resting her hand intimately on his arm and smiling up at him; only then did she turn to Marisa and say with honeyed venom, 'You must let me introduce you to my dressmaker in Winchester, Miss Brooke. I gather you only came into your fortune recently. It must be difficult to adjust to new-found wealth. If I can give you any advice, I will gladly do so.'

Marisa gritted her teeth, gazing pointedly at her opponent's dark, high-necked gown. Then she said, 'Oh, but I wouldn't dream of asking for your advice. You see, Mistress Henshawe, where I come from, it is by no means considered usual to dress for a party as if one were about to enter a nunnery.'

Caroline Henshawe looked a little pale, apart from the spots of anger that burned on her beautifully elegant high cheekbones. Delsingham intercepted smoothly, 'Well, now. I think we should raise the stakes a little, don't you? This looks like being an interesting game.'

Richard Henshawe, a plump, nondescript man who was already rather drunk, came alive at that and said, 'Hey? What's that you say? Capital idea, Delsingham. Five shillings a point, d'you think?' And play began.

Marisa wanted to win this game. She wanted to humiliate Caroline Henshawe, who looked down her long aristocratic nose at her as if she'd crawled out of the gutter. And to make matters worse, the hateful woman was coolly possessive about Delsingham, touching him at every opportunity and smiling at him with obnoxious familiarity. So engrossed was Marisa in her resentment of her opponent that it took her some time to realise that Delsingham was watching her, Marisa, with a strange intensity as he examined his cards. And then he said, quite inconsequentially as he sorted his hand, 'How warm the weather is at present. I wonder if the sunshine will last.'

Richard Henshawe mumbled something banal back, but Marisa, whose turn it was to lead, gazed at him transfixed, her heart suddenly beating rather fast. Why would he make such a trivial, boring remark? Unless . . . He was looking at her again; she thought she saw him nod imperceptibly. 'How warm,' he'd said. H for heart . . .

She led with a low heart, the four, and he won the trick for them with the ace, following with a king. Her pulse started to race. Was she mistaken? Was it just a coincidence? He played skilfully, winning trick after trick. Then it was Marisa's lead, and as she hesitated, he said thoughtfully, 'Supper should be ready soon, I think. But we've time for a few more minutes' play.'

Marisa led with a seven of spades, knowing that the highest cards in that suit had already gone, and Delsingham won with a knave. She was right; he was using one of the oldest and simplest tactics for cheating at whist, prefacing his remark with the letter of the suit he wanted her to play. Simple but effective; together with their mutual card-counting skills and total recall of what had been played, they were devastating partners. Suddenly feeling happy and confident, Marisa met his eyes and saw them sparkle in answer. Suppressing her smile, Marisa lowered her eyelashes demurely to her cards, and together they continued like two conspirators to roundly trounce Caroline Henshawe and her husband and deprive them of a not insubstantial sum of money before supper. Marisa felt the old, familiar elation of successful trickery. Lord Delsingham was a superbly subtle player, and together they were unbeatable.

At last Caroline Henshawe stood up, her elegant face tight and frosty. 'Time for us to get some supper, I think, Richard,' she told her bemused, half-inebriated husband. Then she turned with an icy smile on Marisa. 'Well, Miss Brooke,' she drawled. 'You're certainly successful at cards, aren't you? I wonder where you learned so well.

I'd almost suspect you of hiding the cards somewhere about your person, except,' and her eyes raked Marisa's flimsy muslin dress with scorn, 'there isn't really anywhere to conceal them, is there?'

With that, she turned to go. Marisa hissed and started after her, hands clenched into fists, but Lord Delsingham's fingers bit into her gloved arm.

'Leave her be,' he said quietly. 'Her husband is a drunken, impotent boor. Mistress Caroline, I believe, finds consolation by taking her pleasure with servants. You'll find some way soon to get your own back on her, I'm quite sure.'

Marisa said through gritted teeth, 'I'm going to find a way now, this minute.'

He chuckled. 'Isn't winning 50 guineas off her enough?'

She turned to gaze levelly up at him. 'No. Five hundred guineas wouldn't be enough. You meant what you said? That she's addicted to serving men?'

'I did indeed.' His dark eyebrows gathered. 'Dear Marisa, what are you plotting now?'

'Something I'm quite capable of managing on my own, thank you.'

'I'm sure you are, and that's the trouble.' His eyes danced. 'By the way, you play a marvellous game of whist.'

She flashed a brilliant smile back up at him. 'So do you, my lord,' she replied quickly, then hurried off with the cold light of determination in her eyes to find John the coachman.

Caroline Henshawe wandered slowly out into the private, walled gardens of Southlands Grange to get away from her boring husband, whom she'd left with a full plate of food in the dining hall. She brought her brimming glass of wine with her, knowing that she'd already drunk enough to set her blood racing with dark thoughts and make her judgement a little suspect, but she was past caring. She was hot and angry at the memory of that half-clad little blonde bitch who'd somehow cheated her at cards and made a fool of her. And sitting next to Delsingham had made her fatally aroused, even watching his strong, graceful hands as they expertly dealt the cards had made her feel quite weak. She'd surreptitiously pressed her knee against his well-muscled thigh beneath the table, but he'd pretended not to notice.

That little blonde newcomer, with her big, innocent blue eyes and disgusting dress, was making a play for him; of that she was quite certain. The slut might even have bedded him already.

The soft night breeze was cooling on her hot cheeks as she wandered into the clipped yew gardens. Her body was burning, on edge at the thought of Delsingham and that slut. How had they managed to win so easily? She'd seen the looks they exchanged, knowing, intimate looks. She imagined Delsingham pleasuring the little bitch, taking her roughly from behind with his beautiful lengthy penis darkly erect, and she felt faint with need. At this moment she wanted nothing more than a man, a sturdy, well-endowed, virile man.

She drank down the rest of her wine, feeling a little unsteady. She must have consumed the best part of a bottle. She would have to be careful, or her eyes would be bloodshot, and people would know.

'Now, then.' A man's voice, rough, uncultured, exciting, came from the shadows somewhere behind her. 'Were you out here looking for something by any chance, Mistress Henshawe?'

She turned with a little gasp, her hand to her mouth. A man was walking slowly between the high, clipped yew hedges towards her, a big, stocky man with sun-streaked brown hair, dressed like a servant in his leather jerkin and coarse knee breeches. His linen shirt was open at the neck, and she could see the enticing gleam of his bronzed chest; he looked young, muscular, fit. He was grinning as he walked slowly towards her, and his thumbs were locked loosely into the waistband of his breeches. He stopped when he was a few feet away, and she saw with stunned disbelief that he was starting to rub slowly, meaningfully at himself through the thick fabric of his clothing. She let out a little scream and leaned faintly back against the wall, only too aware of the outline of his knotted penis moving, swelling as he touched himself. He must be huge, she thought weakly, rough and brutal and huge. She opened her mouth to scream again, but then she stopped, because he was unbuttoning himself now, and as she gazed breathlessly at his busy fingers, he parted his breeches and drew out his thickly erect penis. Immediately it sprang towards her, jerking with hungry life.

Caroline shut her eyes and opened them again, quite unable to look anywhere except his groin. His shaft was long and thick and meaty, gnarled with veins, the purple tip glistening with moisture. He continued to rub it luxuriantly as it reared from the nest of hair below his belly. She felt her breasts tingle and ache in response as her nipples peaked, and was aware of a sudden trickle of moisture between her thighs.

'Well, now. Is this what you want, my beauty?' the man said, grinning.

She swallowed hard, her hand at her throat. 'Oh, yes,' she whispered. 'Yes, yes.'

There was a little summerhouse in the garden, perhaps twenty yards away from them, set in the middle of the scented rosebeds. As Caroline moved towards the man, the door of the summerhouse opened very quietly and a slender, shadowy figure slipped quickly inside, but Caroline Henshawe was too entranced by her mysterious admirer to notice.

The shadowy figure belonged to Marisa Brooke. Marisa knelt carefully on the cushioned window seat of the little circular summerhouse and leant her elbows on the sill, gazing out raptly into the moonlit garden. The air was thick with the scent of roses, and she breathed in deeply, realising that she had a perfect view of everything. So far, her plan had worked brilliantly.

After leaving Lord Delsingham, she'd gone quickly to find John, who was in the back kitchen drinking Sir Andrew's potent ale with the other coachmen. She'd drawn him to one side and whispered to him to follow the haughty Henshawe woman everywhere she went until he had a chance to get her on her own. And things had worked out beautifully, even better than Marisa had dared to hope, because the woman had not only obligingly wandered out into the garden, but was also, it seemed, in a pleasant state of drunkenness. John had seized his chance with admirable style, and now Mistress Henshawe looked as if she couldn't wait to get her dainty hands on his stalwart great prick as he meaningfully rubbed at its exposed bulk. Marisa didn't blame her. His penis was already massively engorged, and as he gently stroked the foreskin up and down, the glans seemed to swell yet further, and Marisa saw the beading of moisture at its glossy, bulbous tip.

She felt the familiar tightening in her abdomen, felt her nipples stiffening and poking provocatively at the thin muslin of her bodice, and knew it wasn't just the cool night air making them tingle so. John was playing his part so well, she fancied taking him herself.

She drew a deep breath and pressed her cheek against the cool glass of the little summerhouse, noting that John, still grinning, was putting his big hands on Caroline's thin, aristocratic shoulders, then letting his fingers slip downwards so he was roughly fondling her tiny breasts through the thin silk of her high-necked gown. Caroline grabbed his hands, grinding his calloused palms against the hard nubs of her nipples, her face dazed with greedy lust. 'Oh, take me,' she gasped, 'take me now, you big, rough peasant.'

John clutched her to him and kissed her hard, his big tongue thrusting and delving into her open mouth as she lay back dizzily in his arms. Quickly he unlaced her bodice, tugging it away so he could dip his head to lick hungrily at her exposed teats. Though her breasts were small, her nipples were long and stiff, and he was able to push them from side to side with his rasping tongue, while at the same time clutching at her hips and grinding her against his upright penis; her hands slipped tremblingly towards it as it thrust hard against her. 'So big,' she whispered, 'so fine. Oh, let me taste it, please let me taste your big, fat prick . . .' And before Marisa's startled gaze Caroline dropped to her knees, clutching at John's heavy, bulging testicles and leaning forward to lick avidly at his fiercely jutting penis.

John too looked startled, and not displeased. As Caroline struggled to take as much as she could into her eager mouth, he gripped at her shoulders and started to thrust his hips against her mouth, his eyes glazed with lust as her lips slid up and down his glistening shaft. He drew a rasping breath and whispered hoarsely, 'Well, now, my lady. How would you like to feel my big, fine cock up inside you, eh? I'll give you a right good pleasuring, I swear. I last a real long time, I do.'

Mistress Caroline Henshawe, her scarlet tipped breasts gleaming in the moonlight, removed her mouth lingeringly from his throbbing appendage and breathed, 'Yes. Oh, yes.'

John put his hands on his hips, and his penis quivered and swayed with a life of its own. 'How do you like it then, wench?' he grated out.

'I – I'd like you to lick me first, with your big, rasping tongue. And then I want you to do it to me quickly, strongly. And – ' she licked her lips, pale with excitement – 'I want you to call me rude names while you're doing it.'

John laughed huskily. 'So you like to talk dirty, eh, my fine lady?' He stroked his meaty penis meaningfully; it glistened with her saliva. 'Fair enough. So do I.' Still chuckling, he lowered her to the smooth turf of the little hedged garden, pushing back her silk skirts. She'd already parted her thighs, and was eagerly pulling his face down towards her. John grunted in approval, and started to lick thoroughly between her legs as she wriggled and moaned in ecstasy. Marisa sighed a little as she leant on the windowsill, wishing it was her feeling his strong, thick tongue probing between her own heated flesh folds, finding the sensitive nub of her little pleasure bud. Her hand strayed to her swollen breasts, slipping beneath the low muslin bodice to cup them and stroke them tenderly, trying to assuage the ache but only succeeding in starting a more fiery surge of desire deep within her loins.

And then, too late, she felt the sudden whisper of fresh air on her cheek as the little summerhouse door opened quietly behind her, and a strong masculine hand covered her mouth, stifling her instinctive cry of alarm. At the same time, an all-too familiar voice was saying dryly in her ear, 'Miss Brooke, you really are very wicked, you know.'

Delsingham's voice, Delsingham's hand. Hell and damnation. But then the words of indignation died in her throat, because his hands had slipped inside her bodice and were on her breasts, deliciously cooling and firm as they stroked the smooth, swollen flesh, lightly teasing her protruding nipples until the sharp tongues of desire flew meltingly down to the base of her belly, making her moan and shift her thighs together, only too aware of how her secret sexual parts were slick and slippery with her need.

He was nuzzling at the back of her neck with his warm, dry mouth as she kneeled helplessly against the window seat with her back to him. She felt the sudden dart of his tongue, wickedly licking and caressing her neck until she shuddered helplessly, arching back to press her slender, muslin-clad figure against his tense, powerful body. Then she gasped as she suddenly felt cool air on her thighs and buttocks. He was lifting her flimsy skirt high, gently caressing her bottom, sliding her stockinged thighs tenderly apart as he knelt behind her on the window seat while continuing to kiss the nape of her neck. And then, as she caught her breath and pressed her cheek blindly against the window, she felt the most glorious sensation of all – the firm, purposeful nudge of his beautiful, strong

133

penis slipping between her thighs and probing purposefully between her juicy folds of flesh, stroking its way
between the lushly nectared petals of her labia before
slowly, deliciously insinuating itself into her yearning
vulva.

She ground herself back against him, enfolding him,
wanting more and more of him. 'Oh!' she gasped aloud,
gripping the window ledge and writhing helplessly
around on the delicious impalement. His hands reached
round to tighten on her nipples, sending renewed spasms
of exquisite pain-pleasure shuddering through her
exposed body.

'Is this what you were after?' he murmured against the
lobe of her ear, thrusting gently but firmly as inch by
delicious inch he eased his thick, powerful penis deep
inside her.

'Yes,' gasped Marisa despairingly. 'Oh, yes. But wait a
moment, please. I want to see them, out in the garden.'

'A little voyeur,' he murmured, his hands still teasing
her rosy buds. 'Very well. I can wait, if you can.'

Marisa was really not at all sure that she could wait,
but she had to watch, she had to be able to concentrate,
to make sure that her plan was working. Desperately she
strained to look out of the window into the moonlit
garden, conscious of Delsingham's hands still lightly
cupping her breasts, of his strongly erect penis pulsing
gently deep inside her vagina, knowing that all she really
wanted to do was to lean back into his arms, and let him
pleasure her into oblivion.

Frantically she pushed his hands away from her
breasts. 'Watch!' she hissed.

John, good loyal John, had mistress Caroline Henshawe
on all fours now amongst the lavender bushes. He was
kneeling behind her and grinning from ear to ear, gripping her firmly by her slender buttocks as he ravished
her with his fine sturdy shaft. Marisa, dry mouthed,
could see the great meaty length of his member sliding
in and out; it was dark and glossy with feminine juices,
and John's face was going red with pleasure as he

pumped away, his hairy balls swinging between his thighs as he worked. Caroline was thrusting back against him to take as much as she could into herself, her face flushed and her eyes glazed as she moaned out in her refined voice, 'That's it, stick it up me, please. You big, rough stallion. What a wonderful, wonderful penis you have!'

'Enjoying it, wench?' John grinned back. 'Bet you've not had one as good as this for a while, eh?'

Marisa felt her own musky juices flowing freely, anointing Delsingham's shaft anew as he held himself very still inside her. She clutched convulsively with her inner muscles on his lovely bone-hard penis, unable to control her trembling excitement at the lewd sight of John pleasuring the haughty Caroline Henshawe so vigorously. She heard Delsingham chuckle softly in her ear, saying 'Control yourself, sweet Marisa, or all this will be over rather quickly.'

She bit her lip in mortification as he mocked her, trying to fight the dizzying lust that surged through her body just at the sound of his beautiful, husky voice. Then, at last, what she'd been waiting for started to happen. Suddenly the shadowy garden beyond the little summerhouse seemed to be alive with figures moving towards the copulating couple from the tree-filled darkness, with Lucy, wonderful Lucy, leading them all, perhaps seven or eight of them. They moved quickly, silently in the moonlight, as if following some pre-arranged plan, which, knowing Lucy, no doubt they were.

First of all a man stooped in front of Caroline's head so that he was kneeling in front of her crouching figure. Swiftly he drew out his penis and rubbed it quickly into stiffness, then as Caroline gasped in delight at the sight he thrust it into her mouth and she sucked greedily. Two giggling maidservants reached below her to toy with her long, dark nipples while another couple lay on the ground close by and started to engage in eager copulation just in front of her. Lucy watched with her hands on her plump hips, grinning.

Suddenly, John renewed his stalwart attentions, driving his sturdy, long penis deep between Caroline's bottom cheeks. The two women lay on the ground so they could suckle at her breasts, while the man kneeling in front of her steadily slid his cock in and out of her mouth, groaning as she avidly licked it. Another man masturbated just beside her, pumping away at his engorged shaft with glazed eyes and shouting out as his seed started to spurt against Caroline's face. Another woman had slipped behind the thrusting John, and was reaching between his muscular thighs to stroke his heavy balls as they tightened with excitement. And Caroline Henshawe, taken to the very extremity of degradation, was starting to have the fiercest orgasm of her life. She sucked avidly at the man's cock in her mouth as his seed spurted to the back of her throat, while John, at the brink himself as the woman behind him stroked and fondled his velvety balls, continued to pound away at her with deep, ravishing thrusts. Caroline cried out and trembled convulsively as she felt the women beneath her tugging at her distended nipples with their greedy mouths, her whole body awash with rioting sensations as they all moved in on her, while John gritted his teeth and started to climax with a great roar of pleasure.

And Marisa too felt her last resistance ebb away as Delsingham's strong, gentle fingers renewed their assault on her incredibly sensitised breasts, and his rampant penis began to move slowly, deliciously within her very core.

'You are delightfully wicked, Mistress Marisa,' he murmured in her ear as the moonlit orgy continued unabated outside, 'and I think it's time now for your punishment. Don't you?'

Marisa leaned back against him, feeling his broad chest pressing against her back and aware of his powerful thighs moving in controlled rhythm as he splayed her legs even further so that she could enfold every inch of his thick, lengthy shaft. Oh, but he was magnificent. An ace indeed. She closed her eyes as she felt his knowing hand slip down to touch her soaking, exposed clitoris and she began to gasp, feeling her abdomen tighten with dark, sweet pleasure around his thrusting penis. At the same time his other hand squeezed and pulled at her pouting nipples, and she threw back her head, feeling him tenderly kissing her tousled hair, her neck, her shoulders. Then she was driving herself hard against him, impaling herself anew as the rapture burst upon her exquisitely tormented body and the warm, blissful waves of pleasure rolled through her as he continued to ravish her with slow, incomparable strokes. Only when he'd drawn every last drop of excruciating pleasure from her shuddering body did he pull her hard against him and thrust deeply, harshly, to find his own release. She heard his rasping breath, and felt his iron-hard penis spasming deep inside her, and she shuddered again in a warm renewal of pleasure. In the silence that followed he held her tenderly, his lips just brushing the nape of her neck, his body cradling hers so that she could feel the strong, steady beating of his heart. Bliss, she thought rather dazedly, utter sensual bliss.

Then he murmured in a low voice, 'I think your little pageant is almost over, my Ganymede. Mistress Henshawe is just starting to come to her senses.'

Marisa opened her eyes rather dizzily and saw that Caroline Henshawe was staggering to her feet, her gown torn and rumpled, while all around her stood the grinning band of servants led by John and the brilliant Lucy, whose arms were folded in satisfaction. Caroline Henshawe looked suddenly aghast, as if only just realising what she'd actually taken part in; her hand flew to her mouth as she stifled a little cry, and John, grinning, said, 'Was I good enough for you then, Mistress Henshawe? Any time you need a fine, sturdy man, just let me know.'

And Caroline Henshawe, looking round rather wildly at them all, let out a strangled sob and fled back towards the house.

Marisa giggled. Lord Delsingham, stroking her disarrayed curls, said, 'That was very naughty of you, sweet Ganymede. I take it you arranged it all?'

'Yes,' Marisa laughed rather breathlessly. 'I spoke earlier to John and Lucy, and they made plans with a few other servants. I couldn't believe it when she came out on her own into the gardens. It was just perfect.'

She'd turned round as she was talking to meet his eyes; she caught her breath as Delsingham, gazing down at her, said quietly, 'Yes. It was, wasn't it?'

She went very still, conscious of his dark, burning gaze that was somehow strangely intent. Suddenly feeling shy, she started to pull her disarrayed bodice up over her breasts, the colour still warm in her cheeks. He drew himself up abruptly, dispelling the strange mood that had fallen over them, and held out his arm to her.

'Perhaps we should return to the house now, Mistress Brooke. How I enjoyed our demure walk through the gardens. Shall we go and partake of some supper?'

'With the greatest of pleasure, my lord,' Marisa responded lightly, and they walked back companionably through the now-silent gardens towards the house to rejoin the other guests, as if they'd partaken of nothing more than a moonlit stroll.

And then, just as they were entering the big, crowded dining-hall, where hams and pies and all kinds of succulent delicacies were spread out on the large oak table, Marisa saw that Sir Julian Ormond was there, engaged in earnest conversation with Lady Blockley. His pale blue eyes seemed to flicker a little as he saw her enter the room with Delsingham. For some reason Marisa hesitated, then she moved quickly towards his elegant figure with Delsingham following more slowly.

'Why, Sir Julian!' she exclaimed. 'I didn't realise you would be here.'

He bowed to her, smiling. 'The pleasure is all mine at seeing you,' he said. Then he acknowledged Delsingham.

The two men bowed stiffly, and Delsingham said, with unmistakable coolness, 'Your servant, Ormond.' He turned to Marisa. 'I regret that I must leave now, Miss

Brooke. It's later than I realised.' Marisa gazed up at him in perplexity, aware of a sense of crushing disappointment at his abrupt announcement. Then he smiled, and said quietly, so that only she could hear it, 'I enjoyed our moonlight stroll.'

Before she could say anything he was gone, his tall figure cutting a swathe through the crowded, noisy room. Marisa, pulling herself together, turned back to Ormond.

'How pleasant to see you here,' she said brightly, hoping that Lord Delsingham would look back and see that she wasn't put out in the slightest by his abrupt departure.

Ormond bowed his smooth fair head. 'And you, Mistress Brooke. You look enchanting.' His cool eyes flickered over her lightly clad figure, making Marisa uneasy, as if he somehow guessed about her and Delsingham, out in the garden. But of course, he couldn't have any idea, could he? They chatted inconsequentially for a little while, with Ormond giving her advice on buying a closed carriage, and where to get someone to replace a slight leak in the stable roof. 'And remember,' he added, 'if you ever need any help with your financial affairs, I'll be only too glad to oblige.'

'Thank you. You've been more than kind.'

He hesitated. 'If you truly regard me as a friend, then I hope you will forgive me for being so personal. But I couldn't help noticing that Lord Delsingham was paying quite a lot of attention to you earlier. You do realise, of course, that he has rather a reputation?'

'I'd be disappointed if he didn't,' Marisa said lightly.

Ormond's eyes narrowed as he poured her more wine and handed her back her glass. But he said nothing else about Delsingham, and shortly afterwards, Sir Andrew Blockley came over to claim her as his partner for another game of whist. She took great care to play rather badly, so that Sir Andrew was able to give her lots of avuncular advice and pat her shoulder fondly in consolation at having lost. Then it was time for the dancing sets to be drawn up, and Marisa, who could fling an Irish reel with the best of them in the Old Cider Cellar in Maiden Lane but knew nothing of the intricate steps of the gavotte or the minuet, quickly made her excuses and left.

John drove them home, and the cool night air was fresh on their faces as Lucy and Marisa sat side by side in the open carriage. Lucy was chuckling softly at the recollection of Caroline Henshawe's humiliation out in the gardens.

'I declare, she couldn't speak for excitement when she saw us all moving in on her,' grinned Lucy. 'And John, you were wonderful, to keep her on the brink for so long, giving us all time to come out and join you.'

John, sitting up on the box, blushed proudly in the darkness. 'I know my duty, I hope.'

'You performed admirably, John,' said Marisa, but her mind was elsewhere. She was thinking, rather too much for her own peace of mind, of Lord Delsingham.

Marisa half expected Delsingham to call on her during the next few days, and one morning, when she was disturbed by the clatter of a horse's hooves in the yard, she hurried downstairs from her chamber, hoping that it might be him. She was aware of a rather unsettling sensation of disappointment when she heard John open the door, not to Delsingham, but to Sir Julian Ormond – on a neighbourly visit, he said.

Marisa, who was fortunately dressed most demurely in a high-necked morning gown of dove-coloured silk, received him in the sunlit drawing room, and Lucy served them neatly with coffee and little cakes. Ormond had brought lots of papers and other documents, and he began to talk to her about investments.

'You did say', he reminded her earnestly, 'that you would be glad of my advice regarding your finances, Miss Brooke.'

Marisa stiffened warily. Her money was hers, and hers alone, besides which, she hoped very much that he wouldn't expect her to read anything, because she didn't want him to realise how ill-equipped she was to deal

140

with formal documents. She began to feel nervous, but Ormond, settling himself elegantly into the chair she offered him, had already started to talk.

'They say that wool and iron are bound to take off in a general revival of trade now that the war in Europe is over,' he told her. 'My adviser in the City, who's a three-star East India man, has put fifty thousand pounds of his own money into the woollen industry.'

Marisa listened with an effort, finding herself distracted by the sun glinting on the yellow roses that nodded against the outer casements. A three star East India man? What on earth did Ormond mean? He was talking about another world, a world she didn't understand. 'Perhaps,' she said abstractedly, 'I'd better discuss it with my attorney, Mr Giles, when next I'm in London.'

Ormond laughed dismissively, drawing out his laquered snuff box and taking an elegant pinch. 'My dear Miss Brooke. I mean no disrespect, but do you really think a backstreet attorney could know more about such matters than my friends in the City?'

Marisa gazed at him coolly, not liking his patronising tone. 'Lord James Delsingham also offered to advise me. I might just discuss your proposal with him.'

Ormond's brow lifted in surprise, and he looked concerned as he started to gather up the papers he'd strewn across the small inlaid table. 'But Lord Delsingham won't be in the neighbourhood for some time. Didn't he tell you he was going away?'

Marisa felt her fingers tighten on the arms of her velvet-upholstered chair. 'No doubt he did. But I don't remember exactly.'

'He's gone to Bath,' continued Ormond smoothly, 'to visit Lady Henrietta. You did know, of course, that Delsingham is engaged to be married?'

Marisa felt rather as she had done when footpads came upon her one dark night in Drury Lane and struck her a blow on the head with a cudgel before running off with her purse. With a supreme effort, she sipped calmly at her little china dish of coffee, but it tasted sour on her tongue. 'Of course I knew about it,' she lied calmly. 'He told me all about her, actually. She sounds quite charming.'

'I'm glad he's told you about her,' Ormond said quickly, his smooth forehead furrowed in concern. 'Lady Henrietta is in Bath at the moment, taking the waters. She comes from a very well-bred family, you know, and has connections with the highest in the land. I've heard that she's extremely beautiful and accomplished.'

What in? thought Marisa viciously. Sex? Sword-play? Card sharping? Oh, no. Lady Henrietta was probably accomplished in playing the piano, and dancing the minuet, and painting delicate water-colours, all the insipid arts that were reckoned to be important in a future bride. Well. She took a deep breath, and smiled brightly at Ormond's concerned face as she toyed with her coffee cup. Of course a man like Delsingham would be engaged. He was wealthy, titled, and handsome, and had no doubt had all the eligible brides in the land chasing him for years. And she, Marisa, had no intention of marrying anyone, ever, so why did this news shake her so badly? She struggled to pull herself together, realising that Ormond was still talking suavely as he sharpened the quill pen to which he'd helped himself from her little bureau.

'Delsingham has gone to Bath to discuss their impending marriage, I believe. I would assume her parents are eager for the nuptials to proceed as soon as possible. Delsingham is quite a catch, after all, despite his – ' and he coughed gently, 'despite his reputation for having rather liberally sown his wild oats.' He leant forward earnestly. 'Miss Brooke, I really would advise you to take advantage of this investment opportunity. My friend in the City tells me that within a week or so, all the options will be taken up. There will never be a chance like this again.'

Marisa hardly heard him. She felt dazed. Damn Delsingham. And he had had the gall to warn her against Ormond, when he himself was playing a double game.

'I'm sorry?' she said quickly. 'What did you say I have to do?'

Ormond pushed the quill pen and ink towards her quickly. 'Just sign here, my dear Miss Brooke,' he said softly. 'Unless, of course, you want to read through it all first?'

Marisa shook her head quickly, the familiar panic washing through her at the sight of all those lines of print. 'No. No, that won't be necessary.'

'Then just sign. And later, of course, you will need to instruct your bank. I'll help you with that as well if you like.'

Marisa picked up the pen distractedly. She didn't want to think any more about stocks and shares and the East India company. All she could think of was Delsingham, and how stupidly eager she had been for his advances that night in the little summerhouse. Well, it was the last time ever, because no-one made a fool of her and got away with it. She scribbled her name quickly, and didn't notice how Sir Julian Ormond seemed to let out a little sigh of relief as he drew the papers back towards him.

Chapter Seven

*T*he next few days dragged badly for Marisa. The weather had changed at last, and she awoke each morning to see a solid, drenching curtain of rain outside her window that seemed to engulf all the surrounding areas of parkland and turn the former sylvan landscape into a monotonous, dank prison of dripping greenery. The house itself seemed empty, cold and damp, and even though she ordered John to light fires everywhere, his attempts did little to relieve the gloom. Marisa wandered restlessly around her rural domain, unable to settle to anything. The furnishings seemed heavy and dark to her. The oak panelling that had glowed so welcomingly on her first evening here now seemed oppressive and old-fashioned.

She found herself thinking longingly of London. She missed the noise, the crowds and the dirt of the place, missed the coarse cries of the pedlars and the crossing sweepers, and she missed her dissolute friends from the Blue Bell.

Then suddenly the rain stopped at last, and the sun broke through, sparkling on the leafy trees and lawns, bringing the old house to life again as it poured through the diamond panes of the old, mullioned windows. Several rolls of exciting new dress fabrics that she'd ordered arrived, and Marisa, bored with moping, decided that Lord James Delsingham was nothing but a conceited fraud, and not worth spending her valuable time on. Lucy further helped to restore her temper by telling her some of the tales she'd picked up from the other servants on the night of the Blockleys' ball. Marisa was particularly amused by Lucy's account of a popular dancing master from Crayhampton, who was apparently a great favourite with the local gentlewomen in spite of his miniature stature. 'He can scarcely be five foot tall, ' giggled Lucy. 'His name is Monsieur Gaston – he claims to be French, you see. And his favourite saying is, "Little dogs have long tails."'

Marisa grinned. 'I do believe I could do with some dancing lessons, Lucy. I wonder where he is to be found.' Then she noticed that Lucy was blushing, and she said accusingly, 'Lucy, I have a strong suspicion that you have already met Monsieur Gaston. Well, is it true? Is the diminutive gentleman's reputation well-founded?'

Lucy giggled. 'Indeed, it is. I encountered him the other day in Crayhampton, when I bumped into Jenny, Lady Blockley's maid, on her afternoon off. We called at Monsieur Gaston's apartments in the High Street, and, my dear, I have never seen such a small gentleman, and so well hung! When Jenny asked him about his private parts, he showed us willingly, and the sight of his great long shaft and heavy balls made me feel quite faint.'

'And?' said Marisa narrowly.

'Well,' went on Lucy rather breathlessly, 'Jenny shrieked and vowed that she failed to see how any woman could enfold such a massive weapon. But Monsieur Gaston showed us this delightful little accessory he has, a cunningly formed wooden chair with an aperture in the middle on which the lady seeking to pleasure herself with him can sit astride, quite demurely. Jenny obediently placed herself as she told him, and Monsieur Gaston wriggled beneath her. At first, he tongued her through the secret hole, until poor Jenny was quite red in the face with pleasure, and then I saw him grip his mighty purple weapon and slide it up through the aperture in the chair, and Jenny, feeling his hardened flesh slip into her eager lips, went quite, quite silent.' Lucy swallowed hard, her own eyes bright with lust. 'She bounced herself into a state of extreme pleasure, of course, and the arrangement seemed to work very well.' She stopped, and lowered her eyes demurely.

Marisa said dryly,'And you, of course, Lucy, left at this point?'

Lucy grinned wickedly up at her. 'Oh, no, Mistress Marisa. After witnessing such a fervent pleasuring, you can imagine that I too wished to take my turn on Monsieur Gaston's fine pleasuring couch, and he pumped his mighty staff into me until I was faint with pleasure. We galloped a fine gavotte together, I tell you.' She dimpled. 'And Jenny tells me that he has many more intricate dances in which he instructs his students.'

Marisa laughed, and after that, believing her spirits to be quite restored, she arranged to go into Crayhampton herself, not to meet with Monsieur Gaston, as Lucy teasingly suggested, but for a leisurely dress fitting at the fashionable milliner's in the High Street. She also spent a small fortune on silk shawls, and fans, and dainty slippers for dancing, along with parcels full of stockings and lace and all sorts of other fripperies. Afterwards, she visited the carriage-makers that had been recommended by Sir Julian Ormond, and purchased a fine travelling coach with handsome navy blue paintwork and beautiful velvet upholstery. It had only recently been built, she was assured, for a gentleman of the very highest quality, who had unfortunately lost a fortune at gambling.

'Cards, you know,' confided the carriage-maker to Marisa in hushed tones. 'Dear me. Such a dreadful curse of our times, Miss Brooke.'

'Indeed,' agreed Marisa rather breathlessly, running her hands over the beautiful brass adornments of the carriage with sensual delight. She would have a riding habit made to match her new carriage, she decided; navy-blue velvet would set off her blonde colouring exquisitely. After that, she went to dine at the Bull and Crown, feasting in the private room with Lucy off pheasant, and strawberries and cream, and a wickedly expensive claret that was like velvet on the tongue. By the time John drove them back in the new carriage, it was early evening, with the sun slanting low over the fresh green countryside. Marisa and Lucy, reclining back against the padded velvet of the upholstery, were surrounded by exciting parcels and packages and hat boxes, and Marisa, feeling her spirits surge, decided that she had quite got over Lord Delsingham. So he had a fiancée, more fool him, she thought derisively. Lady Henrietta was probably prim, demure, and virginal, and altogether utterly boring, even if she did come from one of the best families in the land. Well, if Delsingham decided to come to her, Marisa, for a little light relief, then she would treat him with the contempt he deserved.

The sun had almost set behind the trees when they got back to Melbray Manor at last. Marisa and Lucy started on a fresh bottle of wine and, settling themselves in the cosy front parlour, gleefully began to open all the parcels. Marisa tried on a new white muslin gown, with fashionably long, close-fitting sleeves and a jonquil coloured overtunic of fringed satin, while Lucy pirouetted around in a flimsy dress of almost transparent cream tulle with little puff sleeves, draping a long silk shawl in kingfisher blue dramatically around her arms. 'Do you think Monsieur Gaston would approve of me in this?' she grinned mischievously.

'I think he'd prefer you out of it,' said Marisa, helping herself to more wine.

John lit the candles and laid a fire to ward off the evening chill, watching them all the while with an eager eye as they examined all their new finery. No doubt he anticipated more entertainment later. And then, suddenly, they heard the big knocker being rattled against the front door, startling them all into guilty silence.

John, whom Marisa had equipped with smart formal livery as befitted his role as her personal manservant, went to open the door as Marisa and Lucy, both quite tipsy by now, quickly tried to gather up the flimsy gowns and shawls and undergarments that were scattered around the parlour. But they were too late, because in came three women, all demurely dressed in grey shawls and gowns and bonnets, their prim faces bright with visiting smiles. To do them credit, they hesitated only slightly when they saw the empty bottles and glasses, and the discarded clothing strewn about the candlelit parlour. Then the foremost one, a big, strongly made, middle-aged woman in a severely cut riding habit, stepped forward brightly, holding out her hand.

'My dear Miss Brooke, I do hope we haven't called at an awkward time. Just a neighbourly visit, you know? My friends here and I organise a few small functions around the parish. Cynthia here is the churchwarden's wife. We hold sewing groups, musical afternoons, charitable works and so on, and we wondered if you might be interested in joining us.'

Marisa shot a fiery look at Lucy, who was desperately trying to stifle a giggle as she stood there half-naked in her flimsy tulle gown. Then she stepped forward to return the rather firm handshake, feeling decidedly inebriated.

'How – how very pleasant of you to call,' she replied a little faintly. 'Do please sit down. Can I offer you some refreshments? Tea, perhaps?'

'We haven't got any tea,' hissed Lucy in her ear.

Marisa gestured rather helplessly towards the scattered wine bottles. 'Some wine, then, ladies?'

There was a deathly silence. Then one of the three women, who was thin and bespectacled with her brown hair drawn back in a bun, said rather breathlessly, 'I would love some wine. I only ever get a glass at Christmas, at my brother's. With the goose, you know,' she added rather sadly.

'And there's the communion wine,' said Cynthia the churchwarden's wife darkly. She was plump and quite pretty, with faded fair hair peeping out from beneath her grey silk bonnet. 'But my husband always locks it away. He says it's to stop the servants drinking it, but I know it's because he doesn't want me to enjoy myself.'

Lucy was already handing out glasses, and filling them with the remnants of the dry white wine she and Marisa had been drinking. The women tasted it avidly, their faces bright with excitement. The tall one in the riding habit drank hers down in one go and turned confidingly to Marisa.

'We saw you at Sir Andrew Blockley's house the other week,' she confessed. 'Saw that some of the women were a bit frosty to you. They're like that round here with newcomers. But we thought, now, there's someone who'll liven things up around here.'

The thin shy one with the brown hair pulled back in a bun drank her wine reverently. 'Oh, I do hope so.' she whispered, gazing at Marisa.

Marisa took a deep breath. Then she turned to John, who'd been standing impassively by the doorway. 'John,' she said quickly, 'I think we bought some champagne today, didn't we? Bring it in, will you?' She turned back with a winning smile to her visitors. 'I think we ought to make one another's acquaintance in style.'

John bowed and turned to go. Marisa had fitted him out in a short, close-fitting beige jacket in the military style, so that his high-waisted, slim breeches emphasized his muscular buttocks and strong legs quite deliciously. As he went, Marisa noted that three avid pairs of female eyes were most definitely fastened on his retreating backside, and her mind began to run riot.

The bottle of champagne was opened, and then another, and soon their visitors were extremely inebriated. Marisa, watching the three women pityingly, decided that they probably hadn't had so much fun in years. They told her all about their insipid village scandals, and the servant problem, and the attempt at amateur theatricals last winter that had resulted in the new curate running off with the squire's flighty younger daughter. Hannah, the big woman in the riding habit

149

who'd first introduced herself, turned out to be passionate about hunting. She was married to the local magistrate, Sir Henry Davenport, whom she spoke of with dismissive scorn.

As John piled up the logs on the fire and drew the curtains across the windows, the candlelit room grew cosy and warm, and the women giggled like girls as they drank more and more of the champagne. The one with the bun, Emily, looked quite young and pretty as her brown hair slipped slightly from its pins, and Marisa felt so sorry for them, with their drab lives in which a glass of champagne was a rare treat, that she longed to liven up their evening somehow. Then she saw how Cynthia and Emily were enviously fingering the new clothes that she and Lucy had unwrapped so haphazardly.

'Go on,' she urged, laughing. 'Try them on. They'll come to no harm. Choose what you fancy, and try it.'

John thoughtfully retreated to the hall, and in no time at all they were all parading around in clouds of muslin and tulle, under the encouraging guidance of Marisa and Lucy. Cynthia, the churchwarden's wife, thoroughly drunk and with her fair curls in disarray round her plump shoulders, paraded round in a calf-length silk chemise and pale stockings; the thin, brown-haired Emily, whom Marisa assumed was a spinster, undressed rapidly and rather dizzily tried on a lovely brocade dressing robe embroidered with Chinese motifs, while Hannah, the magistrate's wife, who was rather too big for most of the garments, wore her own stiff-boned corset under a long, floating tulle wrap. When the women got onto the subject of men, Marisa and Lucy's eyes met in bright speculation. Cynthia had draped herself across a velvet settee and was downing her champagne straight from the bottle, in between complaining about her straitlaced husband in a rather slurred voice. 'He regards sex as a marital duty, you see. He doesn't like me to move, and he doesn't like me to see him. Just think, girls,' and she giggled, rather hysterically, 'I've never, ever in my life seen an erect penis!'

Hannah the huntswoman snorted as she lay back in a big carved chair, her tulle wrap falling apart so they could see her big, billowing breasts above the line of her buckram corset. 'You want to see my husband's? Blink, and you'd miss it. And it's all over so quickly; a quick push and a grunt, girls, and he's finished. What a fuss about nothing. How I'd love to spend some time with a real man!' She looked assessingly towards John, who had wandered in again to pour out champagne when needed. Marisa and Lucy caught that look, and their eyes met conspiratorially.

Emily, the little spinster, was quite pink from the unaccustomed champagne. Her rather pretty brown hair had fallen loose from its bun and lay around her shoulders, and her dainty voice was a little unsteady as she knelt on the rug before the fire, stroking the thick brocade of her embroidered dressing robe. 'They say', she whispered, 'that Lord James Delsingham is a wonderful lover. They say that if you spend one night in his arms, you'll experience utter bliss.'

Marisa froze, but Hannah laughed aloud. 'Poor Emily. Aspiring rather high there, aren't you, m'dear, seeing as you've never been ridden by a man in your life? Delsingham's rather out of your sphere, Emily, though I've heard similar stories myself.'

'One can dream, Hannah,' said the pink-faced Emily, with a certain amount of dignity; the others laughed at her, teasing her. Such was the noise and chatter that none of them heard the fresh knocking at the door, except for the alert John. He went to answer it, then came back quickly and murmured to Marisa, 'Some men to see you, my lady. Say they know you.'

Marisa, glad to get away from the talk about Delsingham, moved quickly out into the shadowy hallway and stopped in amazement. 'Seth!' she gasped out in delight.

It was indeed Seth, the gypsy from Vauxhall Gardens, standing there in the doorway and gazing at her, with his dark curls, his golden earring and his warm brown eyes. Just behind him she could see big, bearded Caleb, with shy, youthful Tom grinning at her bashfully. Seth smiled, his teeth white in his suntanned face.

'I've brought you this little trinket,' he said, holding out her precious gold ring.

'Thank you, oh, thank you,' breathed Marisa, taking it happily. 'But how did you find me, Seth?'

'We Romanies have our ways,' he replied quietly, folding his arms across his chest as he gazed down at her. He was wearing a loose, white cotton shirt tucked into tight cord breeches, and a short sleeveless jerkin. Beneath his loosely tied red neckerchief his shirt was unbuttoned, and she could see a heart-stopping triangle of bare brown skin. She remembered the feel of his lithe body, the silky sensation of his beautiful cock caressing her breasts, and the champagne sang deliciously in her blood. She suddenly wanted him very much. 'I also heard,' he went on, his dark eyes holding her thick-lashed blue ones, 'that the beautiful new mistress of Melbray Manor might be in the way of wanting some reliable manservants. There's myself, of course, and Caleb, who's big and strong as an ox, and Tom, who's young but learns quickly.' His eyes twinkled. 'We'll work round the estate, or the gardens, or stables – anything you want.' He paused meaningfully, his eyes resting on her beautiful gown, drinking in the sight of her. 'Anything at all.'

Marisa was aware of a breathless hush in the room behind her, and realised that Lucy and her three visitors had moved out silently into the hall to absorb the unexpected sight of the three handsome, stalwart gypsies. She gestured towards the fire-lit parlour and said huskily, 'Come in, Seth, Caleb, Tom. I do believe I have work for you already.'

Her three female vistors were suddenly shy, trying desperately to draw their disarrayed garments around themselves, but Marisa could tell by the way they looked at the young, virile gypsies exactly what they were thinking of as the champagne they'd consumed raced around their fevered blood. She went slowly round the room to blow out all but two of the candles. Darkness, she knew, was a friend to decadence.

'Ladies,' she said softly into the breathless hush that surrounded her, 'I wish to propose a game.' She was aware of Seth's beautiful mouth twisting in a mocking smile, but she turned to him quickly and murmured, 'No cheating this time, I promise.' He bowed his head in acknowledgement, and her flesh tingled as she once more remembered his lovely, long cock rubbing yearningly across her breasts. No cheating, but she'd make sure she had Seth tonight, one way or another. She went across to the little walnut bureau in the corner to fetch two dice while the women watched her, quite breathless with anticipation.

'We're going to have an auction,' said Marisa. 'Here we have four lovely men: Seth, Caleb, Tom, and of course John. All my manservants, and all under orders to give you exactly what you want.' She paused, allowing time for the frisson of unspeakable excitement to ripple round her guests. Then she went on, 'Yes, an auction, ladies. Only instead of paying for these lovely men, we'll dice for them.'

'Four men, five women,' pointed out Seth quietly.

She smiled back at him. 'I can wait. For a little while.'

Someone coughed nervously, and Emily, the shy spinster, looked ready to faint. But then the inimitable Lucy sprang forward eagerly to take the ivory dice from Marisa's hand, and John went round filling up their glasses, fetching more for the gypsies, and they were away. Marisa curled up on the velvet settee beside the fire, smoothing her clinging muslin gown around her legs, and surveyed them all contentedly, quite happy to watch and wait for a while. She sipped her cold champagne and relaxed.

Lucy, wonderful, exuberant Lucy, her plump breasts already falling out of her low-cut bodice, made Tom stand up first. He grinned sheepishly at the women, who gazed on him in silent excitement; he looked endearingly sweet, with his soft brown hair and slender, wiry body.

They all threw, and Emily won. She was so drunk from the unaccustomed wine that she almost fainted with delight, having no idea at all what to do, but Tom carefully removed her spectacles, unpinned the remaining strands of her hair, and kissed her gently. Her long brocade robe fell back, exposing a slender, surprisingly youthful body with small but firm breasts. She just wanted the young gypsy to kiss her, but Tom, who obviously found her appealingly pretty, had other ideas, and lowered his head to gently kiss her bosom, letting his tongue flick over her soft pink nipples until they stood out stiffly at his caress. She went very still, then clutched his face hard against her breasts. 'Oh,' Emily gasped aloud. 'Oh, nobody's ever done that before. How wicked. My God, how very, very wicked – please, don't stop.' Tom mouthed her for a few moments more as she shuddered and gasped. Then he took her hand, and pressed it against his groin, so she could feel his hardening flesh stir beneath his breeches. The colour rushed to her face, and she started to pull his clothes off frantically.

Cynthia the churchwarden's wife won John, and she was ecstatic. She made him take his clothes off slowly, providing a delicious erotic spectacle for the rest of them, because John stripped with calm, self-confident ease, knowing that his muscle-bound body was a treat for any woman. When he slid his breeches down, Cynthia leant forward, breathless with delight, her eyes fastened on his thick, lengthy penis which was already stirring with promise as it hung down between his thighs. She pressed her hands to her burning cheeks in delight. 'A man,' she crowed, 'a real, live man. Oh, let me get my hands and mouth on you, you beauty.' She dropped to her knees in front of him, stroking his penis with fluttering fingers, and then, as John's mighty rod surged into its full glory, she reached to kiss it, avidly tasting and licking its thick, veined length so that John had to brace himself against her ministrations. Gasping with pleasure at the taste of him, she began to frantically pull off her thin chemise so she was clad in nothing but her pale silk stockings, exposing all of her plump, fair body to him. She rose on her knees a little, gripping his springy cock and rubbing it against her heavy breasts, cushioning his shaft between her nipples as John fought for control. 'Oh, you lovely man. What a beautiful cock. How I love the feel of it against my tits.'

Caleb and Seth were still to be played for. Marisa, reclining on her settee, forced herself to stay calm and not to join in, though she couldn't stop herself from becoming rapidly aroused as she watched the others in their decadent play. Tom, who had lowered Emily onto the rug in a dark corner of the room, was gently easing his slender cock between the woman's thighs, caressing her and encouraging her; she was breathless with delight as the tip of his penis slipped into her, making little moaning sounds and running her hands all over his supple, naked back and buttocks. John, less subtle, had roughly turned Cynthia the churchwarden's wife onto all fours and was grunting with pleasure as he ravished her plump, quivering bottom.

Caleb was up for the taking next. Lucy threw two fives for him and so did Hannah, the horse-riding magistrate's wife. Lucy gazed at Caleb's strong, virile figure with hot eyes and said to Hannah, 'Well, now. He looks as if he's got a fine meaty prick on him, doesn't he? Let's see if he can manage both of us.'

Laughing and giggling, the two women flung off the remainder of their clothes and then began on the willing Caleb, tussling him to the floor and stripping him, laughing as they exposed his huge purple appendage already thrusting blindly from his hairy loins. Hannah gasped with delight at the sight of him, while Lucy, cried out, 'Oh, I love men with beards. Pleasure me, gypsy, pleasure me with your hot tongue.' Quickly she sat on his face, wriggling about with her swollen vulva pressed against his mouth until his lips and tongue found her hardened nub of pleasure and he greedily started to lap away. Lucy threw back her head in delight and played with her own plump breasts, drawing out her long nipples and thrusting avidly at his face with her hips as his long, stiff tongue drove between her fleshy labia. Caleb grunted, thrusting high up into her juicy vagina and then wriggling about until she shouted with pleasure.

Hannah the horsewoman jumped astride his hips, her powerful thighs flung apart and her buttocks towards Lucy's face. She shouted aloud in delight as she lowered herself carefully and felt his ravening, gnarled penis impaling her eager flesh. She bounced up and down, hissing out her delight at the feel of that great, stiffened shaft sliding up inside her, shouting out, 'Now, that's what I call a real man. Stick it up me, Caleb, you wonderful boy; drive it all into me – oh, yes, yes.' And she bounced about deliriously on his rampant penis, reaching with eager fingers to stroke at the fat, hairy sac of his semen-filled balls.

Marisa bit on her soft lower lip as she watched them, her body quickening with desire. They were all eagerly pleasuring one another, heedless of the rest of the company. Tom was showing the flushed spinster Emily how to lick his cock, while John was making the churchwarden's wife masturbate him. She was eagerly rubbing his foreskin up and down while he whispered rude words in her ear. Caleb, meanwhile, was keeping his two women happy with amazing vigour. Lucy was already flushed and breathless with the pleasure of his big, skilful tongue lapping hungrily at her secret parts, while Hannah was lifting herself high on the thick, throbbing stem of his penis then pounding down again, rubbing voraciously at her own clitoris as her fierce orgasm started to envelop her.

Marisa swallowed, feeling her own secret flesh to be moist and pulsing. Her breasts were a warm, throbbing ache beneath her muslin dress, and her nipples were tight and painful. The tension was building up inexorably in her body, and she was desperate for release. Suddenly she saw that Seth was moving towards her in the candlelit shadows. He poured out a fresh glass of cooling champagne and handed it to her, then poured out some for himself, and sat beside her on the velvet settee.

She smiled at him, liking him. 'You weren't angry with me that night in Vauxhall Gardens, were you, Seth?' she said. 'For running away?'

'No, I wasn't angry,' he said quietly. 'In fact, I thought you were quite wonderful. That was why I decided to find you again.' Gently he put his arm round her, and slipped his hand inside her low-cut bodice so that Marisa gasped in delight at the feel of his strong, cool fingers against her swollen flesh. Carefully easing her breasts out of the constricting garment, he turned her towards him so he could use both his hands to cup them and soothe the swelling globes. With the ball of his thumb, he gently rolled her straining pink nipples, and a languorous tremor ran through her.

'I'm glad you did,' she whispered, her blue eyes shadowy with desire and her lips tremulous as she thought of his kiss. 'I was sorry to have to leave, believe me.'

'I think we have unfinished business, you and I,' he said, his lean brown fingers tightening round her rosy nipples.

She leant back then against the settee, her eyes half closed in pleasure, and she let him touch her and kiss her and lick her all over as he eased off all her flimsy clothing except her stockings and the delicate, lacy corset she wore beneath her breasts. He took off his clothes too, and she gasped aloud at the beautiful silken texture of his sun-browned, firm body. Pulling him towards her, she rubbed her eager breasts against the hard muscular wall of his chest and shuddered as she felt the meaningful rasp of his powerful, hair-roughened thighs against her stockinged legs.

He laid her back on the cushioned settee and lifted her knees high, then crouched between them so he could lick at her nectared labia, parting the petal-soft folds with his tongue and trailing its tip lightly along her urgently throbbing clitoris. She could see his lengthy penis strain-

157

ing with dark promise at his groin. She moaned aloud and drew her sharp fingernails along his rippling shoulder muscles, unable to conceal her need. Sensing her urgency, he moved upwards again to kiss her, his tanned, handsome face all wet with her juices. He whispered dark Romany words to her that she couldn't understand but could guess at, and she shivered with delight as she felt the long, hot rod of his pulsing manhood rubbing insistently against her taut stomach.

At last, he lifted himself over her, and was in her, slipping deliciously between her parted, swollen sex-lips. His phallus was strong and silky and satisfying, just as she'd known it would be, and better. She clutched her inner muscles tightly round him, relishing the male thickness within her, and wrapped her legs around him as he drove deeper and deeper inside her with gentle yet devastating thrusts. She felt the hard, sweet pleasure gathering in her womb, and as that great, stiff rod of flesh expertly ravished her inner core, Marisa gasped and arched herself desperately to meet him, feeling how her clitoris was pressed and rolled against the base of his shaft. Then she was there, at the pinnacle, and she shimmered into a febrile dance of ecstasy as he drove faster and faster and convulsed with a hoarse shout deep within her spasming loins.

She felt his long penis continuing to twitch inside her and sighed contentedly, still quivering with the aftermath of rapture. Good, so good. His lips were still nuzzling lazily at her sated breasts; her body was fused to his with a light sheen of perspiration. She stroked the dark curls at the nape of his neck and uttered a sigh of sheer bliss.

Slowly, with amusement, she began to realise that the other occupants of the room were still busy. Several more bottles of champagne had been emptied, and all her guests were now thoroughly drunk. Emily, totally naked, was eager to show off her new-found skills, and was going round the room, avid to taste all the men's penises. Tom had initiated her well, and she looked pink-cheeked and pretty with her shiny brown hair tumbling round her shoulders. Hannah had harnessed up Caleb with his own leather belt, buckling it around his chest and under his armpits, and now she was gleefully riding astride him as he crawled round the room on all fours. With an eager yelp, Emily spotted his long, thick cock dangling between his legs as he moved, and she wriggled beneath him, licking at it avidly until it started to surge and grow with fresh vigour. Hannah slapped at his rump while Emily sucked, urging him on. Cynthia was leaning back against the wall with glazed eyes, and muttering, 'Yes, faster, damn you, faster,' as John thrust himself hard into her, and Lucy and Tom were writhing happily on the rug before the glowing fire, as Tom rubbed himself urgently and spurted his hot seed all over Lucy's bouncing breasts.

Seth was watching them all too, and laughing softly under his breath. 'Your new neighbours?'

'My new neighbours. They came to invite me to join their sewing group. The country is full of surprises.' Marisa stroked his shoulder gently. Glancing down at his hips, she saw that his penis, still thick and firm, lay heavily against his thighs, beneath it the twin globes of his testicles looked velvety, vulnerable, exquisite. He looked as if he would be ready for more quite soon. She gazed up at him steadily. 'You'll stay?'

'I'll stay, and gladly.' He put his hand over hers, caressing it. 'But only for a while. Gypsies never stay long in the same place.'

'Of course.' Marisa smiled. 'Neither do I.' Then she remembered something, and said, 'At Vauxhall, Seth, you had two women with you. Where are they?'

'Oh, they're nearby.' He reached out and began to lazily pull on his shirt and breeches. 'They're working for some fancy gentleman over the other side of the valley. He sounds rather twisted, but he pays them well, and they're enjoying themselves.'

Marisa lifted her delicate eyebrows and cupped her chin in her hands. 'Really? How very intriguing. I didn't realise there was anyone as interesting as that around here.' Her eyes roved round the room. 'But obviously I was mistaken.'

Seth laughed. 'As you say, the country is full of surprises.' He poured them both more wine, and Marisa nestled against his arm, feeling relaxed and happy.

At long last their female guests left, rather dazedly vowing eternal friendship to their new neighbour Marisa. John, whose powers of recuperation were considerable, offered to drive them back. There were comfortable servants' quarters at the back of the house, and Lucy, giggling over her role of housekeeper, showed the gypsies to their sleeping quarters, though Marisa guessed that Caleb would probably be vigorously enjoying the pleasures of Lucy's bed before too long. She herself toyed with the idea of inviting Seth to her own bedchamber, thinking that it would be comforting to sleep with a man's arms around her, and Seth was nice. But she decided against it, partly because she needed time to think, but mainly because it was one of her rules not to commit herself too much. One could get too used to sharing a bed. Marisa liked to limit her liaisons with men to the purely physical, to sexual satisfaction only. Anything else led to trouble. She needed time to be herself, time to stretch out and think and dream.

So she went up to her rose-scented chamber alone, and washed herself luxuriously with the ewer of warm water Lucy had thoughtfully remembered to bring up for her. She slipped on her filmy lawn nightgown, then knelt on the velvet-padded window seat, drawing back the heavy curtains and gazing out at the moonlit gardens and the wooded parkland beyond.

Tonight had been fun. At least three of her new neighbours were glad she was here, and she knew that they would never breathe a word of their adventure to anyone, least of all their inadequate husbands. She was willing to wager that they would be stealing back to Melbray Manor for more of the same very soon.

Somewhere out in the darkness an owl cried out, and she shivered suddenly at the melancholy sound, wrapping her arms across her still-sensitive breasts. Seth was a beautiful, considerate lover, well above her minimum of ten. He was possibly even a king. But he wasn't an ace, like Delsingham.

She frowned. Too bad. When he came back – if he came back – after visiting his simpering, aristocratic fiancée, she would refuse even to see him, let alone allow him to tempt her into intimacy again.

Out there in the gardens, just beyond the shrubbery, she thought she saw something move. Stupid, of course. Probably just some small animal, or even the breeze moving the bushes. But she felt suddenly cold, and turned quickly to climb into her big four-poster bed, where she fell into a deep, languorous sleep.

With Seth, Tom and Caleb joining the household at Melbray Manor, Marisa began to feel really in charge of her wonderful inheritance. During the long summer days, the men worked hard, reclaiming the overgrown gardens, felling storm-damaged timber and repairing the walls and fences that secured the parkland while their bodies grew sinewed and bronzed in the sun. Lucy was quite besotted with them, so Marisa salved John's slightly dented pride by putting him in charge of the stables, which now housed two fine bay carriage horses and a big sturdy hunter for John, in addition to the beautiful mare that Ormond had insisted she keep. Lucy, meanwhile, dressed with alacrity in her pretty housemaid's outfit and took in a couple of girls from the village, who walked over for a few hours each day to clean and sweep and do the washing, as well as working in the kitchen to help Lucy fill the ovens and pantries with all sorts of good food.

Marisa dressed like a fine lady, outwardly demure, though her cornflower-blue eyes sparkled from Seth's tender lovemaking. She paid sociable morning calls on her new-found friends, Hannah, Cynthia and Emily, and received visitors herself. Sir Julian Ormond called round occasionally, making brief enquiries as to how she was faring, and offering helpful suggestions as to the management of her land. She transferred some of her substantial capital in order to honour the promising investment he'd made for her, and he assured her he'd let her know more soon about some of the profitable shares a banker friend in the City had whispered to him about.

Ormond was never anything but polite and courteous, but as he left one day, Lucy pronounced darkly, 'I don't trust that one. There's something strange about him; he's too smooth by far.'

Marisa laughed, stubbornly pushing her own doubts to the back of her mind, because in accepting Ormond's help she was resolutely defying Lord Delsingham, and that was all that mattered to her. 'Dear Lucy, your imagination's running riot. You must be getting bored with country living.'

Lucy grinned at her, her brown eyes very bright. 'Me, bored? Oh, no, miss Marisa. I've never been less bored in my life.'

Lucy and Caleb seemed pretty well besotted with each other. Lucy couldn't get enough of the big, bearded gypsy, and Marisa wondered briefly if John would be jealous, but then she found him one day in the butler's pantry, leaning back against the table with the two giggling village maids on their knees before him, taking it in turns to stroke and lick his throbbing member, exclaiming happily over its size and vigour. After that Marisa stopped worrying about him. And of course she herself had Seth, who was a tender and virile companion. Often in the evenings they would drink wine in front of the log fire in the parlour, just the two of them, or sometimes they played cards, and Marisa showed him how her little ring worked. In turn, Seth told her about Romany ways, and the places he'd visited, and showed her just a little of what he could read in the cards.

She lay beside him one evening on the thick rug before the fire, watching his slim brown fingers as he thoughtfully dealt and turned over the three cards that he'd teasingly said were supposed to reveal her fortune.

'This is your first card, Marisa,' he said. 'The ace of hearts, symbol of wealth, and love.'

She laughed, her blue eyes glinting with pleasure. 'How true. And the next one. Turn over the next one, Seth.'

His face darkened slightly, and he hesitated. Marisa pushed his hand away from the card, and saw the knave of diamonds. 'What does it mean?' she said quickly.

'It means you have a hidden enemy, Marisa.'

'What nonsense!' she laughed. His Romany eyes rested on her thoughtfully, and then he turned over the third and final card.

The ace of spades. She felt the colour rise slowly in her cheeks as he fingered the card. 'The third card stands for the man in your life,' Seth said. 'Do you know who it is?'

'Of course not,' she said a little shakily. 'After all, it's all nonsense, Seth, isn't it?'

He kissed her tenderly, and they made love in front of the fire, but she was aware all the time of the discarded cards on the floor beside her, mocking her.

Chapter Eight

When Rowena heard that the gypsies had moved into Melbray Manor, she felt the hot rage burning up inside her. She'd sneaked out of Ormond's house one night and headed for the gypsy encampment on her own, hoping for a good few hours of pleasure with Seth, but when the other gypsies told her where he and the others had gone, the thought of him rutting with the cunning blonde whore made her feel quite sick.

She'd headed back for Greenfallow Park in a daze, and entered, as she usually did, by the back staircase, but she must have been careless, because she was only halfway up the stairs when she realised that Ormond himself was there, blocking her way. He was gazing at her with that cold, vicious look that made her stomach leap with fear.

'Where have you been?' he said softly.

'Out!' Rowena retorted defiantly, tossing back her loose red locks as his eyes raked her gaudy gypsy finery. 'I couldn't sleep, see? So I went out for some fresh air. It's strange for us Romanies, to be sleeping under a roof all the time.'

He'd reached out to grip her arm, not hurting her, but the warning was there, in his fingertips. 'I hope,' he said curtly, 'that you're not thinking of stealing anything. You see, I don't like people who take what's mine.'

'Of course not,' she replied quickly, her heart suddenly pounding in fear, because in fact she and Matty had a tidy little store of trinkets and silver hidden under their mattresses. 'You can trust us gypsies, my lord, you know you can.'

'Really?' His lip curled. Rowena, in a sudden moment of wild defiance, blurted out, 'Why not, my lord? After all, that fine lady at Melbray Manor trusts everything to a band of gypsies. Why, she even has them in her bed.'

There was a sudden, sharp silence, and a look appeared in his cold, smooth face that made her shiver. 'What are you saying?'

His hands gripped her more tightly now, but Rowena lifted her head defiantly. 'Didn't you know, my lord? That fine Marisa Brooke is taking her pleasure with a band of gypsies.'

He seized her wrist then, and pulled her quickly up to his private rooms. Rowena stumbled after him, her mind racing. He was livid with rage. Why? Somewhere, here, there must be a chance for revenge. Once in his bedchamber, he let her go of her arm, and she sank to the floor with her shoulders against his heavily draped bed, her green eyes smouldering up at him, waiting. He stood over her, his breathing jerky. 'If you're lying . . .'

She licked her lips. 'Oh, no, my fine lord. I'm not lying. Ask anybody.' She saw then that his pale eyes had fastened on her luscious, lace-covered breasts. Slowly, deliberately, she started to pull down her blouse, revealing the ripe globes to his hot gaze. 'It seems that Mistress Brooke enjoys being mounted by the gypsy men. Doubtless they've got real long cocks, like gypsies do, and no doubt they know lots of secret little tricks that the fine ladies love, like sucking at them and tickling their bottoms and whispering dirty Romany words.'

Still fondling her breasts until the long brown nipples stood out stiffly, she saw how Ormond's face had gone quite white in the shadows. She reached up to stroke one hand along his thigh and saw the unmistakable knot of hard flesh where his breeches were drawn tight across his groin. Oh, yes. There was mischief to be made out of this, somehow.

'And that slut, the lady at Melbray Manor,' she whispered, 'I bet she just begs them for it. She sounds real fancy, but she's just a high-class whore. I can just see her, as she crouches on all fours and pleads with one of them to slide his fine big cock up her, while she plays with the other two, and sucks them off, and gets them to spurt their hot seed all over her.'

Ormond was shaking now. 'No. It's not true.'

Rowena reached up, her eyes glittering, and gently unfastened his breeches. He groaned aloud as his slender, angry penis jerked free, and tenderly she started to rub it.

'Oh, it's true,' sighed Rowena. 'Me and Matty, we've seen these gypsies in action, you see. Real dirty, they are. You'd like to see them at her, wouldn't you?' Raising herself a little, she dreamily rubbed his quivering shaft against her overflowing bosom, catching the tip of it along her hard brown nipples. 'Just imagine: three of them, all fucking her, all playing with her fine titties, sticking their mighty cocks up her dark little bottom hole. The one she's chosen as her favourite, he's got a lovely thick, silky cock – bet you'd like to feel him up your tight arse, wouldn't you, my lord? He'd do it, too, if you paid him enough – he'd pleasure you real good.'

Her lips fastened suddenly over Ormond's thrusting member, licking salaciously as he shuddered and gripped her bare shoulders. At the same time, she was thinking furiously. Money, she thought, that was behind it all. That blonde slut Marisa must have paid the gypsies really well, otherwise her fine Seth would never, ever have gone with her. She must have paid him lots of gold to ravish her dainty arse, damn her.

'She's a slut,' Rowena gasped aloud, pulling her face away from Ormond's rampant weapon and starting to fiercely caress his tight balls. 'A filthy slut, who needs endless pleasuring. Just think of her, my lord, in her fine silks and satins, writhing around on a lovely gypsy prick as it dances and leaps inside her – oh!'

She broke off because Ormond was starting to climax furiously beneath her ministrations. Clasping her heavy breasts swiftly around his jerking shaft, she caressed him tenderly as his semen spurted hotly over her quivering nipples. He gasped aloud, calling out her name as the sweat beaded on his forehead, and then, when he'd finished, he said in a low voice, 'You're sure about this?'

'About the gypsies and Marisa Brooke? Oh, yes,' said Rowena bitterly, gazing up at his drained face. 'It's true all right.'

'This is too much. She must be stopped.' He seemed, for a moment, to have forgotten that Rowena was there. She crouched silently at his feet, letting his seed trickle coldly down her bare flesh. Then he drew himself up and said sharply, 'Enough. Get out of here.'

She scurried back quickly to her own room, the one she shared with Matty, half exultant and half afraid.

A few days after Seth had drawn the cards for her, Marisa was frightened badly. She'd been out riding by herself through the parkland a couple of miles from the house, close to the boundary with Delsingham's land. She'd just forded the little stream, when the silence of the hot August afternoon was shattered by the crash of a nearby gun. The rooks rose clamouring in protest from the trees overhead, and Marisa's horse reared, nearly throwing her; she clutched wildly at its mane, and then she heard the clatter of another horse's hooves whirling to a stop just beside her. Seth was there sliding off his little pony and yelling out, 'Marisa, Get down. For God's sake, get down!'

He was pulling her so roughly off her horse that she tumbled gasping to the ground and lay there in his arms, all the breath knocked from her body as her mare cantered wildly off and Seth's little pony whinnied in alarm. Another shot rang out, this time whistling just above her head; she felt the breeze of it against her hair.

Absolute silence followed. She lay stunned and trembling. Seth soothed her as he would a frightened colt. 'There, there, my lovely one. It's all right, now. It's all right.'

She drew herself up, her blue eyes wide and dazed in the whiteness of her face. 'Someone was trying to shoot me, Seth.'

He frowned, looking anxious, but then he said quickly, 'Nonsense. Just some crazy poacher, perhaps. I'll send Tom and Caleb through the woods to hunt him down, but first I'm going to take you back to our home. You're shaking. And, Marisa, you must promise me. Don't ever ride out on your own again, without me or John or Caleb with you. Do you give me your word?'

'Yes,' she whispered rather faintly as Seth whistled back her terrified horse and soothed it with expert hands and voice before calmly helping her back into the saddle. She suddenly remembered the other accident, when she'd fallen from her horse. Delsingham had said the strap was cut, and she'd laughed at him, but she didn't feel like laughing now. She remembered, too, the cards that Seth had drawn for her, and the gypsy's disturbing silence as he turned over the knave of diamonds. A hidden enemy, he'd said.

Dear God, Marisa thought rather dizzily, I've faced the gambling dens and brothels of backstreet London, and I've outfaced gangs of Covent Garden ruffians, but I've never, ever been as scared as I am now!

She took Seth's advice seriously, and two days later, when she rode over to a nearby farm to order some supplies of corn, Seth himself accompanied her. The farmer promised to provide exactly what she wanted, and at a good price, so after drinking a glass apiece of his wife's creamy, home-brewed ale, Marisa and Seth set off for home in the late afternoon sunshine. The trees were heavy with summer foliage, and the air was scented with the fragrance of hedgerow flowers. Distant cattle grazed contentedly in the drowsy heat, and swallows swooped low over the river, chasing the clouds of dancing gnats.

Seth started to sing some gypsy songs as they rode along, in his own tongue. He had a sweet, mellow voice, and Marisa listened, entranced. When he had finished she grinned at him and responded by singing an extremely licentious lyric about a young lady who used to frequent certain bordellos in Leicester Fields. They laughed together, taking it in turns to make up more and more outrageous verses as their horses ambled along the dry, dusty track that led through the woods towards Melbray Manor.

Their singing was abruptly interrupted by the sound of horses crashing through the undergrowth alongside the track. Seth's hand was on his pistol. He hissed out, 'Marisa, ride for your life!'

He was too late, because four big, roughly dressed men on horseback had already surrounded them and were pointing guns at their heads, while one of them, a ginger-haired man with a cruel face, was saying to Seth, 'Just drop that pistol of yours, gypsy scum. Don't try anything, or you'll be dead, and so will this fine whore of yours.'

Seth hissed out, and urged his horse suddenly forwards towards the man who spoke, but another of the ruffians rode up beside him and struck him on the back of the head with the barrel of his gun, and Seth fell heavily from his horse.

Marisa let out a low cry, controlling her own frightened mare with difficulty. The men looked coarse and brutal; they wore rough, tattered clothing, and their hats were pulled low over their faces. Two of them dismounted quickly and hurried towards the groaning Seth as he lay on the ground, while the other two made their way purposefully towards Marisa and dragged her struggling from her horse. She lashed them verbally with a stream of vicious invective and tried to hit them with her riding whip, but one of them pulled it easily off her and laughed.

'Fancy you knowing such words, darling, and you so innocent-looking too. Just keep nice and quiet, now, and you'll come to no harm.'

'Then let me go, damn you!' hissed Marisa, still struggling fiercely as the two of them pinioned her. 'What do you want – jewels, money? I've not got much on me, but you're welcome to it. Just let me and my manservant go.' She was conscious that her hat had slipped off, and her blonde curls were tumbling around her face as she pleaded with them. They stared at her, their eyes hot on her breasts, which were outlined by the tight jacket of her riding habit. One of them said, 'We don't want your money or your fancy jewels, Miss Brooke. Hold that gypsy tight, Varley, won't you?'

No ordinary footpads these. They knew who she was, and they wanted something. Marisa began to feel really frightened.

Seth was struggling too, but to no avail. The man with the ginger hair, whom the other had addressed as Varley, pinioned the gypsy's arms roughly behind him, laughing to Marisa, 'Your manservant, eh, my lady? Is that what you call him? He's your filthy gypsy lover. You let him share your bed, don't you? Has he got a fine, stalwart cock on him, then, as well as a handsome face? Do they do things differently, the Romanies? I've heard they've got lots of fancy little tricks to keep their ladies happy in bed. Has he shown you them?'

Marisa had gone quite white as she saw how the man twisted Seth's arms behind his back, forcing him to the ground on all fours. Seth's face was gaunt with pain.

'Let him go, you filthy cowards,' she breathed. 'He's a better man than any of you.'

Varley, who seemed to be the gang's leader, laughed unpleasantly. 'You think so? Perhaps we'll try him out. And maybe by the time we've finished with him, you won't be quite so hot for him, my fine lady. He's a horse thief, aren't you, pretty lad?' His brutal grip tightened on Seth's arms. 'People are hanged for less. A vicious horse

170

thief, who's been taking his pleasure a bit too freely. We've orders to punish him so he doesn't dare to show his Romany face in these parts ever again.'

'Whose orders?' cried out Marisa, but the man just laughed. Seth's face was white as they dragged him along and tied him face down against the sturdy stump of a recently felled oak, securing him with thick rope one of them produced so that he was kneeling over the tree with his cheek laid helplessly against the smoothly-sawn surface. Marisa struggled again with the two men who held her, and wondered if there was any trick she could employ, but they were big and muscular, too formidable by far for any of her ruses. She felt sick with unknown fear for poor Seth; something terrible was going to happen to him, she knew. She said, as steadily as she could, 'If you release him and let him go unharmed, then I'll make sure you get a lot of money, I promise you. I'll pay you in gold for his safety.'

They laughed. Varley mocked her. 'My, my, he does mean a lot to you, doesn't he? But we're already being paid, thank you kindly. Paid more than enough, eh, lads?'

Marisa moistened her dry lips. 'Paid to do what?'

Varley laughed again. 'Watch, and find out. Our orders were pretty clear, so we'll do it with great care, believe me. Maybe you'll enjoy it.'

Marisa felt sick at the cruel mockery in the ruffian Varley's words. The warm, earthy depths of the forest that had earlier been so tranquil suddenly seemed full of menace. The light breeze had dropped, making the air almost suffocating, and even the birds had stopped singing. Varley was starting to rip Seth's clothes from his pinioned body, tearing off his shirt so that the gypsy's tautly muscled brown back was exposed, every sinew stretched by the ropes that bound his arms and wrists to the gnarled roots on the other side of the stump. When Varley pulled out an ugly knife, Marisa felt the blood drain from her face, and then realised that he was using it to cut at the belt of Seth's cord breeches, ripping them away from his kneeling body so that the gypsy's tight, smooth buttocks were exposed to the leering gaze of the men. Someone laughed, and muttered something to Varley; Varley nodded and started to pull off his own leather belt, stroking it meaningfully.

'Know what we do with gypsy horse thieves round here, pretty lad?' he said softly to Seth. 'We leather their arses, just gently, you understand. Just a warning. And you know what we do with gypsies who are bold enough to pleasure our womenfolk with their dark Romany cocks? We teach them a different kind of lesson, lad; one you might even enjoy. The lady's watching you, gypsy. Let's see what kind of performance you put on for her this time, shall we?'

And, his face grimly intent, he drew back the leather belt and started to swing it across Seth's bared bottom-cheeks.

Marisa cried out as the leather landed on Seth's firm, tender flesh, and felt sick as she saw the red weal spring up across his beautiful body. She saw him shudder in his bonds, not so much with pain, because they weren't aiming to hurt him physically, but with the degradation of it. His head was bent against the stump of the tree; his arms were outstretched, and bound at the wrists. She could see that his eyes were shut; his face set tense against the kiss of the belt as it sang through the air, again and again. His buttocks were taut and reddened. Between them was exposed the dark, shadowy cleft, lightly kissed with tendrils of body hair, and she could glimpse the tender pink bag of his testicles dangling helplessly between his thighs.

And then the man called Varley paused, letting the belt dangle heavily in his hands. He laughed unpleasantly and said, 'Enjoying it, lad? Is this something your fancy lady likes to do to you?' He nodded to one of his grim-faced companions. 'Loosen his bonds a little and turn him round. Let our lady get a good look at him.'

The other man did exactly as he was bid, leaving Seth's

arms bound but twisting him round roughly at the hips. Varley had ripped the gypsy's breeches down to his knees, and as Seth's body was forced round, Marisa saw with a stab of shock that his penis was already darkly turgid, stirring with secret excitement as it hung down between his thighs. The man who'd turned him saw it too. He laughed unpleasantly and gripped Seth's member in his big fist, rubbing it up and down with coarse skill. Marisa, scarcely breathing, saw poor Seth's face twist away in agony as his penis swelled inexorably and stiffened in pleasure at that lewd caress.

'No,' breathed Marisa, 'no.' The men holding her tightened their grip on her arms, and one of them said, 'Be quiet, and enjoy it, my lady, or we'll make things worse for him, mark my words. Besides, can't you see the pretty gypsy lad's enjoying himself?'

Marisa bowed her head in despair, still straining silently against the men who held her in their rough grip. But at the same time, she felt a dark wave of shameful, degrading desire wash through her as she saw that what they said was true, that Seth, poor Seth, was indeed aroused by that vile man's attentions, that his beautiful, lengthy penis was continuing to thicken and stiffen into helpless erection as the man brusquely stroked it up and down, pulling the foreskin along the bone-hard stem while grasping with his other hand at Seth's velvety testicles until the fully engorged shaft was rearing up hungrily beneath his rough but accurate ministrations. Marisa glimpsed the angry, dark plum at its tip that continued to swell and redden, and she felt the soft flesh at the juncture of her own thighs quiver at the thought of that hot, hungry penis sliding up inside her. Even here, in front of these hateful men, the idea excited her desperately. Her breasts ached remorselessly, her nipples were like heavy stones dragging at the swollen creamy flesh that surrounded them. She was unable to pull her eyes from his helplessly quivering rod as his tormentor stroked him, soothed him.

'There. Enjoying that, my lad, aren't you? No wonder

the fine lady's so fond of you; it's a pretty toy you've got there. Pays you well, does she? Makes it worth your while?'

Another man laughed and called out, 'How much do you gypsies charge the ladies for a good fuck behind the hedges, eh?'

Seth's eyes flashed as the man crudely fondled his penis. Suddenly he lifted his head and said clearly to his tormentors, 'Try asking your own womenfolk. They'll know the price well enough.'

The men drew back from him with a swift hiss of anger, and Marisa, gazing in despair, saw the ginger-haired one, Varley, step forward threateningly. He said, 'You shouldn't have said that, gypsy boy, about our women. Oh, no.' And while Marisa watched, her throat dry with horror, he grimly unfastened his own rough breeches and drew out his own penis from its bush of wiry red hair. She saw, with fascinated revulsion, that it was already jutting fiercely upwards, throbbing with arousal. He too, it seemed, had been enjoying Seth's humiliation. He fondled his penis himself, lovingly strok-ing the thick shaft until the veins stood out. Then he said suddenly, 'Turn him back round. Make sure he's secure.'

The other men quickly did as they were told, tighten-ing the rope round Seth's wrists to force him into submission. And then Marisa saw Varley spit calmly into his palm and anoint his own penis with saliva, rubbing it lovingly until it was engorged with blood, a dark and angry shaft. Then he knelt behind the pinioned Seth and gripped the gypsy's tight bottom-cheeks, fondling and stroking roughly and pulling them apart until his anal aperture was just visible, a tiny, pouting bud. With a grin, Varley leant forward, gripping his own penis mean-ingfully as he gently prodded and probed between Seth's cheeks. Marisa gasped and tried to break free, but one of the men holding her said, 'No, my pretty. He's enjoying it. See how the gypsy's cock quivers anew.'

Marisa watched dry mouthed as Varley's penis slipped at last into the tight aperture. She saw, too, because her

174

captors made sure she could see it; how Seth's erection throbbed and beat against his own belly at the fresh stimulation, saw how the gypsy threw his head back, his mouth contorted as the dark, forbidden pleasure of penetration assailed him. Varley, his penis gripped by the gypsy's tight anal ring, began to move slowly, carefully between Seth's muscled buttocks, and the other men watched with hot excitement as Varley murmured lovingly between thrusts, 'You're enjoying this, aren't you, my fine gypsy lad? Enjoying being mounted by a good, strong man, enjoying feeling my mighty cock in your tight little hole . . .'

And as his penis slowly slid in and out of Seth's exposed bottom cheeks, Marisa felt the hot waves of despairing excitement flood her own body. She longed to throw herself beneath Seth, to take his beautiful, straining penis with her lips and tongue, and feel his tormented shaft thrusting to sensual oblivion deep within her mouth until his seed was all spent and his agonised face was bathed in bliss. But the men tightened their grip on her, their faces dark with lust as they watched their leader take his pleasure. 'Enjoying it, lady?' whispered one of them softly. She threw her head back in defiance, her lips pressed tightly shut, determined not to let them see how shamefully aroused she was by the animal lust being displayed before her eyes.

Varley, still thrusting with keen pleasure, was near the point of release. His face was dark as he drew out his glistening, meaty penis with slow relish before avidly driving himself back in. Seth was gasping as he crouched, the sweat beading his forehead, his own penis darkly distended. Varley's rough companion suddenly dropped to his knees beside him, laughing crudely. 'Nearly ready, gypsy lad? Let's give you something to really remember us by, shall we?' and as Varley pounded faster and faster into him from behind, the other man gripped the gypsy's straining phallus and swiftly squeezed and pumped at the distended flesh until Seth gasped harshly and his semen started to squirt in dark, shameful rapture. The man behind him suddenly pulled out his penis and orgasmed between Seth's clenched thighs in his own frenzy of lust, his hips thrusting frantically, and Marisa, unable to help herself, felt a violent, helpless spasming at her own core as her body went into involuntary climax. She did her very best to hold herself rigid, squeezing down on her throbbing womb and praying that the men who held her were too hotly aroused themselves by the playing out of the lewd scene before them to notice her secret, despairing ecstasy.

Silence fell. The air seemed hot and heavy. Seth's head was bowed in agony after the sweet pleasure of release. Varley got slowly to his feet, fastening up his breeches as he did so, his face still flushed. 'Let's go,' he snapped to his men. 'I think we've taught the gypsy a lesson he won't forget for a while. And as for you, lady,' and he turned to Marisa, 'let's see if you fancy him so much after seeing what he really enjoys, eh? It's well known that the gypsies will do anything for a penny or two, like letting the gentry stick their cocks up their tight Romany arses. Folks round here don't like ladies who rut with gypsies. Find someone of your own kind to take your pleasure with in future.'

'A filthy animal like you, you mean?' said Marisa with blazing eyes, her body still trembling from the secret, shameful explosion that had taken her by storm.

'Oh, lady,' said Varley, fingering his groin as he fastened his breeches, 'I wish we could teach you a lesson as well.' His hot eyes were on Marisa's panting breasts. 'But that wasn't in our instructions, much as you would have enjoyed our attentions.' He grinned. 'Let's go, lads. We've done as we were bid.'

Quickly they went to their horses and mounted up, galloping off into the dark cover of the woods. As the hoof-beats died away, Marisa ran over to Seth and frantically untied the bonds that still held his wrists. He got quickly to his feet, pulling at his torn clothes to cover his body. She saw that his face was drawn with tension

176

as he said quickly, 'You're all right, Marisa? They didn't hurt you?'

'No. They didn't touch me, except to force me to watch. Oh, Seth, the things they did to you – we must report it to someone.'

He laughed bitterly, his face set and tight. 'You think the magistrates would be interested? As those brutes were at pains to point out, it could have been worse, much worse. Gypsies are supposed to put up with anything, remember? And do you really want them looking into your past, Marisa?'

She was silent, knowing he was right.

'And did you hear what they said?' he went on. 'Someone was paying them to do what they did; they were under instructions from someone.'

'Who could hate you so much, Seth?' she said with a shiver, reaching up to stroke his cheek.

He took her hand, and replied grimly, 'No, you've got it wrong, Marisa. You see, it's not me they hate, but you.'

They rode back together in silence in the low, sultry heat that carried the promise of a thunderstorm. As they dismounted in the stable yard, Lucy came rushing out anxiously with the news that one of the local magistrates, Sir Henry Davenport, the husband of Marisa's new-found friend Hannah, had ridden round that afternoon to ask sternly if there were gypsies living at the house.

'I told him there were, Marisa,' Lucy cried out, twisting her hands and glancing apologetically at Seth. 'Because it seemed to me as if Sir Henry knew all about them anyway. I said they were here quite rightfully, because they were employed by you.'

'It's all right, Lucy,' said Marisa soothingly as she dismounted, though her heart was beating uncomfortably fast. 'What else did he say?'

'He said – he said as how there'd been horse thieving in the district, and the local landowners were complaining that the cows had stopped giving milk. Last night a mare lost her foal over at the Blockleys' place, and folk are saying the gypsies are putting a curse on the neighbourhood. The magistrate said it was best that you all leave, Seth, before local folk take matters into their own hands.'

Seth stood steadily beside Marisa as he listened. 'I'm not going anywhere,' he said. 'Neither are Caleb and Tom. You need us here, Marisa.'

Marisa turned quickly to him. 'Seth, you must go. It's not safe for you here. It sounds as if Sir Henry was trying to warn you. Please listen to him.'

Seth put his hands on her shoulders, gazing into her troubled blue eyes. 'Marisa, it's you, not me, who's in danger. I told you that before. Remember the gunshots, the riding accident you told me about when your saddle leather was cut – and now this. I'm not going anywhere.'

There was a heavy silence, then Marisa said shakily, 'Then you're dismissed. All three of you.'

His hands dropped to his sides. 'What?'

'You heard me,' said Marisa, gazing defiantly up into his shocked face. 'I want you off my land by sunset, Seth. I'll pay you well for what you've done for me.'

His face grew dark and stormy. 'I don't want your damned money.'

'And I don't want you to stay,' she shouted back, 'and perhaps be killed next time. Do you think I want to see you punished again, as you were this afternoon?'

He was silent, his dark eyes blazing. She shook her head slightly and her lip trembled as she gazed up at him. 'Seth, Seth. You must go, please. I can look after myself. I still have John to protect me.'

He lifted his shoulders in a tiny shrug. 'Very well. Since you're the one in charge, we'll go. But remember, Marisa, we'll be around if you ever need us.'

He went to find the others, and they packed their few belongings and loaded them on their ponies. Marisa watched them go from the drawing-room window, gazing after them until they disappeared behind the sweeping curve of the chestnut-lined drive. The sky had grown unnaturally dark. She could hear the distant, ominous rumble of thunder, and she suddenly felt alone and frightened. And yet she knew, somehow, that she'd done the only thing possible. Seth had been right; his dreadful humiliation that afternoon was because of her. The cards had correctly foretold that she had a secret enemy, and she couldn't bear to put Seth further at risk. Who was it? Who hated her so much that he'd punish Seth in such a degrading way? She remembered the darkly erotic scene out there in the silent woods, with Seth desperately climaxing beneath the ministrations of the two big, coarse men, and she shivered, aware of her own shameful arousal still stirring at the pit of her belly.

She hardly slept that night. The next morning she arose unrefreshed and heavy-eyed, already missing the comforting presence of the gypsies, and when Sir Julian Ormond called round, she was quiet and abstracted. He bought her good news, he said, about her investments, but she found it difficult to concentrate on what he said. After glancing at the papers he showed her, and feeling the old familiar helplessness start to overwhelm her at the sight of all those tortuous words, Marisa quickly agreed to place yet more of her capital in his hands, and was glad to see him go.

Time seemed to pass slowly, as if she were waiting for something, or someone. She wandered restlessly around the big, empty house, and wondered about going back to London, if only for a short stay. She missed her friends in Maiden Lane; she missed the vivid taproom ruffians of the Blue Bell, and she missed the quiet sophistication of friends like David Valsino. Soon, she resolved, she would return to the city. But why not now, why not today? She shivered. She wasn't waiting for Delsingham, was she? If so, then she would be waiting a very, very long time.

Rowena, on hearing that Seth and the others had left Melbray Manor at last, hurried from Ormond's house late one night without Matty and sneaked over to the gypsy encampment, where the three men had taken up their old place again. Seth seemed strangely distant,

179

though Rowena did everything she could do get his attention, even offering to spend the whole night with him.

'There's no need,' he said. 'You have to get back to your fine master, don't you? Or you'll lose your post.'

'He won't notice I'm gone,' she said defiantly. 'Besides, Seth, it's you I want. I've really missed you.'

She bent to fondle him, pulling out his somnolent penis and licking it until it grew into stiffness. He responded then and gripped her head, thrusting violently against the back of her throat while she used all the tricks she knew to tease and excite his throbbing shaft. He was lovely, her Seth. His penis was so manly and long and straight, and his balls were velvety hard, bursting with hot seed, a delight to touch. While she was working on him, Caleb came up and took her from behind, and she could tell that Seth was excited by the sight of her being so crudely pleasured by Caleb's big, meaty prick, because his own strong penis grew even longer and harder, so she had to take the remaining inches of it in her saliva-moistened palm and caress him that way while her tongue danced around his swelling tip. It was wonderful, to be pleasuring Seth so and feeling his body stiffen and jerk as he finally lost control and shot his seed into her mouth with a great gasping cry, while from behind Caleb's mighty penis was ravishing her thoroughly, its ridged thickness sliding steadily in and out of her juicy sex-lips. Rubbing her breasts avidly against Seth's face, she pushed her dark brown nipples right into his mouth and moaned happily into orgasm while Caleb thrust away dementedly behind her and came with a great shout of satisfaction, his heavy balls bouncing against her buttocks.

Caleb left, and Rowena stayed with Seth, wanting badly to sleep in his arms, because he still seemed cold somehow.

'You don't still love the blonde bitch at Melbray Manor, do you, Seth?' she murmured sleepily, snuggling against him as they lay on a blanket in the shelter of the caravan.

'You don't still think about her? She'll have found herself a new lover by now; hot for sex, she was, anyone could see that. No doubt she's found some fine lord to pleasure her fancy arse, and give her lots of money as well. That's why she got rid of you, my love. Now she's a great lady, she thinks you're not good enough for her.'

Seth turned suddenly, gripping her by the arms so hard that she was frightened. 'Shut up, Rowena,' he said. 'You know nothing about her. Marisa Brooke is brave and honourable, and I'd go back to her any time, believe me. So don't push your luck. You're good company, and you know how to pleasure a man well, but so do lots of women. So keep your mouth shut, unless you want me to kick you out.'

Rowena was silent then, but her green eyes glittered with hatred as she thought of Marisa. So Seth was still besotted with the fancy bitch, was he? She'd have to do something about that. The rage burned steadily within her. She decided not to spend all night with Seth after all.

It was John, doing his usual slow rounds of the house before locking up at midnight, who first saw the flicker of embryo flames glinting from the direction of the stable block. Then he smelled the acrid smoke and roared out in alarm, rushing towards the pump in the courtyard, and Marisa and Lucy, who had been talking lazily over a late night bottle of wine in the drawing-room, ran out to help him, hurling bucket after bucket on the smouldering hay while the horses stamped and whinnied in alarm. Smoke-blackened and soaked, the three of them soothed the panic-stricken horses into placidity again and gazed at one another silently.

'You were just in time, John,' Marisa said quietly. 'That straw had only just caught. A few minutes later, and we wouldn't have been able to do anything to stop the whole stable block going up in flames.'

John was rubbing his hand slowly through his soot-blackened hair, his face puzzled and anxious. 'I don't understand it, my lady. I never take a light near the stables, never, not even a lantern, in case a spark should drop on the straw. Somebody must have slipped in here and lit it deliberately.'

Lucy gave a little whimper of terror, and Marisa, who'd already come to that unpleasant conclusion herself, felt the cold renewal of the fear that she'd been trying for so long to put to the back of her mind. They checked that the horses were all right, and were just preparing to go back inside when Marisa's eye was caught by something on the ground. Bending to pick it up instinctively, she saw that it was a tiny bundle of twigs, carefully tied with twine. Just right, she thought rather dazedly, for lighting a fire.

Lucy saw what she was holding and grabbed it from her with a little cry. 'That's elder wood, Miss Marisa. The gypsies say that to burn it brings the Devil into the house. It's like a curse on the place.'

Marisa said calmly, 'Nonsense, Lucy. That's just old superstition, and you know it.' But Lucy was still shivering, and as she hurled the tiny, sinister bundle of twigs into the darkness, Marisa suddenly remembered Seth's quietly ominous words: 'It's not me they hate, Marisa, but you.' Who hated her? Who was her secret enemy?

It was well past midnight when Rowena got back to Greenfallow Park. She could tell by the absence of his carriage that Ormond was out late, but then he often was, drinking or gambling with his fancy friends somewhere in the neighbourhood. She tiptoed up the stairs, seeing with a sigh of relief that everything was in darkness, and tumbled wearily into her little bed, after glancing quickly across at Matty to see that she was asleep and gently snoring.

Several hours later, while it was still dark, she awoke with a cry of alarm as the bedroom door softly opened, and then she gave a sob of fear as someone stepped into the room. Ormond. Damn him, but he was back late, and he looked as if he'd been drinking. He also looked as if he wanted something from her, and she knew what that might be. She raised herself quickly, wishing she'd washed the smoke stains from her face and hands, and tried a sultry smile.

'What's your pleasure, my lord?' she whispered enticingly, keeping her voice low so as not to wake Matty.

He was in a hurry. His face tight with urgency, he pulled down his breeches, and pushed her head down onto his slender, straining cock, making her take him in her mouth. She enjoyed this, and was good at it, enjoying her feeling of power over him, and imagining the familiar tension on his pale, agonised face as he drove his rampant penis between her lush lips.

Then, suddenly, he pulled himself out, and gripped her wrists, turning her hands over to inspect them. They were dirty from charred kindling. He touched his finger against the smoke stains on her cheek and hissed softly, 'Where have you been, gypsy slut?'

'Nowhere,' she stammered. 'I – I was just laying the fires for tomorrow, and I was that tired, my lord, I forgot to wash properly.'

'Liar,' he said, still gripping her wrists. 'There's been a fire over at Melbray Manor tonight. It was you that started it, wasn't it? It was you . . .'

Rowena began to whimper. 'Don't report me to the magistrates sir, please. Don't – they'll hang me, for sure.'

He slid his hand beneath her nightgown and took her brown nipple between forefinger and thumb, pinching slightly so she moaned with delicious arousal, her eyes travelling greedily to his still-throbbing penis. 'I won't report you to the magistrates. But you've made a mistake, Rowena.'

She gazed at him speechlessly, not understanding.

'Yes,' he went on, 'you've made a mistake. It's Marisa Brooke who must be destroyed. But not Melbray Manor – you understand?'

No. She didn't understand at all. But it looked as if he wasn't going to report her, as if he was almost pleased with her.

She watched his set face, half horrified, half fascinated as he slowly gripped his slender shaft and pushed it towards her heavy breasts. 'Melbray Manor is special, Rowena,' he went on softly. 'It's mine. And I want that bitch out of it.'

His penis was angry and hot against her cool flesh. Rowena smothered a low cry of fear as he gripped her shoulders. Then swiftly he turned her over, so she was crouching on all fours on her tiny bed in the darkness. Her body began to beat with the dark throb of arousal as she felt him thrust his stiffened shaft avidly, desperately between her lush thighs. He lasted only a moment before he pulled himself out and started to cream over her buttocks with a groan of despair. As soon as Rowena felt him jerk and spasm against her sensitised flesh, she began to desperately rub her long, brown nipples against the rough wool of her bedspread, at the same time reaching down with one hand to rub hungrily at her soaking clitoris. Immediately she felt the excitement gather in her loins, and she rose to silent orgasm as the last of his seed spurted voraciously over her bottom-cheeks. His ominous words rang through her as she shuddered in the very throes of climax.

So Marisa Brooke had another enemy, and a dangerous one at that.

Chapter Nine

*A*fter the fire, Marisa herself went round late every night with John, making sure that all the doors and windows were secure. She knew she needed more men-servants, but she wasn't sure who to trust, and mean-while, even though she chided herself for being stupid, the feeling that she was being watched grew more and more intense.

Then she remembered that there was a gun-room at the back of the house, approached by a small staircase that led up from the main, first-floor gallery. She'd scarcely been in it, except to lay her precious foils up there when she first arrived, but after the incident of the fire she decided to explore it more carefully, finding the keys to the dusty glass-fronted cases and meticulously examining the contents. They contained mostly old sporting guns, heavy and slow, but she also made the discovery of a pair of silver-mounted flintlock pistols, which she carefully cleaned and oiled, making sure that the powder and balls were nearby and that both John and Lucy knew how to use them. She also still had her father's pocket pistol, which she started to keep by her bedside at night. Some-one was trying to drive her away from her inheritance, and of one thing she was certain; they wouldn't succeed. Returning to London wasn't an option now.

One afternoon, when John and Lucy had driven into Crayhampton for household supplies, Marisa felt a sudden urge to take her rapiers out and feel their familiar suppleness in her hands once more. It was late August, and although the heat of summer still lingered, the sky was dark and lowering with the promise of heavy rain later. Shivering a little, Marisa lit a candle against the unaccustomed afternoon gloom and went up to her bedchamber, where she swiftly changed into tight buckskin breeches and a man's silk shirt that felt cool and free against her warm breasts. She pulled her loose blonde curls back into a black velvet ribbon, and slipped her silk-stockinged calves into the soft, leather top boots that she'd had specially made for her in Bedford Row. In the easy garb of a man, she immediately felt more confident, more in charge. Picking up her father's pistol from her bedside table, she took her candle in the other hand and hurried up the narrow flight of stairs to the gun-room.

This was a spare, masculine room, with a high ceiling and tall windows. The floor was of bare wood, while the whitewashed walls were adorned with nothing but rows of metal hooks for the storing of old-fashioned weaponry and harness. There were no other furnishings except for the gun cabinets, a big oak table in the centre of the room, and an old carved settle set beneath the window. The air was redolent with the distinctive aromas of smoke-stained panelling and oil and gunpowder. Carefully she set down her flickering candle on the oak table, glad of its light because the sky was now almost black and the heavy raindrops were already beginning to beat against the leaded windowpanes.

Eagerly she unlocked the case that contained her precious rapiers and examined them critically, balancing the familiar metallic weight in her hand. She tried a few delicate moves, letting the blade become part of her again, feeling her supple body seem to come to life as the blade danced in the shadows. Carefully she balanced her weight on her slender hips, feeling her wrist sinews tingling as she straightened her arm, imagining that

David Valsino was there watching her and murmuring curt words of encouragement. 'Speed and accuracy, Miss Brooke.'

'There's no replacement for speed and accuracy!' she laughed aloud, throwing her weight onto her left foot to make a straight thrust. 'Prepare for the *en garde*!'

And then, above the drumming sound of the raindrops against the window-panes, she suddenly heard something else, the sound of a door opening and shutting quietly somewhere down below. A shiver of alarm trickled like ice down her spine, and then, to her horror, she heard the sound of footsteps, slow, steady, deliberate, climbing up the narrow stairs to the gun-room. Marisa stood transfixed, the fine hairs prickling at the back of her neck. Someone was coming up here. And that someone was neither Lucy nor John, because she would have recognised their footsteps immediately. Whoever it was was getting nearer now; the big oak door was slowly opening. With a little sob, she quickly positioned herself with her foil outstretched, her arm poised, ready.

The door opened wide, and Lord James Delsingham stood there, filling the doorway. His brows arched, just a little, when he saw her in her man's garb with her blade held ready. Then he murmured, 'Well, Ganymede. I'm glad you're so pleased to see me. Is this how you usually welcome your guests?'

Marisa caught her breath, conscious that her outstretched arm was beginning to tremble. 'Guests are invited,' she said in a low voice. 'Who let you in?'

'Nobody. I let myself in; the door was unlocked, you see. You really should be more careful, Ganymede.' He wandered over to where the other foil lay on the oak table and picked it up thoughtfully. 'A trifle overlong, aren't they? And the hilt is somewhat heavy; however, that's a matter of opinion.You play with these toys?'

After her earlier shock at his intrusion, Marisa found herself growing more and more enraged at his calm possessiveness. 'Try me and see if I play, Lord Delsingham.'

He turned to face her. He was wearing a loose but superbly cut grey coat over his ruffled silk shirt; his close-fitting nankeen breeches were tucked into glossy black hessians, and he looked effortlessly graceful. His cropped hair was black from the rain, emphasizing his dangerous good looks. She felt a little weak, because she'd forgotten how physically devastating he was, six foot of hard-packed muscle and bone that made her own slender feminine frame seem quite diminutive. He responded to her fevered challenge by saying carelessly, 'You're serious? I must warn you: I have some skill in fencing.'

'No, I must warn you, my lord,' she said through gritted teeth. 'So do I,'

He stroked the blade he was holding carefully, feeling its edge with the ball of his thumb. 'Well,' he said, 'since you're obviously not going to put your rapier down until someone disarms you, I suppose I'd better oblige.' And he eased off his coat, unwittingly displaying his tall, wide-shouldered frame to perfection. Marisa hated him, wondering if he'd done it deliberately to weaken her, then realised that he'd done it quite unselfconsciously, because he was without any kind of peacock, male arrogance. Staring at him without realising it, she suddenly caught the laughing mockery in his eyes as he waited for her to recollect herself, and she felt the blind rage spill through her again. Carefully she rolled up her shirt sleeves, then she hissed venomously, 'Prepare for the *en garde*, my lord!' and their swords flashed in brief, hostile salute.

Delsingham was good; she realised that quickly. She'd hoped his size would be a disadvantage, but he was surprisingly speedy and graceful for so tall a man. But she was good too, well taught, with quick reactions and plenty of courage, and her much smaller size enabled her to move deftly to avoid his blade. Even so, after a few moments she was brought to realise that she had perhaps met her match, and he didn't seem to be even trying particularly hard, damn him! She lunged forward suddenly on her right foot, delivering a lightning thrust in tierce that she hoped would catch him unawares, but he parried and countered with a scuffling of blades, saying, 'A good try, Ganymede. But it's too well known a trick; try something different. And remember to play from your wrist, not your shoulder.'

Marisa gritted her teeth, her breathing by now coming quick and hard. She could see the sinewy muscles of Delsingham's forearm rippling in readiness, could sense the wily, skilled strength that informed every shift of his glittering blade, and suddenly she wanted more than anything in life to beat him, to humiliate him. Swiftly shifting her balance, she attempted a flanconnade, but just at that moment Delsingham disengaged, giving way with the point of his blade, so that Marisa's foil spun glittering from her grip and landed with a clatter on the bare floorboards.

Marisa hissed out an oath as she grabbed for her fallen blade. Delsingham leaned calmly against the big oak table, examining his hilt, and saying, 'Gently, now, my dear. Your flanconnade was premature, you know. Try a little more subtlety next time. You really are quite a capable opponent – for a woman, that is.'

Marisa lifted her reclaimed rapier threateningly. By now her hair was falling from its ribbon, and she could feel the perspiration wet on her palms. 'Damn you, Delsingham, don't patronise me.'

'Patronise you? I wouldn't dare. Play on, my dear.'

Marisa gasped another oath and lunged again, clumsily. Her hilt was slippery with sweat, and as her foible was raked by Delsingham's forte, she realised, in a flash of instinctive alarm, that the protective button had slipped from her point, so that her blade was naked, lethal. Delsingham saw it too. Parrying with cool precision, he took a step backwards and said quickly,

'Draw back your blade, Marisa. Your point is uncovered.'

But Marisa was wild with rage and humiliation. Crying out, 'What does it matter, when I've come nowhere near

189

you anyway?' she began to press him steadily backwards towards the door, intoxicated with her advantage at last, feinting and thrusting with her arm muscles stiff and outstretched. She saw a flicker of real concern cross his hard face as he slowly gave way, concentrating solely on his defence against her whipping, deadly blade. She saw the light perspiration sheening his clean-shaven jaw, saw the play of the powerful muscles beneath his thin silk shirt as their blades grated and jarred.

'Come to your senses, Marisa,' he snapped, as the point of her blade caught at his shirt just below his armpit and a ragged tear exposed his gleaming, muscle-padded ribcage. Marisa paused, breathing hard, secretly aghast at the dangerous folly she was indulging in. Another half inch and she'd have caught his flesh, drawn blood. And she was endangering herself, because now she could see that he was no longer lazily detached, but was cold, angry, purposeful. Suddenly he whipped up his point deliberately against her forte so that his own protective button flew off. He said between gritted teeth, 'So we're playing that kind of game, are we?' and there was a dazzling glitter of steel and a sliding of his booted feet sideways as his blade caught in the thin silk of her shirt and split the fabric from shoulder to waist, so that her left breast was completely exposed. 'A hit,' he said.

Marisa drew in a deep, shuddering breath, feeling the cool air kissing her pink nipple as it protruded shockingly from the torn fabric. 'You – you could have killed me,' she gasped.

Delsingham smiled, a dangerous, lupine smile. 'Oh, no,' he said softly. 'If I wanted to kill you, then I would, believe me. Are you ready to disarm yet?'

'No, damn you!'

'Very well. If this is how you want to play, then so be it.'

Their blades clashed once more. His point glittered in the shadowy candlelight, slithering lethally down her forte. Marisa wrenched it free with a little sob of indrawn breath, but not before he'd caught at her billowing sleeve with his blade and ripped it almost away. Her upper half virtually naked, she gritted her teeth and lunged forward on her right foot, delivering a lightning thrust in carte. There was a scuffle of blades and she lunged again, her point catching in his loose shirt just an inch above his breeches. She whipped it away, slicing a foot-long scar through the silk, so she could see the flat, hard muscle of his belly tensing as he moved. He swore softly under his breath as they disengaged, and, with his blade lowered and his eyes all the time on Marisa, he deliberately ripped away the last remnants of his torn shirt. Marisa watched him, breathing hard, feeling her heart thudding against her ribs, and not just with exertion. He was magnificent, this beautiful, half-naked male animal who stood before her in the darkening gun room. Her whole world seemed to have narrowed down to a breathtaking vision of those wide, powerful shoulders that tapered enticingly down to his sinuous hips. Inevitably her eyes flickered towards the all too evident bulge of masculinity at his groin, confined into a hard, challenging knot by the tightness of his breeches, and she felt quite faint.

By now her own shirt was in tatters from Delsingham's subtle play, and damp with perspiration. Her upper body was all but naked now, like his. She could feel his eyes on her breasts as they thrust out high and provocative from between the remnants of her slashed shirt. Beneath his dark, purposeful gaze she could feel their pink crests stiffening involuntarily, but the sight didn't put him off his stroke, damn him, as his own body put her off hers. Apparently quite impervious to her near nudity, he was moving again already, and their swords rang together with wrist-bruising ferocity, scraping fiercely before the inevitable disengagement. Delsingham was beginning now to press the attack, but still Marisa fought on more and more wildly, her slim wrist numb from the jarring blows, until she knew with despair that she was tiring, making mistakes. She was also more than a little distracted by the sight of Delsingham's naked torso, and by the sight of his powerful muscles sliding and coiling

191

beneath his perspiration-sheened skin. She backed up further, her eyes on his dangerously exposed blade, knowing with despair that the wall was only a few feet behind her. Already she could smell the musky, virile heat of her opponent's body as he relentlessly pressed on with his attack. No escape. The end must be near, she thought desperately.

He made a sudden feint, and she parried a fraction of a second too late. It was what he'd been waiting for, and his point flashed in under her guard. She tried to counter his attack, but he was bearing her wrist irresistibly upwards until she thought that the delicate bones would snap with the strain, and then, in blind despair, she felt her foil spin away from her aching hand and heard it land with a sickening crash on the floorboards.

She leant back against the wall to steady herself, her legs trembling and her fists clenched, trying to conceal her wild panting. Delsingham was still advancing on her slowly, his sword outstretched. He seemed to tower above her, and his body looked lithe and dangerous.

'The disarm, I think, Miss Brooke. You concede victory?' he said softly.

Her blue eyes blazed up at him. 'No. You took advantage of me. You cheated.'

'How?' he frowned, tossing his blade with a clatter to the floor. He was only inches away from her now. Her eyes were on a level with his chest, and as she gazed helplessly at the enticing curves of gleaming male muscle, the fierce desire licked at her stomach, dragging away the last of her strength. 'By – by distracting me,' she retorted helplessly.

He laughed. He leant slightly forward, resting his hands against the oak-panelled wall on either side of her head so that his wrists were just above her shoulders, while his slate-hard eyes devoured the sight of her small, pouting breasts as they rose and fell rapidly beneath the tattered remnants of her shirt. 'Am I to take it, then, that you don't consider yourself to be a distraction, Miss Brooke?'

Feeling quite faint with wanting him, scarcely able to stand, she tossed back her blonde head defiantly. 'Obviously I'm not a distraction,' she snapped back sharply, 'as you seem able to disregard me quite easily, for weeks on end.'

His grin showed his even white teeth. 'So you've missed me, sweet Marisa?'

'Of course not.'

There was a silence. 'I've missed you,' he said.

She caught her breath. 'What?'

'I've missed you,' he repeated. He was gazing down at her; she could see the golden sparks dancing in his intense grey eyes. 'Oh, my dear, how delicious you are when you're angry.'

And before she could think of escaping, he'd cupped her face gently in his hands, and bent his head to kiss her. His mouth was firm and warm and strong as it persuaded her tremulous lips to part. Then he drew his tongue lightly, caressingly along the line of their parting, and took possession of her, his teeth nipping gently at her silken inner lip, his tongue moving wickedly to ravish her moist inner place with cool masculine intent. Marisa shuddered, feeling her own tongue entwining helplessly with his as his hands slipped round her shoulders, pulling her firmly against him so that her breasts were pressed against his naked chest. She could feel the hardness at his loins nudging with increasing urgency against her slender hips as she arched with instinctive longing towards him.

As if sensing her surrender, he gave a low sigh of triumph, and Marisa froze suddenly. How dare he! How dare he leave her for weeks, without a word, to go and visit the woman they said he was going to marry, only to return, and think he could take her, casually repossess her, just as if she was nothing, just some slut of a backstreet girl whom he could carelessly discard until he felt the need to sate his restless loins on her again. No-one treated her, Marisa Brooke, like that – no-one.

Well, there wasn't much time to prove her point.

Delsingham's breathing was growing heavier, slower as he pressed intimate kisses against her face and throat. His hand had slid from her shoulder to fondle her breast, rubbing at the nipple, and sending shivering darts of longing down to her abdomen. Fighting back her own betraying lust, Marisa stretched her hand behind his back, reaching towards the oak table on which her father's pistol lay. She fumbled for a moment or two, her senses in disarray from his caresses, but at last her fingers fastened round its familiar cold smoothness. She lifted it up, and flexed her wrist to press the pistol's muzzle against his naked back.

His mouth moved away from her throat in stark surprise at the kiss of cold metal against his ribs. 'Marisa?'

'Get away from me,' she said.

He twisted a little, then saw the pistol and laughed. 'Sweet Marisa, what joke is this? You want a duel with pistols now?'

'No,' she replied evenly. She drew the pistol close to her body and pointed it steadily at his chest. 'I want to remind you that this is my house and my property, Delsingham, and I'm not some cheap little doxy you can come to visit whenever you can't think of anyone else to sate your lust on.'

He put his hand out defensively. 'Marisa – '

She cocked the pistol. 'I'm warning you, my lord. I know how to use this toy. Another useful lesson my father taught me.' She fingered the pistol thoughtfully. 'An unfair advantage, strictly speaking, but as you're twice as heavy and powerful as I am, I think I deserve a little assistance, don't you?'

His body was poised and still. 'What are you going to to with me?' he said quietly, watching the gun.

Marisa shrugged. 'I suppose I could just ask you to leave. And yet . . .' Her blue eyes glinted wickedly. 'I'd like you to know how it feels, I think. How it feels to be used, as if you were just some cheap, impulsive purchase, and then discarded without a thought.'

194

And then, as she paused, she heard the voices down below. Lucy and John were back. Her wide blue eyes gleamed maliciously: oh, perfect timing. Keeping her gun pointed on Delsingham, she backed towards the doorway to call out to them, and immediately they came up the stairs, still chattering and laughing together. When they saw Marisa's state of undress, and saw Delsingham pinned against the wall, they fell silent, and Lucy's eyes grew suddenly hot with lust as they alighted on his superb torso.

'Lucy,' said Marisa silkily, 'as you see, we have a surprise visitor. He wasn't invited, Lucy. So we're going to teach him a little lesson, about manners.'

Lucy licked her lips. 'Beautiful,' she murmured, still gazing at Delsingham, her eyes flickering from his starkly muscled chest down to the skintight breeches that covered his well-muscled thighs. 'Quite beautiful. What are we going to do with him, Marisa?'

Marisa gestured to the corner of the gun-room, where the leather harness and belts that were used to store the old weaponry were slung on iron hooks. 'You're going to tie him up, so he can't move. John, help her.' Delsingham made an involuntary move towards the door, but Marisa levelled the gun at him. 'Oh, no,' she said softly. 'You're not going anywhere, my lord.'

Delsingham's face was still as Lucy and John advanced towards him, but he remained silent. Marisa felt herself quicken with excitement as she watched them spreadeagle his arms, and carefully secure each of his wrists to the wall by twisting the supple leather harness around the hooks until the sinews of his shoulders stood out like steel cords. With a surge of power she saw that his arousal had, if anything, increased; the bulge of his genitals against the tight crotch of his breeches was unmistakable.

Still levelling the gun at him, she said steadily, 'I'm going to make you beg me for release, Delsingham. You're a bit too used to people begging you for the favour of your rather splendid cock, my lord, but now you can feel what it's like to wait in humble silence, to be tormented until you can't stand it any more.'

He said nothing but just watched her, a pinioned, silent prisoner who nevertheless dominated the shadowy room with his breathtaking male beauty. Lucy couldn't drag her eyes from him, but John was watching Marisa, his hot eyes feasting on her naked breasts and her loose blonde hair curling round her slender shoulders as she lounged casually on the window seat with her pistol in her hand. Outside, the rain was drumming down coldly against the leaded glass panes, but in here the warm air was tense and expectant.

Marisa was conscious of an insistent beat of excitement throbbing at her own loins. She wasn't quite sure what was going to happen yet, but she knew it was going to be good. And then Lucy came sidling up to her. 'Please. Oh, please, Marisa. I've got an idea.' She whispered carefully in Marisa's ear so Delsingham couldn't hear, and Marisa smiled grimly. 'Go ahead,' she said. 'Do whatever you like.'

Delsingham knew. He could tell, she knew, what he was in for. He kept himself very still in his bonds, but she saw a muscle pulse in his lean jaw. Her eyes slid downwards to the delicious knot of male flesh at his groin, somehow obscenely prominent against the backdrop of his slender, snakelike male hips. The greatest humiliation for him would be that he would enjoy everything they did to him. Lucy would make quite sure of that.

Marisa settled herself back against the window ledge, her booted legs slightly apart, her arms folded across her naked breasts. There was no need for the gun now, because he was trapped. The rain beat down outside as the afternoon light faded, and the solitary candle guttered warningly. The room was filled with the pungent scents of oak, resin, and gunpowder, and the strong musk of heated sexual arousal.

Lucy knew what to do only too well. She sidled across to the spreadeagled man, pulling coquettishly at her own

196

tight bodice and slipping out her full breasts to cup them lusciously in her hands. As she drew near to Delsingham Marisa saw a tremor run through his lean, pinioned frame. Lucy, mimicking the enticements of a Covent Garden flower girl to perfection, jiggled her breasts inches from his face and simpered, 'Well, my fine gent. You're a handsome specimen and no mistake. Like the look of my rosy teats, do you? Like a taste?' She rubbed her breasts mockingly against the hard wall of his chest until her nipples hardened with excitement. He shuddered involuntarily, his eyes half closed, and Lucy, seeing it, laughed. 'I think you do like me, my lord. Let's see what's happening to your beautiful cock, shall we? But first, I think you'd like to take a better look at me.' And with a mischievous smile, she slithered completely out of her dress, letting it rustle to the floor, and stood there clad only in her laced white corset and her silk stockings.

Lucy was plump but shapely. The corset, which was cunningly stiffened with buckram to push her full breasts up and apart, was laced tightly down the front, and came to a point just above the enticing dark curls of her pubic hair. Her thighs were round and creamy above her garters, and her bare bottom-cheeks below the tightly waisted corset were deliciously dimpled. Marisa heard John's grunt of excitement from the shadows as Lucy paraded slowly before the helpless Lord Delsingham, the heels of her little laced-up ankle boots clacking on the floorboards.

'Like what you see?' taunted Lucy to her prisoner. 'Like to stick your cock up me, would you?' Still Delsingham was silent. With a wicked chuckle, Lucy dropped to her knees and began to work at the placket of his breeches. Then she gave a gasp of delight.

His penis sprang out fully erect, and Marisa, watching, fought hard against the desperate renewal of desire between her thighs at the sight of that long, thick member, duskily pulsing with power. Lucy stepped back, breathless with excitement at the sight of the superbly built man standing there pinioned, his arms stretched wide and taut as his lengthy, purple-tipped shaft thrust up helplessly from the hair-roughened pouch of his testicles. Ready for the taking, thought Marisa, wildly imagining that beautiful length of flesh sliding deep within her own melting core.

Lucy, regaining her breath, gave a gurgle of delight. 'Oh, it's beautiful! So long, so thick. Let me taste you and lick you; let me feel your mighty cock in my mouth.' And Delsingham closed his eyes as Lucy's vigorous pink tongue darted out and encircled him. Marisa watched, eyes narrowed, as Lucy slid her full lips avidly over the throbbing muscle of his penis and slid up and down the silky rod with little crooning noises, her hands caressing his flat, taut belly and his seed-filled balls.

Then John, who had been standing silently in the shadows with his fists clenched at his sides and his breath coming in ragged bursts, suddenly moved. Marisa, a little dizzy from the sight of Lucy pleasuring Delsingham's shaft, was about to shout to him, to order him back, but then she realised what he intended, and she went very still.

John had knelt behind Lucy and was grunting as he clumsily pulled his thick penis out of his rough breeches. He pumped it quickly into fulness, and then, while Lucy continued to caress Delsingham avidly with her mouth, John grabbed her plump bottom-cheeks where they flared out beneath her tight corset, pulling them apart and thrusting blindly between her thighs until his cock was anointed with the creamy nectar that flowed between her pink sex-lips. Then, pulling back with a groan, his purple member moving and thrusting with a life of its own, he began to prod blindly at the dark cleft between her buttocks, until the glistening tip of his penis found the tiny pink rosebud of her secret entrance and slipped eagerly up into that tightly collared hole.

Lucy cried out in delight as John tenderly started to ravish her, carefully sliding his thick shaft deeper and deeper between her fiercely clenching bottom-cheeks. In a frenzy of delight, she licked and mouthed avidly at Delsingham's straining phallus, grunting out her pleasure in time to John's manly thrusts. By now Delsingham's head was pressed back helplessly against the wall, and his thin, sensual mouth was compressed against the onslaught of rapture as Lucy's wicked tongue snaked up and down the lengthy, rigid shaft of flesh that jutted fiercely from his loins.

Marisa felt faint as she watched them. In the shadowy candlelight, she could see Delsingham's beautiful silken cock sliding in and out of Lucy's greedy mouth; she could see John's muscular, hairy buttocks pounding away at Lucy's rear, his ballocks swaying against her as the fat, purple stem of his cock eagerly pleasured the gasping Lucy. Marisa longed to join in. Her breasts were painfully tight, the nipples tugging like fiery cords at her abodomen, while the moisture seeped wantonly from her swollen labia. She wanted Delsingham's beautiful, captive body so much; she wanted to kiss his agonised face, to take his cock into her aching core, and run her hands over his straining, sinewed torso, to feel the glory of his orgasm exploding all through his beautiful body.

But there was no time. John was shouting out hoarsely now, reaching round to fumble with Lucy's heavy breasts as he pumped faster and faster. Lucy, with a cry of joy, wriggled back against him, relishing every inch of his glistening fat rod as it penetrated her so deliciously. At the same time she continued to rub at Delsingham's saliva-slick penis with eager hands and fingers, and Marisa saw her prisoner go helplessly rigid as his magnificent penis spasmed into orgasm, sending milky jets of semen gushing over Lucy's plump breasts. Lucy, in the throes of climax herself, rubbed frenziedly against his twitching glans, delighting in the floods of hot seed spilling across her engorged nipples, clutching at his tight, thick testicles as the dark pleasure convulsed his powerful body. John, too, was spent at last, and they were all still. Delsingham, his arms still pinioned high to the wall, stood with his head bowed, while Lucy subsided with a contented sigh to the floor, and John knelt beside her, slowly lapping their prisoner's copious semen off her now soft pink nipples with his long, rough tongue.

Marisa felt suddenly tired and drained. The solitary candle had gone out, and outside it was almost dark, with lowering clouds obscuring the last of the daylight. Walking slowly across the room, she said flatly, 'That's all for now, Lucy, John. You can go.' They nodded their heads and scurried off, pulling their clothes around them as they went, their faces still flushed with exertion. As their footsteps faded away down the stairs, Marisa moved across to Delsingham and began to unstrap his wrists. She concentrated steadfastly on her task, avoiding his gaze, and avoiding too the sight of his now-soft phallus as it hung, still thick and lengthy even in detumescence, against the silken-haired skin of his inner thigh.

'You can go too,' she said shortly as the last of his bonds came free.

He began to rub his wrists gently, bringing back the circulation. Marisa trembled, realising that even now, now that she'd humiliated him, she still wanted him as badly as ever. She'd hoped to make him appear lustful and degraded and stupid as her two servants played with him, but instead he'd been magnificent, and the memory of his hard, silken penis spasming with a life of its own across Lucy's swollen breasts still made her feel faint with longing. She wanted to stroke him into arousal again, wanted to take him for herself, to feel his virile shaft tenderly caressing her, filling her, urging her into the realms of sweet, sensual delight she knew he was so superbly capable of providing.

A fantasy. She'd driven him away now for good, and wasn't that what she wanted? She went slowly to pick up the rapiers and started putting them away in their case. 'You heard me,' she repeated tersely, not looking at him. 'You can go.'

But he was walking up behind her. She could hear the soft fall of his leather boots on the floorboards as he came nearer. He put his hand on the rapier case, and said, quite calmly, 'Why, Marisa?'

She twisted round sharply at his words. 'Why what?'

'Why all that charade?' he said softly, his eyes assessing her. 'Why do you hate me so much, when I thought we were friends?'

She laughed scornfully, planting her hands on her slender hips. 'Friends? I thought you would have described me more as some kind of free whore. Someone you could just come to when you felt like a quick bit of fun. Well, you can't! And maybe the memory of that,' and she nodded sharply at the discarded leather straps on the floor, 'will remind you that you can't just go off to visit the woman you're going to marry and then come back to me!'

'The woman I'm going to marry?' he said. 'What do you mean?'

Marisa caught her breath. 'And now you're trying to deny it. How truly pitiful. I mean Lady Henrietta, of course, who I believe is taking the waters in Bath.'

Delsingham gripped her shoulders, his fingers burning her flesh through the tattered remnants of her shirt. His breeches, still unfastened, were clinging by some miracle to his lean hips; his exposed genitals in their nest of soft dark hair were a threatening reminder of his all too potent masculinity, though he himself seemed calmly indifferent to his nakedness. 'Who told you', he said, in a dangerously quiet voice, 'that I was going to marry Lady Henrietta?'

Marisa tried furiously to twist away from his strong grasp, but failed. 'What does it matter who told me, you bully?'

His fingers tightened painfully around her narrow shoulders; his dark eyes burned her. 'It matters,' he said, 'because it's a lie. There was talk, once, of an alliance between her family and mine, but I never took it any further. I'm not engaged to marry anyone, Marisa.'

She gazed up at him, stunned. 'Then – where have you been all this time?'

'Minding my own business,' he said curtly, 'but I can see that I should have been here, minding yours. What's all this I hear about gypsies, and bullets that just miss you, and fires in the night?'

'How do you know?'

'I have my methods,' he replied grimly.

Again she tried to struggle free of him. 'I don't see that any of it matters to you, Lord Delsingham.'

He shook her. 'It matters because you matter to me, Marisa, damn you! Maddening as you are, I find you quite, quite irresistible, as you can see all too clearly for yourself.'

Her eyes dropped once more to his groin, and widened. Her heart was hammering wildly, but she did her best to sneer up at him coldly in response. 'I can see that your powers of recuperation are quite remarkable, my lord, but so are those of a rutting stag. Am I supposed to be impressed?'

'No,' he said, his eyes narrow slits, his voice husky with restrained desire. 'No, but you're supposed to kiss me, damn you.'

'And you,' she replied angrily, 'are supposed to ask me.'

His breath was coming short and hard now: she could see the hot desire burning in his dark gaze. His hands slipped to her breasts, cupping them, twisting at her throbbing nipples. 'When', he said slowly, his eyes glinting, 'did you ever have any time for men who asked you, Marisa?'

She gasped as the fierce arousal leapt through her body at his touch. 'Never,' she said, with a sudden, tiny ripple of laughter. 'Oh, never,' and with a growl of masculine victory he started to cover her face and breasts with burning kisses.

'A hit?' he said softly.

'Oh, yes,' she murmured breathlessly. 'A veritable hit, my lord . . .' And she sighed aloud with delight as his tongue circled and flicked at her tight pink nipples.

He drew himself away, just for a moment, in order to

lay her carefully back against the big oak table, pillowing her hips and shoulders with cushions he pulled almost savagely from the window seat. Then, desperate for the renewal of his touch, Marisa helped him to ease her buckskin breeches from her hips, slipping them completely away so that he could pull her slender thighs wide apart as they dangled over the edge of the table. She knew that her lush, crinkled feminine flesh was already honeyed with moisture. He ran his fingers teasingly through the pale down of her pubic mound, and let the ball of his thumb separate her darkly engorged labia, spreading them like petals and pushing up gently into her yearning sex with his fingers until she cried out and almost climaxed against him. He let his hand slide away, keeping her teetering deliciously on the brink, straining in exquisite torture, and desperately she reached out to feel for his beautiful, thick penis, guiding its solid length towards her churning hips. He laughed gently, saying, 'Patience, little one,' but Marisa had forgotten the meaning of patience, and as he carefully parted her sex lips and slid the swollen head of his dark shaft into her honeyed passage, she clasped him to her, thrusting her yearning breasts against his warm, wet mouth and clamping her hands round the firm globes of his buttocks, gasping with joy as she felt that beautiful, solid shaft of male flesh slowly driving into her. She arched frantically up to meet him and, sensing that she was well past the point of no return, he reached down carefully with one hand to savour her glistening clitoris as it thrust out hungrily from her parted flesh folds, while continuing to drive his lengthy penis deep within her, and pleasuring her into such a wanton frenzy of lust that her splayed thighs trembled and jerked. She clasped him to her, feeling all that delicious length ravishing her, again and again, until nothing else existed but the sweet, hard pleasure of his penis. She cried out his name, engulfed by the white hot explosion that was rippling out in great, sensual waves from her very core.

He drove himself powerfully into her as he too reached

his climax. She stroked his heaving shoulders as he lay against her breast, feeling her womb still pulsing slowly and sweetly around him.

Afterwards he kissed her very tenderly and helped her to her feet. She leaned dizzily against the table, trying to push her disordered blonde curls back from her face. Her hand strayed to the discarded rapiers. 'I rather think', she said a little distractedly, 'that you were the victor in that particular bout, Lord Delsingham.'

They ate alone that evening in the vast dining room, with a log fire blazing in the great hearth and extravagant branches of candles glittering on the fine crystal and silver plate. They'd ransacked the pantry like children, piling up huge platefuls of cold ham and pickled salmon and Lucy's delicious veal pasties; there were peaches, too, from the glasshouse, and late raspberries, washed down with delicious goblets of claret from the cellar. Marisa felt deliciously lightheaded and carefree, until Delsingham sat back and said, 'And now, Marisa, I think it's time you told me exactly what's been going on while I've been away. Don't you?'

She told him reluctantly about her feeling of being watched all the time, and the shots that just missed her, and the fire, although in reality she just wanted to forget about it all. He listened silently and sipped at his wine, showing no reaction until she mentioned the incident with Seth. She didn't tell him everything, but she told him that they'd beaten the gypsy brutally, apparently on someone's orders, and at that his expression grew hard.

'You've no idea who arranged it?'

She shrugged carelessly, trying to seem unconcerned, though the memory of Seth's terrible punishment still made her cold with fear. 'I assumed at first that it must be someone who doesn't like me being here at Melbray Manor. But then, the other night, I remembered that something happened in London, before I even heard about my inheritance.'

He refilled her glass. 'Tell me,' he said.

So she told him about the raid on the Blue Bell, explaining how at first everyone thought it was the magistrates, making one of their forlorn gestures against the illegal gaming dens that infested that part of London, only now they knew that it wasn't, because her attorney Mr Giles had made discreet enquiries, and the magistrates knew nothing about it.

Delsingham frowned, listening to her carefully. 'A private vendetta, then.'

'So it would seem, especially as my rooms bore the brunt of the raid. They stole or destroyed nearly everything. Not that I had much,' she addded wryly.

He said, 'It could well be the same person who's trying to frighten you off here, though I suppose it's always possible you have more than one enemy. You're taking care of yourself, Marisa? Not going out by yourself, and locking up well at night?'

She nodded. 'Yes, I keep my pistol with me all the time. And of course I've got John and Lucy, who are alert and quick witted. It's not as if I've never faced danger before. But – ' and her eyes shadowed suddenly, 'I feel frightened this time, because I feel as if somebody hates me.'

'What, you, frightened?' He touched her cheek gently. 'The girl I first met striding around London in her breeches and greatcoat, exchanging coarse insults with coachmen and defying the world?'

She smiled back, but her eyes were still troubled. 'This is different, James. You see, in London I knew who my enemies were.'

He reached out his hand and put it calmly over hers. 'Then it seems as if perhaps you need a little help from me.'

She drew her hand back quickly. 'I can manage. I can look after myself: I've always had to in the past!'

'I know. But Marisa, let me help you this time. Let me stay with you for a little while, and perhaps together we can track your enemy down.'

She hesitated. The idea was desperately tempting. She imagined sleeping with his arms around her, knowing that he would make her feel safe and exquisitely cherished. But it was one of her rules, to take her pleasure where she pleased, but to sleep alone.

As if guessing her thoughts, he said quietly, 'I'm not asking you for any sort of commitment, Marisa. Neither of us want to lose our independence; we both know that. But I would like to be with you for a while, because I think we can offer each other company, and pleasure.'

She glanced up at him mischievously, her resistance broken. 'Pleasure? Again?'

His mouth twisted into a grin. 'Most definitely. Remember what you said earlier about my powers of recuperation?'

She laughed, feeling suddenly very happy. He got to his feet and swung her up into his arms as if she weighed nothing, then he carried her up the wide staircase to her chamber. There he laid her gently on the bed, then drew the curtains and bolted the door and turned back to her, smiling in the darkness.

Chapter Ten

*T*he bright, lush greens of early summer turned into the heavy ripeness of late August. As the corn turned gold in the fields under gentian-blue skies, and the birds grew silent in the dusty heat, Marisa felt lazy and voluptuous, as if she, too, was ripening in the hot sun.

Lord James Delsingham stayed with her most nights at Melbray Manor. Marisa filled the house with lushly scented roses from the garden, and dressed in flimsy, sprigged muslins and little straw bonnets trimmed with pastel ribbons. When he wasn't there, because of course he had his own, much larger estate and tenant farms to see to, she sat dreaming in the sun, or wandered aimlessly through the cool shrubberies of the garden, thinking of him. He'd sent some of his own men over to work on her land, and, he said, to keep an eye on her. The feeling of being cherished and protected was quite new to Marisa, and she revelled in it.

At night they would make love passionately, and afterwards Marisa would lie on the crisp linen bedsheets with the casements thrown open to the cool night air, gazing at him as he slept. Often he would wake up and turn to her, smiling lazily, and draw her into his arms to kiss her and make love to her all over again. It was a dream-like summer, and Marisa shut the future resolutely from her mind.

During the long, hot afternoons Delsingham taught her to drive his high phaeton. They laughed together as she learned, but she was an apt pupil, and soon she was bowling capably along the leafy lanes of the neighbourhood in the fast, sporty vehicle, showing off the new, dark-blue riding habit she'd had made, which she wore with a ruffled silk shirt and a little velvet hat with sweeping feathers. Delsingham was a member of the Four Horse Club, and renowned as a whip, so when he quietly praised her deft handling of his team she felt a secret burst of pride.

From time to time they were invited separately to social events in the neighbourhood, and they greeted one another with cool politeness, taking pleasure in concealing the intensity of their relationship from their neighbours. Later, alone together, they would laugh at the absurdities of their fellow guests, and Delsingham would chide Marisa for the way so many besotted male guests trailed around after her.

'Their wives hate me,' laughed Marisa. It was another hot, breathless night. They were lying together on her big four-poster bed, with Marisa clad in the flimsiest cream silk wrap and pale stockings, while Delsingham, who had undressed down to his breeches, pulled himself up from the pillows and poured them both chilled champagne. He had filled the little brick-built ice-house in her garden with ice from his own store, and the cold, sparkling wine was one of her greatest pleasures.

He handed her a glass, and watched her as she sipped happily at it. 'Their wives hate you because you're beautiful and clever.'

Marisa gazed at him. 'They also hate me because I've got you.'

The champagne was cool and delicious, and she drank it with relish, feeling the heady bubbles stinging against the roof of her mouth. Then slowly, deliberately, she leant across his groin, letting her hair and breasts brush

208

his hard belly. She unfastened his breeches to cup his already stirring penis in her hands, then slowly she drew her tongue across the dark, wrinkled pouch of his balls, taking them one by one into her mouth and sucking at the tender globes. He gasped, and wickedly she moved her mouth along the silken shaft of his veined phallus, loving the way it sprang and stiffened beneath her caress. He leant back with a little shudder against the pillows, his hands behind his head, his eyes tightly closed in the intensity of his pleasure. Marisa, lifting herself, sipped more of the champagne, then took him immediately in her mouth so that the cold sharpness of the wine cooled his hot penis and made him groan aloud with delight. Tantalisingly she repeated her ministrations, sipping at the champagne to cool her velvety lips and tongue then sliding her mouth up the silky pole of his flesh, feeling it thicken and swell inexorably, grazing the back of her throat, until at last he clutched his hands in her hair and she felt him start to thrust urgently against the back of her throat. Quickly she slid her fingers round his hips to cup his taut, muscular buttocks, then she eased one finger into his tight anal crevice, teasing rhythmically at the quivering little hole while her lips continued to suck on his thrusting penis. He began to shudder in violent ecstasy at the dual assault, and at last she felt his whole body go rigid as he started to spurt his hot seed into her mouth. She swallowed avidly, relishing his ecstasy, loving the movements of his shadowy, convulsing body. He was hers, all hers.

Moments later he laid her gently back against the silk bedspread to reciprocate with his own tongue, driving it deep within her soaking cleft and moving it about with gentle thrusting movements so that she melted with liquid desire, while at the same time he rubbed his high-bridged nose against her throbbing clitoris. She cried out his name urgently and arched into a fierce climax, parting her thighs as wide as she could and grinding her vulva against his delicious tongue and lips, sobbing aloud as he steadfastly extracted every last ounce of pleasure from her trembling body.

Afterwards he poured them more champagne, and Marisa nestled contentedly into the crook of his shoulder, murmuring sleepily, 'You're the ace in the pack, James. Have I told you that? The only one I've ever come across.'

He laughed. 'And are aces high or low?'

'High, of course. That was why I stole that invitation with the ace of spades in the corner. It intrigued me.'

'And I didn't disappoint?'

'Oh, no.' She curled up her smooth, slender legs against his powerfully-muscled thighs, loving the way they caressed her. 'Not at all.'

His arm tightened round her. There was a pause, then he said, 'Marisa. There's something I want to say to you.'

His voice was suddenly serious. Something constricted round her heart like a cold fist, and instantly she was quite sober. He was going to tell her that it was over. Pleasure, no commitment, that was their mutual bargain. Their summer idyll couldn't last for ever.

And didn't she know it already? From the moment she'd met him, she'd known he was wildly beyond her reach. In spite of her inheritance, she, Marisa Brooke, the daughter of a shiftless army deserter, could never belong in his world. She fought down the sudden sick feeling rising in her throat. 'Neither of us want to lose our independence,' he'd warned her. She should never have allowed her to feel like this about anyone, never.

She turned to him with light, laughing eyes, and drawled lazily, 'Dear James, you sound very serious all of a sudden. What is there to be serious about? This is a delicious summer interlude. We both know that very soon it will be over.'

He frowned. 'Marisa, I have to go away for a few days, into Winchester, on business. There are some things we should discuss – '

She pressed her finger lightly against his mouth. 'Let's not shadow the end with discussions and declarations, shall we? I'd much, much rather you kissed me than talked to me.'

Still he hesitated, his dark eyes sombre, but then he kissed her, and they didn't talk any more.

Delsingham had said that he would be back from Winchester in a few days, and Marisa, trying hard to pretend that his absence meant absolutely nothing to her, went out riding by herself in defiance of his instruction that she must never go out alone. By now the days were growing noticably shorter; there was a heavy dew on the lawns in the morning, and the horse chestnuts that lined the sweeping drive were revealing more than a hint of burnished gold amongst their heavy green foliage.

She rode as far as the beech woods, and was just turning her mare slowly back when she caught a glimpse of a shadowy movement in the trees. Her horse shied in alarm, and she struggled to control it, her heart in her mouth, as a man moved quickly out into the open. 'Seth! It's you.' She breathed a sigh of relief as she recognised the gypsy, conscious that her heart was hammering madly.

'Marisa,' he said quickly. 'I'm sorry to have startled you.'

She guided her horse nearer to him and he stroked its neck, calming it with his usual magical skill with horses. 'How wonderful to see you, Seth,' Marisa said warmly. 'How are you?'

'Well enough.' His face seemed strangely closed. 'But I've something to tell you. It's about Lord Delsingham.'

Marisa caught her breath. Something in the way the gypsy said his name warned her that Seth felt no kindness towards Delsingham.

'Yes?' she said quickly. 'What about him?'

He gazed up at her. 'I know how things are between you and him, Marisa. Reckon everyone does in these parts. But I just thought you ought to know that he was seen a couple of days ago, talking to that man with the ginger hair – the man called Varley. You remember him, Marisa?'

Marisa's fingers tightened round her reins. She felt rather dizzy and sick. How could she forget? 'You're trying to tell me that Lord Delsingham was talking to the man who attacked you, Seth?'

He held her gaze steadily. 'Aye, that's right. They were seen together at the fair up Winchester way, two days ago.'

Marisa shook her head, bewildered. 'Perhaps it was just a coincidence, a chance word, Seth.'

'Lord Delsingham gave him money, Miss Marisa. The two of them were seen whispering together for several minutes, then Delsingham passed the ruffian gold. It's the truth. We gypsies have our ways of knowing everything. I thought you ought to know.' He nodded his head and moved to go. Marisa called out rather wildly, 'Wait, Seth, wait! What is it you're trying to say?'

He turned back, gazing up at her steadily. 'I'm trying to say nothing, Marisa, just telling you the facts. Reckon you can draw your own conclusions just as well as me. You'll know well enough that there's some of the gentry who wouldn't relish the idea of a gypsy man taking pleasure with a lady they'd a mind to. Take care.'

Then he went, vanishing like a shadow into the woodland. Marisa couldn't have thought of any words to keep him.

Normally Marisa would have thought nothing of Delsingham's absence, and would simply have busied herself in different kinds of pleasure around her lovely home, always with the awareness at the back of her mind that on his return there would be a delicious reunion. But now she worried all the time, with dark, unstated fears at the back of her mind.

She found it impossible to believe that Lord Delsingham had anything to do with poor Seth's dreadful degradation. But why had he been talking to that hateful man Varley? She remembered Delsingham's frown of concentration when she'd told him just a little about the vile assault on Seth; she remembered how very little he'd said about it, though he questioned her thoroughly about all the other incidents that had worried her. And she suddenly remembered how he'd come quietly and unannounced into her house that afternoon when she was trying out her foils in the gun-room. Had he thought the house was empty? If so, what was he planning?

Suspicion came as second nature to Marisa. She'd found, during her eventful life, that it was a lot safer than trusting people. She suddenly looked at the men that Delsingham had sent over to work on her estate, with a view, he'd said, to keeping an eye on the place as well. They were quiet and self-contained, sleeping in the stable quarters instead of in the main house, and even Lucy couldn't coax a smile from them. Once, Marisa got back early from her morning ride and found one of them coming out of her study, where she kept all her papers and business documents. He'd looked embarrassed, and said he was looking for Lucy, but Marisa knew he was lying. Suddenly, instead of feeling protected by the presence of Delsingham's men, she began to feel spied on, trapped.

Then one afternoon, while Delsingham was still away, Sir Julian Ormond called by to say he was going away for a while. He asked her to sign several papers that were connected, he said, with her latest investment, and Marisa, feeling the familiar panic at the sight of all those close-written words, signed them quickly. Ormond took them back and said after a moment's hesitation, 'Is Lord Delsingham here, Marisa?'

'No,' said Marisa with apparent unconcern. 'He's away for a few days. He had to go up to Winchester on business, I believe.'

Ormond seemed to hesitate. He paced the room a little, and the sun that shone through the tall windows sparkled on the immaculate lace that spilled forth at his neck and wrists. He turned back to her suddenly. 'Marisa, I hate to

213

see you hurt. Delsingham is rather notorious, you know, with regard to women.'

Marisa felt her breath catch in her throat. Then she said, 'A little while ago, you told me he was engaged, but that was untrue.'

Ormond moved forward then stopped, his hand on the back of a chair. 'Only because Delsingham broke it off, a short while ago. Lady Henrietta's family were devastated. London is apparently still ringing with the scandal. Delsingham is very attractive to women, I believe. You really should be wary of him, Marisa.'

Marisa said coldly, 'Is there anything else, or have you just come to regale me with country tattle?'

His face seemed to close up. 'I just want you to be careful, Marisa. You do realise, don't you, that Delsingham has nothing at all to gain by marrying you? He already has enormous wealth, and would only marry for the sake of some connection with one of the highest or most influential families in the land.'

Marisa suddenly moved towards the window, turning back to him with a brittle smile. 'I really must inform you, sir, that I have no intention of marrying anyone, ever. I do appreciate your assistance in managing my finances, but I require no advice whatsoever in the matter of my private life. And now, if you please, I see that the groom is bringing your horse round to the front door. Thank you for your concern, but I consider that my friendship with Delsingham has nothing at all to do with you.'

Ormond bowed his head, and a muscle flickered in his tense jaw. 'Of course. But there is one more thing. I am reluctant to mention it, but I really think you ought to know that Lord Delsingham has made arrangements for an investigation into your financial affairs.'

Marisa, white lipped, took a step forward. 'What?'

'It's true, I'm afraid. I received a quiet word from Newmans, the London bankers who have charge of some of your money, that he's been trying to pry into your investments. Unless – ' and he looked at her sharply,

214

'unless I've made a mistake, and he had your permission to do so.'

Marisa felt dazed, suddenly remembering how she'd caught one of Delsingham's men in her study. 'No. No, he certainly didn't . . .' She moved over to the window so her back was to him, not wanting to be under his anxious scrutiny any longer. When she'd composed herself, she turned back to him. 'Thank you for your visit, Sir Julian. I shan't detain you any longer. Just one thing before you go: I find myself in need of a little of my capital. Could you arrange for some of my investments to be sold, say to the value of two thousand pounds?'

He seemed to hesitate, then said smoothly, 'Of course. But it might take a week or two. Leave it with me.'

He went at last, leaving her feeling restless and unhappy. Later that morning, she summoned the man-servants who had been sent to her by Lord Delsingham, and she dismissed them all.

Late one evening, Lord Delsingham returned. Marisa, who was half-heartedly gossiping with Lucy in the drawing room, heard the clatter of his horse's hooves in the courtyard, and her heart started to thump uncontrollably.

Lucy ran to the windows and pulled back the heavy drapes. 'It's Lord Delsingham,' she cried out happily. 'All by himself. John's out there taking his horse.'

Marisa, getting to her feet, said quietly, 'Perhaps you'll open the door to him, Lucy. I'll see him in here.'

Lucy rushed out eagerly, and a few moments later Lord James Delsingham strode in, his high-crowned hat in his hand.

'Marisa,' he said swiftly. 'Are you all right? I expected to see some of my men here, but John tells me they've all gone. Why? Has something happened?'

Marisa stood very still in front of the fire. She wore a gown of palest green tulle, and her fair curls were bound up loosely in a green satin bandeau. She folded her hands in front of her. 'I sent them away,' she said.

His brow darkened. 'Why? They were there to protect you, Marisa, as well as to work for you. Why did you tell them to go?'

She held her head high to met his burning gaze. 'I need to be independent, James. I need to know what's going on around me. I don't like to be surrounded by someone else's spies.'

He stepped forward angrily. 'Spies?'

'Yes – spies! I – I can't afford to trust anyone. Can't you see that?'

He said in a low voice, 'You don't even trust me, Marisa?'

She shook her head. 'Least of all you. And I think you know why.'

He moved swiftly towards her and gripped her shoulders until his fingers bit into the pale, filmy fabric of her gown, and his face blazed down on hers as he cried out, 'No, I don't know why. Tell me, damn you.'

She held herself rigid in his arms and said, 'You've been investigating my affairs, haven't you?'

He went suddenly still. 'How do you know?'

Marisa felt the onslaught of real despair then, because he hadn't even tried to deny that he'd written to her bankers and set his men to spy around her house. 'Does it matter?' she breathed.

He said heavily, 'No, I don't suppose it does. If you don't trust me enough even to want to talk about it, then there's nothing more to be said at all. And if you trust that crook Ormond with your money, then you deserve everything you've got coming to you.'

Her throat was burning with unshed tears, because she'd never seen him look so angry. 'Why should I trust you,' she breathed, 'when you were seen at Winchester fair, talking to that man who attacked Seth so vilely? How do you explain that?'

He took a deep breath and said through gritted teeth, 'Ever since you told me of it, I've been trying to track down the people who were responsible for that outrage, trying to find out who paid them to do it. You're still in danger, Marisa – don't you realise?'

She shook her head, her face white with distress. 'How can I believe you? You were seen giving money to that vile man. How do I know that you weren't the one who paid him for what he did? I learnt long ago that I can't afford to trust anyone, anyone at all. Can't you see that?'

Slowly he let his hands drop to his sides. His face was harsh and drained as he gazed down at her. At last he said, 'Marisa. If you trusted no-one else, ever, you could have trusted me. Remember that. But I don't stay to argue my case with anyone. I'm going. You've made it quite clear that you value your stubborn independence more than my friendship. You know where to find me if you change your mind.'

He turned and went out, and she heard the big front door thudding behind him. As his horse's hooves clattered away down the drive, Marisa was left standing there white faced, her eyes burning and dry. She wouldn't cry, she told herself fiercely. She wouldn't.

Rowena was back with the gypsies again, and she was glad. Ormond had told her he was going away for a while, to London, so she and Matty were no longer required in his household. Rowena had a feeling it was something to do with Ormond's vendetta against Marisa Brooke, and she was delighted. He'd given her gold too, and she pretended to be sorry to leave, but really it was good to be back with her friends, to be sitting here beside the fire on this warm, still night with the stars out overhead, and the gossip of the other Romanies a distant, comforting murmur. Seth was away buying horses, and his absence disappointed her, but Caleb was here. She sat by the fire with him drinking lots of rough wine, and scornfully told him about Ormond's cold, aristocratic ways, and his fondness for being humiliated. Caleb growled and took her hand, making her feel the hefty bulge at his groin. 'You need a real man, girl, don't you?'

217

'Oh, I do that, Caleb,' she laughed, nuzzling against him. 'I need to feel your big, fine cock up inside me.'

He bent to kiss her roughly, but just then one of the mean, skinny lurchers that encircled the gypsy camp began to bark suddenly. Caleb pulled away, annoyed. 'What's that dog rowing about, blast him?' He went off to investigate, and came back a few moments later, grinning.

'There's a mighty fine gentleman loitering over beyond the trees. Says he has a fancy for a hot gypsy wench.' Caleb opened his clenched fist, letting her see the gleam of a gold coin in his hand. 'He also says there's more where that came from.'

Rowena got hurriedly to her feet, smoothing down her full crimson skirts and swinging her hips. 'Well, now. And what does this fine gent want me to do?'

'Why, tell his fortune, of course,' chuckled Caleb, and patted her behind affectionately as she moved off towards the trees, an anticipatory smile on her face and a nearly full bottle of wine in her hand.

A fine gent. Rowena wondered suddenly if it was Ormond, come back from London, but no, Caleb knew him by sight and would have told her.

She caught her breath when she saw the man standing in the shadow of a clump of birches. A fine gent indeed: tall and handsome as could be, with long, fine legs in those tight breeches and boots, and a ruffled white shirt and cream silk waistcoat that showed off his lovely broad shoulders. Rowena licked her lips. Then she drew nearer, and she realised who it was: Lord James Delsingham, owner of Fairfields, the biggest place hereabouts, and the one they said the fine ladies went wild for, especially Miss Marisa Brooke.

Well, well. And he'd come looking for her. She, Rowena, would certainly give him something to remember. She moved her shoulders slightly so that her smocked blouse slipped down to reveal the creamy upper swell of her breasts in the moonlight, while her nipples were like dark berries, just visible beneath the wispy fabric. She said in her husky voice, 'You wanted me, my lord?'

He gazed down at her, his beautiful mouth curving in a glimmer of a smile. 'Try persuading me,' he said softly.

She sidled up to him, her lips pouting provocatively, and reached up to draw one finger down his lovely lean cheek. Then she pulled lightly at her blouse again, so that it slipped to show all of her breasts, with the tawny nipples already tingling and stiffening. She rubbed them gently against his silk shirt, feeling the long protuberances drag from side to side against his hard male chest in delicious arousal. Reaching up with one hand, still clutching her wine bottle in the other, she pulled his dark head down and kissed him languorously, reaching and probing with her pink tongue and letting its tip flicker in the intimate recesses of his lovely mouth. She gasped when she felt him respond, felt his powerful long tongue thrusting back and entwining with hers, probing in a divine pretence of copulation as he slipped his hands round her back and pulled her towards him.

Rowena gasped at the pressure of his narrow hips, where the exquisite bulge of his hardening genitals was all too obvious through the fine wool of his smooth-fitting breeches. She pulled away a little to get her breath, gazing up at him with glittering green eyes, devouring him. 'Let's go over there, my lord,' she whispered. 'I know a little clearing where we'll be nice and private – as private as you could wish.'

He nodded, and she led him to a moonlit dell in the woods, where the mossy turf was studded with buttercups. She sank down onto the grass, drawing him with her, feeling desperately excited at his proximity, and while he settled himself she took a deep swig of the wine she still held, feeling it race through her blood. Then she handed it to him, enjoying watching the muscles of his throat as he swallowed. Beautiful, she thought dreamily as she gazed at his perfect profile, the most beautiful man I've ever seen. No wonder they say the women run wild for him. She thought suddenly of Marisa Brooke, and her eyes grew hard.

Well, she decided triumphantly, he must have tired of Miss Marisa Brooke, mustn't he? And she, Rowena, would give him something to remember. She reached for his hand to place it on her hot, swollen breasts, and he stroked them softly, pulling at her nipples. Gasping as the tawny crests sprang out at his touch, she let her thighs fall apart beneath her full skirt, feeling the cool night air whispering against the lush folds of her vulva. A sudden fierce spasm of desire shook her and the moisture trickled down her thighs as she anticipated the feel of his beautiful, strong penis.

He was watching her, assessing her as he pulled and teased lazily at her dark, throbbing teats. 'Well, mister,' she gasped a little faintly, 'are you going to get on with it, or what?'

He laughed. 'What a hot little gypsy girl you are.'

With a muttered curse of impatience, she ran her hands up his lovely strong thighs and began to struggle with the fastening of his fancy breeches. At last his cock sprang out, already dark and rigid, and she licked her lips and moaned as she caressed its silky, long shaft with trembling fingers. 'Please, mister,' she whispered, 'take me now! Stick your lovely juicy cock into me. You needn't pay me anything at all. I just want to feel you inside me . . .'

He arched himself over her, and she reached to touch his penis with impatient fingers, pulling back her full skirts with her other hand and rubbing avidly at her own swollen labia. Then she stretched out her thighs and opened herself to him, longing for the penetration of that throbbing, engorged shaft; her pleasure bud was a stiff little rod of tingling sensation, yearning to be caressed. She moaned out as she felt the smooth, rounded glans nudge at her glistening sex-lips, and raked at his shoulders, but he caught her hands, pushing them back to the ground above her head, and kneeling between her thighs, pinioning her as his long, stiffened penis danced just a fraction of an inch away from her soft-petalled vulva. Rowena cried out in longing, trying to lift her hips to meet him and enfold him, but he was powerful, even more powerful than she'd realised, and she was trapped. 'Please, mister,' she begged, her eyes hot, 'don't keep me waiting. Please, stick it up me . . .'

His grey eyes suddenly seemed hard and dangerous, and she noticed how tiny gold sparks seemed to flicker in them, like flames. He said, in a low, clear voice,

'You'll have what you want in a moment, gypsy girl. But first, I want you to tell me a few things.'

Rowena blinked dizzily, trapped beneath his weight, her hands pinioned. There was something inhuman about this one. What other man, with a great, throbbing cock poised just above her parted legs, would want to talk, for God's sake? A little frightened, she said, 'Depends on what you want to know, doesn't it?'

His mouth a thin compressed line, he lowered his snakelike hips, letting his lovely bone-hard cock slide just an inch into her moist, soft flesh. She gasped with delight, clutching at him with her inner muscles, and her gasp turned into a sob of disappointment as he slowly withdrew. He watched her reactions, and said softly 'Tell me a little about Sir Julian Ormond.'

Rowena's eyes flashed defensively. 'Not much to tell,' she said scornfully. 'Oh!' She gasped in delight as his quivering, beautifully controlled phallus nudged again between her silken sex-lips.

'I'm not too interested in the intimate details,' he said, 'but I would like to know what interest Ormond has in Marisa Brooke.'

'How should I know?'

His hands were tight around her wrists. 'I think you know quite a lot.'

'Well, he has her watched, has his men spying on her. Nothing wrong in that, is there?'

'Why?' His voice was hard.

Rowena was suddenly frightened of him. She guessed he knew everything anyway. Why was he asking her?

She went on hurriedly, 'He hates her, of course, because he reckons that the house and everything should have been his. But he seems to think he'll have her out of there quickly enough.'

Delsingham's hands tightened again warningly. 'How? How will he get her out?'

''Cause all her money's gone, or something like that.' Delsingham seemed to swear softly under his breath. Rowena muttered sulkily, 'Are you going to do it to me, or not? Can't wait for ever.'

He ground his penis slowly into her, and lowered his head to her breasts, using his strong tongue to flick her long, straining nipples to and fro. The fierce delight shot straight down to her throbbing clitoris, as if he was actually tonguing that little stem of flesh, teasing it with his teeth, sucking on it with his hot wet mouth. At the same time the sweet length of his penis slid into her, filling her aching void, and she flushed and shuddered against him. 'Oh, yes! Yes, that's better, my beauty – fuck me now, harder, please, I'm nearly there . . .'

He slid out and poised himself above her as she gasped with loss and writhed her hips beneath him.

'And the fire?' he said meditatively. 'The fire that was deliberately started in the stable block at Melbray Manor?'

'He said he'd kill me if I ever told.'

Delsingham moved himself into her again, just parting her puffy, glistening labia, and thrust gently, teasingly in and out of her. She strained towards him, desperate to pull him inside herself as the beautiful, shimmering sensations of fulfilment hovered just out of reach. She lifted her head and saw his penis thrusting wickedly above the fiery nest of her pubic hair, its shaft dark and thick and long. Oh, if only he'd pound into her. If only he'd drive his delicious cock deep within her, so she could fasten herself round it, and feel the blissful waves of release pour through her . . .

'Tell me,' he whispered softly.

'Why, one of Ormond's men started it, of course,' she

lied frantically. 'He wanted to frighten her, to drive her away. It was the same with the broken saddle, and the same with what those men did to Seth.'

'Did you know what they were going to do to Seth?'

'No. I told that bastard Ormond that Seth was with Marisa, because I hated her, but I didn't want them to hurt him. Please, mister, do it to me, let me feel your lovely cock sliding into me . . .'

'Why do you hate Marisa Brooke?'

'Because she's a whore, a filthy little whore pretending to be a fine lady. She gambled with us gypsies at Vauxhall, for sex, that was where she first put her spell on Seth. Loved it all, she did, getting us to play games, making fools of us all. She bared her titties, and let my Seth cream all over them. She's a fancy slut!' Rowena got one of her hands free at last, and grabbed for his hips in desperation. The memory of the fierce pleasuring in Vauxhall Gardens that night, as Caleb took her from behind and the others sported lasciviously around her, had brought her almost to the brink. 'Are you going to punish me now, mister? Don't be angry with me, will you? You've got such a beautiful cock.'

Delsingham said, 'I have my own ways of punishing people,' and then, slowly, unbelievably, he began to get to his feet. Rowena lay there, naked and shivering, her face incredulous as he carefully eased his still-rigid penis back into his breeches and rearranged his clothing.

'What the hell are you playing at?' she demanded angrily. 'You promised me money.'

He casually tossed a gold sovereign; it landed close by her head. 'There you are. Easy money for you, I should say.' And he turned and started to go.

'Damn you!' she called after him. 'Damn you, you're as perverted as Ormond.'

He laughed back over his shoulder. 'Dear God, I sincerely hope not.'

Caleb was waiting a few yards away in the shadows, spying on them, hungrily rubbing at his swollen penis beneath his breeches as he watched their sex-play. Now he was bewildered, because the fine lord had seemed to have changed his mind, and was coming towards him as if he'd known all the time that he was there. Caleb flushed angrily as the man stopped and said, 'Enjoying yourself? I hope so, because you're needed rather urgently over there.' He nodded back towards where Rowena lay, then strolled on. Caleb glared at him suspiciously and hurried down to the little glade.

'That was mighty quick,' he said to Rowena suspiciously. 'Did he pay you?'

Rowena hissed, 'Yes, he paid me, damn him, and that was about all. Quickly, Caleb . . .' Even as he crouched beside her, she was pushing her hand inside his breeches, pulling out his meaty cock and pumping it into full hardness. Grunting with surprised pleasure, Caleb leaped astride her and began to thrust vigorously, feeling Rowena climaxing almost instantly beneath him as she writhed her hips against his big, stalwart penis. Caleb came too, driving himself hard, swept away by her feverish excitement.

'So much for the fine gentry,' he grunted in satisfaction as his lengthy shaft spasmed repeatedly inside her. 'What you needed was a real man up you, eh, my beauty?'

Rowena said bitterly, 'Caleb, you're a clumsy great fool.' She pushed him off, and went to wash herself in the cool little stream that ran nearby. He lay there in the darkness shaking his head, his eyes blank with puzzlement.

Some days later, Marisa stood in the cool oak-panelled hall of Melbray Manor, breathing in the now familiar aroma of the old tapestry hangings, the carved wooden furniture and the dark, smoke-stained oil paintings that were relics of a previous age. From the open door, mingling subtly with the scent of beeswax and wood, came the fragrance of late summer roses and lavender, and she could hear the faint sounds of singing in the distance as Lucy cheerfully polished the copper pots and pans in the old, stoneflagged kitchen. She rested her hand on the carved balustrade and remembered how Delsingham had carried her up the wide oak staircase on that first night they spent together, laughing as she pretended to struggle and protest, silencing her at last with his all too devastating kisses in the shadowy, silk-hung stillness of her bedroom.

Well. That was all over. And now it was necessary for her to pay a visit to her bank in Crayhampton. Several bills were pressing, and Ormond, her adviser, was away from home, having forgotten, it seemed, to provide her with the money she'd asked him for. Letting John drive the carriage, she called in at the offices of Smith and Tavitt, her bankers in the High Street, and enquired discreetly about getting access to the investments Ormond had made for her. She felt nervous, because anything to do with official transactions sent her mind into a state of helpless inadequacy.

The banker checked through the sheaf of papers she silently handed him, and when he'd finished his face was grave. 'You've been badly advised, I'm afraid, Miss Brooke. These shares have collapsed. It's been a bad time for the manufacturing industries. Now the war is over, foreign competition has undermined the trade badly.'

Marisa's fingers tightened round her little velvet reticule, not quite taking it in. 'And my investments in the shipping venture? Are they accessible, Mr Tavitt?'

His earnest grey head jerked up at that, and he leafed through the papers again. 'I have no record of them here. You put your money into shipping? My dear Miss Brooke, I fear that your investments have been catastrophic. You have other capital elsewhere, I hope?'

Other capital? Somewhere outside in the street a dog barked, breaking the heavy silence. 'Why, yes,' Marisa lied, knowing full well that she hadn't. Her own voice sounded strangely distant in her ears. The room seemed to be ebbing and swaying around her. Her money, all her money, gone.

'I'm glad to hear it,' said Mr Tavitt concernedly.

'And of course,' went on Marisa rather breathlessly, 'I

have the house and the land. I could always raise money on them. That's what people do, isn't it?'

Edward Tavitt leaned forward across his desk, his thin, kindly face really anxious now. 'But my dear Miss Brooke, the house and land are already mortgaged up to the hilt.' He pushed a document towards her. 'It's all here. You must have realised that, surely? You signed the papers for that transaction only the other day. Sir Julian Ormond brought them in, saying that you needed the money rather quickly, so you'd asked him to see to it all for you. I was surprised at the time, but I assumed you knew what you were doing.'

Marisa tried to look calm as the rows of incomprehensible words spun once more before her eyes, though she felt ill with shock. 'So you gave Ormond access to the money?'

'Of course. After all, you'd signed the additional papers giving him power as your sole executor. Miss Brooke, is anything wrong? You look quite pale, my dear. Can I fetch you anything? A glass of cordial, perhaps, or some tea?'

Marisa had risen to her feet, controlling herself with a supreme effort, though she knew her face must be quite white. Brandy, perhaps, a rather strong brandy. 'No, I'm fine, thank you. I'm sorry to have troubled you, Mr Tavitt. Everything is quite in order, I assure you. Good day to you.'

She made her way down the narrow stairs in a state of numbness and stood for a moment on the crowded pavement, trembling with cold in spite of the warm sun.

Everything – everything gone. She'd let Ormond dupe her, wilfully trusting him against all Delsingham's advice; in fact, she'd befriended him initially just to spite Lord Delsingham. She'd been too proud, too vulnerable in her own weakness to ask anyone for advice about the papers Ormond was asking her to sign; too proud to admit to anyone that she couldn't even make out half the words, let alone understand them.

Stunned, she rejoined John and Lucy, who were waiting by her carriage, and told John to drive her home. It was no easy task to weave through the narrow streets of Crayhampton, because it was market day, and the pavements were thronged. She gazed silently out of the window, all the figures and faces just a blur to her, until suddenly she stiffened, because she'd caught sight of two young women watching her with bold eyes as her carriage rolled slowly by. They were gypsies to judge by their gaudy dress, one of them slight and dark haired, and the other with flowing red curls. As Marisa met her eyes, the red head's voluptuous mouth twisted in open contempt.

Lucy's hand was suddenly on her shoulder. 'Look, Marisa. Those are the two gypsy girls that Ormond kept for his private pleasure. He's dismissed them now, they say.' She laughed, recalling the vivid servants' gossip she'd heard. 'They were too much for him, I should think.'

The carriage was moving on, but Marisa turned back, her eyes still held by the beautiful gypsy girl's venomous gaze. She knew her, knew them both. Then she remembered the gypsies at Vauxhall. Redheaded Rowena had belonged to Seth. No wonder she was looking at Marisa as if she hated her.

And Lucy's casual words were slowly turning in her whirling mind. Rowena and Ormond: the woman quite open in her jealous hatred, the man quiet, deadly, venomous. Suddenly she remembered the sinister little bunch of elder twigs she'd found by the stables after the fire: a gypsy's curse, Lucy had said. Well, the fire had failed, but together they'd finally finished her off. Ormond, her secret enemy, had made an utter fool of her, ruined her. He'd certainly got his revenge on her for inheriting what he believed should have been his. And she couldn't even accuse him of treachery, couldn't report him for fraud and theft, because after all she'd signed everything he'd put in front of her. He would only have to produce those papers to destroy her case against him completely.

227

When they arrived back she went slowly up to her lovely silk-hung bedroom and began to carefully pack the few belongings she'd originally brought with her from London. As she worked, she had just one burning idea in her mind, driving away everything else.

She would go back to where she belonged, to where she understood the rules and wasn't anybody's fool. And then, she would use every trick she knew to make Melbray Manor totally hers again.

Chapter Eleven

*I*n the upstairs chamber of his elegant house in Park Place, David Valsino reflected ruefully that Lady Georgina Morency was being more than usually demanding this evening. Fortunately he didn't really mind. Although in her late thirties, and rather inclined to plumpness, Lady Georgina was still exceptionally beautiful, and, what was more, exceedingly rich. Her elderly financier husband indulged her besottedly, paying David vast sums for his wife's particular whim – her fencing lessons. Today, they hadn't even got the rapiers out before Lady Georgina had jumped on her tutor, avidly struggling with the buttons of his silk breeches and pulling out his thick, dusky penis. She'd encouraged him swiftly to erection, and bounced about on top of him, coming almost immediately. Now, she seemed to be eager for another bout, but David, lying back against the settee where they'd been exchanging kisses, laughed rather helplessly. 'There's time enough, Lady Georgina.'

'Oh, no, there isn't,' she replied, her eyes fastening greedily on his freshly stirring erection. 'An hour with you is never time enough.' She adored the handsome Italian fencing master. She dreamed every night of his lithe, compact body; of his beautiful bronzed skin with the light matting of hair on his chest, his superbly muscled legs, the dense bush of black hair at the base of his belly from where his lovely instrument of pleasure swelled and grew so willingly. At night, when her elderly husband was asleep and snoring, full up with over-rich food and too much port, she'd pretend that David was with her, and she'd rub herself with hard and hungry fingers, desperately imagining the lovely silken caress of the Italian fencing master's fine shaft inside her as she shuddered into solitary orgasm.

She'd been looking forward to this session all week, and she was going to make the most of it. She eased off her bodice, letting her plump but still firm breasts pout provocatively above her corset, feeling how her stiffening nipples tugged at the creamy skin of her bosom. 'Now,' she crooned, stroking the erect length of David's dark veined weapon and admiring the velvety globes of his testicles, 'now, give me something to really remember, Signor Valsino . . .'

Then the door to the upstairs chamber opened, and the sudden draught blew out all the candles. Georgina gave a little cry of dismay. She dreaded the thought of some- one spying on them. Her husband was fiercely jealous. If he knew of these encounters, she would be banished to the country for sure. David too sprang up, a hiss of anger on his lips, while Georgina, her heart thumping beneath her lush breasts, watched faintly from the settee as a beautiful blonde youth stepped inside the room.

It was almost completely dark in here without the candles, but she could just discern by the dim glow of the street lamp through the window that the intruder wore a long, loose greatcoat over his shirt and breeches, and his blond hair was cropped short beneath a wide-brimmed hat that shadowed his fair, smooth-shaven face. She could also see that in his hand the youth carried a pistol, and it was pointed straight at them. Georgina heard David Valsino let out a hiss of breath, then he went very still.

'Don't let me interrupt you,' said the newcomer in a low, husky voice. 'Carry on.'

Valsino said, 'You must be joking.'

The pistol lifted fractionally. 'Oh, no. I never joke about such things. Do proceed. I hate to interrupt urgent matters. Both of you on the floor, I think, and then I can see you properly.'

Georgina was beside herself with mingled shame and excitement. David, grim faced, reached to touch her arm. Miraculously he still had an erection, which swayed ominously as he said to her quickly, 'Better do as he says. Kneel on the floor, Georgina.'

Georgina gasped, 'He's going to watch us?'

'Unless you want me to argue with that pistol, he's going to watch us, yes. Kneel on the floor, and let me deal with things.'

And suddenly, Georgina was deliciously excited. She crouched rather breathlessly, and shuddered with shame as David lifted her skirts, knowing that the beautiful blond intruder would be watching her firm, ripe buttocks, would be seeing how her heavy breasts hung helplessly, brushing against the floor. Her excitement continued to mount relentlessly as she felt David's strong penis nudging between her thighs, dipping itself in the silky, silvery moisture that seeped from the soft folds of flesh between her legs. Then she heard the youth's voice, light and cool and confident.

'Tell your fencing master what to do to you, Lady Georgina. Tell him exactly what to do.'

Georgina swallowed hard. She was frightened and ashamed, but she was also more aroused than she'd ever been in her life. David whispered urgently in her ear, 'Do as he says. Remember, he's got a gun, and he looks as if he knows how to use it.'

'I'm waiting,' said the voice menacingly from the shadowy pool of darkness by the door.

Georgina cleared her throat, and said rather shakily, 'I – I want you to mount me, David.'

'Louder,' said the voice.

'I want you to mount me,' she cried out desperately. 'I want you to drive your beautiful penis deep inside me. I want you to reach round, David, and play with my breasts, and service me like a mighty stallion, and drive your hot shaft to and fro, and ravish me – oh . . .' She could already feel his lovely, hardened flesh sliding between her pouting labia, burying itself in her moist softness. She shuddered and cried out, gripping herself around him.

'And then?' said came the stranger's soft voice from the doorway.

'I – I want you to squeeze my nipples, and pound into me from behind, while I writhe against you. Then I want you to draw back, and tease me with the tip of your penis, and grip my bottom, and then drive yourself slowly, so slowly, back inside me so I can feel every inch of you . . .' Her voice broke off in a strangled cry of pleasure as David did just that. She could just see the beautiful blond youth leaning casually back against the shadowy door, his big coat hanging loosely to give a glimpse of his lovely, slender figure, but there was nothing casual about the pistol he pointed straight at her in his smooth, elegant hands. Suddenly she wanted him to join in. She wanted to see his lovely Adonis-like face tighten with pleasure, see his slim body melting with rapture, just as hers was. David had gone very still, his penis held steady in her tight love passage, just pulsing gently to remind her he was there. She looked dazedly up at the youth by the door, and whispered, 'Oh, I want you. I want to take you in my mouth while David fucks me. Please . . .'

Georgina heard the hiss of David's exhaled breath behind her and in the silence that followed her heart seemed to stop beating. Then, suddenly, the youth nodded. 'Why not?' he drawled softly, and, thrusting the gun into his pocket, he crossed the floor slowly towards her, and began to unfasten his breeches. Feeling quite faint, Georgina closed her eyes. She had never been so excited in her life. David was still gripping her bottom-cheeks. She could feel his ramrod penis very still inside her juicy love passage, and her inner nectar flowed freely around him. And now the beautiful youth was kneeling before her, reaching with divine skill to play with her hot, leaping nipples, pulling them gently as if he were milking her. She shuddered with rapture as he parted his breeches and she prepared herself to attend to him, knowing he must be as fiercely aroused as she was, as David was.

She felt his hands guiding her head gently towards his loins as he knelt upright in front of her face. And then, the excitement ran through her like a shock wave as she dazedly opened her eyes and saw the lush, crinkled folds of femininity splayed out before her, smelled the sweet scent of womanly arousal wafting towards her from between those slender female thighs, saw the light tangle of blonde down around the throbbing stem of a lustfully exposed clitoris. 'Pleasure me,' said the youth softly.

A woman. An incredibly beautiful, slender young woman, dressed as a man. Georgina's heart gave a great lurch of excitement, and she whispered, 'Who are you?'

The woman was silent, but David, just behind her, was laughing quietly. 'Georgina, my dear,' he said, 'meet Marisa Brooke.'

And then he started to move steadily behind her, filling her, stretching her with his lovely thick penis, and she reached forward in dazed obedience to start tonguing at the soft female flesh that was exposed to her hungry view, feeling how the silken petals parted in welcome, giving her entrance to the dark, honeyed cleft that was the very essence of womanhood. Slowly, deliriously, Georgina ran her tongue up and down those silky folds while Marisa continued to play devastatingly with her nipples and David gripped her buttocks, driving faster and faster from behind. As Marisa squeezed and pulled at her burning teats, Georgina found the other woman's throbbing clitoris, and whipped it with her long pink tongue, slavering at it, feeling it throb and quiver. Then she instinctively fastened her lips round it, and started to suck, hotly, strongly. She felt the exquisite Marisa arch into sudden immobility before crying out and starting to grind her soaking vulva desperately against Georgina's face, coating her with her copious juices. Georgina could feel her open and close like an anemone as the fierce, sweet, pleasure of her orgasm engulfed her, while at the same time David pounded into her from behind, ravishing her with a ferocious strength that sent her own body toppling over the edge. She cried out, 'Oh, yes. Yes! Fuck me, David. Fuck me hard . . .' The pleasure pooled like molten liquid low in her abdomen, and her whole body was wrenched by violent, exquisite convulsions as David's lengthy penis spasmed deep inside her.

David was the first to recover, the first to get up, smiling rather ruefully.

'So you're back, Marisa,' he said.

And Marisa smiled contentedly as she lazily started to fasten up her breeches. She felt at home again now.

Later, when Georgina had left, vowing eternal friendship and making Marisa promise to visit her in her beautiful home in Hanover Square, Marisa leaned back thoughtfully on the little French settee in David Valsino's candle-lit drawing-room and sipped at the goblet of cold Rhenish wine he'd brought for her.

'Where,' she said, 'would a gentleman go if he wanted to win a really large sum of money?'

David leant forward to refill her glass, feeling warm and happy in her presence. Life had been dull without Marisa Brooke. He gathered that she was in some sort of trouble, but he knew her too well to press her for details. 'I take it,' he said, 'that you're not thinking of the reputable clubs in Pall Mall?'

'Oh, no,' she replied scornfully, 'nor the seedy dives in Houndsditch where the butchers' apprentices and the poor city clerks throw away their paltry half-crowns. No, I want real play, David. Deep and dangerous.'

He hesitated, sitting back thoughtfully in his own chair. 'Fashions change in these places, of course. And if they're raided, or if there's any sort of scandal, then they close up pretty quickly. But I did hear, during the summer, that there's a rather notorious club opened up in Albion Place. It caters for jaded aristocrats, mostly younger sons with money to burn who want a taste of danger and excitement. Rumour has it that the Earl of Caterfield's third son won a hundred thousand there one night, and lost it all the next day.'

Marisa nodded. Albion Place. She'd heard of it. It lay in a dark labyrinth of streets somewhere between Whitcomb Street and Leicester Fields. 'What's it called?' she enquired casually.

'It's just known as the Albion, I think, but they keep it very private. Members only, of course, and no women allowed, so you don't stand a chance of getting in, my dear. Anyway,' he added thoughtfully, 'I've heard one or two slightly sinister stories, reports of wild parties and hushed-up scandals. You really don't want anything to do with decadent roués like them, Marisa. Your best bet, if you really want to win some money, is to go to your friends at the Blue Bell and get back into their circle. Either that, or go to some low-class den like the Bedford Arms in Covent Garden.'

Oh, no. She was beyond all that now. Marisa laughed and lifted her glass to drink, eyeing David over the rim. 'Of course I'm aware that places like the Albion are well beyond my reach. I'm just interested, that's all. I like to catch up with the latest scandal.'

'Life in the country's been dull, then?'

'Not exactly,' said Marisa, her blue eyes glinting. 'Sometime I'll tell you all about it. Dear David, you've been such a good friend to me. If I could have a bath, and perhaps a good meal before I go out for the evening, I'd be most grateful.'

David nodded, his eyes straying wistfully over her relaxed, supple figure. Her newly cropped blonde hair added a piquant sexuality to her heart-shaped face, and her slender body looked quite divinely feminine in her shirt and breeches and high leather boots. Lady Georgina had obviously thought so too. He'd been able to watch Marisa's flushed face as she orgasmed beneath Georgina's avidly lapping tongue, and he'd imagined it was Marisa's tightly exquisite loins he'd been thrusting into as he ravished Lady Georgina's plump rear. The memory of that deliciously unexpected threesome was making him grow hard again already. There was no-one quite like Marisa Brooke.

'You'll be back later tonight?' he said hopefully.

She leaned towards him, resting her hand lightly on his thigh. 'I'll see how the evening progresses,' she said.

And with that, he had to be content.

Two hours later, Marisa was busy again. It was just past ten in the evening, and inside the furtive gambling den that nested in a narrow court leading off Drury Lane, there was no sound except the deft slither of cards and the occasional clink of money. A small group of silent onlookers had gathered round one particular table in the far corner, where a final rubber of piquet was being played in the smoky light of some sparse tallow candles stuck into iron holders on the walls. Marisa was one of the players. Feeling well-fed and confident after a generous meal at David's house, she pushed back her tricorne hat and ran her hand through her cropped hair. 'Four in sequence,' she said, calmly surveying her cards. She was winning rather thoroughly, and her opponent, a grizzled veteran of the Peninsular wars, was not happy.

'Your point is good, lad,' he said rather gruffly.

'Very well,' said Marisa. 'Four aces, three kings, and eleven cards played, I think.' The soldier frowned hard at the array of cards which Marisa deftly laid on the wine-stained table. 'I claim repique,' she went on sweetly. 'This time I really think I have you, captain.' The soldier swore coarsely as Marisa reached out to pull a pile of gold coins towards herself and started to get up.

The soldier rasped out, 'Damn you lad, you could at least give me the chance to win some of it back!'

'Oh, no.' Marisa patted her pocket where the coins were. 'This is mine, and now I'm going to find a place where I can win some real money.' Calmly she started to go out through the door, pretending not to notice that everyone else had got up too, their hot eyes fastened on her retreating back, out and up the steps into the comparative gloom of the ill-lit court, where she looked around quickly, and saw more shadowy figures hurrying out of another door to block her exit. She caught her breath sharply. Damn them, but they were quick. They must have been planning to waylay her whether she won or not. She slipped quickly into an empty doorway, and waited resignedly. Soon, the soldier and three of his friends came clattering up the steps after her, all scouring about like hounds after a fox as the others came down the alley to meet them.

'Where is the lad, curse him?' muttered the soldier. 'I want my money back, and then I want him beaten black and blue for his impudence.'

'There,' cried another. 'Just there, in that doorway.'

Marisa slipped her pistol from her pocket and pointed it at them with lethal calmness. 'The first one to come near me gets a bullet in the throat,' she said. 'I mean it, gentlemen. I know how to use this, believe me.'

They hesitated, looking foolishly at one another, none of them wanting to be the first to try her out. Marisa turned with a ringing laugh and ran swiftly on booted feet through the narrow confines of Hartley Court, disappearing easily into the swirling, noisy crowds that surrounded the brothels and wine bothies of Drury Lane.

So far her disguise had worked well. David had smiled at her in reluctant admiration as she left his house earlier that evening. 'Be careful,' he said. 'You make such a pretty lad that all the boy-chasers of Vere Street will be after you.'

'All of them? Well, I'll keep them guessing while I win their money,' promised Marisa. 'Thank you, David. Thank you for everything. I'll see you soon.' With a quick kiss to his cheek, she'd tipped her hat at a jaunty angle and set off into the dark London night, to win back her fortune.

And now, the air of night-time London seemed sweet

and sharp to her nostrils after the leafy, soporific aroma of the Hampshire countryside. Her senses were assailed by the pungent odours of beer and gin and tobacco smoke, by the heavy ripeness of rotting fruit discarded by passing street sellers, by the musky fragrance of the faded prostitutes who lingered in the doorways. And the sounds. The familiar cacophony of the London streets seemed somehow to bring her alive again as she smiled at the coarse cries of passing barrow boys and pimps, and was deafened by the rumbling of heavy cart wheels on the lamplit cobbled streets. She swung jauntily down Drury Lane, conscious that her lovely winnings, just enough to get her into a really serious game, were jingling deep in her coat pocket. Glancing down a dark, unlit passageway, she glimpsed a young sailor vigorously pleasuring a giggling girl as he held her up against the wall, heedless of passers-by. The girl was gasping in delight, her arms clasped frantically round his neck as he pulled up her skirts and thrust into her. The sight excited Marisa, reviving her own sexual appetite, which was already honed by the encounter with Lady Georgina and the thrill of winning at cards.

She thought suddenly of Lord Delsingham, then quickly pushed him to the back of her mind. He'd belonged to another life, another world. Now she was Marisa Brooke again, a child of the London streets. She wore her man's clothes with a swagger, enjoying the sensual feel of the tight breeches enclosing her slender buttocks and the firmness of her high leather boots around her calves.

She took a hackney to the north end of Whitcomb Street, but decided to approach her final destination carefully, on foot, because she didn't know the area well, and here she didn't have any friends to fall back on. Having paid off the cab, she wandered slowly along the lamplit street, wondering how best to get inside somewhere as private, as decadent as this Albion Club. She had no doubt whatsoever that she would succeed. All her confidence, so badly shaken by Ormond's trickery, had come flooding back to her, as if she breathed it in with the familiar sights and smells of London. The streets of this area were alive with the carriages of the gentry, and their attendant hangers-on. She kept in the shadows, watching, waiting her chance.

And then, an elegant closed carriage suddenly pulled up beside her. She saw the coat of arms on the doorway, and her skin tingled with excitement. A man leant out from the window, his face in darkness as he beckoned to her. She sauntered up to the door, her hands in her pockets, her fingers ready on her concealed pistol. The man was young; he had a handsome but weary face, with wine-hazed eyes and lines of gauntness around his mouth that spoke of a life already devoted to dissipation. And he was rich. Marisa gauged quickly that the Mechlin lace at his neck and cuffs was priceless, and in his cravat he wore a glittering diamond pin. Marisa's heart began to thump at the sight of that diamond. She gazed up at him and waited, her mind racing.

'Well, boy,' the man drawled in a smooth, aristocratic voice that was blurred with alcohol. 'You've a pretty face. Not seen you round here before. Come up and keep me company for a few minutes, hey? I'll pay you well.'

Marisa glanced quickly up at the driver on the box, and saw his silent, impassive face as he gazed straight ahead. She would wager all the gold in her pocket that there wouldn't be any interference from that quarter. She drew a deep breath and looked again at the diamond tie pin. Oh, yes, she could deal with this.

'How much?' she said, her blue eyes narrowed in calculation.

The man shook his head, as if he couldn't be bothered. 'Oh, I don't know. A guinea, I suppose. More, if you please me.'

Marisa pulled open the door to leap nimbly in, and the silent coachman moved the big horses off at a slow pace, no doubt used to his master's ways. Marisa sat on the seat facing the fancy gentleman and saw how he was eyeing her hotly from beneath his heavy, aristocratic lids, while his well-manicured hand was already fondling his own crotch with the lazy intensity of the very drunk. 'Such a pretty boy,' he was murmuring as he gazed at her. 'Come over here and feel my cock, suck it for me, will you? And then – and then – '

But he said no more, because Marisa, her blue eyes glinting, had pulled off her hat and was already on her knees before him, quickly dealing with his buttons and drawing out his penis. He was handsomely made and clean, smelling of silks and satin and lots of money; a pity he was a drunkard, or she would have been tempted to take more time with him, but she had other business on her mind. Skilfully she drew out his penis, which in spite of his arousal was still a little flaccid, thanks to too much liquor, but she knew how to deal with that. She bent her head quickly to wrap her tongue around the succulent glans, teasing him. He groaned aloud and clutched her head against his groin, so she was all but stifled by the male smell of his genitals. His shaft began to stir thickly beneath her lips, but he was taking too long, so she reached with cunning fingertips to scratch lightly at his dark, velvety testicles, feeling them tighten excitingly. Then, as his bottom arched towards her, she slipped one finger further back, tickling at the dark cleft between his buttocks. He cried out in dark pleasure, clutching at her hair, and she felt him stir and thicken remorselessly as she softly sucked him in her mouth. She had him now. He was hard and delicious against her lips as her wicked fingers rasped at his scrotum.

He started to thrust towards her as the big coach rumbled slowly along the cobbled back streets, his handsome, aristocratic face gleaming with perspiration. 'Don't stop,' he moaned as her mouth danced along his straining penis. 'You have such soft, soft lips – don't stop. Take it, take all of it, boy, and suck me, hard.' Marisa obediently did as she was told, enjoying her adventure. She squeezed at his hairy balls, fondling the twin globes almost roughly, and bobbed her head up and down his thick shaft while her tongue drew little circles around the

240

fatly swelling plum of his glans. He groaned aloud, and his hips began to spasm helplessly. Quickly she pulled her head away, crouching back in the corner of the carriage, wary and alert. He shouted out, and began milking himself with his desperate fist, rubbing the foreskin feverishly up and down the iron-hard core as his penis began to twitch and jump. Then his hot seed spurted out over his silk breeches, and he wrenched his head back in a fierce rictus of pleasure.

Marisa tore her eyes away from his wildly spasming cock, grabbed her hat and leapt for the door. Flinging it open, she jumped out and landed lightly on her booted feet as the coach rolled on. She started to walk quickly along the pavement in the opposite direction, whistling under her breath, her blue eyes alight because she had the man's fabulous diamond pin clasped tightly in her hand.

Then her pulse quickened in alarm, because the big coach had pulled to a rumbling stop, and now there were heavy footsteps thudding down the road towards her. A rough voice called out, 'Stop him! Stop the wretch who's just robbed my master.'

Hell and damnation. She'd thought she would have all the time in the world to get away. Marisa started to run, throwing a quick look over her shoulder. She caught a chilling glimpse of the big, burly coachman, who was obviously more alert than she'd given him credit for, hurrying after her, raising the hue and cry. There were more people around than she'd thought, stopping to turn and look, and her pistol was of no use to her here, because if she used it she'd only draw more people in pursuit. Panting for breath, she plunged down a narrow, unevenly paved alley that twisted between dark, over-hanging tenements, then sped desperately on through a labyrinth of unlit lanes until at last it seemed safe to stop and listen. Silence. Perhaps she'd shaken her pursuers off. Then she heard footsteps again, rapidly coming closer, and in the same instant she realised that her way

241

ahead was completely blocked by a high, featureless brick wall.

Marisa spun round, her hands clenched at her sides, breathing hard. The footsteps and the voices were getting nearer. Soon, her pursuers would pass the end of this alley and see her, and she'd be trapped. Looking round sharply, she saw then that there were some dark, unlit steps leading downwards, presumably towards the basement of one of the apparently deserted buildings that backed onto this yard. She flew down them, stumbling a little in the blackness because they were slippery with damp, and finding at their base a heavy door, which was unlocked. Wrenching at the handle, she pulled it open and slammed it behind her, leaning back against it and breathing heavily.

She thought she could hear her pursuers moving around in the yard at the top of the steps, their voices baffled and angry. She had to move on quickly, before they too spotted the steps. Pulling her hat securely over her cropped hair and tugging her big coat collar over her chin, she stepped warily forward into the dark passageway, noting yet another closed door, a few yards further on. She pushed it open carefully a few inches and stopped, catching her breath in surprise.

The building was not deserted after all. Beyond this door, the faint glimmer of distant candlelight revealed to her a wide, spacious corridor with oak-panelled walls and rich Turkey carpets adorning the polished parquet floor. Closed rooms lay to her left and right, and from behind them she thought she could hear the muffled, scarcely discernible sound of cultured male voices, and the light chink of wine glasses.

An adventure. She'd got into the very heart of somewhere exciting and rich and exclusive, a private party, perhaps. Marisa's skin tingled with excitement and her blood raced. She moved along carefully, catlike in the darkness, towards the dim glow of candlelight and the husky sound of masculine voices. An open door lay to her right, revealing an unoccupied card room, with the sealed packs lying temptingly on green baize tables in delightful anticipation of play, though it seemed as if all the players were engaged elsewhere at the moment. Marisa crept forward carefully, her back pressed against the wall in the darkness of the corridor, and soon she saw exactly how they were engaged.

A private club indeed. No wonder nobody had heard her come in.

In the heavily curtained, dimly lit room that opened out in front of her were perhaps a dozen men. Most of them were seated, but some were standing with their backs against the wall, their arms folded impassively. Silent spectators, they looked bored and jaded, and yet the warm air of the room was somehow alive with the intensity of their concentration. Marisa followed their eyes, and understood.

The focus of the watchers' attention was a small, raised dais at the end of the room, lit by several discreetly placed wax candles. On the dais, a woman was leaning forward over a curved chaise longue, clad in a demure silken black gown, but her appearance was far from demure: her skirts had been lifted up round her waist, and her black-stockinged legs were spread wide apart to reveal her naked private parts. Positioned behind her was a big, dark-skinned man in the full silk livery and grey powdered wig of a footman, and Marisa watched in dazed fascination as with the utmost control, with scarcely a flicker of his eyelids, he pleasured the girl in front of all those onlookers. Marisa felt a sudden dryness in her throat as she glimpsed his sleek, lengthy penis sliding in and out purposefully between the woman's plump buttocks. The man was quite impassive as he steadily did his work; the woman was less controlled. As Marisa watched, she desperately pulled her breasts out from her constricting bodice so she could rub her distended nipples hard against the brocade chaise longue, and she groaned aloud with pleasure as she thrust her raised hips back against the man, voraciously matching his sturdy, measured strokes. Marisa felt the sudden assault of her own arousal, and wished it was her sprawled against the cool brocade as the big, stalwart footman serviced her so impeccably with his massive rod, his heavy dark testicles swaying rhythmically against the woman's white buttocks in time with his thrusts. Somehow the strangely quiet audience excited her too. No-one moved, no-one spoke, and although she could scarcely discern their expressions, because most of them had their backs to her as she crouched hidden in the darkness, she knew that in spite of their silence, their self-control, they too would be fiercely aroused, and hungry for sex.

She remembered one night after a drunken, dissolute Bartholomew Fair, when she and Lucy had seen a stalwart but simple youth offering to take a group of women in succession for a guinea a piece. The jeering crowd had laughed at him, saying he'd never last through one woman, let alone several, but he proved them all wrong, and on that hot, debauched night the raucous onlookers were soon baying with excitement as the simple beggar lad, the size of whose appendage was legendary, performed happily in public. The local women had queued up for him, breathless with lust at the sight of his meaty, swaying penis as it thrust eagerly out from his breeches. They climaxed quickly, often almost as soon as he penetrated them, already fully aroused by the drunken decadence of the scene, and the crowd howled its approval as the beggar boy pleasured the women with eager joy. The watching menfolk, spilling out of the taverns at the news of the spectacle, played with themselves openly as they watched, or found groups of more than willing women to take their pleasure with. Marisa and Lucy had watched from the shadows, breathless with excitement. But even that crude display wasn't somehow as exciting as this cold, ritualistic coupling.

The woman in the black silk dress was almost at her extremity. Reaching beneath herself and whimpering, she began to rub hungrily at her juicy cleft, just above where the footman's sturdy great cock impaled her.

Marisa felt her own nipples harden against her loose silk shirt and she shifted her thighs uncomfortably, secretly striving to heighten the gentle assault of the tight seam of her breeches against her delicate, already moistening sex. She licked her dry mouth as she saw the grim-faced footman clutch the wriggling woman's bottom-cheeks, and pull them yet further apart, so his audience could see everything as he drew out his long, swollen penis from her vagina. Then he started to speed up, pounding in deliberately, his buttocks tense. The woman bucked against him as the excruciating pleasure overwhelmed her, and she shouted aloud in the delicious throes of orgasm. Still the footman pumped at her, his strength seemingly inexhaustible, though the sweat beaded on his forehead. Then someone in the audience called out coolly, 'Fifty guineas to see you spill your seed, Matthew.'

The man nodded. With incredible control, he pulled out coolly from the whimpering woman and started to rub his long, glistening shaft with loving hands, making sure that his audience could see every inch of its stunning length as it jutted duskily from his loins. Then he lowered himself slightly to let the swollen tip dance against the woman's still trembling buttocks. Suddenly, just as Marisa thought he was going to go on for ever, he gripped harder and his semen started to jet forth in hot, intense spasms of lust, landing on the woman's creamy bottom-cheeks. She saw him rub his spurting shaft with febrile intensity to and fro across her hips, his balls grazing her buttocks, his face distorted with lust. A sigh seemed to ripple through his rapt audience as the last of his seed trickled out from his mighty, twitching member.

At last, he was finished. Marisa, suddenly realising that her own sharp fingernails were biting into the palms of her clenched hands, heard a cool, disdainful smattering of applause from the audience, and she quickly turned her attention to them, wondering what kind of men they could be.

They were undoubtedly rich. With the ease of years of

practice, she narrowly assessed their beautifully cut clothes, their immaculate, lace-edged cravats, the neatly coiffured precision of their fashionably cut hair. Rich, young and handsome, all of them, perhaps it was a condition of membership. The sort of company, she thought rather bitterly, where Lord Delsingham would feel at home. At the thought of her former lover, she felt a quick, painful spasm of acute need at her loins, and closed her eyes, fighting hard to suppress it. And when she opened them again, she caught her breath in sudden dismay, because there were two big footmen, dressed like the one on the stage, standing just in front of her, and their eyes were hostile and unpleasant as they asssessed her boyish frame. One of them gripped her arm roughly. 'Well, lad?' he grated out. 'Enjoy that, did you?'

Marisa uttered a silent prayer of thanks for the shadowy darkness that engulfed this section of the room as she tried to pull herself free. 'Take your hands off me!' she hissed. But then the other one seized an arm too, so that she struggled helplessly between them, and by now the others had begun to notice the disturbance, and were turning well-bred, cruelly refined faces towards her. Marisa felt her senses quicken as she saw their bored faces flickering with sudden interest. Dangerous play indeed.

One of the men was already coming slowly towards her. He had jet-black hair and a thin mouth, and a long, aristocratic nose. 'Well, well,' he said. 'And what brings you in from the alleys, boy?'

Someone followed him, a plump, foppish looking man who regarded her through his quizzing glass and muttered, 'I told you we should have kept that back door locked, Sebastian. He'll have slunk in that way, mark my words.'

The man he called Sebastian turned round on him icily. 'Sometimes we have to get out of this place in rather a hurry. You know that as well as I. I'm not prepared to take the risk of being arrested, even if you are, you fool.'

He turned back to Marisa and said slowly, unpleasantly, 'I asked you a question. Why are you here?'

Marisa drew a deep breath and lifted her face defiantly to meet his chilling gaze. There was no escape, nothing for it but to somehow bluff her way out, and she'd got out of worse places than this. Her mind working busily, she suddenly remembered the empty card room she'd passed and said coolly, 'Why am I here? Because I heard you played for high stakes, and I've come to join you.'

The man laughed shortly. 'Not just anyone can join us here at the Albion Club, boy. We play for high stakes indeed.'

Marisa's heart pounded. The Albion Club. She'd made it! By the sheerest twist of fortune, she'd made it into the secret, exclusive gaming hell where David Valsino had said the play was deepest in all of London. She felt herself tingle with a new kind of excitement as she lifted her chin and said, 'I play for high stakes too.'

The man took a pinch of snuff from a little laquered box, his coldly handsome face sneering as he ran his cynical gaze up and down her slender form swathed in her loose, long coat. 'I somehow don't think you're quite in our league, boy. What kind of stakes do you have in mind?'

Marisa stared up at him challengingly from beneath the brim of her tricorne hat. 'If you tell these apes of yours to let me go, then I might be able to show you.'

The man Sebastian nodded curtly at the two footmen, who released her with obvious reluctance. Marisa dug deep in her pocket for both the diamond pin and the purse of gold she'd won off the soldier, and as she held them out she saw the onlookers' eyes narrow with greed. 'Here are my stakes, gentlemen. Will they do to start with?'

They could, of course, have robbed her and thrown her out into the street, but amongst gamblers there was an unspoken code of honour, which she rather fervently hoped would prevail here. After a chilling pause, the man Sebastian nodded curtly, and the little group moved silently up a small flight of stairs and through an arched doorway into a small, dimly lit chamber hung with heavy drapes. A single branch of candles glimmered from a round, polished table in the centre of the room, and Marisa felt her senses quickening. So it was going to be dice, not cards. As the men seated themselves round the big table, some of them donned old-fashioned leather guards round their foreheads to protect their eyes from the low glare of the candlelight, and Marisa, pretending to feel a similar discomfort, pulled her hat low over her forehead to shade her face. Silent footmen followed with trays of liquor, as did the women, hovering in the shadows in their black silk gowns, reminding her that gambling was not the only entertainment on offer at the Albion Club. A house of secret pleasures, thought Marisa, for the rich and depraved, and, perhaps, a house where she could replenish her lost fortune . . . Her pulses raced.

They were preparing to play hazard. Calmly she took her seat at the table, pretending nonchalance, but at the same time she slipped her hand into her deep coat pocket, feeling for her own secret dice. Then play began.

When it was her turn to take the box, she called her number out confidently, then cast carelessly and lost her stake. Someone sniggered, and she continued, airily, to lose. But as the stakes increased, and the play grew more intense, she began to employ her weighted dice, and the pile of coins at her side began to grow. The men were drinking too much, a fatal mistake in deep play, because it made you over-confident, and as the casters increased their stakes with remorseless recklessness, she felt the heat of success begin to pour through her blood, bringing its own kind of intoxication. Once, as the footman who acted as groom porter was calling out the odds, she noticed the man Sebastian watching her with narrowed eyes as she prepared to call her main.

'You have some luck in this game, lad,' he said softly.

Marisa shrugged, though the prickles of warning went down her spine like ice. Bad luck indeed that he was sitting next to her. 'Beginner's fortune, sir,' she said lightly as she rattled the box. She let herself lose a few times, and then cautiously began to win again.

The stakes were being raised all the time; some of them were starting to write notes on their banks. The murmured mention of a thousand guineas, the kind of winnings she'd only dreamed of, made her head spin. The box was in front of her now, and they were waiting for her call. Slowly she put her beautiful diamond pin on the table. 'You'll match my stake, gentlemen?'

There were growls of appreciation as those who wished to join the game quickly placed their money before them. 'Eleven,' said Marisa quietly, and rattled the box lovingly before casting the dice on the table. Six and five, the most beautiful numbers she knew. There was a hiss of disappointment from the watchers, but Marisa, ignoring them, began to pull the notes and the money and her precious diamond towards her. At a quick glance, she had at least ten thousand guineas here, small fare indeed compared to the fortunes staked nightly at Watier's or White's, but it was enough, enough to make Melbray Manor hers again.

And then the door opened slowly, letting in a waft of chilly air, and Sir Julian Ormond walked in.

He didn't see her. He sat in a chair against the wall, crossing his legs nonchalantly and taking a glass of wine proffered by one of the obsequious footmen, no doubt aware that any interruption of play would be a grave misdemeanour. But he watched them all, with his pale eyes, and Marisa, bowing her head low over the dice, felt her heart hammer sickly against her ribs. Hell and damnation. He wouldn't recognise her. He couldn't. But the risk was there, nevertheless, and somehow she had to get out of here as soon as possible, with her winnings intact. Play had halted for a moment due to a minor altercation over the odds, and Marisa started, very quietly, to get up. There was an open door, just behind her, in the shadows.

She felt a hand on her arm, restraining her. 'We're

ready to continue,' said Sebastian calmly, handing Marisa the dice. 'Your turn to throw, I believe.'

Damn. Marisa said to him in an undertone, 'In a moment, sir. I was just going to relieve myself. Start without me if you like.'

Sebastian laughed. 'No need to miss any of the action, my dear young sir. There's a pot for pissing in just over there, beneath the sideboard.' He spoke loudly, sneeringly, and they all turned to watch her. Marisa sat down again and took the dice box, cursing Sebastian for staying sober and calculating when the rest of his cronies were almost under the table with wine. 'In a moment, perhaps,' she said diffidently, and prepared to cast. Sebastian said, 'Why, I do believe our brave young gentleman is shy,' and Marisa, shaken by the burst of raucous laughter, substituted clumsily for the first time.

And Sebastian, who had been watching her carefully, reached out and put his hand coldly over her fingers just as she was about to throw.

'Well, well,' he said softly. 'Do you know, I think that our unexpected guest is cheating.'

The whole room fell into deafening silence as the weight of his smooth hand pressed her palm down against the tell-tale dice, and she was icily aware of Ormond looking across the room at her with widening eyes. Hell and damnation indeed. 'Of course I'm not,' Marisa said defiantly. 'How could I be?'

With a knowing half smile, the hateful man Sebastian pulled the dice from under her hand and threw. The little ivory cubes landed on the table with a spine-chilling clatter, showing a six and a five. Everyone had gathered round the hazard table to watch, even the women and the footmen, as Sebastian threw a six and a five again and again, with sickening monotony. At last he palmed Marisa's dice, letting them roll mockingly around in his palm. 'As I said,' he repeated gently, 'you're a little cheat, aren't you?'

Marisa swallowed, silent, her agile mind racing for ways to escape. She could still bluff, could still run for it.

And then Sir Julian Ormond, who'd come quietly up behind her, put his hand on her shoulder and said to the others, 'Oh, she's cheating all right, I assure you. After all, it's what she's done all her life. Didn't any of you fools see through her disguise?'

Someone swore in surprise at his words, then they all turned to look with new eyes at Marisa, who twisted violently in his grip. 'It's you who's the cheat and impostor,' she said to Ormond in a cold, venomous voice, but no-one was listening to her, because Sebastian was reaching across to rip her silk shirt open, and there was a gasp of arousal as her small yet exquisitely feminine breasts were exposed to a dozen hungry pairs of eyes.

'You see?' said Ormond, his voice scornful though his eyes too were hot on Marisa's soft pink nipples. 'Your handsome youth is a woman, you fools. Strip her properly and you'll see.'

Marisa tried to run then, kicking and lashing out like a wild animal, and hissing out vicious invective, but the men held her with strong hands, while the women, giggling and exclaiming, pulled off her remaining clothes with deft fingers until Marisa stood naked before them, her small breasts heaving with exertion. Their hungry eyes feasted on her slender curves, on the golden down that peeped between her thighs. They held her so firmly that she couldn't even struggle. Her mind worked feverishly, twisting and turning to find some way out; but this time she feared, very much, that she'd overplayed her hand at last.

And Sebastian said, 'Well. It looks as if we have some rather novel entertainment in store for tonight, gentlemen.'

Chapter Twelve

David Valsino was disturbed at midnight by the battering at his front door. He was in bed with two beautiful girls, twin sisters of one of his clients: one was nibbling at his erect penis, while the other was crooning over his lithe Italian body and guiding his finger gently but persistently into her vagina. He was just wondering rather dazedly how best to bring them both to simultaneous orgasm when he realised he had a visitor.

He cursed at first, and decided to ignore the violent knocking, because one of the girls was doing something rather naughty to his sensitive testicles with her tongue. Then it suddenly occurred to him that it might be Marisa, and the thought made him pull himself away from those tormenting fingers and lips to reach out for his silk dressing robe. If it was Marisa, then he didn't particularly want his manservant letting her in and betraying the fact that he already had company. The girls protested, clinging to his hands as they twined together deliciously on the bed, their long, dark hair falling over their shoulders, and their faces pouting up at him in disappointment.

'I'll be back in a moment,' he promised, pulling the robe over his aching erection. Then, picking up a candlestick on his way, he hurried downstairs and pulled open the big front door.

It was Lord James Delsingham. The nobleman looked big and formidable in the light of the streetlamp. He was wearing a dusty, many-caped travelling coat, as if he'd just driven a long way, and David could see his phaeton pulled in against the pavement, with his liveried tiger holding the lathered horses with some effort.

'Is she here?' rapped out Delsingham curtly.

'Who?' David, pulling his silk robe around him, made the mistake of trying to appear dazed and innocent.

Delsingham said, 'Marisa Brooke, you fool. I know she spent some time here earlier. Where is she now?'

David, suddenly very alert, said quickly, 'I'm afraid I've really no idea. She has lots of friends in London, as I'm sure you know. She could be with any of them.'

Delsingham had moved closer to David as he talked. Suddenly he was pinning the fencing master against the wall, his strong hands digging into his shoulders. He said softly, 'Don't play games with me, Valsino. I have to find her, and quickly. She could be in danger. There's every chance she's in some sort of gaming den. Have you any idea which one?'

David swallowed. 'There – there was some mention of the private club in Albion Place . . .'

Delsingham's mouth thinned. 'The Albion? Did *you* mention it to her?'

'Yes,' David stammered. 'We were talking of places where the play was deep, and I just happened to mention the name – '

Delsingham pushed him away, so that he sagged back against the wall. 'You'll pay for this,' he said quietly, and turned swiftly back towards his waiting carriage.

David went slowly back upstairs, feeling shaken. Delsingham was a dangerous man to antagonise. He hoped to God that Marisa was all right. Then he shrugged his shoulders. Marisa could survive anything, couldn't she?

Even so, he was worried about her, and it took the twin sisters some time to revive his flagging interest in them.

* * *

253

Marisa lay wary and watchful, struggling to keep all her senses about her. They'd tied her down to a couch with silken cords, the same couch on the raised dais where the young maid had earlier taken such lascivious pleasure from the dusky footman. She could still smell the musky secretions of the woman's perfumed body. She closed her eyes scornfully to shut out the hot, hungry gaze of the onlookers, but inside she felt a secret shiver of fear as they tied her wrists behind her cropped head so that her breasts were thrust provocatively upwards. She almost uttered an instinctive cry of protest as they pulled her legs apart and tied her ankles to the clawed feet of the couch, exposing her naked femininity for all to see, but she knew they'd take pleasure in any show of fear, so she clamped her mouth shut tightly.

Then she heard Ormond saying to Sebastian, 'I know this little slut. She's like a bitch on heat, believe me. Take no notice of her protests. She pretends to be all golden-haired innocence, but she'll rut with anyone if the fancy takes her. For the past few weeks, she's hired a band of gypsies for her private pleasure.'

Marisa gazed at Ormond with scornful deliberation. 'I thought you were the one into secret rutting. It's common knowledge, I believe, that you can't get your rather inadequate penis to stand proud unless someone gives you a beating. Shall I tell them about your two gypsy girls?'

It was a wild thrust, but her taunt struck home. Marisa's mouth curled in sardonic amusement as he clenched his fists, his smooth face quite white with anger, and ordered two of the women to tie a silk scarf round her mouth to silence her.

Then she heard Sebastian murmuring something to the hovering women, and suddenly two of them were crouching beside her, fingering and stroking her pinioned body, pulling at her soft nipples until they sprang into hard, defiant life. She pulled at her bonds in protest, trying to fight down the delicious ripples of pleasure as she felt their hot, wet lips attending to her breasts with consummate feminine skill, and then she went very still, her breath catching in her throat.

Dear God, there was no way she could fight this.

Because now she could feel a pink, pointed female tongue stroking lightly at her swollen labia, skilfully parting her dark petals of flesh as they lay exposed between her outspread legs, and sliding along languorously towards the base of her swollen clitoris. She shuddered at the wicked voluptuousness of the caress as the two women at her breasts tugged and nibbled her distended teats, sending fierce strokes of rapture rushing down to join the dark pool of burning need at her tense womb. As they continued to lick, she felt their fingers as well, cunning, busy fingers, fastening something round her. She felt the kiss of cold leather biting into the soft flesh of her bosom, and looked down to see a skilfully made harness of supple straps encasing each breast and pushing them out with lewd wantonness, the swollen flesh white and creamy as it stood proud from the tight leather. She heard the hiss of indrawn breath around the room, and saw that several of the men down in the shadows of the hall were slowly fondling themselves, rubbing surreptitiously at their distended cocks beneath their clothing as they watched her, their eyes glazed over with lust.

Marisa swore fluently at them and twisted in her bonds, desperately aroused in spite of her resistance. The woman crouching between her tethered legs, sensing her weakness, increased her tender assault on her captive's most secret places, darting and licking as Marisa's juices spilled out, then pointing her tongue and thrusting it as far as she could inside Marisa's honeyed sex, filling it with a rasping sweetness and wriggling it about inside her until Marisa moaned aloud and thrust her harnessed breasts up against the faces of the women who were eagerly tonguing her nipples. In spite of everything she could do to resist she was nearly at the point of delicious, rending orgasm, feeling herself about to split like a ripe fruit as she bore down against the thrusting tongue in her vagina, helplessly grinding the plump kernel of her clitoris against the woman's face. Then she was suddenly aware that Sebastian was whispering in one of the women's ears, and he laughed as he met Marisa's burning eyes. 'Do your work, Susannah,' he said curtly.

Marisa felt the sharp tension ripple through her as the maid, Susannah, came lightly towards her, picking up on her way a long, unused wax candle from a gilt holder on a little satinwood table nearby. Slowly she started to moisten it with a bottle of musky unguent, and all the time her hot eyes were on Marisa's secret parts. Marisa watched, her skin prickling with alertness, and then Susannah leaned across her shoulder and whispered, 'Lift your bottom up.'

Marisa shook her head dazedly. 'What?'

'I said, lift your bottom up, dearie.' The woman grinned. 'I'm not going to hurt you. Oh, no. You're going to enjoy this, believe me.'

Still Marisa resisted instinctively, but with deft fingers Susannah and another woman raised Marisa's slender buttocks and swiftly piled cushions beneath her hips, so her body was arched away from the couch. With a thrill of despair, Marisa realised that now all of her most secret places were exposed to the watching company: the pink, fleshy lips of her vulva, the dark cleft of her pelvic floor, even the tight little rosebud hole of her anus. She licked her dry lips, feeling the leather harness bite gently at her swollen breasts, while Susannah stroked and prodded at her exposed anal orifice with her oiled fingers, caressing the little puckered crevice, loving it, teasing it gently. Slowly she pushed her finger in, and Marisa felt her tight ring of muscle flutter and close around it as her whole body shuddered at the deliciously wicked intrusion.

'That's it, my pretty,' murmured Susannah lovingly. 'You've enjoyed this sort of thing before, I can tell. Like it, don't you? Now for the best part.' And even as she spoke, Marisa felt the slender wax candle ravishing her anus like a phallus. She spasmed instinctively around it, her muscles clenching fiercely as the whole of her lower abdomen began to palpitate with heavy, liquid pleasure at the hard penetration and her breasts in their black leather strapping thrust hungrily for release. Susannah, watching her intently, slid the stem of wax in a little deeper, then withdrew it a fraction, and Marisa gritted her teeth beneath the silk gag. She wouldn't submit to them, she wouldn't. And yet, oh, just the slightest pressure on her burning pleasure bud, and she would topple over the edge into sweet, consuming release. She clenched fiercely at the intrusive candle-stem as the warm waves of degradation washed through her.

Then Sebastian's voice penetrated the velvety blackness in which she lay suspended. 'Enough for the moment,' he said. 'Leave her. At least we know she's ready and waiting for us.'

The women fell away from her, leaving Marisa panting, aroused, open. Her tormentor turned round to look at the hot-faced circle of watchers in the candlelit shadows. 'I think you'll agree, gentlemen,' he said, 'that we need to teach this slattern that nobody tricks us and takes our money.'

The others nodded eagerly. Ormond said coldly, 'What shall we do with the slut then, Sebastian? Take her one at a time?'

Sebastian's voice again, cold and chilling. 'No, I have a better idea. Winner to take all. We'll play for her.'

Marisa lay back on her couch, the room swimming about her. For the first time ever, she was beginning to think that there was no way out.

The table was drawn out, the cards were produced in intense silence and they began to play. Marisa twisted her head on the couch as the cards were dealt for vingt-et-un, trying to glimpse the hands nearest to her, but concentration was difficult with the slender wax phallus seeming to throb like a live thing in the tense passage of her rectum, keeping every one of her senses on edge. Soon, unless some miracle happened, she would be publicly taken, in front of all these people. She pulled in vain at her tight silken bonds. Dear God, there must be some way to get out of here, there must be.

Then the door opened slowly. She turned her head to look, as did everyone else in the room, and her heart seemed to stop as a man came in, tall and formidable in the shadows. She saw his darkly expressive eyes flicker momentarily as they scanned the candlelit room, and then they finally came to rest on her tethered, almost naked body.

Delsingham. Lord James Delsingham. Marisa's eyes blazed with scorn at the realisation that he too belonged with this decadent, debauched set of men. Somehow she'd thought he was different, but then, hadn't she misjudged him all along? For a moment their eyes met and held, but then Delsingham let his bored gaze wander back to the card party, and Marisa saw how Ormond's face flickered with a sudden, intense hatred which he quickly concealed. And then Delsingham drawled, 'Sorry I'm late, gentlemen. I see you've been enjoying yourselves. Any chance of me taking a hand?'

Sebastian gestured smoothly to the empty chair beside him. 'Take a seat, Delsingham. We've only just started.'

Delsingham took off his big coat and eased his tall, athletic frame into the proffered chair. The candlelight burnished his glossy black hair and flickered on the clean-cut lines of his darkly handsome face. Marisa saw with narrowed eyes how the women watched him hungrily, wanting him. 'The stakes, gentlemen?' he enquired lazily, lifting his first card.

Sebastian smiled thinly. 'We're playing with tokens only.' Delsingham raised his eyebrows. Sebastian went on, 'The prize, you see, is rather unusual. The winner gets to enjoy this rather delectable female intruder, whom we caught spying on us earlier.'

Delsingham's eyes flickered once more up to Marisa on the dais. She felt the cords bite into her limbs, felt the harness lewdly pushing out her naked breasts, and hated him for seeing her like this. He said softly, his eyes lingering on the wax phallus protruding from between

258

her uplifted buttocks, 'Well. In that case, I'm definitely glad I arrived in time.'

So he was going to play too, thought Marisa scornfully. He was hateful, hateful. Just as bad as all the rest, only worse, because he pretended to be different.

The cards moved fast. She could see Delsingham clearly. He seemed to pause, very slightly, each time it was his turn, and she saw how his hooded eyes swept the upturned cards with every move. He was counting the cards, she realised narrowly, being only too familiar with that procedure herself. And then she saw something else, something that almost made her forget her predicament and caused her heart to thud slowly, painfully against her ribs. He was wearing her ring, her beautiful gold ring on the little finger of his left hand.

He was using it too. No-one but she would have known it, but from where she lay she could just detect the tiny, almost imperceptible movement as he used the retractable pin to mark the corner of certain cards as they passed through his hands on the deal. Casing the pack wasn't enough for Delsingham; he was really making sure of winning this time. The others were watching him too, hating him for winning so easily, but were unable to detect anything compromising in his steady play. He didn't even bother to lose a few times to confuse his opponents, thought Marisa rather dazedly, as he calmly doubled his stake and displayed an ace and a ten. There was a growl of disappointment from the remaining players as his long, elegant, manicured hands, edged with beautiful Brussels lace that spilled from his cuffs, moved in confidently to pull in the tokens. The other players threw in their cards and scattered their tokens in angry disappointment. He'd won. And his prize was her, Marisa. She held herself very still, hardly breathing.

'She's all yours, damn you, Delsingham,' growled Sebastian, leaning back in his chair, his face drawn with tension. Ormond said nothing, but just watched his enemy with burning, heated eyes.

Delsingham said, 'Here? Now?'

'Those were the terms of play. If you don't want her, someone else will oblige.'

'Oh, I want her,' said Lord James Delsingham. He pushed back his chair and casually strolled across to the dais, his long boots thudding softly on the smooth floorboards. Then he stood looking down at her, his hands on his lean hips, his face expressionless.

'Get on with it, Delsingham,' growled someone from the table, thick-voiced with lust. 'Pleasure the wench, will you? Either that, or let someone else claim her!'

Delsingham stooped to carefully remove the gag from round her mouth, letting his long fingers brush her swollen lips. He had his back to the card table, and she realised that he was deliberately blocking off the other men's view of her face. 'Can you bear it,' he said to her very quietly, 'if we get on with the business in hand here and now?'

Marisa gazed up at him, her eyes burning. 'In front of these animals? I didn't realise your tastes ran to such depravities, Lord Delsingham.'

His mouth thinned. 'They don't,' he said.

'Then get me out of here, damn you.'

He drew a deep breath and said, 'My Ganymede, that's not possible without fulfilling the terms of the game. Our friends over there would feel cheated, and they might cause trouble.'

'They're your friends, not mine. You can deal with them.'

'They're not my friends. And normally I would never set foot in a depraved place such as this.'

Marisa stared at him. 'Then why – '

'I'm here because I was trying to find you, to extricate you from whatever trouble you'd plunged yourself into,' he replied shortly. 'And believe me, I'm regretting it more and more each minute.'

The pack was starting to close in on them. The men's mood was getting restless and ugly. 'Damn you, man,' an onlooker was protesting indignantly. 'Why did you ask to be dealt into the game, if you didn't want the little slut?'

Another man had wandered over to leer at Marisa. 'Perhaps Delsingham can't get it up. Perhaps he ought to let me poke the wench instead.'

Delsingham whipped round at that, and lifted the man who'd just spoken by his high shirt collar, so he couldn't breathe. Then he threw the man aside so that he thudded, dazed, to the floor, and the room fell silent.

Delsingham turned back to Marisa. 'Let's get this over with, Ganymede, shall we? You never know, we might even enjoy ourselves.'

Her eyes narrowed. 'Conceited as ever!' she spat out.

He laughed, 'Of course,' and then he bent to kiss her gently. 'Aren't you glad I won?' Even as he spoke, his hands moved to caress her leather-bound breasts, cupping each globe of constricted flesh while his lips moved to lave at her nipples, his tongue stroking and pulling at both yearning crests until they were hard and stiff.

'What do you think?' she whispered, her eyes suddenly sparkling. And she arched suddenly towards him, heedless of the silken cords tightening relentlessly at her wrists and ankles, melting at his familiar masculine touch, at his scent, as his hard, lithe body pressed against hers.

They had shut everyone else out. His hands continued their delicious work on her breasts as the tight leather harness bit into their swelling flesh. Gently he shifted the silk cushions beneath her hips, lifting them higher, and she felt herself moisten sweetly for him as her thighs fell apart still further. Carefully he moved the slender shaft in her rectum, reminding her anew of its sweet, heavy penetration; she moaned aloud in pleasure at the intimate caress, catching her lip between her teeth to stifle her cry. In the midst of her own excitement, she was dimly aware that he was attending to his own clothing with skilful fingers, finally drawing out his lovely thick penis, which was dusky and already rigid. 'You're ready?' he said very quietly.

'Yes,' muttered Marisa, her eyes on his face, her body melting with exquisite impatience. 'I'm ready. Take me, damn you.'

He arched over her, his substantial frame protecting her from the avid stares of the onlookers. 'That's my intention, my sweet,' he murmured, and she gasped aloud at the wonderful sensation of that thick, lengthy shaft of flesh sliding deep inside her very core. She was doubly filled, her aroused body squeezing and relishing the invasion of her secret flesh. Delsingham rocked gently, moving his powerful member with exquisite skill, and at the same time he drew on her stiffened nipples with his fingers, pulling and rolling at the dark teats and making her gasp as the tingling pleasure-pain shot through her body. Then he clasped her bottom-cheeks up towards him, reminding her of that other, wicked penetration at her rear. She gasped as the heavy sensations rolled through her, but he kissed her to stifle her cries, and proceeded to drive her to sweet distraction with his beautiful firm penis, sliding it deliciously in and out of her quivering flesh until she moaned and bucked wildly against him, shuddering into dark ecstasy as her buttocks clenched around the thin, smooth shaft that penetrated her rear. Gently but strongly he continued to ravish her, his penis a mighty rod of pleasure around which she convulsed and trembled as the languorous waves of bliss crashed through her pinioned body. Harder and harder he drove himself, his tongue darting and tugging at her distended nipples, and she felt his penis plunging at her very heart as his own silent ecstasy consumed him. His hips clenched and jerked above her, and just for a moment his self-control was gone. Marisa felt herself pulsing round his powerful phallus, draining his very essence, holding him deep inside her as the longed-for bliss lapped in slow, caressing waves around her.

She was brought back to stark reality by a slow, calculated burst of clapping from the shadowy figures who surrounded them. Slowly Delsingham raised himself, silently pulling out the invasive wax stem from

262

between her bottom cheeks as he did so and casting it to one side. Marisa shivered, suddenly chilly in the oppressive heat of that richly furnished room. She heard Sebastian's hateful voice saying coldly, 'Well done, Delsingham. The bitch was certainly hot for you; you pleasured her well.'

And then she heard Ormond's voice, cold and snake-like. 'Of course she was hot for him. These two already know each other well. Didn't you realise?'

Delsingham ignored him. He was slowly untying Marisa, his eyes tender as he worked at the cords. He said to her very quietly, so no-one else could hear, 'Your clothes are nearby?'

Marisa nodded: 'Just within reach.'

'Good girl.'

And then Marisa was aware that Ormond was saying in a louder, deadlier drawl now to his companions: 'I tell you, they know each other. This whole thing was set up between them, if you ask me, with Delsingham arriving when he did. The girl is a cheat, and so is Lord Delsingham. You've all been cheated of your pleasure.'

Delsingham swung round to him. 'You want me to tell them about your ideas of pleasure, Ormond? The other day I had a most interesting conversation with one of those gypsy girls you kept closeted in your quarters for a while. Now, she had some tales to tell, believe me.'

Ormond forced a defiant shrug, but Marisa saw the sudden flicker of fear in his pale eyes, and he went silent. So Delsingham knew about the strange alliance between the gypsy girl and Ormond and their plans to destroy her. Had he known about it all the time? Her mind raced, but there was no time for anything now, because at last Delsingham had untied all of her bonds, except the intricately buckled leather harness around her breasts. As Marisa drew herself up on the couch, fighting for alertness, only too aware of the resurgence of menace in the air, he reached to hand her her coat, which lay discarded on the floor beside her, and said very quietly

263

so no-one else could hear, 'Pull this on, then your breeches and boots. And be ready to run.'

'But how – '

'No time for arguments, my sweet. Just do exactly as I say.'

Marisa nodded. Already she could hear the low growling and muttering of protest coming from the crowd of men who were watching. Ormond was silent, white-faced, but she could hear the cold voice of Sebastian rising above them to say clearly, 'You should have left the wench where she is, Delsingham. I've a feeling we were all entitled to try her, just as we originally planned.'

They were advancing towards the couch where she was hurriedly pulling her boots on, their faces mean and ugly with frustrated lust. Marisa felt her heart racing. And then Delsingham, already on his feet and calmly slipping on his own loose greatcoat, reached into his deep pockets and pulled out two pistols. He raised them almost casually, and said, 'I shouldn't try anything, gentlemen, if I were you. I really shouldn't.'

Marisa, hastily buttoning up her coat beside him, murmured calmly, 'I'm ready.'

'Then make for the door,' he rapped out, and as she hurried to open it, he began a slow, measured retreat, walking backwards with his pistols levelled at the thwarted faces of their enemies.

Marisa was already by the door, holding it open, waiting as he retreated towards her with what seemed to be agonising slowness. 'Where now?' she asked tersely.

'Up those stairs behind you,' snapped Delsingham over his shoulder. Marisa nodded and hurried on up, with Delsingham following her. One of the men lurched forward angrily, and Delsingham whipped his pistol towards him. 'I really would enjoy using this, believe me.'

The man fell back, uncertain. They were almost at the top of the stairs. Delsingham said quickly, 'Make for that door down at the end of the corridor, Marisa. It should take us out of this place. Pray God it isn't locked.'

It was. Marisa saw Delsingham's face tighten as he pulled and strained at the handle. She turned sharply and saw the men, led by Sebastian, coming towards them down the shadowy corridor with the greed of approaching victory in their faces. Delsingham whirled round to face them, and said to her, between gritted teeth, 'I might be able to hold them off for a few minutes, while you try to find another exit. Don't worry about me, just run.'

And then Marisa laughed softly. 'No need to be heroic, my dear Lord Delsingham. You see, I think I've got the key.' She fished in her deep coat pocket to pull out a heavy iron key, and with their furious pursuers only yards away, she eased back the lock triumphantly and they plunged into the street outside, slamming the door behind them and locking it from the outside. The rain was pouring down into the silent London street, and with a wide grin, Marisa threw the key over her shoulder, so that it landed with a splash in a puddle. Delsingham was running his hand through his hair, watching her perplexedly. 'How in damnation did you get that key?'

'I picked that oaf of a footman's pocket earlier, when he was manhandling me. He never even noticed,' she announced triumphantly 'They'll have another key, of course, but it might take them a little while to find it.'

'Do you always pick people's pockets?'

'Oh, yes. It's a habit of mine. You see, you never know when it will come in useful.'

Delsingham, his hands on his hips as the rain streamed down his face, began to laugh softly. 'Magnificent, my dear Ganymede. Quite magnificent.'

Marisa grinned back up at him, suddenly feeling very, very happy.

But they didn't get much time. Another door opened somewhere further down the dark lane, and they heard shouts behind them. 'This way. They must be along here somewhere.'

Quickly Delsingham and Marisa began to run through the rain-soaked street, their boots splashing in the puddles. For a moment, Marisa hesitated in dismay as she realised they were in another dead end, but then Delsingham grabbed her hand and pulled her into the warm, hay-scented darkness of a stable, where horses stirred restlessly in the shadows. Somehow he found a wooden ladder up into the hay loft and pushed her up there, following speedily and pulling the ladder up after himself. Marisa, gasping with exertion, lay in the hay, while he put his arm round her protectively and listened at the hatch. 'They've gone on past,' he said. 'We should be all right now.'

'They might call out the constables.'

'I doubt it. When they come to their senses, they'll realise they would be somewhat foolish to draw attention to the rather sordid activities of their club.'

Marisa sat up rather sharply, starting to brush the hay from her face and hair. 'Presumably you too have enjoyed those rather sordid activities, as you call them.'

He shook his head. 'Never. Believe me, I've no fancy to lose a thousand guineas at a sitting. And as I told you, normally the kind of depraved pleasures they offer are rather beyond me. Though not tonight.' His eyes gleamed wickedly as he assessed her slender, rain-bedraggled figure, with her blue eyes wide and strangely vulnerable beneath her close-fitting crop of wet blonde hair. 'You're all right, Ganymede?' he said suddenly, his hands on her narrow shoulders. 'They didn't harm you?'

Marisa smiled a little shakily, then her eyes glittered with familiar mischief. 'No, indeed. They were a bunch of drunken fools, all of them. Though,' and a frown darkened her face, 'I hadn't realised how much Sir Julian Ormond hated me. Do you think he can still cause trouble for me?'

'He's facing complete ruin,' said Delsingham shortly, 'and if he has any sense at all, he'll keep very quiet about his dealings with you.'

'He must have really hated me, from the beginning,' shivered Marisa. 'He must have been responsible for everything: the ransacking of my rooms in London, that fall I took on the horse he lent me, the terrible attack on Seth, even the fire . . .'

'I did try to warn you about him.'

Her eyes glinted with sudden mischief. 'You think I'd take any notice of you? Anyway, I would have dealt with him somehow. Nobody gets the better of me!'

'So I'd observed,' he murmured rather faintly.

'And see. See what I've got here.' Marisa thrust her hands into her deep pockets and pulled out fistfuls of coins, bills, and IOUs, with the beautiful diamond pin glinting on top of the pile.

Delsingham caught his breath. 'I take it you cheated rather expertly?'

'I think they got good value out of me,' she laughed. Then she added regretfully, as she fingered the notes, 'I suppose they'll refuse to honour these, won't they? And the man I stole the diamond from might set up a chase for me.'

Delsingham shook his head, examining her booty. 'No. I don't think any of your victims will dare to dispute their losses in the cold light of day, otherwise we'll threaten to reveal where and how you acquired them. They have much more to lose than you, because some of these men have formidable reputations to keep. You'd be surprised at the exalted positions some of them hold in society. I think they'll stay quiet. And lots of them are so wealthy that they won't miss a few hundred guineas.'

Marisa gazed up at him steadily. 'You make it sound like nothing,' she said. 'But this diamond alone will make sure that I can keep Melbray Manor.'

He smiled down at her, the rain still streaking his dark hair. 'Still want to play the fine lady, Marisa?'

Her face tightened stubbornly. 'Yes, and why not?'

'Why not indeed? I think you're the most wonderful lady I've ever met in my life.'

Marisa stared at him, looking for tell-tale signs of mockery, but there were none. Then, still distracted, she suddenly realised that her coat had fallen apart as she crouched there in the hay, and she remembered that she was wearing nothing underneath but the tight leather harness that the women had fastened round her breasts. Delsingham had just noticed it too. She felt his eyes glide appraisingly over her small, creamy breasts, upthrust and conical in their thin black strapping. She felt a warm tongue of desire assaulting her senses, making her weak; her nipples hardened slowly and shamefully beneath his thoughtful gaze. She wanted him, damn him, wanted him again quite badly, and it unsettled her. She said rather shakily,

'I don't suppose many fine ladies go around dressed like this.'

'True,' he said. 'But most of them would look ridiculous in such attire. Whereas you, my sweet, look quite, quite delicious.'

Marisa moistened her lips. She was suddenly frightened of the power this man had over her. No-one else had ever been able to make her a churning mass of desire just by looking at her. Determined to regain control, she peered down through the hatch in the hayloft a little nervously as the horses down below stirred and whickered. 'I can't hear anything from outside,' she said with a pretence at calmness. 'They must have given up the hunt long ago. I think we ought to go.'

'Oh, no,' he said seriously, drawing her back up beside him. 'They'll still be looking, I'm quite sure of it.'

'Well, then,' she persisted stubbornly, 'even so, perhaps we ought to make a run for it.'

'I think,' he said, 'that we ought to stay.' And he pulled her hand down gently, pressing it against the warm, swelling bulge at his groin. Marisa caught her breath at the feel of that delicious rod of flesh, but she wasn't giving in, not yet.

'Dice for it,' she declared stubbornly. 'Best of three. If you win, we stay. If I win, we go.'

He laughed. 'Oh, no. Dice with you, Miss Brooke? They'll be weighted, crooked, whatever. By the way, did you like the way I used your ring?'

'Yes,' she said impatiently. 'You were almost as good

as me. Look, if you don't want to dice, then we'll toss a coin. Agreed?'

'Agreed,' he said warily.

Marisa pulled a silver coin swiftly from her pocket. 'Tails,' she said.

It was heads. 'We stay,' Delsingham said softly, and Marisa, with a show of reluctance, subsided obediently into his arms.

He kissed her, lapping the rain from her face and throat with his tongue, then entering her mouth with deep, tender strokes that were urgent with passion. He paused to ease off his coat and lay her down on it, dipping his head to caress her wonderfully aching breasts until she was moaning aloud with liquid desire, longing for him to take her with his lovely, silken cock which was already sliding languorously across her taut belly. She struggled to pull off her boots, ripping her breeches down impatiently so she could welcome him into her very heart, and as his wonderful penis slid deep within her, she shivered with rapture, wrapping her arms and legs round him and letting her inner muscles flutter and ripple around that solid shaft of flesh. His strong hand moved lightly down across her belly to tangle in the blond down of her pubis and stroke lightly at the base of her straining little bud of pleasure. She cried aloud, almost on the brink already as the delicious feather-strokes of his fingertip circled and caressed so lightly while his thickly solid penis continued to move slowly, purposefully within her. For a moment, his dark gaze burned into her flushed, melting face. 'Marisa,' he said. Then he started to drive strongly, passionately into her, his hand still lightly caressing her clitoris, his mouth rasping at her straining breasts. She lifted her hips, clutching deliriously round his iron-hard penis with her greedy inner muscles, feeling his moist, velvety mouth rubbing against her breasts and his pointed tongue tugging at her distended teats. She reached down to caress his tight, hard balls as they filled with his seed. With a low growl he drew himself out almost to his extremity, lifting himself so that she could glimpse the darkly masculine root of him, breathtakingly powerful and long, the sleek, veined shaft shiny with the flowing nectar of her inner core. She gasped aloud, writhing her hips, yearning wordlessly for him to possess her, and he smiled and plunged his penis in slowly, inch by delicious inch, stretching her, filling her. Rising with a cry to meet him, her whole body tightened and exploded in dark, wanton rapture as he drove himself to his own harsh, passionate climax.

She lay dazed in his arms, still feeling the gentle spasms of his sated member deep inside her as he kissed her softly. Outside the rain poured down on the cobbles of the dark London street, and she heard the faint cry of the watch in the distance. 'One of the clock, and a fair night.' Languorously she opened her eyes, feeling blissfully content as they lay in the hay-scented darkness. An ace. Quite definitely an ace.

'Marisa,' Delsingham was saying softly, 'Marisa, my precious, it really wasn't like you to misjudge the fall of that coin. You must be losing your touch.'

She smiled up at him, her thick-lashed eyes hazy with calculated pleasure, and showed him the two-headed silver coin she always carried in her pocket. 'I cheated,' she said contentedly, and nestled into his arms.

Visit the Black Lace website at
www.blacklace-books.co.uk

FIND OUT THE LATEST INFORMATION AND TAKE ADVANTAGE OF OUR FANTASTIC FREE BOOK OFFER! ALSO VISIT THE SITE FOR . . .

- All Black Lace titles currently available and how to order online
- Great new offers
- Writers' guidelines
- Author interviews
- An erotica newsletter
- Features
- Cool links

BLACK LACE — THE LEADING IMPRINT OF WOMEN'S SEXY FICTION

TAKING YOUR EROTIC READING PLEASURE TO NEW HORIZONS

LOOK OUT FOR THE ALL-NEW BLACK LACE BOOKS – AVAILABLE NOW!

All books priced £6.99 in the UK. Please note publication dates apply to the UK only. For other territories, please contact your retailer.

EVIL'S NIECE
Melissa MacNeal
ISBN 0 352 33781 8

The setting is 1890s New Orleans. When Eve spies her husband with a sultry blonde, she is determined to win back his affection. When her brother-in-law sends a maid to train her in the ways of seduction, things spin rapidly out of control. Their first lesson reveals a surprise that Miss Eve isn't prepared for, and when her husband discovers these liaisons, it seems she will lose her prestigious place in society. However, his own covert life is about to unravel and reveal the biggest secret of all. **More historical high jinks from Ms MacNeal, the undisputed queen of kinky erotica set in the world of corsets and chaperones.**

LEARNING THE HARD WAY
Jasmine Archer
ISBN 0 352 33782 6

Tamsin has won a photographic assignment to collaborate on a book of nudes with the sex-obsessed Leandra. Thing is, the job is in Los Angeles and she doesn't want her new friend to know how sexually inexperienced she is. Tamsin sets out to learn all she can before flying out to meet her photographic mentor, but nothing can prepare her for Leandra's outrageous lifestyle. Along with husband Nigel, and an assortment of kinky friends, Leandra is about to initiate Tamsin into some very different ways to have fun. **Fun and upbeat story of a young woman's transition from sexual ingénue to fully fledged dominatrix.**

Coming in April

VALENTINA'S RULES
Monica Belle
ISBN O 352 33788 5

Valentina is the girl with a plan: find a wealthy man, marry him, mould
him and take her place in the sun. She's got the looks, she's got the
ambition and, after one night with her, most men are following her
around like puppies. When she decides that Michael Callington is too
good for her friend Chrissy and just right for her, she finds she has bitten
off a bit more than she expected. Then there's Michael's father, the
notorious spanking Major, who is determined to have his fun, too.
**Monica Belle specialises in erotic stories about modern girls about town
and up to no good.**

WICKED WORDS 8
Edited by Kerri Sharp
ISBN O 352 33787 7

Hugely popular and immensely entertaining, the *Wicked Words*
collections are the freshest and most cutting-edge volumes of women's
erotic stories to be found anywhere in the world. The diversity of themes
and styles reflects the multi-faceted nature of the female sexual
imagination. Combining humour, warmth and attitude with fun,
imaginative writing, these stories sizzle with horny action. Only the most
arousing fiction makes it into a *Wicked Words* volume. This is the best in
fun, sassy erotica from the UK and USA. **Another sizzling collection of
wild fantasies from wicked women!**

Coming in May

UNKNOWN TERRITORY
Rosamund Trench
ISBN O 352 33794 X

Hazel loves sex. It is her hobby and her passion. Every fortnight she meets up with the well-bred and impeccably mannered Alistair. Then there is Nick, the young IT lad at work, who has taken to following Hazel around like a lost puppy. Her greatest preoccupation, however, concerns the mysterious Number Six – the suited executive she met one day in the boardroom. When it transpires that Number Six is a colleague of Alistair's, things are destined to get complicated. Especially as Hazel is moving towards the 'unknown territory' her mother warned her about. **An unusual sexual exploration of the appeal of powerful men in suits!**

A GENTLEMAN'S WAGER
Madelynne Ellis
ISBN 0352 33800 8

When Bella Rushdale finds herself fiercely attracted to landowner Lucerne Marlinscar, she doesn't expect that the rival for his affections will be another man. Handsome and decadent, Marquis Pennerley has desired Lucerne for years and now, at the remote Lauwine Hall, he intends to claim him. This leads to a passionate struggle for dominance – at the risk of scandal – between a high-spirited lady and a debauched aristocrat. Who will Lucerne choose? **A wonderfully decadent piece of historical erotica with a twist.**

VIRTUOSO
Katrina Vincenzi-Thyne
ISBN 0 352 32907 6

Mika and Serena, young ambitious members of classical music's jet-set, inhabit a world of secluded passion and privilege. However, since Mika's tragic injury, which halted his meteoric rise to fame as a solo violinist, he has retired embittered. Serena is determined to change things. A dedicated voluptuary, her sensuality cannot be ignored as she rekindles Mika's zest for life. Together they share a dark secret. **A beautifully written story of opulence and exotic, passionate indulgence.**

Black Lace Booklist

Information is correct at time of printing. To avoid disappointment check availability before ordering. Go to www.blacklace-books.co.uk. All books are priced £6.99 unless another price is given.

BLACK LACE BOOKS WITH A CONTEMPORARY SETTING

☐ THE TOP OF HER GAME Emma Holly	ISBN 0 352 33337 5	£5.99
☐ IN THE FLESH Emma Holly	ISBN 0 352 34498 3	£5.99
☐ A PRIVATE VIEW Crystalle Valentino	ISBN 0 352 33308 1	£5.99
☐ SHAMELESS Stella Black	ISBN 0 352 33485 1	£5.99
☐ INTENSE BLUE Lyn Wood	ISBN 0 352 33496 7	£5.99
☐ THE NAKED TRUTH Natasha Rostova	ISBN 0 352 33497 5	£5.99
☐ ANIMAL PASSIONS Martine Marquand	ISBN 0 352 33499 1	£5.99
☐ A SPORTING CHANCE Susie Raymond	ISBN 0 352 33501 7	£5.99
☐ TAKING LIBERTIES Susie Raymond	ISBN 0 352 33357 X	£5.99
☐ A SCANDALOUS AFFAIR Holly Graham	ISBN 0 352 33523 8	£5.99
☐ THE NAKED FLAME Crystalle Valentino	ISBN 0 352 33528 9	£5.99
☐ ON THE EDGE Laura Hamilton	ISBN 0 352 33534 3	£5.99
☐ LURED BY LUST Tania Picarda	ISBN 0 352 33533 5	£5.99
☐ THE HOTTEST PLACE Tabitha Flyte	ISBN 0 352 33536 X	£5.99
☐ THE NINETY DAYS OF GENEVIEVE Lucinda Carrington	ISBN 0 352 33070 8	£5.99
☐ EARTHY DELIGHTS Tesni Morgan	ISBN 0 352 33548 3	£5.99
☐ MAN HUNT Cathleen Ross	ISBN 0 352 33583 1	
☐ MÉNAGE Emma Holly	ISBN 0 352 33231 X	
☐ DREAMING SPIRES Juliet Hastings	ISBN 0 352 33584 X	
☐ THE TRANSFORMATION Natasha Rostova	ISBN 0 352 33311 1	
☐ STELLA DOES HOLLYWOOD Stella Black	ISBN 0 352 33588 2	
☐ SIN.NET Helena Ravenscroft	ISBN 0 352 33598 X	
☐ HOTBED Portia Da Costa	ISBN 0 352 33614 5	
☐ TWO WEEKS IN TANGIER Annabel Lee	ISBN 0 352 33599 8	
☐ HIGHLAND FLING Jane Justine	ISBN 0 352 33616 1	
☐ PLAYING HARD Tina Troy	ISBN 0 352 33617 X	
☐ SYMPHONY X Jasmine Stone	ISBN 0 352 33629 3	

WICKED WORDS 7 Various   ISBN 0 352 33743 5

THE BEST OF BLACK LACE 2 Various   ISBN 0 352 33718 4

A MULTITUDE OF SINS Kit Mason   ISBN 0 352 33737 0

BLACK LACE NON-FICTION

THE BLACK LACE BOOK OF WOMEN'S SEXUAL   ISBN 0 352 33346 4   £5.99
FANTASIES Ed. Kerri Sharp

To find out the latest information about Black Lace titles, check out the
website: www.blacklace-books.co.uk or send for a booklist with
complete synopses by writing to:

Black Lace Booklist, Virgin Books Ltd
Thames Wharf Studios
Rainville Road
London W6 9HA

Please include an SAE of decent size. Please note only British stamps
are valid.

Our privacy policy
We will not disclose information you supply us to any other parties.
We will not disclose any information which identifies you personally to
any person without your express consent.

From time to time we may send out information about Black Lace
books and special offers. Please tick here if you do <u>not</u> wish to
receive Black Lace information.   ☐

Please send me the books I have ticked above.

Name ....

Address ....

....

....

....

Post Code ....

Send to: Cash Sales, Black Lace Books, Thames Wharf Studios, Rainville Road, London W6 9HA.

US customers: for prices and details of how to order books for delivery by mail, call 1-800-343-4499.

Please enclose a cheque or postal order, made payable to Virgin Books Ltd, to the value of the books you have ordered plus postage and packing costs as follows:

UK and BFPO – £1.00 for the first book, 50p for each subsequent book.

Overseas (including Republic of Ireland) – £2.00 for the first book, £1.00 for each subsequent book.

If you would prefer to pay by VISA, ACCESS/MASTERCARD, DINERS CLUB, AMEX or SWITCH, please write your card number and expiry date here:

....

Signature ....

Please allow up to 28 days for delivery.